T0304381

The
Little Lost
Library

Also by Ellery Adams:

The Secret, Book, and Scone Society Mysteries:
The Secret, Book & Scone Society
The Whispered Word
The Book of Candlelight
Ink and Shadows
The Vanishing Type
Paper Cuts
The Little Lost Library

Book Retreat Mysteries:
Murder in the Mystery Suite
Murder in the Paperback Parlor
Murder in the Secret Garden
Murder in the Locked Library
Murder in the Reading Room
Murder in the Storybook Cottage
Murder in the Cookbook Nook
Murder on the Poet's Walk
Murder in the Book Lover's Loft

THE
LITTLE LOST
LIBRARY

ELLERY
ADAMS

KENSINGTON PUBLISHING CORP.
www.kensingtonbooks.com

KENSINGTON BOOKS are published by

Kensington Publishing Corp.
900 Third Avenue
New York, NY 10022

All Kensington titles, imprints and distributed lines are available at special quantity discounts for bulk purchases for sales promotion, premiums, fund-raising, educational or institutional use.

Special book excerpts or customized printings can also be created to fit specific needs. For details, write or phone the office of the Kensington Special Sales Manager: Kensington Publishing Corp., 900 Third Avenue, New York, NY, 10022. Attn. Special Sales Department. Phone: 1-800-221-2647.

KENSINGTON and the KENSINGTON COZIES teapot logo Reg. US Pat. & TM Off

Library of Congress Control Number: 2024939440

ISBN-13: 978-1-4967-4379-4
First Kensington Hardcover Edition: November 2024

ISBN-13: 978-1-4967-4381-7 (ebook)

10 9 8 7 6 5 4 3 2

Printed in the United States of America

For Mom, who started this whole thing by giving me a miniature book.

The older I get, the more I'm conscious of ways very small things can make a change in the world. Tiny little things, but the world is made up of tiny matters, isn't it?

—Sandra Cisneros

The Secret, Book, and Scone Society Members

Nora Pennington, owner of Miracle Books
Hester Winthrop, owner of the Gingerbread House
    Bakery
Estella Sadler, owner of Magnolia Salon and Spa
June Dixon, Guest Experience Manager, Miracle Springs
    Lodge

Relevant Miracle Springs Residents

Sheriff Grant McCabe
Deputy Jasper Andrews
K9 handler Paula Hollowell
Sheldon Vega, Nora's friend and bookstore employee
Jack Nakamura, proprietor of the Pink Lady Grill
Gus Sadler, Estella's biological father

The Wynter Family

Hugo and Helena Wynter
Lucille and Lynette Wynter (Hugo's daughters)
Lucille's children:
    John Steinbeck, "Beck"
    Harper Lee
    Samuel Clemens, "Clem"
Frederick Vandercamp (Lucille's husband)

Chapter 1

*A hermit is one who renounces the world of frag-
ments that he may enjoy the world wholly and
without interruption.*

—Khalil Gibran

Nora Pennington parked her 1973 mail truck in front of the
town's haunted house and cut the engine.

Her truck, which was canary yellow with a rainbow of
colorful books dancing across both side panels, looked out
of place on the lonely street. A funeral carriage drawn by a
pair of black horses would be more fitting.

Nora grabbed the paper shopping bag stamped with the
MIRACLE BOOKS logo and let out a sigh. It had been a long
day and she was ready to go home. Instead, she was delivering used books to one of her most eccentric and unusual customers.

Few residents of Miracle Springs, North Carolina, had
seen the woman who lived alone in the Gothic mansion next
to the old cemetery. Because of that, all kinds of rumors surrounded Lucille Wynter.

People called her a snob. They called her a witch. They
decided she was too ill or too infirm or too paranoid to leave
her crumbling estate. They complained about her over-

grown yard and the deplorable condition of her house. Children dared one another to touch the front door or batter the shale-gray clapboard with raw eggs on Halloween.

Nora had been delivering books to Lucille for several years now, and after visiting her once or twice a month, she'd learned that the old woman was a recluse. She never left Wynter House. Never. And no one was ever invited inside.

Not even Nora.

Though she was one of the few people who regularly visited Lucille, she'd never made it past the boot room. This small, square chamber behind the kitchen was uncomfortably cold in the winter and oppressively stuffy in the summer. The only furniture was a pair of cane chairs and an old piano stool that served as a table. A threadbare rug covered the dusty floorboards. Cobwebs gathered in every corner and clung to the window glass. Insect corpses cluttered the sills.

Year after year, the room remained unchanged. As did Lucille's rules.

From Day One, she'd told Nora to do exactly as she said. If Nora made a single misstep, she'd no longer be welcome on Lucille's property.

The first rule was to enter the boot room and ring the doorbell outside the kitchen door. After that, she was to sit down to wait, anywhere from five to fifteen minutes.

Lucille Wynter was old and frail. She did not move quickly, and her routines were as rigid as a steel beam. For example, she always asked Nora to identify herself before she'd crack the kitchen door. After peering out to confirm that Nora was who she claimed to be, Lucille always said, "Stay where you are. I'll make the tea."

The preparation would take another five to ten minutes, but eventually Lucille would appear in the doorway, a dainty porcelain teacup balanced in her trembling hand. The cup would rattle on its saucer until tea sloshed over the rim, but Nora had learned to stay seated and to keep her mouth shut. Lucille didn't like anyone to come too close, and offers of assistance put her in a foul mood. "My home is my whole world," she told Nora the first time they'd met. "I don't want outsiders in my world. That chair is for outsiders. You can sit there—and only there." She'd pointed at the chair closest to the back door. "That's as close to the inside of my house as you'll ever get. Don't ask to use the phone or the powder room. Don't ask if I need help carrying things. The answer to all of those questions is no."

Lucille was a tiny woman. Her body seemed as light and hollow-boned as a bird's. Her hair, which she wore in a Gibson girl bun, was white and wispy. The scent of rose eau de toilette clung to her moth-eaten cardigans and corduroy skirts. Beneath the heady floral notes was the fragrance of decay. And of loneliness.

It was the old woman's solitude and fragility that brought Nora to her door once or twice a month. She'd sit in her chair and drink weak tea and eat two of the four Lorna Doone cookies Lucille arranged on a dessert plate. The teacups, saucers, and plates never matched. Though often chipped or riddled with hairline cracks, they were still beautiful.

Lucille's financial situation was a mystery to Nora. She had no idea if the old woman was filthy rich and extremely frugal or living on a fixed income. The only thing she knew for certain was that Lucille Wynter wasn't a fan of change.

Like Miss Havisham, she wore clothes from earlier decades. She didn't care what colors or patterns she paired together, whether her blouses were missing buttons, or if her house slippers were held together by duct tape.

Wynter House was as disheveled as its mistress. It, too, was worn at the edges and spotted with age. Its unkempt lawn led to a tall, tangled hedge border. Tulip poplars lined the driveway, their branches creating a disjointed archway over the sparse gravel. Crows haunted the trees. Bats roosted in the attic. Snakes slipped through the tall grass, hunting the mice nesting in the basement.

There were only two structures on all of Still Wood Lane. Wynter House and a small stone chapel overlooking the town's oldest cemetery.

"The best neighbors are dead neighbors," Lucille liked to say.

Though the old woman seemed lost in time, she knew how to use a computer. Whenever Nora updated her used-book inventory, Lucille received an email notification. She'd immediately peruse the newest titles, make her selections, and add them to her online shopping basket. She never chose books costing more than five dollars and, nine times out of ten, paid her bill by applying credits she'd received the previous month by selling other, and sometimes more valuable, used books directly to Nora.

There was no telling what Lucille would offer Nora in exchange for a bag of fairly unremarkable books. Most often, she sold back the titles she'd bought from Miracle Books, but every now and then, she offered Nora something truly unique or valuable.

Nora was no saint, and there'd been times when she resented having to spend thirty minutes in Lucille's grungy boot room just to earn a few bucks, but she kept returning to Wynter House. And as the years passed, she added goodies to every bag of books.

Today, for example, she had a box of homemade lemon poppy-seed shortbread cookies, courtesy of Hester, owner of the Gingerbread House Bakery. And Nora's friend June had knitted Lucille three pairs of socks. June suffered from insomnia, and when she couldn't sleep, she either went out for a late-night stroll or worked on a knitting project while watching survival reality TV shows.

Lucille accepted Nora's offerings with minimal thanks. Nora knew she'd wear the socks and eat the cookies, but she only became animated when Nora presented her with the books she'd ordered.

The old woman's face would light up like a child's as she rummaged through the bag. It wouldn't matter if the book was a James Patterson hardback from 2010, a mass-market Harlequin paperback with yellowed pages, a Pulitzer Prize winner, Oprah's book club pick from March of last year, or a collection of stories by relatively unknown writers. She gazed at each book like it was made of gold.

Lucille loved every format and all genres. She read fiction and nonfiction. The only thing she wouldn't buy were books for young children.

"I get through them too quickly," she explained. "Except for the old fairy tales. I like those. When I was young, I was like the pretty maiden in my tower, waiting for my prince to come. Now I look more like the fairy godmothers. Or the witches. But I love a story with a quest. A hero determined to save the girl or find the treasure. Those have always been my favorite, even though I don't want to be rescued and this house is already full of treasure."

This statement had raised so many questions, but Nora had learned to curtail her curiosity. Lucille wasn't looking for a friend or confidant. She was a very private person and used her words sparingly. She would talk about books and that was all. She didn't care about Nora's personal life, and she didn't care about what was going on in the outside world.

She served tea because she was a Southern lady and the rules of hospitality were too deeply ingrained in her to be ignored. And while she never seemed especially glad to see Nora, she was always openly delighted to receive her new batch of books.

Hoping to bring a smile to Lucille's face, Nora had added two free mass markets to today's order.

She climbed the back steps, noting that another brick was loose on the top step, entered the boot room, and rang the doorbell.

She sat in her chair for five minutes. Then ten.

After fifteen minutes, she moved to the kitchen door and called, "No Lorna Doones today, Ms. Lucille! I have something even better!"

When there was no response, she returned to her seat, took out her phone, and began reading her new email messages.

When another fifteen minutes passed, with no sign of Lucille, Nora rang the doorbell again.

Putting her ear to the kitchen door, she listened for sounds from inside the house. There was nothing.

An eerie stillness had settled over the whole place.

Get a grip, Nora told herself. *It's seven o'clock at night. The heat hasn't let up all month. Everyone's inside, trying to stay cool. Lucille's probably napping and can't hear the bell over the hum of some ancient fan.*

Nora wished she had a fan. Or a cold drink. The air was as thick as oatmeal. Air-conditioning units were whirring all over town.

But not at Wynter House.

Here, nothing stirred. It was closed up tight, as if bracing for a storm. There were no cracked windows. No doors were thrown open, with only a flimsy screen door guarding the inhabitants from the bugs. No thrum of spinning ceiling fans.

Lucille didn't own a cell phone. Nora knew this because the old woman often came out to the boot room with the handset of her 1990s-era cordless phone poking out of the pocket of her cardigan.

Nora once asked her if she had a way of calling for help during a power outage or a medical emergency.

"I have a rotary phone in my bedroom," she'd said. "It's

such a pretty thing. White with pink roses. And a gold dial. I've had it for ages, but it works just fine. They made things better in those days, you know. Things were solid. Now everything's made of plastic. It's all junk. My father made so many beautiful things with his own two hands. He inherited his skills from my grandfather. He even designed this house. *My* house."

Lucille never missed the opportunity to remind Nora that Wynter House was hers.

Nora didn't mind. She could see why Lucille was so attached to the place. She and the house were like two aging spinsters. They'd been together for so long, Nora couldn't imagine one without the other.

The house sheltered Lucille. It kept her warm and safe and dry. In return, she padded over its floors and gently opened and closed its doors. Her breath drifted up to its ceilings and her voice sank into its walls.

Still, Nora worried that the old mansion wasn't structurally sound. Because no one was allowed inside, neither repairs nor routine maintenance had been done to the furnace, the fireplaces, or any of the appliances. Electrical or plumbing issues were left unresolved.

Nora pictured uneven floorboards, frayed wires, and clogged chimneys. She imagined loose stair treads, shaky banisters, and slippery tile. She heard dripping taps and the groan of rusted hinges.

Standing outside Lucille's kitchen door, Nora wondered if the old woman had had an accident. She'd never taken this long to come to the door.

"That's it. I'm breaking a rule." Nora took out her phone and logged on to Miracle Books' website. Because she was the site administrator, she was able to look up Lucille's account. In addition to her purchase history and street address, the account included her phone number.

Nora dialed the number and heard a phone ring from somewhere deeper inside the house.

It rang and rang.

Ten times.

Then twenty.

"Where are you?" Nora murmured into the sticky air.

Finally she hung up. Pocketing her phone, she tried to peer through the window panel into the kitchen, but the glass was completely covered by a shade, which had turned a brownish yellow with time. The color reminded Nora of a nicotine-stained tooth.

Nora tried to recall if Lucille had ever missed an appointment before, but she knew she hadn't.

Something was wrong. She could feel it in her bones.

Nora banged on the door. She called Lucille's name. She pushed the doorbell again and again. When the house remained quiet, she took out her phone and called the landline again.

It rang and rang. And then, abruptly, the ringing stopped.

With the phone pressed to her ear, Nora strained to hear a noise on the other end of the line. All she heard was the sound of her own breathing.

She went very still. And in the stillness, she felt a presence.

Someone was in the house.

Someone had answered the phone.

"Lucille?" Nora whispered.

A weighted silence echoed through the phone speaker. It was like the hush of dead air in the middle of a broadcast.

In the silence, Nora heard someone draw in a soft breath.

"Lucille? Can you hear me?"

A faint whimper whispered through the line.

"Lucille!" Nora raised her voice. "It's Nora Pennington. Can you answer me?"

Nora held her breath and waited for a response, no matter how subtle.

And then she heard a soft exhalation. It sounded like someone blowing a dandelion seed off their palm. A word was carried on the back of this sigh. "*Help.*"

"Okay, Lucille." Nora spoke calmly and clearly. "I can hear you, and I'm going to call for help. I need to put you on hold, but I'll be right back—"

Lucille whined like a terrified dog. "*Help me. Please!*"

The urgency of Lucille's plea struck Nora like an arrow. Was she hurt? Or scared? Or both? Nora had to call 911. She had to get help. And yet she didn't want to leave a terrified old woman whispering into the silence.

"Hold on, Lucille. Help is coming."

Nora switched her phone to speaker mode and reached out to press the hold button when Lucille spoke again. Her voice sounded so small and distant that Nora wasn't sure she'd heard anything at all. But then the words sank in, and Nora's blood turned to ice.

"Too . . . late."

"No," Nora argued as she dialed 911. She explained the situation to the emergency dispatcher as quickly as she could before switching back to the other line.

"Hold on, Lucille! Please hold on!"

A map of Miracle Springs popped into Nora's head. She saw the closest fire station. It was almost ten minutes away. The sheriff's department was fifteen minutes.

"Too late," Lucille had gasped.

Nora couldn't let that be true. She couldn't stand outside her door and wait for someone else to get to the old woman. She had to act. She had to break every promise she'd made to Lucille. Every one of her rules.

She had to get inside Wynter House.

Nora was a middle-aged bookseller. Before that, she'd been a librarian. She had no experience forcing her way into someone's home. However, she'd been in a relationship with Sheriff Grant McCabe long enough to know that there was a strategy to kicking in someone's door. She could hear his voice, quiet and calm, telling her exactly what to do.

"Kick as close to the knob as you can. You're trying to dislodge the locking mechanism without breaking your ankle. Use the heel of your strongest leg."

"I'm coming, Lucille!" Nora shouted.

She raised her right leg and sent her foot crashing into the door.

The wood cracked in protest, and she felt something give under her shoe, but the door didn't fly open like it did in an action movie, so Nora kicked it again.

This time, there was a splintering sound. The door gave way, revealing a gap half a foot wide.

Nora widened the gap and stepped inside.

"Oh, my God," she gasped.

She scanned the room, her eyes confused by what she saw. And then the smell hit her.

She clamped a hand over her mouth as a wave of nausea rolled up her throat. She gagged once, drew in a breath through her nose, and moved forward.

In the next room, which she assumed was the dining room based on the chandelier dangling from an ornate ceiling medallion, she picked her way over a well-worn path in the floral rug, removing her hand just long enough to call Lucille's name.

Through the door at the other end of the dining room, she entered a dimly lit space with a staircase to the right and darkness to the left.

"Lucille!" she shouted.

Her voice didn't echo up to the high ceilings. It sank like a stone in water.

As she moved toward the staircase, which hugged the left wall and curved away into blackness, she saw Lucille.

The old woman was crumpled at the bottom of the staircase.

"Lucille!"

Nora turned on her phone's flashlight and held it over Lucille.

A moan rose from Nora's throat as she took in the paper-white oval of Lucille's face and the unnatural slackness of her jaw. Her lips were parted, but when Nora lowered her cheek to Lucille's mouth, she couldn't feel even a whisper of air. The old woman stared up at the ceiling, her glacier-blue eyes fixed on some point beyond Nora's comprehension.

"No, no, no." Nora took Lucille's bony hand in hers. It was still warm, which meant Nora had waited just a few minutes too long. "I'm so sorry."

She didn't know how long she sat there, holding the old woman's hand and crying, but when someone spoke her name, it seemed to come from very far away.

It took a light touch on her shoulder to bring her back to herself.

Nora turned to find Deputy Jasper Andrews leaning over her.

Speaking in a hushed tone, Andrews said, "Ms. Wynter. Is she gone?"

Nora nodded.

The town recluse had finally left the confines of her house, floating away from all that once held her to the earth. But as Nora glanced up at the narrow staircase, it occurred to her that the old mansion was far more than Lucille's home.

It had been her prison.

Chapter 2

*I have read my books by many lights, hoarding
their beauty, their wit or wisdom against the dark
days when I would have no book, nor a place to
read.*

— Louis L'Amour

Andrews took Nora's elbow and helped her to her feet. He
kept holding on after she stood up, and for a long moment,
they both gazed down at Lucille's body.

"Did you know?" he asked softly. "That she lived like
this?"

Nora glanced up the staircase. There were stacks of books
on every step. Clothes were draped on top of the books, as
were linens, hangers, shoes, tissue boxes, food containers,
and more.

"I had no idea," she said.

Andrews followed her gaze. "She kept that path next to
the railing clear, but it's so narrow. If her foot caught on the
edge of one of those book piles, she could easily trip. Honestly, it's surprising she didn't lose her balance before now."

"But she begged for help," Nora protested. "She answered the phone and begged for help. Then she told me it
was too late. I didn't get to her soon enough."

"I need to know everything that happened, but not here. Come outside with me." He put a hand on Nora's back and steered her toward the dining room.

This room, like the center hallway and staircase, was also a repository of books, clothes, and miscellaneous household items. It looked like a tornado had ripped through the house, picked up everything Lucille owned, and deposited the whole mess right back where it came from.

Outside Vanderbilt's library at Biltmore, Nora had never seen so many books in someone's home. Most of the piles were waist-high. Other stacks were over six feet tall. Nora didn't know if there was a dining table under the mound of old paperbacks that rose toward the ceiling like a cresting wave, but it had to be stronger than Atlas to bear the weight of a thousand romance novels.

The path leading to the kitchen was lined by encyclopedia sets. There were blue ones, black ones, brown ones, and red ones, stacked without any sense of order. Volume 14 from one set was sandwiched between Volumes 2 and 9 from two other sets.

"My gran had the same ones," Andrews said, pointing at a pile of red books. "She was so proud of them, even though they were all missing pages. Turns out, Gran ripped out entries from every volume. She said certain people didn't deserve to be in the Encyclopedia Britannica, so she took them out."

Something cracked under Nora's foot. The noise startled her, and she jerked sideways, knocking into a tower of encyclopedias. They wobbled precariously, but she pressed the length of her body against them, holding them in a lover's embrace to keep them from falling.

When she raised her foot, she saw that she'd stepped on a plastic water bottle.

"This place is a minefield," said Andrews. "Let's get you outside."

They picked their way through the dining room and into the kitchen. They'd just entered the cramped and dirty space when two men in EMT uniforms appeared in the boot room.

"Hey, Andrews. Where's our patient?" asked the older of the two men.

"Let Ms. Pennington get outside. Then I'll show you," said Andrews.

The EMT gave Nora a once-over. "You okay, ma'am?"

"I just need some water. I have some in my truck." Eager to take a breath of fresh air, she brushed past the EMT. "If Andrews needs to talk to me, that's where I'll be."

"Is your truck parked out front? The one with all the books painted on it?" asked the younger man.

Nora nodded.

He gestured toward the dining room. "She buy all these books from you?"

The hint of accusation in his tone nettled Nora. "No. I brought her a bag a few times a month, but she sold books back to me too. I have no idea where all of these came from."

"You never asked her?" the man pressed.

"I didn't see them because I've never been inside. If I knew she was living like this . . ."

She let the thought dangle because the truth was, she had no clue what she would've done other than share her concerns with Grant. He would've contacted social services. He would've followed up with Lucille Wynter's caseworker. He would've used all of his connections to ensure she got the help she needed.

Why didn't you do something? taunted her guilty conscience.

The answer wasn't a pretty one. Nora had convinced herself that she hadn't questioned Lucille about the holes in her sweater or the spider web crack in her reading glasses because she didn't want to upset the old woman, but the truth was, she didn't ask because it was easier not to know. *I brought her cookies I didn't bake. Socks I didn't knit. And books. I thought they'd ease her loneliness. I thought they were enough.*

The older paramedic gazed into the dining room and whistled. "Looks like Ms. Wynter tried to wall herself in. I used to make forts out of junk when I was a kid. I thought it would keep the monsters out." He turned back to Nora and said, "We'll take good care of her. You go get that water."

Monsters, Nora thought as she waded through the soupy air.

Inside her truck, she put the windows down and drank her tepid water. The ambulance had blocked her in, and when she realized she wouldn't be going anywhere soon, she folded herself over the steering wheel, rested her head against her arms, and closed her eyes.

In the silence, she considered the EMT's words: "Looks like Ms. Wynter tried to wall herself in."

Lucille was afraid to go outside. Nora already knew that, but she had no idea why Lucille had turned her home into a death trap in an effort to feel safe.

Nora had watched dozens of documentaries about hoarding, and in every episode, the hoarder could always go back in time and pinpoint the moment when their need to accumulate stuff began to outweigh all other needs.

Their behavior was often a result of trauma, and many of the hoarders felt compelled to surround themselves with mountains of things as a coping mechanism. The chaos in their homes became a reflection of the chaos in their minds, and Nora felt sorry for every one of these people. At the same time, she felt a voyeuristic fascination watching these shows. She was riveted by the extent of their hoards and by how they continued to add to their collection despite protests from family, friends, landlords, and neighbors.

She knew these shows were scripted and carefully edited, but the pain in the hoarders' eyes was always genuine. Like Lucille Wynter, they'd used things as a means of separating themselves from the rest of the world. In their labyrinth of material goods, they thought the monsters couldn't find them.

Except the monsters were already inside.

The thought made Nora feel itchy, so she grabbed her water bottle and wandered into the backyard to wait for Andrews.

A round cement table sat in the middle of a brick patio overrun with weeds. Nora sat on one of the attached bench seats and stared at the gurney parked at the bottom of the stairs leading to the boot room.

She wanted to call Grant, but he was having a beer with a friend he saw only a few times a year and she didn't want to ruin their time together. She could tell him later, after he came home smelling of smokehouse ribs and onion rings, the traces of laughter still lingering in his eyes.

A car door slammed, and minutes later, Nora heard shoes crunching over gravel.

When Deputy Paula Hollowell rounded the corner of the house, a soft groan wheezed like a deflating balloon through Nora's lips.

Hollowell darted a glance at the gurney parked outside the boot room before marching over to Nora. She put her hands on her hips and smirked. "Well, well. What have we here?"

It was such a ridiculous B-movie line that Nora had to suppress the urge to roll her eyes. Instead, she gestured toward the back of the house and said, "Andrews is inside."

"I hear you called it in. What happened?"

Nora wasn't inclined to give Hollowell more than a quick sketch, so she explained how her concern for Lucille's welfare had led to her entering Wynter House and finding Lucille at the bottom of the stairs.

"*You* kicked in the woman's door?" Hollowell raked her gaze over Nora's legs. "Are you working out now?"

Seeing a grown woman channel a playground bully would have been laughable if that woman wasn't wearing a badge and carrying a gun and a Taser.

Nora had disliked the newest member of the Miracle Springs Sheriff's Department from the moment they'd met. The feeling was clearly mutual.

Hollowell had burgundy hair, deep-set eyes, and a changeable face. She treated most women with either coldness or derision and didn't have a single female friend. When she was around men, however, she dropped her haughty glare and softened her entire demeanor. She was warm, jocular, and occasionally flirty. Her male coworkers had quickly accepted her into the fold, while the women at the department kept their distance.

Hollowell was one of the younger deputies who'd been hired to replace the vacancy left by the previous K9 officer. She came to Miracle Springs with her own partner, a black German shepherd named Rambo, and when the pair walked the streets, people gave them a wide berth

Nora liked dogs well enough, but with a handler like Hollowell, Rambo made her nervous.

Hooking her thumbs through her utility belt, Hollowell glared down at Nora. "This is what I heard from dispatch. You broke into an old woman's house because she didn't answer her phone and, after illegally entering her home, you found her dead at the bottom of the stairs?"

"She asked for help. I tried to give it to her, but I was too late."

Hollowell put her foot on the bench, inches away from Nora's hand, and dusted a blade of grass off the toe of her polished boot.

"What *really* happened? Did the old lady owe you money? Or were you hoping to get your hands on some of her books? I mean, you must've known all about her treasures." Hollowell straightened. "Maybe she was gone by the time you reached her or maybe, once you realized she was in a bad way, you just let nature take its course. You had a good, long look around before dialing 911, and you didn't even attempt CPR. So, what really happened? She didn't have anything worth stealing?"

Nora spread her arms wide. "Your detecting skills are off the chart, but before you take me downtown and book me, you might want to take a peek inside the house. After that, you can tell me what you'd steal if you were me."

Hollowell was about to respond when the EMTs shuffled out the back door, carrying a body bag. They descended the stairs and gently eased Lucille Wynter onto the waiting gurney. Andrews trailed after them, holding his hat in his hands out of respect for the dead woman.

Spotting Nora and Hollowell, he approached the table.

He greeted Hollowell first. "Evening, Deputy."

She flashed him a wide smile. "Evening, Jasper. I heard you were here, so I thought I'd stop by to lend a hand."

"Well, I wouldn't mind having some company when I notify Ms. Wynter's next of kin. This kind of thing can be easier when there's a lady present." Andrews pointed at the garage. "Her son lives in an apartment in the back. His name's Clem. You've probably seen him in the drunk tank. He spends the night with us at least once a month, usually after finding the bottom of a Wild Turkey bottle."

Nora couldn't believe what she was hearing. "Lucille has a *son*? And he lives on the property? How could she be living like that with him right *here*?"

"Living like what?" asked Hollowell.

Andrews jerked his head toward Wynter House. "Go see for yourself."

Hollowell clearly didn't want to leave Nora and Andrews alone, but curiosity won out, and she jogged up the stairs and into the boot room.

Andrews waited for several heartbeats before pulling an object wrapped in a plastic grocery bag from his uniform shirt pocket. "This was in the kitchen, next to the teakettle."

Nora saw that an envelope bearing her name had been taped to the plastic bag.

"I didn't open it. I assumed she owed you money," Andrews said.

"Yes, but not much. She mostly paid in books, but sometimes she'd give me cash. Five or ten bucks." Nora held the bag to her chest. "Andrews, this doesn't make sense. She asked me for help, told me it was too late, and then tripped on the stairs? I mean, there's no way she could've been talking to me after she fell, is there?"

"No. The phone's broken. Probably happened during the fall."

"Then why did she say it was too late?"

Andrews watched the EMTs load the gurney into the ambulance. "She was probably dizzy or confused when she was talking to you. She was old, Nora, and there's hardly any light on those stairs. Look at her living conditions. There's no way she was healthy."

"Living in those conditions, I guess not."

Andrews put a hand on Nora's arm. "None of this is your fault. It's a sad situation, and even though it'll probably be ruled an accident, we're going to do a complete investigation. I already took photos and we'll be back here in the morning. I'll make sure we know what happened to her, okay?"

The beeping of the reversing ambulance drew their attention to the driveway, and they both watched as the rig backed out onto the street and slowly drove away.

"I need to talk to Clem," said Andrews. "You should go home."

Just as Nora got to her feet, a man appeared from behind the garage. "Hey!" he shouted, lurching in their direction. "What the hell's going on?"

Andrews held up his hands. "It's okay, Clem. I was on my way to talk to you."

The man came to a stop a good ten feet from where Andrews stood. He wore a Looney Tunes tank top, baggy athletic shorts, and Dollar Store flip-flops. His eyes were at half-mast, and he had the flushed face of an alcoholic. His pigeon-gray hair, which clung like a horseshoe to the lower half of his skull, stuck out in all directions. There were crumbs in his beard and his teeth and fingernails were nicotine stained.

Clem's eyes slid from Andrews to Nora. "Who the hell are you?"

"This is Nora Pennington," Andrews said. "She owns the bookstore. She and your mom met a few times a month."

Clem's expression sharpened. "Has she been giving you books to sell?"

Nora nodded. "A few."

"How much do you get for them?" Clem demanded, slurring his words.

Sensing danger, Nora looked to Andrews for help.

"Listen, Clem. Your mom didn't come to the door when Nora rang the bell, so Nora called her on the phone. Your mom answered and asked for help, so Nora went inside the house. She found your mom on the floor at the bottom of the stairs. It looks like she had a bad fall—a fatal fall. I'm sorry to tell you this, Clem, but your mom is gone."

Clem dug the heels of his palms into his eyes. He took several deep breaths before lowering his hands and vigorously shaking his head. "Wait. Wait. I don't understand. Are you saying my mama's dead?"

"Yes. I'm sorry."

Suddenly Clem's hands were everywhere. They raked his hair, tugged his beard, and grabbed the neck of his shirt. They were birds let loose from a cage, frightened by their sudden freedom. He turned his back to Andrews, then swung around to face him again. His mouth worked, but no sound came out.

Andrews took a step toward him. "Hey, man. It's going to be okay. Do you want to sit down?"

"No!" Clem held out his arms as if warding off an attack. "No! No! No!"

His eyes were wild, and his breath was coming so fast that he was practically panting. He rocked from side to side, like a cornered animal waiting to bolt.

Feeling her own anxiety rise, Nora darted a glance at Andrews.

Andrews stretched out a hand, palm up. "It's going to be okay, Clem. But you've got to calm down. Can you focus on my face and take a slow breath?"

"Get outta here," Clem murmured, his gaze shifting from Andrews to Nora. He threw his chin up toward the sky, filled his lungs, and screamed, "GO AWAY!"

Suddenly Hollowell was beside Andrews. "Who's this guy?" she asked in a low voice.

"Samuel Clemens Wynter. He goes by Clem. I just told him about his mom, so he's understandably upset."

Nora wondered why Clem used his mother's maiden name as a surname instead of his father's, but didn't think this was the time to ask.

"He's also high as a kite."

Andrews whispered, "We need to calm him down. Look at his face. His blood pressure must be through the roof. Why don't you try?"

Hollowell nodded and took a step closer to Clem. She

then put her hands on her heart and said, "Mr. Wynter? I'm Deputy Paula Hollowell, and I'm here to help you."

Hollowell's soft, musical tone surprised Nora. Every time she ran into the deputy at the station, the woman spoke to her in a cold, flat voice.

She must save the nice voice for the men she flirts with and the dogs she trains.

"Where'd *you* come from?" Clem cried. "Why are you all here? What do you want?"

He started backpedaling toward the garage, his hands flapping near his head. His muttering intensified. Sweat beaded his forehead and his skin was now the color of a ripe tomato.

Hollowell was about to pursue him, when Andrews told her to stand down. "Go on back inside now, Clem. You need to calm down. Go on. We're not going to follow you."

"Just leave me alone!" he shrieked before turning away. He lurched behind the garage and out of sight. A few seconds later, a door slammed.

"Can you radio dispatch? We're going to need EMTs to give us a hand with Mr. Wynter."

When Hollowell moved off a few paces to make the call, Andrews looked at Nora. "It's time for you to go before this gets really wild."

Nora glanced at the garage. "Will he be able to take care of Lucille's arrangements? He doesn't seem like he's capable of taking care of himself."

"It'll work out. Go get some rest."

Andrews was telling her as politely as possible to get lost, so she wished him luck and did as he asked.

Despite the heat, she drove home with the truck windows down. She wanted the air to whip her whiskey-colored hair around her face. She wanted the sounds of downtown to swirl around the interior cabin. Having just witnessed death, she wanted to be surrounded by life. She wanted it to stream in her window and curl around her.

As she sat at a red light on Main Street, she heard music and laughter coming from the outdoor dining area of the vegetarian restaurant. People milled in front of shop windows or strolled purposefully down the sidewalk toward the Pink Lady Grill or one of the higher-end eateries that required a reservation.

Summer was the height of the tourist season and even though it was the last weekend of August, Miracle Springs was still packed to the brim with people who'd come to bathe in the revitalizing waters of the hot springs, participate in sunrise yoga classes, and drink green smoothies. They'd come for therapeutic massage, meditation sessions, weight-loss programs, detox cleanses, couples counseling, terminal illness support groups, and women's retreats.

Long before Europeans stepped foot on American soil, the Cherokee were reaping the benefits of the mineral waters that gave the town its name.

Eventually the tribe was driven out of the area. European settlers built roads and erected an inn at the crossroads. Travelers on their way to South Carolina, Tennessee, Virginia, or North Carolina's Piedmont or coastal regions were encouraged to stop for a night of rest and a revitalizing dip in the hot springs.

Other businesses and homesteads followed the inn, and three centuries later, Miracle Springs was known across the globe as a center of healing.

Luckily, the town was located in a valley, which meant the suburban sprawl was limited. One could only build so much in a place surrounded by mountains. Vacation homes and timeshare condos now dotted the hills, but the powers that be held fast to tough restrictions and rules when it came to tree clearing and the preservation of green spaces. In a country where capitalism was king, this was a rare occurrence.

And while Miracle Springs didn't have fast-food chains, lots of big-box stores, or dozens of cheap apartment complexes, most of its residents prospered. They weren't wealthy, but they lived comfortably, and most were content with their lot.

People came from all over to experience the serenity of the little town, and Nora tried to soak up every ounce of that serenity before turning into the parking lot behind Miracle Books.

Like Nora, the building had lived a previous life. Before it became a bookstore, it had been a train station. And before her tiny house perched on the hill behind the shop became her home, it had been the caboose of a passenger train.

She climbed up the stairs to the deck and unlocked the front door. Dumping her purse on the sofa, she went straight into the kitchen to pour herself a glass of wine. She then sat at her little table, wineglass at the ready, and put the package from Lucille on the place mat.

She opened the envelope first and pulled out a note written in gorgeous calligraphy.

> *Dear Nora,*
> *Thank you for spending time with an old woman. Thank you for your kindness. Your visits meant a great deal to me, as did the books you brought. They kept me company all these years. They were my friends. My family.*
> *Please accept this book as a token of my appreciation. It's the only one of its kind and is very precious to me.*

Perhaps you'll brew a cup of tea and place two Lorna Doone cookies on a pretty plate before you read this, my favorite book. If you read it as it was meant to be read, you will know my whole story. I've never shared it with another soul, but the time has come.

Yours,
Lucille Wynter

Bemused, Nora opened the plastic bag. Inside she found a thin book with a brown cloth cover. The book was roughly the size of her hand and had deckled edges. It smelled old and musty, like the pages were aching to return to the soil.

But the book had been precious to Lucille, which meant it was now precious to Nora.

She opened to the first page, which was blank. Though the paper bore the yellowed patina of time, it was of the highest quality. Nora could see the individual fibers running up and down and back and forth. And as she traced one of these lines with her fingertip, she heard a sound like wind whispering through dry leaves.

The next page was the title page. The words had been pressed deep into the paper. The ink was cave black and every letter with an ascender or loop, such as the *T, h, b,* and *y,* had a dramatic swoosh. The rest of the letters were leaning slightly to the right as if too tipsy to stand up on their own: *The Little Lost Library.*

Below the title, in a much humbler font, was the author's name: *Hugo Wynter.*

Intrigued, Nora turned to the next page. This contained a woodblock engraving of a bookshelf stuffed with books and the lines:

I have lost my little library.
Would you find it for me?
I put it down, but I don't know where,
Perhaps in a vase or on a chair,
Perhaps on the chimney on top of the
*   house,*
Or inside a nest made by a mouse.
I miss my books, for they are my friends,
They are adventures that never end.

Nora heard the jangle of keys on the other side of the front door and reluctantly closed the book. She wanted to see Grant. She wanted to feel his arms around her. But she also wanted to keep reading. She wanted to know exactly how one lost a library and, more important, how one found it again.

Glancing down at Lucille's letter, she considered how much it sounded like a goodbye. But how could Lucille have known that she was about to die?

Unless she did.

Chapter 3

You get old and you realize there are no answers,
just stories.

—Garrison Keillor

Sheriff Grant McCabe was skilled at reading faces, which was why Nora hid hers behind a Jodi Picoult novel. She knew she needed to rearrange her features before McCabe entered her house or he'd see that she was upset. She didn't want to ruin his rare night out by appearing grief-stricken and morose.

Long before they'd become lovers, Nora and McCabe had been friends. They'd met when McCabe first came to Miracle Springs to serve as the interim sheriff after the previous sheriff was arrested. McCabe had wasted no time cleaning house. He'd hired new deputies, changed the department's culture, and gained the respect of the community.

Nora had warmed to McCabe from the get-go. She liked his sharp mind and dry sense of humor. She admired his dedication to his office and how his face lit up when he talked about his sister and her children. He and Nora had bonded over their love of food. Both were adventurous eaters and mourned Miracle Spring's shortage of ethnic restaurants. In search of new eateries, they drove to neighboring counties once a month.

During these casual lunches, Nora would share anecdotes about the bookstore, while McCabe would tell her about life as a divorced man, cat dad, and sheriff. In the beginning, he was Sheriff McCabe, but as they grew closer, he became just McCabe.

Nora lay back against the pillow and raised her book up until it covered her face. She hoped McCabe would see the wineglass and lit candle on the coffee table and assume Nora was having a quiet evening on the heels of a long, busy day.

McCabe was whistling "Sweet Caroline" as he unlocked her front door. Judging by the jauntiness of his song, he'd had a grand time with his friend. He was relaxed and happy, and Nora wanted him to keep whistling. He would find out about Lucille soon enough.

"There's my girl!" he said, dropping on the sofa. He picked up her legs, scooted closer, and draped his arms over her thighs. "Would you like a sloppy, beer-hoppy kiss from your man?"

Nora smiled and lowered her book. "Who would resist such an offer?"

McCabe leaned over and kissed her on the neck, just below her earlobe. After tracing a line of feather-light kisses from her neck to her lips, he whispered, "What page are you on?"

"Ninety-six."

"Remember that number." He closed the book and put it on the coffee table. "Wanna make out on the sofa? We can pretend we're teenagers."

Nora didn't want to, but just as she opened her mouth to demur, McCabe stretched out on top of her.

"Oof," she gasped, unable to fully inflate her lungs. She gave him a push, and he immediately rolled off her onto the rug. Sitting up, he gave Nora a goofy grin and laid his head in her lap. "I forget how many pounds I've put on since I was a teenager."

"I've seen photos of you when you were that age, and you're much hotter now." Nora ran her fingers through McCabe's salt-and-pepper hair. It was soft as kitten fur.

"I had such a good time tonight," he said, grabbing Nora's hand and planting a kiss on the inside of her wrist. "Quentin was in fine form. He had all kinds of stories about the new casino and about this huge fight that broke out in the DMV—man, I haven't laughed so hard in weeks. We were sitting outside so he could smoke his cigars, and I almost died when the waitress called him Boss Hogg."

Nora laughed. "From *The Dukes of Hazzard*?"

"You got it. Anyway, Quentin told the waitress that the citizens of Haywood County would never elect a man like Jefferson Davis Hogg, but she called him 'Boss' for the rest of the night. I guess he liked the attention because he left her a cigar and a thirty percent tip."

McCabe refilled Nora's wineglass and shared more anecdotes from his night out. His ebullience was contagious, and for a little while, Nora was able to push Lucille and Wynter House to the back of her mind.

Eventually McCabe ran out of stories and asked about her day.

"It was a day, and the best part of it is happening right now because you're here with me."

McCabe cupped her hand in his. "Want to watch a show?"

Nora doubted she could concentrate on anything, but nodded and passed the remote to McCabe. They'd been watching *Unforgotten* together, so he started the next episode and rubbed her feet while DSI Cassie Stuart worked another cold case.

McCabe dozed off long before Cassie brought closure to a grieving mother after thirty-plus years. When his head lolled against the back of the sofa and his body went limp,

Nora turned off the TV, carried her wineglass to the sink, and then gently nudged McCabe's shoulder.

He came awake with a start. "What'd I miss?"

"Nothing you can't catch up on tomorrow. Time for bed."

McCabe rubbed his eyes. "I've got a staff meeting tomorrow. It's my turn to bring the snacks, and I have to swing home to feed the cats first."

"The Gingerbread House's muffin of the week is strawberry and cream. I had one the other day. It had little pieces of fresh strawberries and white chocolate chips. Delicious."

"Way better than the grocery store donuts I was going to buy." McCabe lumbered to his feet and slipped his arm around Nora's waist. "You make my life so much easier." He gave her a quick squeeze before letting her go. "I'm going to make you a nice pot of coffee before I leave tomorrow. I promise I'll only take half of it with me when I go."

Nora pointed at the magnetic calendar affixed to her fridge. "Just remember that tomorrow's storytime at the bookstore. If you don't leave me enough coffee, I won't be held responsible for what happens when Sheldon passes out cups of glitter to twenty toddlers."

"What is it with that man and glitter?"

"He likes shiny things. Glitter, disco balls, Elton John's suits, muscle cars with chrome bumpers—he's a human magpie."

McCabe headed into the bathroom to brush his teeth. As Nora changed into her pajamas, she couldn't help comparing her small, tidy home to the large, overstuffed rooms of Wynter House.

Who's going to clean up that mess? she wondered.

Long after McCabe fell asleep, Nora lay awake, thinking about Lucille and her son. When she finally drifted off, she dreamed of books. Stacks and stacks of books towering so high that they blocked out the light. She sensed she was in a huge room, though she couldn't see any walls or a ceiling. All she could make out were the shadowy shapes of books. Suddenly she heard the sound of books falling. It began as a rumble, like a train approaching from a distance, but as the noise increased in volume, she knew she was in danger. One of the book towers had fallen, and the rest would soon follow. There was nothing to stop the domino effect, and Nora knew she was minutes away from being crushed under the weight of a thousand books.

She tried to run, but a mass of snarling, twisting roots shot out through the floor, grabbing at her ankles. She struggled to free herself, to no avail. She couldn't move.

The sound of cascading books grew thunderously loud, and just when she thought she'd be flattened, the roots released her. She fled from the books, bursting through a door that appeared in the darkness. On the other side was Lucille Wynter's kitchen. Lucille stood at the stove, calmly waiting for a kettle to boil.

"We have to go!" Nora's dream self shouted, but Lucille couldn't hear her above the kettle's sudden shrieking.

Behind Nora's tiny house, the two A.M. freight train whistled as it emerged from the tunnel just past the Miracle Springs station. It clattered down the track dividing Nora's house from the woods, and the noise wrested her from her nightmare.

Sighing in relief, Nora nestled closer to McCabe. She listened to the train pass, comforted by its familiar sound and the steady rhythm of McCabe's breath. When she eventually sank back into sleep, her arm was locked around McCabe's waist, as if his body were an anchor that kept her from floating too far into the dark.

* * *

Pale threads of light were just beginning to slip through the blinds when McCabe woke her.

"What time is it?" she grumbled, slitting her eyes.

"Nora. Why didn't you tell me about Lucille Wynter?"

The mention of Lucille's name chased off any residual sleep. Images flashed through Nora's mind. Lucille's body on the floor. Her slack face. Her bony hand. The stench inside her house. The mounds of stuff.

Nora opened her eyes and sat up. She turned on the lamp with a shaking hand, nearly knocking over the coffee cup perched on the edge of her nightstand.

McCabe sat down on the bed. "I just talked to Andrews. He wanted to give me a heads-up about Clem and to see how you were doing. Why didn't you say anything last night?"

Nora's voice came out as a croak. "I wanted you to have a night off from being the sheriff." She paused to grab a quick sip of coffee. It was so hot that it scorched her tongue. "You've been working so many extra hours—covering all kinds of shifts so that other people can take vacations. You've been having meeting after meeting to plan for all the upcoming festivals, and, well, you're exhausted, Grant. Last night was the first time in months I've seen you relaxed and happy."

"That's not true. I'm happy all the time around you."

"I'm not talking about us. We're good. I'm talking about you running on fumes. I knew you'd hear about Lucille this morning, and I wanted us to have a few hours of peace before that happened."

McCabe shook his head. "You can't make those choices for me. I'm the sheriff. If someone dies in my county and my partner is involved, then I need to know about it *right away.* I can't afford to be blindsided. It makes me look incompetent."

"I was thinking about you as my McCabe, not as Sheriff McCabe. I'm sorry. I should've told you last night." Nora reached for McCabe's hand. "Do you want me to tell you now?"

"As quickly as you can. I have to leave in ten minutes."

Nora gave him a succinct account, skimming over the enormity of Lucille's hoard and focusing on Lucille's plea for help and how Clem had fallen apart after hearing about his mother's death.

"I never knew about her living conditions. Or that she had a son." Nora pictured the back side of Wynter House. The overgrown yard. The cement patio table. The deep garage. "It was all there. All those signs of decay. Of trouble. I saw them, but didn't do anything about it."

"Hey." McCabe squeezed her hand. "The whole community let Ms. Wynter down. Usually, we hear about people living in unsafe situations because the neighbors alert us, but Ms. Wynter didn't have neighbors. Still, Clem has spent so many nights in the drunk tank that it's practically his second home. We should have done more to find out what his *actual* home life was like. If we had, we could have helped Ms. Wynter. Gotten her out of that house before it killed her."

Nora thought of the path running through Lucille's dining room. She remembered how little free space had been left on the stairs. There were obstacles everywhere. Every time Lucille moved, she risked a fall. How had she survived in such a state? How had she supported herself? And what about Clem? Where did he get the money to fund his benders?

Getting to his feet, McCabe pointed at the coffee cup on the nightstand. "I made it strong today. We're going to need it."

Question after question formed in Nora's mind, rising and

thickening like a loaf of bread, but she pushed them aside. She had something more urgent to convey to McCabe.

"Lucille left me a book," she said, catching him before he could leave the room. "And a note. They were in a bag in her kitchen. Do you want to see them?"

"Later. I've gotta go."

McCabe had left without kissing her goodbye, and she almost called after him. She wanted to tell him about Lucille's letter—about its prescient tone—but the front door slammed before she had the chance.

While her coffee mug spun around in the microwave, she re-read the note. It unsettled her just as much as it had the night before.

And then there was the book.

Lucille had given Nora vintage books as payment for a bag or two of gently used books, but she'd never gifted a book to Nora. The timing felt strange. Had she meant it as payment for the bag of books Nora delivered?

"It's as if you knew you'd never be able to read them," Nora murmured.

She must've been sick. No surprise there. She was an old woman living in unsanitary conditions. The house smelled of mold and feces. The air was fetid. She didn't go to the doctor or the dentist. She was probably malnourished.

Nora remembered holding Lucille's small hand. It had been as light as a house sparrow. The bones had felt hollow. Touching her was like touching onionskin.

"Help"—the plea echoed in Nora's head.

The microwave beeped. She carried her coffee and Lucille's old book to the café table out on the deck.

The sun was slowly working its way above the tree line. As it climbed over the peaks of the blue mountains, sunbeams cut through the pines, exposing squirrels moving through the canopy and birds darting from limb to limb.

The drone of cicadas drowned out all other sounds. Dew clung to the spearpoints of the parched grass, and the air was already heavy with moisture. It was going to be another hot, humid day.

As the sun fell on Nora's face, she wondered if Lucille had stolen a few minutes here and there to sit at the cement table in her garden. Had she left the suffocating rooms of her house to sip tea and read a book in the fresh air? Had she stared at her house and remembered it in its former glory? Had she ever wondered what her life would look like if she'd left Wynter House and ventured out into the world? Or were such thoughts too frightening?

A cardinal trilled nearby. A male, red as a toy wagon, was perched on the lip of the tray feeder at the far end of the deck.

The Cherokee believed the cardinal was a sacred animal. The bird's presence indicated that it had a message to deliver. It could also mean that someone Nora knew had recently died, and the cardinal was carrying the person's soul to the creator.

"Is that you, Lucille?" Nora asked.

Though Nora didn't share all of the Cherokee's beliefs, she knew the universe had many ways of conveying information to those willing to keep their minds and hearts open.

She held up the book. "Thank you for this. I imagine it was very special to you."

The cardinal let out a loud chirp.

Nora lowered the book and went very still. "Did you know that the end was coming?"

The cardinal cocked his head, his black eyes studying her. Then he raised his head and whistled three times. He seemed to be demanding something, but Nora had no idea what it was.

Suddenly a shadow crossed over the deck. Nora glanced up to see a red-tail hawk swoop low over the deck before diving straight down into the grass. It pinned something beneath its talon and bent its head toward its prey, poking with its arrow-sharp beak.

The hawk's proximity had spooked the cardinal. Nora scanned the surrounding trees for a splash of red, but it was gone. She picked up *The Little Lost Library* and read it for the second time.

The children's story, written completely in verse, told of a magnificent library that was accidentally lost when a wizard's magic carpet abruptly tilted to avoid a midair collision with a flock of swans. The library had been packed into an enchanted box for the journey, and because the box could change its size and shape to blend in with its surroundings, it was almost impossible to find. Only a person with a vivid imagination would succeed:

> *"You must first learn how to look
> To discover this treasure trove of books."*

It was a charming story that reminded Nora of Victorian morality tales. The young heroes of these stories were all brave, kind, and charitable. They always met with many hardships, but never gave up. And while the child in *The Lost Library* was never identified, Nora liked to think that it was Lucille.

She'd told Nora many times that her father had designed Wynter House. Maybe the hiding places really existed. Maybe Hugo Wynter created them.

Nora wished she had time to get her laptop and run a search on Hugo, but she didn't. She needed to get ready for work.

Forty minutes later, Nora unlocked the back door to Miracle Books and stepped into a haven of cool air and quiet. After putting her lunch in the fridge, she stood just outside the ring of mismatched, well-worn chairs known as the Readers' Circle and breathed in her store's signature scent of book pages, coffee, and possibility.

She turned on the lights and placed *The Little Lost Library* under the checkout counter. If she could steal a few moments between storytime and the after-school rush, she'd learn what she could about Hugo and the rest of the Wynter family.

For now, she needed to get the coffee started. The ticket agent's office was Sheldon's domain, but on Thursdays, Nora had to take over as barista while he hosted storytime.

Nora hoped her only employee wouldn't be late, but because Sheldon suffered from acute arthritis and fibromyalgia, his punctuality wasn't guaranteed. Often his pain and inflammation were so bad that he couldn't get out of bed. On good days, he stopped by the bakery to pick up pastries on the way to work and charmed every customer in the store.

At quarter to ten, Nora was just starting to worry that Sheldon might not show up, and then he breezed through the door.

"I'm here, and I've got the carbs!"

Sheldon Vega appeared in the ticket agent's office, arms laden with bakery boxes. He put the boxes on the counter and moved to the sink to wash his hands.

"There's an extra box," said Nora.

"Nothing gets past you, boss." Sheldon flashed her a grin as he dried his hands. "Hester's using our customers as guinea pigs again. She sent the strawberry-and-cream muffins you ordered, plus a box of peach basil muffins."

Nora arched a brow. "Peach basil? I'm intrigued. Wanna split one?"

Sheldon already had the box open. "As if you had to ask."

The muffin was a surprise. It was buttery and sweet, with

just enough basil to balance the natural sweetness of the peaches.

"I like it, but I doubt parents will buy them for their toddlers."

"Not a chance. I've gotten all the kids hooked on the Shel Silverstein," he said.

The café at Miracle Books had a limited menu. There was coffee, tea, and a small selection of espresso drinks. The food choices were either a book pocket—a soft pastry with a chocolate or raspberry filling—the muffin of the day, or the Shel Silverstein, which was Nutella on toasted Cuban bread.

Sheldon baked the Cuban bread from scratch, using his grandmother's recipe. He'd inherited his love of food and music from his Cuban father and his love of reading and fussing over people from his Jewish mother. With his wavy silver hair and glorious mustache, Sheldon looked like a sixty-something Clark Gable. He had a penchant for bow ties, sweater vests, reality dating shows, contemporary fiction, and, of course, Nutella.

Everyone loved Sheldon. On his good days, he was gregarious, patient, and kind. When he was hurting, he stayed in bed and cursed the world.

"How are your hands today?" Nora asked. "They look good."

"My knuckles are as nimble as a Cirque du Soleil performer. These hands are ready to swipe lots of credit cards."

"That's what I like to hear. Can I help you set up for the craft?"

Sheldon glanced at his watch. "No, but if you could put the pastries in the case and pour me a coffee, I'll love you for life."

"You already love me."

"Nothing lasts forever," Sheldon teased as he scurried into the Children's Corner.

His comment made Nora think of Lucille. She wanted to tell Sheldon everything that had happened after she'd closed the shop yesterday, but now was not the time.

It was ten o'clock on the dot when she unlocked the front door to welcome her first customers of the day. Even though there wasn't a cloud in the sky, the woman and her little boy wore yellow rain slickers.

When a man carrying a little girl in a ladybug raincoat followed close behind, Nora decided that Sheldon must be hosting a rain-themed storytime.

As more children and their parents or caregivers filed in, Nora took up her position in the ticket agent's office. Most of the adults liked to drink coffee and chat when storytime was over, but a few wanted a caffeine fix as soon as they walked through the door. She managed to serve coffee or espresso drinks to at least a dozen customers before Sheldon banged a small gong, signaling that storytime had officially begun.

"Good morning, friends," he intoned in his low, velvety storyteller voice. "I hope you're ready for some *crazy* weather because today is going to be cloudy with a *very* good chance of meatballs! I see you all wore your raincoats, which is very good, and we're going to make our own umbrellas to keep the meatballs from falling on our heads. Do you want meatballs on your head? Because *I* don't! Okay, get comfy. Let's find out how these meatballs got in the sky in the first place."

While Sheldon read, Nora helped the non-storytime customers. She also filled in holes on the new release table and switched out the endcaps in the mystery and romance sections.

She was trying to decide whether to put Louise Penny or Lisa Jewell in the last space in the endcap when the noise level in the Children's Corner went from library whispers to monster-truck-rally-loud.

The kids were throwing red pom-poms in the air and squealing. Sheldon, who was now wearing a steel colander as a helmet, kept reaching into a saucepot and tossing more pom-poms onto the floor.

After several minutes of mayhem, he asked the kids to collect eight meatballs each. The cacophony immediately faded as the tiny tots focused on counting. Their next task was to glue the pom-pom meatballs to their paper plate umbrellas.

Nora had a no-food rule when it came to the Children's Corner, but no one, including Sheldon, paid much attention to this. Sheldon asserted that he had to blackmail the kids with edible treats to conduct a successful storytime, and today was no different. As each child finished their craft project, Sheldon rewarded them with a small bag of fruit-shaped gummies.

"Listen, friends. It's super fun to try new foods, so I want you to try one new thing this week and tell me all about it next Thursday. And since you did such a great job today, I'm going to tell you a very special secret about next week's storytime. Want to know what it is?"

"Yeah!" the kids shouted in unison.

"We're going to have a teddy bear picnic, which means you can bring your favorite stuffed animal from home—it doesn't have to be a bear, any furry friend will work—but we're going to learn what real bears eat, and which bears live in North Carolina. And if you *really* want to, we can go on a teddy bear treasure hunt in the store."

Judging by their raucous cries, the kids were very keen on the treasure hunt idea.

For the rest of the morning, Nora shelved, recommended, ordered, and rang up books to the accompanying hum of the espresso machine, the hiss of the milk frother, and one of Spotify's coffeehouse playlists.

When she finally had a breather, she slipped into the ticket agent's booth to load dirty mugs into the dishwasher.

Sheldon wiped the counter and then pointed at the pastry case. "We only sold two peach-and-basil muffins, but the strawberry-and-creams are all gone. And yes, there are crumbs *everywhere.* I know you hate a dirty floor, so—hey, what's wrong?"

"I was thinking of another place with a dirty floor. Wynter House."

Sheldon stared at her. "Wait. You went *inside* the haunted mansion of Miracle Springs?"

"Yes, but—" Nora stopped when she heard the jingle of sleigh bells attached to the front door.

"Don't leave me hanging." Sheldon clamped a hand around Nora's forearm. "Tell me everything! Was it full of priceless antiques? Candelabra draped in cobwebs? A pipe organ that played a single note when no one was in the room? Scary portraits with eyes that followed you wherever you went? I'm so jealous! I never thought Lucille would let you in."

A woman's face appeared in the ticket agent's pass-through window. "May I have a chocolate book pocket, please?"

"Sure thing. Would you like me to heat it up for you?"

"That'd be great. I'm just going to grab a book I saw on my way in."

Sheldon popped the pastry in the microwave and set the timer for twenty seconds. Then he focused on Nora again. "Why did she let you in? Or did you just kick the door down?" When Nora didn't reply, he stared at her, aghast. "*Dios mío,* is that what happened?"

"Yes. She didn't answer the door, so I called to see if she was okay. She begged me for help, but . . . I was too late. She was dead by the time I got to her."

The microwave beeped, but Sheldon ignored it. He wrapped Nora in his arms and held her tight.

"I'm sorry, *mi amor*. That must have been terrible for you. I guess it was just her time."

Stepping out of his embrace, Nora said, "I'm not so sure that it was."

Chapter 4

*When you know you are of worth, you don't
have to raise your voice, you don't have to
become rude, you don't have to become vulgar;
you just are.*

—Maya Angelou

"I don't like this," Sheldon said after reading Lucille's note. "This feels like a goodbye to me. Do you think she knew she was sick? Maybe she was in pain. Or terribly dizzy. So she asked for help, but then . . . just let herself fall?"

Nora shook her head. "No one in their right mind would end things like that. She might've broken her hip or back and lain there in agony for hours."

"She answered the phone when you called and she asked for help, so no matter what this letter says, it must've been an accident." Sheldon folded the piece of paper in half, as if hiding Lucille's handwriting could dispel the uneasiness her words had evoked.

Though Nora could leave it at that, she needed to give voice to her fears, and she knew it was safe to share them with Sheldon. "What if someone else was in the house?"

To Sheldon's credit, he gave this serious consideration before responding.

"*Mija*, I know you've seen things. I know violence has left its mark on you, and I'm not just talking about these." He brushed the burn scars on her right arm. "For whatever reason, you seem to get caught in the gravitational pull of way too many criminal investigations. It's something you can't help, but that amount of exposure to violence makes you more suspicious, don't you think?"

Nora sighed heavily. "I'm not looking for drama, Sheldon. I don't want this to be anything but an accident. Still, my gut says that Lucille was trying to tell me something in the letter. And by giving me that book. Because of those, I can't shake a sense of doubt."

Sheldon gestured toward the front of the store. "Then go get your Google on. Things are pretty quiet, and I can steer the ship until Davis comes in. He wants to have a coffee and a chat. About what? I don't know, nor do I care. As long as I get to sit there and stare at his beautiful face, he can talk about tax law and I'd be happy."

"You might want to find a nook with some privacy," Nora cautioned. "He's only come out to a few people, and you know how many women in this town want him to swipe right on their dating profiles or fix him up with their sister, daughter, or BFF."

"You don't need to tell *me* about those women! Half of the ladies in June's knitting circle *still* think they can reverse my asexuality by showing me pics of some honey in a teeny, tiny bikini. I can't get them to understand that being sex-repulsed means that I'll never be tempted to get it on with another human being, no matter how hot they are."

Nora cocked her head. "Not even Davis?"

Sheldon knew Nora was teasing, but he answered, anyway. "Davis is beautiful inside and out. He's a smart and successful lawyer. He's funny. He's generous. He has tons of hobbies. I haven't had a romantic relationship in fifteen years, and that was with a woman, but I could fall in love with Davis Godwin." Sheldon held out a finger. "I'm *not* going to fall in love with him, because he needs more than I can give, but a boy can dream."

Nora left Sheldon to his fantasies as she helped a customer find a copy of Daniel Mason's *North Woods*. After that, she took up her position behind the checkout counter, leaving the other customers to wander through the shop at their leisure.

Miracle Books had the perfect layout for wandering. The shelves were laid out with labyrinthine corridors and dead ends. Nearly every genre had its own cozy space, complete with special displays and reading chairs. Fairy lights illuminated the darker corners. Colorful mobiles hung from the ceiling.

There was always so much to see in the stacks. The books, of course, were paramount, but the shelves also held decorative objects Nora dubbed "shelf enhancers." These were not the plastic figurines so prevalent at other bookstores, but rather eclectic, vintage items Nora found at the flea market and local estate sales.

Nora priced the shelf enhancers to sell quickly, which kept the store feeling fresh and exciting. Her last trip to the flea market had yielded a brass compass in a display case, cast iron bookends shaped like angelfish, a porcelain ginger jar, a set of appetizer dishes with fruit designs, a copper teapot, a glass elephant, and framed silhouettes of a family of six, including their dog and cats.

It was only Thursday, and half of these items were already gone. Nora wanted to hit the road after the flea market on Sunday and go thrifting in Asheville, and she was hoping McCabe would come along. They could spend the afternoon visiting antiques malls and consignment shops and then eat at one of Asheville's excellent restaurants. It had been decades since she'd had Ethiopian food, but she remembered the platters of *kitfo* and *doro key w'at* she'd shared with her college roommate as if it were yesterday. She was eager to savor the unique spices and throat-warming heat of those dishes again and to share the experience with McCabe.

Pulling out her phone, she sent him a quick text, asking if she should make reservations for Sunday evening.

Three dots surfaced on her screen. As she waited for McCabe's reply, Nora opened her laptop and typed Hugo Wynter into Google's search box. When she glanced back at her phone, the three dots had disappeared.

"That doesn't bode well," she grumbled.

She didn't fixate on McCabe's silence for long. The moment she began reading about Hugo Wynter, she became completely absorbed.

Hugo was born in the small town of Clyde, North Carolina, in 1899. His father, who worked in the paper mill in a nearby town, groomed Hugo from an early age to follow in his footsteps. However, the onset of the Great War changed Hugo's future. He joined the army and was sent to France. A year later, injuries from an exploding artillery shell cost him his right foot, and he was sent home.

With the shortage of qualified workers at the paper mill, Hugo's head for numbers and leadership skills landed him a management position. He stayed at the mill until the Great Depression shuttered its doors for good.

Hugo didn't want a new career, so when the economy bounced back, he took out a loan and opened his own mill a stone's throw from Miracle Springs. He named it Pisgah Mill after the Pisgah Forest. Hugo married a debutante from a well-to-do family in Asheville and built Wynter House as a wedding gift for Helena, his bride.

Hugo and Helena had two daughters, Lucille and Lynette. The girls grew up in the house their father designed, and

Lucille remained there after her marriage to Frederick Vandercamp, her father's right-hand man at the mill. Not long after her marriage, Hugo retired.

The name Vandercamp gave Nora pause. It was uncommon for women to retain their maiden name back then, so why was Lucille known as Lucille Wynter and not Lucille Vandercamp? Nora wondered if the couple had gone through a nasty divorce or if Frederick Vandercamp had been a bad egg. That would explain why Clem went by his mother's maiden name.

Nora pushed these questions aside and continued reading about Hugo Wynter.

She learned that the passion Lucille's father felt for paper didn't diminish upon his retirement. A lifelong book collector, Hugh purchased several printing presses and started to publish beautiful books in his own basement.

Each book had a very small, very costly print run. Hugo used the best paper on the market and Helena designed intricate engravings to accompany each collection of poetry or children's storybook. Hugo was fifty-five when he suffered a fatal heart attack. His wife found him bent over one of his beloved printing presses.

Cancer claimed Helena two months later.

Returning to the search results, Nora saw a hit with the headline THE PISGAH PAPER MILL SCANDAL.

She clicked on the link and was shocked to learn that Hugo Wynter had been accused of embezzling a large sum of cash from the mill. Though he was never arrested, and the money was never recovered, he immediately retired from the mill and from public life. Three years later, Hugo and Helena were both dead.

Lucille was probably in her early to mid-twenties when she lost her parents and became mistress of Wynter House, Nora thought. *All that, and a scandal. Poor Lucille.*

The sleigh bells rang, jerking Nora back to reality. She glanced up to see Davis Godwin enter the store. He flashed his thousand-kilowatt smile and tapped the brim of an imaginary hat.

"Afternoon, Nora."

"Hey, Davis. Nice to see you."

And it was. Not only was Davis one of the best-looking men in Miracle Springs, but he was one of the best-looking men Nora had ever met. At forty, Davis looked just like Denzel Washington's son John David Washington. Davis was the town's top defense attorney, but he had the charisma and killer smile of an A-list actor.

Nora had gotten to know him when she'd found herself unexpectedly needing his services. He wasn't much of a reader, but he joined Sheldon's Blind Date Book Club to widen his social circle. In no time at all, he and Sheldon had become close friends.

"Sheldon's in his lair," she told him.

"Before I get my coffee on, I wanted to get your feedback on an idea that's been bouncing around in my head for a while." Hearing the bells, he swung around to see who'd entered the shop and gave a friendly wave to a pair of teenage girls. They giggled and clung to each other as they disappeared around the corner of the stacks.

Davis grinned. "We were like that once, long, long ago. Awkward and confused. Our bodies changing and our futures looming. It's a tough time. This summer, I had a string of clients who didn't look old enough to shave. Money's tight for many of their families, and the kids think they can make things better by boosting a car or dealing dope. They're looking for quick fixes—something to keep the wolf from the door—but then they get arrested, and it all just piles on. Most of these kids will go to juvie, which is where they stop being kids. It's where they lose hope. They get hard and angry. I'm not naïve. I can't help all of these kids, but I can help some of them."

"What do you have in mind?"

"I know it sounds crazy, but I want to start a book group. I want to go in once or twice a month and talk about a certain book—something that these kids can relate to. I want them to know they're not alone." Davis splayed his hands. "I'll buy the books, of course. There's no way the state will fork over any money for this, but I don't care. I'll need your help figuring out which books to pick. I can't go in there with twenty copies of *Invisible Man* or *Native Son,* or I'll scare every one of them off, but I can't go in with a picture book either."

"What about a graphic novel? I can make you a list."

Davis snapped his fingers. "Yes! *Yes!* That's perfect. I knew you'd have the answer."

The sleigh bells jingled again, and Davis turned toward the sound. A young woman with hazelnut skin and a head full of copper-colored braids hesitantly stepped into the shop. She drew her shoulders inward as she carefully closed the door.

"Batrice!" Davis called out. "What's going on, girl?"

The young woman smiled shyly. "Nothing much. How 'bout you?"

Davis put a hand on Nora's shoulder. "Having a tongue wag with my friend. I'm about to go back and have the best iced decaf latte this town has to offer. Can I get you one?"

Batrice nodded and followed Davis into the fiction section.

Nora spent the next thirty minutes flitting between the espresso machine and the checkout counter. Because it was after three, Sheldon was officially off the clock, but he interrupted his conversation with Davis and Batrice to serve the last book pocket to the teenage girls who'd emerged from the YA section, carrying an armload of fantasy titles. While Sheldon chatted with the girls about their favorite books, Nora helped a harried mother of three find a cookbook featuring quick and easy recipes, bagged an older gentleman's special order of Horatio Hornblower novels, and introduced a nine-year-old to Nancy Drew.

At four o'clock, the high school students trickled in. They loved hanging out in the Readers' Circle and were disappointed to find it occupied by three adults. To placate them, Nora cut up the rest of the peach-and-basil muffins and offered free samples. They disappeared in a matter of minutes.

Eventually Batrice left her seat to wander deeper into the stacks and Davis headed back to the office. Sheldon crooked his finger at Nora, beckoning her to follow him to the ticket agent's office.

"I know I've said this before, but I need you to hear me," he began. "It's time to hire someone. It's four o'clock and this place is jumping. Look at all these kids. I bet one of them would love to work here after school. You can't keep flapping around like a flustered chicken. You'll wear yourself out. Worse, you'll lose sales. That girl, Batrice, needs your help. She's going to walk out any minute now, but you'll be too busy to notice."

Nora leaned against the fridge and sighed. She didn't want anyone to leave her store feeling unseen or unheard. "I'll put a sign in the window before I close tonight."

"Good. And keep an eye on the YA section. There are too many books scattered on the floor and too many backpacks for them to disappear into. That section has been hit the hardest by our 'freetail therapist.'"

Anyone who ran a retail business faced shrinkage, but the losses to Nora's inventory because of theft had always been relatively small. Until recently.

When Nora closed Miracle Books in July to do a thorough inventory, she'd been shocked by how many books were unaccounted for. The number of damaged books hadn't changed. Most of these were children's books, but there were also a few that arrived from the publisher with dented or torn covers. This was usually a result of poor packaging.

Nora could recoup her losses on items damaged during shipment, but kids' books riddled with bite marks, torn pages, or mystery stains found their way into the used-book section and were sold at a loss.

Shrinkage due to theft was hard to take because every stolen book bit into the store's profits. It had never been a serious problem until July, and by the middle of August, it was clear that the booknapper was still active.

When Nora griped about the situation to McCabe, he recommended security cameras.

"Even if they're not turned on, their presence is a deterrent."

Nora had immediately rejected the idea. "Security cameras would ruin the vibe of Miracle Books. It's a place to escape the outside world and relax. No one wants to feel watched while they're trying to find a little peace. Some customers are nervous about buying certain self-help books or study guides. They feel ashamed or embarrassed. If they know they're on camera, they'll probably buy those books online. They need to feel safe in my store. They need to trust me, which means I need to trust them too."

After mulling this over, McCabe had said, "What would you do if you saw someone steal a book?"

"I'd confront them in a casual way. I'd say something like, 'Oh, it looks like you forgot to pay for the book in your bag. I get it. I did the same thing at the flea market. I popped a candle in my purse to free up my hands. I grabbed two more, and by the time I went to pay, I'd totally forgotten about the candle in my bag.'"

"That's a solid approach," McCabe said. "What if they deny it?"

Nora had frowned. "In a different town, I'd suggest they go to the library and borrow books, but since we don't have a library, I'd recommend they check out the used section next if the new books are too pricey."

"It's going to be tough to identify your thieves. You have kids who come in with backpacks, the Monday mom groups carry giant purses, the parents have diaper bags, and every day, you get tourists from the Lodge carrying their teal tote bags. Unless you start asking people to leave their bags behind the counter, you'll have to catch shoplifters in the act."

"I am *not* going to ask customers to check their bags," she said emphatically. "I need to figure out what's motivating the thief. Are they selling the books online? Is there a shoplifting trend on TikTok? Is someone doing it compulsively? Sheldon and I just need to keep our eyes open."

But when the shop was teeming with customers, two pairs of eyes weren't enough. Even though Nora wandered throughout the store, showing people books, reshelving strays, and completing the checkout process, Sheldon was usually stuck in the ticket agent's office. His view from there was limited, and the store had plenty of nooks with just enough privacy to make stealing all too easy.

Sheldon's right. I need to hire someone.

Ignoring the mound of dirty coffee cups in the sink, Nora headed into the stacks in search of Batrice.

She found her in the self-help section, looking defeated.

Nora had been in business long enough to know that Batrice wasn't ready to ask for assistance, so she simply said, "I hope you didn't feel like you had to give up your chair. The high schoolers are way too territorial when it comes to the Readers' Circle."

Batrice smiled. "I can see why. That purple chair is so soft.

I could've taken a nap there." Her smile wobbled as she added, "It's been a long week and I still have one more day to go. I'm not lying when I say I live for the weekend."

"Work getting you down?"

"Kinda. It's not the job. That's okay. It's some of the people I work with."

Nora pointed to a book with *Toxic People* in its very long title. "Are they like that?"

"Yeah, I guess. It's not really people, though. It's just one person. A woman." Batrice folded her arms across her chest. "We used to be close. When I first started the job, I saw her as an ally. We're the only two Black women in the company, and we have so much in common. We went to the same high school, we love podcasts, and we're both into photography. We used to hang out at lunch and grab drinks after work. That was before we both went after the same promotion."

"That's when things changed?"

Anger flared in Batrice's honey-brown eyes. "Yep. The bi—" Batrice stopped herself, took a breath, and started again. "This *woman* started a rumor that I had an alcohol problem. I never have more than one glass of wine, while her Gucci bag jingles like Christmas bells because of all the mini bottles of vodka she carries around. She didn't stop there either. A coworker asked me if I had something going on with my previous boss. Something romantic." She shook her head in disgust. "The man's old enough to be my granddaddy! Guess who put that idea in his head?"

"Did you ask him?"

"He said he couldn't remember. He hasn't talked to me since." Tears beaded Batrice's long lashes. "I can't file a complaint about her without proof that she's behind the rumors, but if she gets the promotion, she'll make my life a living hell. I don't even know if I want to stay at this job. I feel like my life is a total mess, and I don't know how it happened."

Nora touched Batrice's arm. "Can I show you something?"

Nora led Batrice to the fiction section and pulled a book off the shelf. It was *Wahala* by Nikki May. "Have you heard this word before?"

"No."

"It's Nigerian for 'trouble,' and one of the women in this book is nothing but. She acts like a friend, but it's just an act. There's something broken in her that makes her create chaos. She is *wahala*. She reminds me of your coworker."

Batrice was already reaching for the book. "Does she get run over by a bus? Because I will read this tonight if she does."

Nora laughed. "The other women in her sphere figure out how to handle her. Why don't you have a seat and read a few pages? See what you think. While you're doing that, I'll grab a few other titles. If any of them resonate with you, you can take them home. Or you can read them here anytime you want."

Leaving Batrice to select a chair in one of the reading nooks, Nora moved purposefully around the stacks. She deposited Jessica George's *Maame* and two nonfiction books about toxic personalities on the table next to Batrice and returned to the ticket agent's office to serve another customer.

Batrice bought three of the five books. Handing Nora her credit card, she said, "I know Davis from church. When he told me to tell you what's been going on, I thought he was crazy. I didn't think you'd understand, but I'm glad I came. I like the vibe here."

"Good luck with everything," Nora said as another customer lined up behind Batrice.

The rest of the afternoon passed quickly. Business was steady enough to keep Nora occupied from the moment Sheldon left until closing time.

Usually, Nora watched the last customer leave before locking the door and flipping the sign in the window from OPEN to CLOSED, but she was still in the YA section, trying to figure out if there were too many holes on the shelves compared to the number of YA titles sold that day, when the sleigh bells indicated that the last customer had just walked out.

Nora didn't want to move until she straightened the three shelves with the most holes, so she squatted down and tried to figure out which books were missing. All the books in T.J. Klune's The Extraordinaries series were gone, but that was okay because Nora remembered selling them to a high schooler with green hair. However, the hardcover copies of Rebecca Yarros's *Fourth Wing* and *Iron Flame* were gone, and Nora definitely hadn't sold those books in the past twenty-four hours.

Moving through the stacks toward the Readers' Circle, Nora was dismayed to see large holes in the contemporary romance section too. She knew she'd bagged one or two Colleen Hoover titles over the course of the day, but at least six of her books were missing from the shelves.

"What is wrong with people?" Nora muttered angrily.

She stomped behind the checkout counter to print a sales report. Tomorrow she'd come in early and take inventory of all the titles written by the authors who'd been so popular today.

"I need to catch this scumbag," she muttered angrily.

A shadow darkened the doorway and Nora hurried out from behind the counter to stop the potential customer from coming inside.

She wasn't fast enough, and a slim woman in a white sundress opened the door.

The woman took two steps inside and slapped a hand over the sleigh bells, instantly silencing them. "Are you Nora Pennington?" she demanded.

Nora had never seen the woman before. She was in her early fifties and obviously took good care of herself. Her long hair, which was the color of corn silk, fell over her tan shoulders in soft waves. She wore a full face of makeup and gold jewelry. Nora recognized Chanel's trademark double Cs on her earrings and necklace. Diamond rings sparkled on her fingers and from the crystal face of her gold watch. Her handbag cost more than Nora's truck.

A rich woman from out of town, Nora thought, hoping the woman would make a quick purchase and leave. It had been a long day and she was ready to go home, pour a glass of wine, and flop on the couch with her current read.

"I'm Nora. Can I help you with something? We're closed right now, but if you're looking for a specific title, I can see if I have it in stock."

The woman's mouth puckered in disgust. "I'm not here to get a book. I *hate* books. I'm here because you're the last person my mother talked to before she died." Squaring her shoulders, she pointed an acrylic nail at Nora's chest. "I want to know *exactly* what she said, and I'm not leaving until you tell me."

Chapter 5

All parents damage their children. It cannot be helped. Youth, like pristine glass, absorbs the prints of its handlers.

— Mitch Albom

Nora didn't like this woman.

She didn't like her haughty tone, the way her Gucci bag dangled from her upturned wrist, or her flashing diamonds. She acted like she was in charge—like she owned everything she saw. Nora's proprietorship of Miracle Books was irrelevant in the face of her demands.

To quell her annoyance, Nora focused on the human being behind the tone and status symbols. This woman had woken up this morning to a new world—a world that no longer included her mother. She'd answered a phone call from the sheriff's department and was told that her mom was dead. It didn't matter if the two had been close—and Nora suspected they hadn't—Lucille was her mother.

And now, she was gone.

"Would you like to sit down?" Nora waved toward the back of the store. "We have a seating area in the back."

"No, I wouldn't like to sit down. I'd like for you to answer my question."

Nora had lived in Miracle Springs for over a decade, and one of her favorite things about her town was its gentility. The people raised in these parts were polite. Well mannered. They were "please" and "thank you" people. They smiled or waved in passing. They held doors. Helped seniors load groceries into their cars. They were courteous to visitors—even the rude ones—but the moment these people were out of earshot, the locals would mutter, "You were *not* raised right."

Lucille had never mentioned her children to Nora. Not once. She'd never given the slightest hint that her adult son was living in an apartment in the back of the garage. Nor had she breathed a single word about her daughter.

Maybe that's why this woman oozes anger out of every pore.

"What's your name?" Nora asked her.

"Can you just answer my question?"

Nora gave up. She couldn't force this woman to be civil, so she'd tell her what she wanted to know and show her the door.

"She asked for help. I called her because she didn't show up after I knocked on the kitchen door. I waited, but didn't hear any noises from inside the house. So I called her and let the phone ring and ring. When she finally picked up, she said, 'Help.' I told her help was coming. Then she said, 'Too late.' I called 911 and kicked in the door. I got to your mom as fast as I could, but she was already gone. I'm really sorry."

The woman stared. "She asked for help and then told you it was too late? You're *sure* that's all she said?"

"Yes."

"What about the other times you saw her? You've obviously been selling her books, despite her situation."

Now Nora understood the source of this woman's hostility. "Yesterday was the first time I stepped inside Wynter

House, so I had no idea she owned that many books. We always met in the boot room."

"And what did you talk about?"

"Book plots. Characters. Favorite stories. She was very private about her personal life, though sometimes she'd talk about her father."

The woman rolled her eyes. "Oh, yes. Her precious, perfect daddy. What else?"

"That's all. She didn't like to talk about herself. If I asked questions about her life, she'd change the subject."

"What kind of questions? What were you hoping to learn?"

But Nora had had enough. "Look, I'm very sorry for your loss, but I'm going home now. You're welcome to come back in the morning if you want to talk some more."

"Oh, I'll be back. You're a book person. If my mom shared her secrets with someone, it's got to be you. What time do you open?"

Nora thought of the little book stashed under the checkout counter and the letter folded inside its pages. They were within easy reach. All she had to do was walk behind the counter and get them.

But something stopped her. A niggling feeling told her to keep these items to herself. Better yet, she should hide them. She should bring them home and hide them in one of the storage nooks inside her tiny house.

"We open at ten, but if you want to talk, come at nine thirty. That way, we can sit down, have coffee, and chat without being interrupted."

The woman turned to go. "I'll be here at nine thirty, but you can skip the coffee. I'm not here to make friends. I'm looking for information. When I've got what I need, you won't see me again. Goodbye."

And with that, she left the shop without closing the door behind her.

"Her name is Harper Wynter," McCabe said as he ladled Bolognese sauce over Nora's spaghetti. "Fifty-two. Divorced. She dropped her husband's surname, which was Hamilton, two years ago. Like Clem, she uses her mom's maiden name. When I asked why, she said that she didn't want anything from her deadbeat dad, including his name."

"Sounds like some family drama."

McCabe grunted. "The only families without drama are on TV. Anyway, Harper owns an interior design firm called Wynter Designs in Dallas. She's named after Harper Lee, but has never read *To Kill a Mockingbird*."

"Seriously? Wow."

McCabe added sauce to his own bowl before returning the pan to the stovetop. Scanning the counter, he mumbled, "What did I do with the sprinkle cheese?"

"It's on the table."

McCabe sat down with a sigh. "It's been a day." He spooned ground Parmesan on top of his pasta and then passed the bowl to Nora. "Too bad she didn't show up at the store a few minutes later. Talk about ending on a sour note. And it doesn't sound like tomorrow will start with rays of sunshine either."

"At least I know what to expect." Nora spun spaghetti around on her fork. "Was she brusque with you too?"

McCabe grunted. "If that's code for bitchy as hell, then yes. She blazed into my office, demanding to know exactly when, where, and how her mother died. When I asked her to identify her mother's body, she told me to look for a tattoo saying 'Worst Mom in the World.'"

Nora managed to swallow a bite of salad before whispering, "Damn."

"I know. Ms. Wynter didn't want to hear about her brother either. She had no intention of bailing him out or taking care of the rehab paperwork. She made it very clear that Clem was not her problem. She was in town to bury her mother, learn the contents of her will, and deal with the house."

"Has she been to Wynter House yet?"

McCabe nodded. "She went there straight from the airport but didn't stay long. She said she'd go back tonight after buying gloves and coveralls from Walmart."

"I don't blame her for that. I wouldn't want to spend time in that house without gloves, a face mask, and all the doors and windows open. It smells worse than a landfill."

McCabe made a noise of approval. "Whoever inherits that place will have to hire a professional cleaning crew. It's going to be a big, expensive job. Are you tempted by the books?"

"I don't know what she has, but the ones I saw in the dining room are destined for the trash. You can't save a moldy book. God knows what kind of filth is under the books in the kitchen, especially the ones on the floor." She held up both hands. "Let's not go there. I don't want to put us off our dinner."

"I'm in law enforcement. Nothing puts me off my dinner."

Nora wanted to tell McCabe about Lucille's letter and show him the copy of *The Little Lost Library*, but didn't want to risk getting Bolognese sauce on the book. As soon as their meal was over and they'd finished cleaning the kitchen, she'd retrieve both from her purse.

She was loading the dishwasher when McCabe's phone chirped. Ignoring it, he popped the cap off a bottle of Gaelic Ale from Highland Brewing and took a long pull.

When his phone chirped again, he tapped the screen and read the text message. "No way."

Nora turned off the water and reached for the dishrag. "What?"

"There's a third sibling. Beck Wynter is at the station right now. He wants us to keep his siblings out of Wynter House until his mother's will is read." McCabe shook his head. "He's asking us to put seals on the doors—treat it like a crime scene. But only to keep his siblings from digging through Lucille's stuff. He's gung-ho to get a cleaning crew in there."

Suddenly the food in Nora's belly felt very heavy. "I need to show you something."

"I don't like the sound of that," McCabe said, following her into the living room.

Nora removed the fabric book sleeve she'd tucked inside her purse and handed it to McCabe. "Be gentle. The book is old. There's a letter inside too. That's what I really want you to see."

McCabe carefully eased the book out of the sleeve and examined the cover. Cradling the book's spine in his left hand, he flipped through the pages. Then he removed the letter and read it. Nora could tell when he reached the end because a deep groove appeared between his brows. He shot her a worried glance before reading it a second time.

After setting the letter aside, he read the entire book. When he finished, he placed the book and letter, side by side, on the kitchen table. Resting his chin on his folded hands, he stared into the middle distance for nearly a minute.

When he turned to Nora, the crease in his brow was still there. "Did Lucille ever say anything about owning valuable objects? Art, jewelry, rare books?"

"She told me there was a treasure trove inside the house, but I think she was talking about her hoard. She bought used books from me, Grant. She never spent more than five dollars per book. She had holes in her sweaters. Her shoes were worn. An arm of her glasses was taped on. The Lucille I knew was frugal and eccentric." Nora's eyes slid to where the book lay on the coffee table. "Then again, after seeing the inside of her house, I realize I didn't know her at all."

McCabe tapped Lucille's letter with his fingertip. "What was your gut reaction to this?"

"I made me feel . . . uneasy. It sounds like she knew her time was up."

"Maybe she did. She was eighty-three, and her living conditions were a health risk. Maybe she hadn't been feeling well for days. Weeks, even. I haven't gotten the medical examiner's report yet. She had a bad migraine yesterday and had to go home, so she's running behind today."

Nora gazed at Lucille's signature. "I wonder what happened between her and her kids. And why does Beck want to keep his siblings out of the house?"

"Who knows? There could be valuables inside."

"There must be. Harper only wants to talk to me because she believes her mom told me her secrets. About what, I don't know."

McCabe picked up *The Little Lost Library* and cradled it in his palms. "Could this be what they're both after?"

"I don't think so. Lucille treasured that book because her father made it. After selling his paper mill and retiring, he printed children's stories and volumes of poetry using a printing press he kept in the basement. His wife, a talented artist in her own right, made all the engravings. According to what I read online, Hugo Wynter made little to no profit from these books. He gave most of them away. I found only two records of Wynter House Press books sold within the last ten years, and they didn't sell for much."

McCabe's shoulders relaxed and he smiled. "I can see why

she gave you this book. She knew you'd read it and recognize how special it was to her. I know you feel guilty about selling books to her, but I bet she treasured being your customer. You gave her something to look forward to, and after you left, she had a new book and a new memory. Those are good things, sweetheart."

Nora laid her palm against McCabe's cheek. "I love you so much."

"I love you too." McCabe grabbed her hand and kissed it.

"Do you want to check out that true crime series on Netflix everyone's been talking about, or do you need to deal with Beck's request?"

Reaching for the remote, McCabe said, "Fuentes is handling it, but let's watch the Harlan Coben series instead. I've seen enough true crime."

The next morning, Harper Wynter rapped on the bookstore's front door.

"Even her knock sounds obnoxious!" Sheldon groused.

Once again, Lucille's daughter looked flawless. Today's dress was blush colored with ruffles on the sleeves and hem. Her hair was swept up in a loose bun, and a pair of designer sunglasses perched on top of her head. Her strappy gold sandals looked like something a Greek goddess would wear.

Nora waved at the fiction section. "The seating area is in the back. The coffee offer still stands if you're interested. We also have tea, pastries, and muffins."

"I already ate at my B and B—a place that didn't exist when I lived here. I can't believe so many people visit this dump of a town. There are no miracles in these springs."

"How long has it been since you were here?"

Harper snorted. "A few years after graduating college. As

soon as I finished at the University of Texas, I started working at a design firm. I got engaged and was looking at houses, with my fiancé, when I got a call from my brother Clem. He was in jail on possession charges. My mom wouldn't leave the house, and my older brother had just started his practice and couldn't leave his precious clients in *pain*, so I took a week off work. I got Clem into a top-notch rehab and hired a professional organizer to help my mother. She didn't want help. She told me to leave her alone—not very nicely, either—so I did."

Harper's tone and expression were completely bland.

Over the hiss of the milk frother, Nora said, "That must have been hard on you. But like I said last night, your mother and I talked about the books we'd read or wanted to read. Occasionally she'd mention one or both of her parents. That's it."

"What about Wynter House?"

Inside the ticket agent's booth, Sheldon tamped the espresso beans with more fervor than usual. Harper didn't even glance in his direction.

"She told me her father designed the house and that it was a blend of styles. Though mostly Gothic revival, it had a few Victorian and Art Deco features too. She also said she'd never lived anywhere else. She talked about it like it was a person. If she was tired, she'd say it was because the house had been talking in its sleep. The house could be grumpy because of the humidity. Or happy because the magnolia trees were in bloom."

Harper twisted one of the rings around her finger. "She always talked about the house like that. Did she mention specific rooms or architectural features?"

"Not really. I asked her once if she had a library, and she said that she had more than one."

Harper went very still. "Go on."

"I told her she was lucky, and she agreed and changed the subject. She was very private about her personal life. With me, at any rate."

"You sold her books for *years*. She *must* have told you more about the house."

Nora shook her head. "Only that Wynter House was hers. She made a point of telling me that many times. I really didn't know her. I had no idea she had a family other than her parents."

Harper flicked her hand in impatience. "If she didn't talk to you about the layout of the house or something she was keeping hidden, then you can't help me. I'm due at the attorney's office in a bit, so I'll show myself out."

With her purse hanging limply from her wrist, Harper marched away.

"Have a blessed day!" Sheldon called after her in a loud, singsong voice.

Nora followed Harper to the front. When she opened the door to let Harper out, she saw that it had begun to rain. The scent of wet grass and damp pavement drifted inside. A rainy end-of-summer Friday would bring in more customers than a hot and sunny day, and Nora wanted to check the YA inventory before the crowds rolled in.

"I hope you find what you were looking for," she told Harper.

Harper paused on the threshold. "What makes you think I'm looking for something?"

"Because you asked me if your mother talked about particular rooms or told me secrets. If she hid something in that house, I have no clue what it is *or* where it is. She was good at keeping the world out."

"Yes," Harper agreed sourly. "It was the only thing she did well."

Nora barely waited for Harper to step outside before firmly closing the door. She turned the dead bolt and watched Lucille's daughter scuttle up the sidewalk, her shoulders hunched against the rain.

Thinking of the Wicked Witch of the West, Nora whispered, "Better hurry, or you'll melt."

It was seven in the evening and Nora was putting away strays when she heard Hester shout, "Hello! Where are you?"

Nora pushed *Hello Beautiful* into its place on the shelf and stood up. It was an hour past closing and she still hadn't vacuumed or wiped down the counters in the ticket agent's booth.

"Be right there!" she shouted back.

By the time she shelved three more books and returned to the center of the store, June arrived. Balancing a cardboard box in her arms, she darted into the ticket agent's booth

"I'm coming in hot—literally!" she cried.

Hester pushed a scattering of dirty coffee cups to the side to make room for June's box and then poked her head through the pass-through window. "Busy day?"

"Crazy busy." Nora sagged against a chair. "I'm *so* glad it's Friday night. I need some girl time."

"I hope you're hungry. I made baked grits with ham, corn, and a truckload of cheese. I just love me some breakfast for dinner," June said. "What's tonight's mocktail?"

Nora joined her friends in the kitchen area. "Mimosas. I'm mixing OJ with Perrier."

"Estella's bringing green bean salad, and I've got dessert covered, so we're good to go." Without being asked, Hester loaded the dirty cups into the dishwasher and hung the clean ones back on the pegboard.

No two mugs were alike. Many had bookish themes. Some featured superheroes. The ones favored by Nora, Sheldon, and most of their customers featured snarky text. Sheldon indulged children when they asked for a Hello Kitty or Batman mug, but adult customers never made requests. It was more fun to see which mug Sheldon would randomly grab off the pegboard.

Nora suspected Sheldon's picks weren't always random, like the time he served a cappuccino to an elderly judge in a mug that said I WOKE UP SEXY AS HELL . . . AGAIN. Luckily, the judge thought the mug was the funniest thing he'd ever seen.

Occasionally, chipped or cracked mugs were thrown out, and Nora would scour the flea market for worthy replacements.

Hester examined the newest mug, which featured an image of Michael Myers and the text KILLING IT SINCE 1978, before putting it in the dishwasher.

She tucked a honey-colored curl behind her ear, closed the dishwasher door with her hip, and frowned at the mocktail Nora handed her.

"I'm ready for Estella to have this baby so our book club can be boozy again!"

"Rough day?" Nora asked.

Hester looked aggrieved. "I'll tell you after Estella gets here."

Estella showed up five minutes later, wearing a chic black pantsuit and a jubilant expression. "I felt the baby today!" she told her friends. "She fluttered like a little butterfly."

June put her hands on her hips and scowled. "I knew you'd have a Hollywood pregnancy. Your bump is adorable, your skin looks amazing, and you haven't puked once, have you?"

Preening, Estella smoothed her auburn hair and said, "Nope." When her eyes met June's, they were no longer shining. "One of my clients told me that morning sickness is a sign of a healthy baby. Is it bad that I don't feel sick?"

Wagging her finger, June said, "I told you. When you start showing, everyone will tell you everything they know about pregnancy. Facts, superstitions—everything. You run a salon, which means every woman who comes in for a balayage or root touch-up is going to share her own pregnancy story with you."

"That's going to get old fast," Hester muttered.

June snorted. "For real. After they've told you about their own experiences, they'll tell you about their sister-in-laws', aunts', and cousins'. After that, they'll start in on celebrity pregnancies and finish off with a generous helping of advice. People who've never even held a child will suddenly have all kinds of wisdom to impart." She laid her hand on top of Estella's. "Honey, I know you're nervous because you're forty, but you need to tune out the unsolicited advice or comments. This is *your* pregnancy. *Your* baby. And the village you need to raise this child? It's right here. It's us and Jack. And your dad. No one else matters."

"Here." Nora thrust a mocktail into June's hand. "You must be thirsty after that speech."

June swatted Nora with the dishrag. "Go sit down so I can dish out these grits."

The four friends carried their plates to the Readers' Circle and sat in their favorite chairs. June always took the purple velvet chair. "If Crown Royal made a throne, it would look like this," she'd once joked.

At fifty-five, June was the oldest member of the Secret, Book, and Scone Society. Nora and Estella were both in their forties, and Hester was in her late thirties. The four women had crossed paths around town for years, but it had taken the suspicious death of a visiting businessman to truly bring them together. Now they couldn't imagine a life without these deep and abiding friendships.

Friday nights were sacred to all four of the women. It was their night for sisterhood and books. For food and gossip. For whispered confidences and banshee shrieks of laughter. Tonight they'd talk about their men and their jobs. And in between voicing concerns or sharing anecdotes, they'd discuss that week's book pick.

June was the first one to put her fork down and reach for her copy of Barbara Kingsolver's *Demon Copperhead.*

"I knew this one was going to be tough for me, and it was. I cried at least three times reading this, but it made me see how easily a person can lose themselves to drugs. I thank God that my son came out the other side of all that pain and shame, but it hurts my heart to think about what he went through."

Nora said, "When this book first came out, you said that you never wanted to read it. What changed your mind?"

"Tyson. He listened to the audiobook, and he wanted to talk about it with me." June gave a dry chuckle. "I never thought I'd be doing a buddy read with my grown son, but we learned things about each other because of this book."

Hester flipped to the pink page tab sticking out of her book like a snake tongue and said, "I was blown away by how Kingsolver described OxyContin. She says OxyContin was a shiny thing, and 'God's gift for the laid-off deep-hole man with his back and neck bones grinding like bags of gravel.'"

"Anything to dull the pain, right?" Estella said softly.

Nora couldn't listen to the discussion without thinking of Clem Wynter, so she told her friends about Lucille's passing, what she'd learned about her grown children, and the visit from Lucille's curt daughter.

"You actually waited until *this moment* to tell us something this huge?" Hester gawked at Nora.

"I wanted us to finish talking about *Demon Copperhead* first. I feel like I've interrupted too many book discussions with my drama," Nora said.

Estella gestured around the circle. "We're here for the drama. Always. So, can we see the book Lucille gave you?"

Nora retrieved it from its place under the checkout counter and handed it to Estella. "Could you read her letter too? All of you? I'd like to hear everyone's take on it. I'll clean up while you're doing that."

She cleared the dinner plates, washed them, and brewed a pot of decaf. She then carried Hester's caramelized fruit tart to the Readers' Circle, but her friends weren't interested in dessert. They were completely focused on *The Little Lost Library* and Lucille's letter.

"The letter makes me sad," Hester said. "But this book? I love the idea that these riddles could lead to a lost library. I wish it were real."

June opened to the middle of the book. "Maybe it is. This line about the place where the wood gets very hot and where, once upon a time, Ma would hang a pot, could be a fireplace. What if this book is a scavenger hunt?"

"Lucille's dad must've written this for his family," said Estella. "No offense, Nora, but why did she give this to you? Wouldn't it mean more to someone who grew up in Wynter House?"

Nora shrugged. "I've wondered the same thing. Maybe she gave it to me to safeguard. I don't know about Lucille's sons, but Harper hates books."

Hester passed Nora a fork. "Wouldn't it be cool if you could get inside the house and look for the lost library?"

"Harper made it pretty clear that I was persona non grata." Nora used the side of her fork to guillotine the tip of her tart. "I doubt I'll ever see the inside of Wynter House again."

Nora would later look back on this conversation and wish that she hadn't been so completely and utterly wrong.

Chapter 6

It takes so little to make a child happy, that it is a pity in a world full of sunshine and pleasant things, that there should be any wistful faces, empty hands, or lonely little hearts.

— Louisa May Alcott

Between Friday night's book club meeting and a Saturday marked by banner sales, Nora had shaken off some of the shock and sorrow of Lucille Wynter's passing.

As she walked to the Pink Lady Grill to meet McCabe for dinner, she smiled and waved at acquaintances, other merchants heading home after a long day, and regular frequenters of Miracle Books.

The humidity that had weighed everyone down for the past eight hours was being swept away by the mountain breeze. It ruffled women's skirts and dried the sweat on hikers' brows. It carried the scent of sun-warmed pine needles and honeysuckle from the forests, teasing people with hints of autumn.

Nora was a little early for her date, so she meandered through the memory garden on the far side of the diner. Created by Jack Nakamura, owner of the Pink Lady and the love of Estella's life, the garden was a small oasis nestled between the diner and a parking lot.

Though Jack had lost his mother to breast cancer many years ago, he never stopped fighting the disease. He donated a portion of his monthly profits to cover the cost of early-detection screenings for area residents, gave free food to the monthly support groups, and hung letters and photos on the bulletin board known as The Wall of Warriors.

The Japanese-style garden next to the diner was not only a tribute to Jack's late mother but also a place where anyone could write the name of a loved one on a small rock and add it to the river of stones flowing through the center of the garden. Visitors could ring the little bell hanging from a post by the red bridge and listen as the high, clear notes drifted into the sky.

Under the bell was a plaque inscribed with a Matsuo Bashō haiku. Nora paused to read the familiar lines:

> *The temple bell stops—*
> *but the sound keeps coming*
> *out of the flowers.*

She was admiring the snowball-sized flowers on the hydrangea bushes when she heard the crunch of gravel. Seeing a figure approaching from behind a stand of bamboo near the entrance, she decided to move away from the bell in case the newcomer wished to ring it.

Nora sat down on a bench shaded by an ornamental cherry tree and studied the torn leaves of the hosta plant near her feet. Insects had been ravaging the cluster of plants, leaving ragged holes and misshapen gaps near the veins in every leaf.

A movement at the base of one of the healthier leaves caught her eye. A praying mantis lumbered up the stalk, and just as Nora spotted a beetle in its path, the mantis struck, pinning the beetle against the leaf with a single foreleg.

Nora's knowledge of plants was limited, but she suspected the beetle had been feeding on the hosta. She found it oddly satisfying to watch the praying mantis slowly devour its meal, beginning with the beetle's head.

Glancing back toward the red bridge, she saw a man holding one of the small, smooth stones. He turned and, catching sight of her, gave her a wave.

"Hi. Sorry, but do you know if it's okay to put someone's name on here if she didn't have cancer?"

Nora gave him a nod of encouragement. "It's definitely okay. The man who built this garden meant it to be a place where loved ones are remembered."

The man uncapped a black paint pen and wrote on the stone. He gazed at the stone in his hand for a long moment before looking at Nora again. "Can you remember someone you never really knew? Someone you were supposed to love—and who was supposed to love you. I wasn't a good son. I let my mom push me away. I'd tried to help, but I didn't do enough. No one did."

The last remnants of daylight slanted through the bamboo and burnished the man's flame-colored hair, which was streaked with bits of silver. He removed his tortoiseshell glasses and wiped his eyes with the back of his hand. Then he gently placed the stone on the edge of the river of stones, adding another name to be bathed in sunshine and starlight.

"I'm sorry," the man said as he straightened. "You probably came here to reflect, and I intruded on your thoughts."

Nora got to her feet. "Not at all. I'm meeting someone for dinner, but I'm a bit early." She gestured at the bench. "This is a nice place to sit. The lightning bugs should be coming out any minute now, and it's beautiful to watch them fly over the river."

A wistful smile appeared on the man's face. "I haven't seen a lightning bug in years. I used to love catching them in my hands and then letting them go. Other kids would put them in jars, but we—my brother, sister, and me—just wanted to see how many we could catch each night. At the end of the summer, whoever had the most was the winner. The winner got a huge ice-cream sundae."

This man's mother just died. He has two siblings. A brother and a sister.

"I hope I'm not being rude, but your mom—was her name Lucille?" Nora asked softly.

The man's eyes flew open wide in surprise, and he took a step toward Nora. His expression was eager. Almost desperate. "Yes. Lucille Wynter. Did you know her?"

Tiny needles of guilt pierced Nora's heart. "A little."

The man extended his hand. "My name's John Steinbeck Wynter, but most people call me Beck."

"I'm Nora. I own the bookstore here in town, and I, um, delivered books to your mom one or two times a month."

It was the first time Nora's voice didn't ring with pride when mentioning her store. She saw her role as a bookseller as integral to the overall health and happiness of those living and visiting Miracle Springs. Her store was a gathering place. It was a haven and sanctuary. It was a source of information, entertainment, and guidance. It was the steady and dependable beating heart of the town.

Nora was a purveyor of books, a noble and important profession to most. But to Lucille's children, she wasn't that different from a drug dealer. She'd fed their mother's addiction. Reinforced her unhealthy behavior. Added to her hoard.

"I'm so sorry," she said lamely. "I didn't know she had so many books."

"You have nothing to be sorry about. My mom bought books from lots of places. At least you took the time to deliver them. Clem told me that you'd sit and have tea with her in the boot room. Thank you for that."

Nora couldn't respond; she was too unnerved by the idea that Clem had been watching her.

"Clem isn't a bad guy," Beck said, as if hearing her thoughts. "He's just lost. Mom started hoarding when we were kids. Her behavior affected us all."

Nora liked order. She liked filing cabinets and card catalogs. She liked the Dewey Decimal System. She liked alphabetizing. She couldn't imagine growing up in a home where one couldn't see the furniture or use a kitchen or bathroom counter because it was buried by a mound of stuff or was too unsanitary to touch without gloves.

"I'm oversharing. Sorry." Beck put a hand over his heart. "Listen, Nora, I know I have no right to ask, especially after Harper was so rude to you, but I was wondering if you'd be willing to help us deal with Mom's books. Harper would rather toss the whole lot in the trash, but I know there are some valuable books in the library. If the dust and mold didn't ruin them, we could sell them."

Nora was already shaking her head. "I don't have that kind of time. I'm at the bookstore six days a week, and even though I was only in the house for a few minutes, it looks like there are piles and piles of books to sort."

"I won't lie. There are thousands of books. Mom left the house and its contents to the three of us, but after we hire a cleaning crew to haul away the junk, we're going to be stuck with a huge bill. But if we don't clean it up, the town will fine us because the house is now officially condemned."

Unable to stop herself, Nora said, "What will happen to the house after it's cleaned out?"

"We'll put it for sale, and someone will probably buy it for the land. The house might be too far gone to save, so my guess is it'll be torn down."

It was a sad thought. Wynter House was a fixture in the landscape of Miracle Springs. It was the town's haunted house. It loomed over the street, comfortable in its proximity to the graveyard. It was the source of gossip, conjecture, and ghost stories. Children dared each other to step on the property. Teenagers went as far as the front door, but only on Halloween night.

The thought of the historic mansion being razed to the ground—removed like a decayed tooth—didn't sit right with Nora. Not when Lucille had loved the house so much that she'd entombed herself within its walls.

Demolishing Wynter House felt like erasing Lucille too.

Nora couldn't solve Beck's problems, but she could offer him a glimmer of hope. "I might know someone who can help you. An antiques dealer. Books aren't her specialty, but she can help you with furniture and accessories. Her whole family is in the business, so she'd be a great resource." She passed Beck her phone. "Give me your contact info and I'll pass it along to my friend. Her name is Bea."

When Beck handed her phone back, Nora caught a glimpse of the time.

"Shoot. I'm late for dinner. I'll have Bea call you," Nora said before hurrying inside the Pink Lady to meet McCabe.

As usual, a crowd swamped the hostess podium. As Nora politely made her way to the front of the line, she saw the long list of names on the clipboard and knew the wait was easily thirty minutes. Luckily, counter seats were first come, first serve, but the man in a brown uniform parked in McCabe's favorite stool wasn't McCabe. It was Deputy Jasper Andrews.

The beer by Andrews's right hand suggested he was off duty. Unlike his boss, Andrews wasn't on a dinner date.

Even though it looks like he is, Nora thought as she studied the woman with the possessive hand on his shoulder, who didn't have Hester's creamy skin or honey-colored curls. This woman's hair was the shade of a heavy red wine—a Malbec or Pinot Noir—and her long nails were a flashy silver. They glinted like a new dime as her fingers danced over Andrews's back.

Deputy Paula Hollowell was not in uniform. She wore jeans so tight that they could've been made of neoprene and a cropped tank top that emphasized her muscular arms and flat belly. A tornado tattoo made of chaotic black lines spiraled upward from her waist to her rib cage.

How fitting, Nora thought as she stole up behind Andrews and said a loud, cheerful "Hello."

Andrews jerked like he'd been poked by a cattle prod, causing beer to splash over the rim of his pint glass. Hollowell lowered her hand, but made no attempt to create distance between herself and Andrews. She directed a triumphant smile at Nora, while Andrews mopped up the beer he'd spilled.

"Hey, Nora. How are you?"

"Great. McCabe and I have a date tonight. What are you up to?"

Andrews shifted on his stool. "I'm just grabbing a cold one before I head home. Paula and I have been talking about hunting dogs. I'm this close to getting one."

Looking beyond his pinched fingers, Nora saw the blush rise on Andrews's cheeks. "That's exciting. Is Hester going to fence in her backyard?"

The blush on Andrews's face deepened. "Uh, I haven't talked to her about that yet. I wanted to visit the breeder Paula knows first—see the puppies for myself."

A hand landed on Nora's arm and McCabe said, "What puppies?"

Hollowell backed away from Andrews and smiled at McCabe. "I'm trying to talk Jasper into getting a Mountain Cur. They're great hunting dogs. They're also smart, playful, and make excellent watchdogs."

"If you get a puppy, Hester might start baking fancy dog

biscuits, like my sister gets for her dogs," McCabe told Andrews. "She spoils those things rotten. Every week, she drives them to the doggie bakery. Last time I visited, I ate one of the dog cookies by mistake. The thing looked so good that I'd eaten half of it before I realized it didn't have any sugar."

Andrews chuckled while Hollowell laughed like she was in the audience of a sitcom. Then, still grinning, she scooped her keys off the counter. "I've got the early shift tomorrow, so I'm going to bounce. Y'all enjoy your dinner."

She glanced from one man to another, but let her gaze slide over Nora, like she wasn't there.

"I'd better roll out too," Andrews said after Hollowell walked away. "You guys should grab these stools. Looks like a packed house tonight."

Andrews placed a twenty on the counter and left. After Nora took a seat, she peeked at his check and saw that he'd paid for both beers.

"Are you double-checking his math?" McCabe asked.

"No. I was wondering if he bought Hollowell's drink."

McCabe gave her a quizzical look. "Why?"

"Because they weren't acting like two coworkers grabbing a beer at the end of their shift. Hollowell was touching Andrews in a way that Hester wouldn't appreciate. And he didn't seem to mind. Quite the opposite, in fact." She pushed Andrews's empty glass toward the back of the counter. "I have a feeling that I saw the beginning of something—something that could rip my friend's life apart."

McCabe covered her hand with his. "I know you're not fond of Hollowell, but I haven't seen her treat Andrews in any way that could be construed as unprofessional. Maybe the brief moment you saw doesn't mean what you think it does."

"Maybe. But what if it does?"

"I'll keep my eyes open at work. I trust your instincts, honey, but I really hope you're wrong about this."

Nora sighed. "Me too."

Their server bustled over, cleared the pint glasses, and recited the specials.

"You had me at chimichurri," McCabe said when she was done. "Can we get a half bottle of the Spanish red while my lady decides what to order?"

When Nora set out for the diner, she'd been craving blackened catfish and greens, but after meeting Beck, and seeing Andrews and Hollowell together, all she wanted now was comfort food.

"I'll have the shrimp and grits," she told the server when he returned with the wine.

"Buttered biscuits or corn bread?"

Nora chose the biscuits. Jack's biscuits were the best she'd ever had. They were soft, flaky, and buttery.

"Are you gonna share?" McCabe asked.

"Yep."

McCabe touched the rim of his glass against hers. "To buttered biscuits and Saturday nights."

In between sips of wine, Nora told McCabe about meeting Beck in the garden.

"He's got a lot to handle right now. His mother just died, his brother's an addict, and his sister's perpetually angry. *And* he's got to get that house cleaned out. I feel for the guy."

"Same here. That's why I'm going to see if Bea can lend him a hand. It's a big house, and if all the rooms are like the ones I saw, it'll take an army to clean out the hoard."

McCabe drained the rest of his wine and refilled their glasses. "I was there today, and I've never seen anything like it. The books are everywhere downstairs. Even in the bathroom. Upstairs has fewer books, but loads of other stuff. Clothes, art, sewing supplies, picture frames. There's a whole room downstairs that's full of clocks. None of them work, but there must be thirty or forty of them. In all sizes and shapes."

"Where did Lucille sleep?"

"In this tiny corner of a room at the front of the house. It must've been the living room at one time because her bed was an old couch. The cushions are practically flat and the fabric's stained with God knows what." His chest contracted in a sigh. "It reminded me of a nest. She had this little clearing in the middle of all the chaos. I wonder if she felt safe in that spot, surrounded by walls of stuff."

The server arrived with their food and they both tucked in. Five minutes later, Jack pushed through the swing doors dividing the kitchen and dining area and made a beeline for the counter.

He grinned as he smoothed his starched apron. "How's my cooking tonight?"

"Better than ever," Nora said. "Your child is going to have the best food. How many kids have a dad who cooks better than Gordon Ramsay and a granddad who can out-bake Paul Hollywood?"

Jack's gaze roamed around the room. "It's an honor to cook for people, whether they're strangers or family. For me, it's an act of joy. I can't wait to make farm animal–shaped pancakes or fill a bento box with rice balls and chicken teriyaki bites. I've even been thinking about updating our kids' menu to make it more adventurous."

McCabe held out a finger. "Just don't take away the mac and cheese. I don't want a riot in my town."

"And I don't want a thousand bad Yelp reviews," Jack said with a laugh. "I'm not getting rid of the staples, but I'd like to offer healthy sides. Fruit kebabs, cauliflower tots, broccoli au gratin—stuff like that."

The hostess caught Jack's eye and he nodded in acknowledgment. "Looks like the mayor is getting tired of waiting for her table. I need to pacify her with a strawberry milkshake. Enjoy your meal."

McCabe watched him walk away. "You always hear about the pregnant woman's glow, but that man's face could light up this whole place."

"They're going to be such great parents," Nora said. "Estella's nervous because her mom was such a mess. She's nothing like her mom, but I can understand her anxiety."

"At least she has her dad."

Estella's father, Gus, had just finished serving a fifteen-year prison sentence for killing a man. He'd caught this man physically abusing his daughter, and though he'd walked out on his wife and child without a backward glance years before the incident, he came home in time to rescue Estella from a terrible fate.

It had taken a good part of that fifteen years for Estella to forgive her father for his long absence. After many letters, phone calls, and visits, the two had become very close. Gus now lived with Estella and worked part-time at the Gingerbread House. He was a gifted bread maker, and Hester loved having him in her kitchen.

"I keep wondering what happened between Lucille and her kids," Nora said. "And what about her husband? What was his story?"

"According to Harper, he left Lucille and the kids when she was nine and Beck was eleven. Clem was still a baby. They never saw him or heard from him again."

Nora put her fork down. "That's awful. Lucille must've been totally overwhelmed. Three little kids. That huge house." She pictured Wynter House from the outside. How long had it taken for its gutters to snap like fractured bones or for the paint to peel like dead skin? When had the porch sagged like a pair of drooped shoulders, or the windows turned filmy like eyes clouded by cataracts?

"I've heard that hoarding stems from trauma," she said. "Maybe the grief was too much for her and she lost her way. Those poor kids. I bet they had to grow up so fast."

McCabe pushed his plate away and balled his paper napkin in his fist. "I know you, Nora, and I know you're going to want to help Lucille's kids. But it's better if you keep your distance. Let them find someone else to deal with the books."

Nora saw the tightening of McCabe's jaw. The napkin was still captured in his fist as if he were afraid to let it go. "What aren't you telling me?"

"Not here," he said.

After that, their conversation ground to a halt. McCabe paid the bill and put a hand on Nora's back as they squeezed past the knot of people waiting to be seated.

Once outside, Nora took McCabe's hand and led him to the garden. She was too restless to sit on the bench, so she walked to the center of the little bridge and waited for Mc-Cabe to speak.

Staring down at the river of stones, he said, "I met with the ME today. Lucille had injuries consistent with a fall, but that's not what killed her. Her hyoid bone was fractured and there was bruising around her neck."

"What are you saying?"

"The hyoid fracture and bruising indicate strangulation."

The truth pierced Nora like a needle. "She was murdered."

McCabe nodded solemnly. "We're launching a full investigation. This is why I want you to stay away from the Wynter siblings. And that house."

Nora didn't reply. She stared at the river of stones and heard Lucille's meek cry for help replay, over and over again, in her mind.

Murdered.

"Who would kill an old woman?" she whispered to the uncaring night.

McCabe gave her space to process the news, but eventually he coaxed her away from the stones and led her out of the garden.

Later, as she lay next to him in bed, one of his cats climbed over his slumbering form and nuzzled Nora's hand. She caressed its soft fur without opening her eyes. Its rumbling purr sounded like a train in the stillness, but Nora found it comforting.

The cat, who was called Magnum after the fictional private eye, pressed his back against Nora's belly and languidly stretched. His front paw landed on her chin, the claws immediately retracting, and his purrs became even louder.

Nora buried her face in the cat's fur, wishing his contentment would seep into her skin. But the movement unsettled the little tabby, and he relocated to the foot of the bed, turning around several times before curling into a tight ball that McCabe referred to as a "kitty croissant."

As the night dragged on, and Nora's mind refused to shut down, McCabe slumbered without stirring.

She was glad he was getting good rest, because when morning came, he'd wake up to a day filled with questions that needed to be answered. He'd be hunting for evidence, motive, and opportunity. He'd be making lists, interviewing people, examining photographs, and peering into the past.

Nora had the day off, which meant she'd be conducting a hunt of her own. But her search would take her to estate sales and the flea market, where she planned to tell Bea about Wynter House.

Despite McCabe's warnings, she couldn't turn her back on Lucille's children. Lucille's final words continued to haunt her, and she couldn't deny her desire to know if something valuable was inside Wynter House—a treasure worth killing for—hidden among thousands of books.

Nora planned to be completely transparent when she

spoke with Bea. She'd be honest about the state of the house. She'd tell her that it was the scene of a crime, the center of a murder investigation.

Nora hoped Bea would take the job. She was a friend, which meant she'd let Nora examine the books. Bea would give her leave to search for what was hidden in that crumbling mansion.

A fortune in books.

A lost library.

Chapter 7

Outside the leaves on the trees constricted slightly;
they were the deep done green of the beginning of
autumn. It was a Sunday in September.

—Ali Smith

Nora was first in line when the doors to the big red barn were unlocked that Sunday morning. It was Labor Day weekend, which meant the flea market would be even more crowded than usual. Nora would have to move fast if she wanted to find the best items for the best prices.

Once inside, she zipped by the vendors near the front door. Most of these booths catered to visitors, and though Nora loved the quilts, stoneware, and wood items created by local artists, they were too expensive for her to purchase for resale.

The candlemaker in the fourth row was a different story.

Scented candles were a big hit at Miracle Books, especially since Nora had asked the candlemaker to start making custom scents with names like Rainy Day Reads or Tea & Books.

This week, the candlemaker had four new products earmarked for the bookstore.

Nora uncapped the first candle, which was called Miracle

Books in Autumn and inhaled the scents of fall leaves and apples.

"Wow. This makes me believe that it's October, not the last weekend in August."

The Children's Corner was the color of cornflowers and smelled like a snickerdoodle, while Cozy Reading Chair was a peachy pink, with notes of Earl Grey, wood, and honey. Finally there was Book Therapy. This ivory candle had a clean, bright fragrance. The aroma of sun-dried linens, combined with a hint of jasmine, gave Nora an instant energy boost.

After handing the vendor a check, Nora promised to pick up the boxes of candles on her way out and walked deeper into the barn.

Several items caught her eye as she made her way to Bea's booth. A vendor specializing in vintage ceramics had a fabulous display of Franciscan Apple cups, plates, and bowls for sale. Nora really wanted the teapot, but the vendor wouldn't reduce the price by more than ten percent, so she had to settle for a set of cups and saucers, a sugar dish, and a pair of water tumblers.

At another booth, she picked up an assortment of Fiestaware creamers. She knew the bold colors of these little pitchers—daffodil, juniper, paprika, and scarlet—would brighten the dark spines lining the shelves in the mystery and thriller section.

When she arrived at Bea's Bounty, a U-shaped booth in the back of the building, Bea was holding a magnifying glass over the bottom of a silver candlestick for the benefit of a man on a mobility scooter.

"That mark don't look right to me, so I'll give you sixty for it," the man said with an air of practiced disinterest.

There was nothing Bea liked better than a good haggling session, but she had little patience for customers who tried to convince her that her wares weren't what she claimed them to be.

"This is a bona fide Sheffield silverplate biscuit warmer from the early 1900s. The William Hutton and Sons stamp proves it. And here's the Sheffield, England, stamp too. Not a thing wrong with the mark or dish, *and* it's in great condition. I can sell this today without taking a dime off the asking price, so I'm gonna pass on your offer."

The man glared at Bea over the rim of his half-moon glasses. "I know my silver makers."

Bea's translucent blue eyes flashed. "So do I, which is why the price I quoted is firm."

The man reddened, muttered something about the "expert opinion from a piece of trailer trash," and put his scooter in reverse.

Bea was still holding the dish when the scooter slammed into her table. Silver pieces and glassware toppled in every direction. Something crashed onto the concrete floor, very close to where Bea stood, and the crack of shattered porcelain silenced everyone in the vicinity.

The man sped off in his scooter, driving down the middle of the aisle without much regard for the people pushing strollers or wheelchairs. Nora heard a collection of indignant shouts as she rushed to Bea's side.

"Are you okay?"

"I'm fine." Bea scowled. "But my vase is a goner. I'm down fifty bucks and the day's just started."

She squatted down and began collecting triangular pieces of white porcelain. They looked like teeth scattered across the gray concrete.

While Bea cleaned up the broken vase, Nora began straightening the items on the table. Most of the candlesticks, glasses, and tall vases had toppled over, but it looked like nothing else had been damaged.

"I don't think this was an accident," Nora told Bea. "He didn't get what he wanted, so he lashed out. I heard what he said to you."

Bea tossed the plastic bag of broken porcelain into a cardboard box under the table. "That jackass can't offend me. I'm proud to be 'trailer trash.' My double-wide is my castle, and I've got ten acres with a big garden and an above-ground swimming pool. Plenty of room for my dogs to run. Nobody gets in my business. It's my Eden."

The vendor from across the aisle came over to see if Bea needed any help, but she waved her off with a smile. "Thanks, but I'm good. You know folks get fractious this time of year. People have a lot going on with school starting and whatnot. But for others, it's just the end of another season. They've got nothing on the horizon and that makes them want to dim everyone else's lamps."

"I feel like the world would be a better place if we all had an excuse to go back-to-school shopping," said Nora.

Bea laughed. "You got that right! You can't be unhappy with a new box of crayons and some scented markers in your cart. Add a pack of stickers or a cute notebook and you've got everything you need."

"I feel the shopping dopamine hit every Sunday, thanks to you," Nora told Bea.

"Don't butter me up until you see what I put aside for you."

Bea gathered her stringy hair into a ponytail and secured it with a hot pink scrunchie. From a distance, the blonde looked like a teenager, with her tan skin, tiny frame, and cutoffs, but up close, every one of her fifty-plus years showed on her face. Smoking and sun damage had given her a weathered appearance, but Bea didn't seem to care. She was a no-nonsense country girl whose life was centered around three things: her family, vintage housewares, and trips to the beach.

"You'll like some of the stuff. The prices? Not so much. It's getting harder and harder to find a good deal. I was on the road all last week, but pickings were mighty slim."

A group of high-school girls floated over to Bea's booth, drawn to her display of vintage dresser boxes. The girls' voices seemed unusually loud and their hands seemed to be everywhere. It was hard to keep track of the boxes because the moment one girl put one down, another girl picked it up.

Without moving from her spot, Bea said, "Hello, ladies. Those boxes are perfect for jewelry storage. Just be careful because someone already broke one of my treasures today, and it's put me in a foul mood."

The girls didn't bother to reply. They simply drifted off to another booth to resume their grabbing and giggling.

"They're looking for pocket-sized goodies," Bea said. "All the vendors know their game. Four of the girls distract the seller, while the fifth does the swiping. The thief rotates every week. I don't think they give a damn about what they're stealing either. It's probably some stupid dare or social media challenge—something to post on TikTok."

Nora thought about the missing YA books. None of the flea market girls looked familiar, but she kept watching them until Bea tapped her on the arm.

"Here's your box. Take a look and see what strikes your fancy."

Nora immediately passed on the first item—a collection of souvenir spoons. After much consideration, she also put aside an old pair of binoculars and a John Deere toy tractor. She kept a bronze hand sculpture, since it could double as a bookend, two pieces of embroidery hoop art, and a set of vintage ice-cream bowls.

"I knew you'd like those. That blue glass will look nice on a bookshelf," Bea said. "I thought you'd want the binoculars for sure."

"I'm just not feeling them. Sorry. But I love these." Nora

held up three magnifying glasses. Two were made of heavy brass and the third had a bone handle.

Bea gazed around her booth. "See what I mean? Slim pickin's."

Seizing the moment, Nora told Bea about Lucille and Wynter House. She was in the middle of describing her conversation with Beck Wynter when a customer pointed at the binoculars and asked if they were for sale. Five minutes later, they'd been wrapped in white paper and placed in a bag. The customer thanked Bea, turned away, and then swiveled around again.

"Do you sell any miniatures?"

"Like, for a dollhouse?"

The woman nodded. "Yes, but also child-sized items, like miniature tea sets, doll furniture—anything in a smaller scale. My friend is a collector and her birthday's coming up."

Unwilling to lose a potential sale, Bea said, "I have a doll's picnic basket, but it's in my truck. If you give me a few minutes, and my friend is willing to watch my booth, I can run out and get it."

"Does it come with plates?"

"Yep. Little utensils too. It's real cute."

The woman said that she'd look at a few other booths and circle back to Bea's when she was done. By the time she returned, Bea had fetched the basket from her truck and Nora had finished explaining why Wynter House was currently a crime scene.

"This is darling! My friend will be so tickled," said the woman. After paying top dollar for the picnic basket, she gave Bea her contact info. "In case you find other tiny treasures in the next two weeks. If you do, call me and I'll put you in touch with my friend's husband. He has no idea what to get her for her birthday, and my bestie is turning forty, so it's kind of a big deal."

She walked away, leaving Nora and Bea to haggle over the price of the ice-cream bowls and magnifying glasses.

"I want the job," Bea said after they came to an agreement.

Nora's heart jumped. She hadn't realized until this moment how badly she wanted to return to Wynter House.

"I want you to know exactly what you're in for," she told Bea. "The house smells disgusting. You'll have to wear a mask and gloves. There's mold, animal droppings, and God knows what else. And Lucille's collection might be pure junk—a total waste of your time."

Bea shook her head. "If nothing's changed inside for fifty years, then at least some of the items are antiques. I want to be the first one to see what's there. Being the first person in an untouched estate is a seller's dream."

A man paused to admire a group of tobacco tins. Bea threw a smile his way before turning back to Nora. "This could be my chance to earn some real money. I can charge the family an hourly rate *and* make it clear that I'll only take the job if they agree to sell the good stuff through my cousin's auction place in Radford. He's a full partner now, which means he can pay me a fat finder's fee. I need that money because my aunt has a hospital bill longer than my arm and no health insurance. Our whole family's gonna have to work together to pay it off."

"I know you have relatives in the business, but will they want to tackle this job? It's a huge house, and most of the work will be carrying rotten books and other trash to the dumpster."

Bea grinned. "My niece runs a cleaning-and-hauling company called Junk Hunks. Between her, my auctioneer cousin, and the younger kids looking to pay off student loans, I'll have it covered. Gimme Beck's number. I want to call him before he has the chance to hire someone else."

"What about the books?" Nora asked.

"After we toss the ones we can't sell, you can look over the rest. Shoot, you can come over whenever you want. I owe you big time for this one, girl. If that means giving you a set of keys to the castle, I'm happy to do it."

This was exactly what Nora wanted to hear.

"Is there any wiggle room on this price?" asked the man examining the tobacco tins.

"For you, honey, you bet there is!" Bea exclaimed.

Turning away, Nora said, "Let me know if you get the job."

"I'll get it. Don't you worry about that. We're gonna make some money and help three grown children say good-bye to their mama. We might even find the clues your man needs to solve the mystery of the old lady's death. There's no telling what we'll find once we start digging."

After loading up her flea market finds, Nora ate a sandwich in her truck and drove to a tag sale starting at one.

She liked shopping tag sales because the items were usually inside someone's home, and the prices were clearly labeled. During a two-day sale like this one, the items that were full price on Saturday would be a fraction of the price today.

The house was in a neighborhood undergoing gentrification. Small cottages inhabited by the same residents for decades were being either scooped up by upper-middle-class families and renovated or demolished to make way for new builds.

As Nora waited to enter the house, she saw real estate agents and young couples circle the exterior like vultures vying for position around the corpse of a dead animal.

The front door opened and a man carrying a side table shimmied through the doorway.

"Not much furniture left," he told Nora on his way out.

Entering the house,, Nora saw that this was true. Her footsteps echoed as she moved through the living room, passing by a pair of floor lamps and a threadbare rug. The knickknacks lined up on the mantel were of no interest either, so she headed into a small dining room.

The remaining pieces of dinnerware were either too big to fit on a bookshelf or too damaged to resell, but a glass basket caught Nora's eye. It was the color of amethysts and large enough to hold a bouquet of flowers. She could picture it gracing the shelf where the Mary Stewart books lived.

An old woman shuffled into the room and pointed at the basket. "I used to keep mints in there."

Nora covered the awkwardness she felt by smiling at the woman. "Is this your house?"

"For the past forty-seven years. My Jimmy carried me over the threshold when I was a bride. We raised our boys here. Had our grandkids over every Christmas. But Jimmy passed two years ago—just slipped away watching baseball in his favorite chair." Her gaze traveled to the living room and Nora imagined she didn't see it as a sad, empty space, but as a repository for memories. "My son built a little cottage for me on his property. It's real nice."

After introducing herself, Nora asked if there were any books for sale.

The woman, whose name was Ida Fleming, shook her head. "Jimmy was the reader of the family. My boys cleaned out his books after he passed. But come on through to the bedroom. You might find something for your shop in there."

Ida prattled on about how much the neighborhood had changed as she led Nora through the kitchen, a narrow hall, and, finally, into a bedroom.

"I thought someone would snap up my old Singer table right away, but maybe folks don't sew anymore." Her stooped shoulders rose and fell in a shrug. "Jimmy worked at the paper mill. After they closed, he became a mechanic. I made his first pair of coveralls. Even stitched his name over the front pocket."

Nora ran her hand over the table's smooth, worn surface. "Did you know Lucille Wynter?"

Shadows pooled in Ida's rheumy blue eyes, and she pinched her lips into a tight line. Nora could sense an avalanche of words gathering on the old woman's tongue.

After a long moment of silence, she said, "I knew her from my schoolgirl days. From the time I was knee high, Lucille and I were the best of friends. I went on my first double date to the soda fountain with Lucille. I went to her wedding. A year later, she was my maid of honor. I saw her obituary in the paper this morning." She put a wrinkled hand to her chest. "It hit me hard."

"Were you two still close?" Nora asked, suspecting she already knew the answer.

Pain deepened the lines around Ida's mouth. "I haven't seen her for a very long time. Not since the scandal. Right after Lucille got married, her daddy stole money from the mill—money that was meant for his employees. He denied it, of course, and he wasn't arrested because there wasn't enough evidence. But everybody knew it was him. He was the only one with the combination to the safe."

"Did he pay his employees in cash?"

"It was their Christmas bonus, plus a bunch of money set aside to pay local vendors. It was a terrible shock, and Hugo stepped down, retiring early. After that, the Wynters barely left the house. I tried to visit after her son was born, but she sent me away. Years ago when our children were in school together, I went to see her. She wouldn't invite me in." Ida lowered her gaze. "She said she wasn't interested in being friends. And that was that. So many years have gone by since then—too many to count—but I still remember how much it hurt when she closed that door in my face."

Nora nodded in sympathy. "I brought books to Wynter House a few times a month. Lucille always talked about her father like he walked on water."

Ida's smile was wistful. "Hugo doted on his two girls, there's no doubt about that. They had the prettiest dresses and all sorts of luxuries. Dolls from England and boxes of chocolate. When the girls got older, he bought them French perfume and jewelry. All those airs and graces, and you'd think they'd have married some cosmopolitan fellows. Lucille's sister, Lynette, moved away a year or so after Lucille and Frederick were married, but Lucille never left Miracle Springs."

A man in khakis and a red polo shirt knocked on the open door. "There you are, Ms. Fleming. Do you have a sec? A lady's interested in buying the lawn mower and some tools."

"I'll be right there." Ida turned back to Nora. "It's funny that you mentioned Lucille. I started collecting perfume bottles because of her. Just this morning, I decided I wanted less clutter in my new house, so I decided to sell them. You're welcome to take a look."

Ida pointed at a box on the floor. Nora thanked her and unwrapped the first bottle she touched. It was a lovely Art Deco atomizer in malachite with gold trim. The next bottle featured hand-painted roses. The one after that had sky-blue glass. Nora decided to make an offer on the entire box and, after negotiating with the man in the red shirt, carried her purchases to the truck.

She drove to Miracle Books, unloaded her finds from the day in the stockroom, and went home to start a load of laundry. After that, she went on a grocery store run followed by a late-afternoon hike. By five o'clock, she was wiped out.

Flopping on the sofa with her current read and a glass of sparkling water, she tried to lose herself in the story, but the words weren't soaking in. When her phone buzzed, she let the book rest on her chest while she read a text from McCabe.

She wasn't surprised to learn that he'd be working late and planned to spend the night at his place. This didn't bother Nora a bit. Not only did she enjoy her own company, but there were times when she just wanted eggs or cereal for dinner and didn't want to cook something else for McCabe. Unlike Nora, who'd happily eat breakfast food at any meal, McCabe believed omelets and pancakes should be consumed only before noon.

I wonder what he's doing right now. Interviewing Lucille's kids? Meeting with her attorney to review her will? Searching the house for clues?

Nora sent a reply saying that she'd miss him and to call if he wanted to talk, but she had a feeling she wouldn't hear from him until tomorrow.

She picked up her book again, but it was no use. Her thoughts had turned to Lucille and Wynter House, and no work of fiction could compare to the real-life mystery of a dead book hoarder and her dilapidated Southern Gothic mansion.

Retrieving *The Little Lost Library* from its hidey-hole—a space behind one of the floating bookshelves on the wall dividing the living room from the kitchen—Nora re-read the first two pages.

She wished she could participate in this scavenger hunt in verse. Because every page directed the reader to a different location inside Wynter House, Nora didn't think she could puzzle out the rhyming riddles from outside the home. Most were too vague to be solved from afar.

"If only I could get back in there," she said as she studied an illustration of a skeleton key tied to a length of ribbon.

The sound of her phone's ringtone startled her. She was equally surprised to see Bea's name on the screen.

"Guess where I am," Bea said before Nora could even utter a word.

Nora didn't need to guess. "Wynter House."

"Yep. Started working an hour ago. Me and the Junk Hunks team are already kickin' ass. Even with folks from the sheriff's department telling us where we can and can't go and what we can and can't touch, and making sure we're only tossing old food, broken plates, and mouse turds, we've cleared most of the trash from the kitchen. It was real bad, but we've got the windows open and some fans blowing, so you can actually spend thirty seconds inside without gagging. Wanna come over?"

Nora sprang off the sofa and grabbed her car keys. "Yes, I do. I'll be there in ten minutes."

"Okay, then. I'll tell the skeletons to stay in the closets until you get here."

Chapter 8

*Don't own so much clutter that you will be
relieved to see your house catch fire.*
— Wendell Berry

Nora had never seen so many cars in front of Wynter House. There were sheriff department SUVs, half-a-dozen cargo vans and commercial pickup trucks featuring the purple Junk Hunk logo, and Bea's old VW bus.

Nora parked by the cemetery and hurried down the street. The fatigue she normally felt at the end of a busy day was absent. Her whole body buzzed with excitement. She couldn't wait to see the rest of Lucille's house.

A pair of huge dumpsters sat in the middle of the driveway. Though Nora couldn't see inside, the smell wafting out of them was so rank that she clamped her hand over her nose and mouth.

The backyard looked like the scene from an outdoor flea market. Several canopy tents with folding tables were lined up in a tidy row. Some of the tables held piles of books. Others were empty. A steady stream of people wearing purple shirts, work gloves, and face masks carried items to the tables while a short, round woman with a purple headband directed traffic.

Two deputies wearing gloves and masks were also present. One was flipping through the books while the other stood next to the woman with the purple headband.

"That's all trash," she told one of the Junk Hunks, waving him on with her clipboard.

A man pivoted a cardboard box to show her the contents. "What about this?"

The woman pointed at the tent closest to the garage. "Auction."

The man waited for the deputy to nod his head in approval before walking away.

Nora felt the magnetic pull of the books on a nearby table. The tall, uneven stacks looked like a city skyline.

"Hey, there! You must be Nora." The woman with the clipboard directed a grin her way. "Bea said you'd be drawn to these like a bee to a flower. I'm Cricket, Bea's niece. Bea told the deputies you were on our team, so you can look around, but don't touch anything without protecting your hands and making sure it's okay with one of the deputies inside. We were hired by the family, but we can't do a thing without the blessing of the sheriff's department."

Nora promised to respect any boundaries put in place. As much as she wanted to see Lucille's things, she wanted to see her killer brought to justice even more.

"There's a box of gloves and masks near the back door," Cricked continued. "You'll see some Vicks VapoRub too. We got the worst of the smelly stuff out of the kitchen, but it's not gonna smell like fresh laundry in there anytime soon. If you dab a little Vicks under your nose, you'll be good to go."

"Thanks. Have you found anything interesting yet?"

"Not yet. It's really hard to move around in there, so we're bringing stuff outside for sorting. At this point, ninety percent has gone into the dumpster. There's some old glassware and a few copper pots from the kitchen that's saleable, but most of the stuff was chipped or cracked."

A veritable mountain of a man approached Cricket, his arms laden with encyclopedias.

"Did you carry the whole set, Saquon? Leave some for the other guys, would you?"

The man's laugh was a rumbling waterfall. "You said you wanted to clear most of the dining room before supper. Well, *I'm* hungry!"

Cricket turned to Nora. "I'm sure Bea's told you about our Sunday suppers. Saquon married my little sister back in June, and it's their first time hosting a family meal. You think he's sweating now? Wait until my whole family shows up at his house later tonight."

Saquon groaned as he headed for an empty table, but after checking with the deputy, Cricket told him to dump the books in the recycling bin. Another man approached, carrying a cardboard box, and while Cricket's attention was diverted, Nora slipped into the boot room.

As she looped the strings of a disposable mask over her ears, she noticed the absence of the two chairs and the little side table. The place where she and Lucille always had their tea and cookies was gone.

Lucille is gone.

Staring at the space where Lucille's chair had been, Nora felt sadness settle on her shoulders like a heavy coat.

She'd been eager to wander through Wynter House, but her excitement was suddenly tempered by her memories of the person who lived here. For decades, Lucille had been amassing a collection of objects. She'd put them in piles, touched them, and learned to maneuver around them. She'd hidden away in her fortress, in her hoard, and become invisible to all but a small number of people.

Nora wondered if Lucille's collection would reveal long-buried secrets. By sifting through the artifacts of her life, would they learn the reasons behind her terrible death?

One of the Junk Hunks exited the kitchen with a garbage bag in each hand. His eyes were watering as he hurried past Nora, leaving the stench of dead animal in his wake. The odor lingered in the kitchen and was strong enough to permeate Nora's mask and the barrier of Vicks VapoRub.

Moving deeper into the room, Nora was momentarily shocked by the sight of the tile floor and the clear countertops. The Junk Hunks had unearthed a freestanding butcher block in the center of the room, as well as a brick fireplace.

The space was a long way from being clean, but someone had swept the floor and wiped the worst of the grime from the counters, stovetop, and sink. Despite these attempts, nearly every surface was discolored by stains. Years of dirt, spoiled food, and mold had marked the room like lesions on a leper's skin.

The fridge was gone. The cabinets were empty. Nora opened the door of a narrow broom cupboard and peered inside.

"Nothing in there either," said Bea. "We went through this room like a swarm of locusts."

Nora glanced around. "You're not kidding. But how did you get the green light from the sheriff's department? Don't they want to look through everything before it gets trashed?"

Bea jerked her thumb toward the dining room. "We've been working with them every step of the way. They look at everything we're sorting and tell us what goes where, but at this point, it doesn't take a brilliant detective to know that there aren't any clues hidden in a box of broken dishes or a bag of rotten food. But just so you know, we're not allowed to go into the hall or upstairs. Officer Fuentes is making sure no one goes where they aren't supposed to. Your man and a few of his officers poked around for two days and didn't find anything helpful."

"Did Fuentes say what they were looking for?"

"All I know is that we need to give any personal papers to

him. Letters, bank statements, tax records—stuff like that. Photos too. We can't throw a single book away until we've made sure there's nothing stuck in the pages, which is why Cricket's team has to bring everything outside to be checked by the deputies in the tents."

Nora thought of the encyclopedias in Saquon's massive arms. "Every book?"

"Every book. No exceptions." Bea put her hands on her hips. "Wanna see what I found in the dining room?"

"You know I do."

Following Bea into the room, Nora felt an overwhelming sense of misplacement. When she'd been here before, she'd had to turn sideways to squeeze past towers of books and junk. Seeing the wide expanse of floor and high ceiling threw her for a loop. The fireplace was massive. Nora only had to crouch down a little to fit her whole body inside it.

"Isn't the wallpaper wild?" Bea asked.

Nora examined the Greco-Roman design. The linear pattern featured toga-draped figures, harps, birds, and amphorae. The faded maroon, beige, and moss-green colors gave the room a solemn air.

"Nothing like having the gods of Olympus watch you eat." Nora pointed at the table. "I bet that was a lovely piece once."

"Yeah, it used to be gorgeous. Mahogany. Circa 1910. All those books broke its back. It's split right down the middle. When you're done looking through these books, and Officer Fuentes said you were cleared to look, we'll move the table out and call it a day."

The books waiting for Nora were arranged, spine up, on a piece of brown paper in the middle of the table.

They weren't encyclopedias. The matching blue cloth covers indicated they were part of a set, and after reading the gilt lettering on one of the spines, Nora smiled.

"A Jane Austen Winchester edition. All twelve volumes."
Gingerly she picked up *Persuasion* and opened to the title
page. "1911"

Some of the pages had foxing and every cover had bumped
corners. The spines showed some fading, and dust had yellowed the exposed page edges. Overall, the set was in good
condition, and after using her phone to do a quick search on
AbeBooks, Nora told Bea that the books were worth at least
a grand, maybe more

"Beck will be happy to hear that, but he needs us to find
more Jane Austens and less garbage to cover the costs of
this job."

"Is he here?"

Lowering her voice, Bea said, "He's at the station. Both
him and Harpy."

"Is that what you call Harper?"

"Damn right. I bet that woman's portrait is somewhere in
this wallpaper—maybe next to the guy with the bull's head
or that three-headed dog. Before they left, she and Beck
were holed up in the library with another officer. We can't
go in that part of the house, so I don't know what they've
been doing in there."

Though Nora wanted to tour as much of the house as she
could, she was reluctant to revisit the place where she'd
found Lucille's body. Someone from the sheriff's department had strung yellow caution tape across the door leading
from the dining room to the hall. Black-and-orange DO NOT
ENTER signs framed the doorway.

Bea rested a hand on Nora's back. "You okay?"

"I know you and Cricket have everything handled, but I
want to help. I owe Lucille."

"You can help us with the books," Bea said. "Tell us
which ones should go to auction, which ones should go on

eBay, and which ones can be sold at your store. I'll give you a good price."

Bea winked and Nora couldn't stop a laugh from escaping. The sound bounced off the empty walls like a tennis ball.

A face appeared behind the yellow barrier tape. Waving Nora over, Deputy Fuentes said, "You part of the cleanup crew? I don't see a purple shirt."

Though Fuentes was wearing a mask, there was no mistaking the glint of humor in his eyes.

"I just couldn't stay away from so many books," Nora said with a smile. "Which reminds me. Your special order arrived this morning."

Fuentes was always buying books for his baby sister. While he chatted about his extensive family, Nora's gaze moved over his shoulder to where the staircase rose from the gloom like some prehistoric sea creature.

Seeing her face fall, Fuentes said, "I'm sorry you had to find her. This whole thing—the way she died, the state of this house—it's crazy sad."

"It is," Nora agreed, her eyes returning to Fuentes's face. He was a good man, and she was glad he was on duty instead of Hollowell. "How'd you end up with this assignment? Did you draw the short straw?"

"Nah. I switched shifts with Andrews. I want off next Sunday because my family's going to the lake, and he had something going on today."

I wonder if that something has to do with Paula Hollowell.
"Where's Hollowell?"

"On patrol. Why? You wanna bring her coffee and a donut?" Fuentes's eyes crinkled. "What? You thought I didn't know? It doesn't take a seasoned detective to figure out you don't like the woman."

Nora didn't want to talk about Hollowell, so she pointed at the closed door behind Fuentes. "What's in there?"

"Here's the two-cent tour." Fuentes turned toward the front door. "The parlor's at that end. Behind me is the library. There's a closet under the stairs too—totally stuffed with books and boxes." He gestured at the card table, folding chair, and desk lamp to his left. "And this is my office. I need to look at every scrap of paper and check the contents of every bag and box before the Junk Hunks haul it outside. I've been at it for hours, and, man, I'm ready for some fresh air."

"We're wrapping up," Bea assured him. "Ten more minutes and we'll be out of your hair."

Fuentes saluted her before returning to his chair. Retrieving a stack of envelopes from the box near his feet, he opened the first envelope, read the letter, and placed it in a box marked BILLS.

"I hear she owed lots of folks," Bea whispered. "Uncle Sam, mostly, but a bunch of credit card companies too. She left her kids a helluva mess. I'm hoping the goodies in the office will help them clear some of their mama's debt. Come on, you've got to see this before you leave."

When Bea opened a door on the rear wall, the movement roused a tornado of dust motes. The room was cave black, but Bea stretched out her arm and turned on a banker's lamp. The green shade glowed like a traffic light on a dark and lonely road.

"We haven't removed many boxes, so there isn't much room to move, but there's a really cool collection on the shelves in the back. The lamp is all the light we've got, so you'll need this to see what I'm talking about." She held out a battery-powered lantern. "Meet me outside after you've had a look."

Nora raised the lantern and slowly moved it left to right.

She saw more waist-high stacks of books. More box towers. More bulging bags. More hoard.

And then, her light snagged on something shiny along the back wall. Something winked in the darkness. Something made of bronze or gold. Something with a white face.

Nora shuffled forward until a stack of boxes prevented her from taking another step. She placed the lantern on top of the stack and waited for her eyes to adjust to the dimness.

Bookshelves emerged from the semiblackness. Lined up, shoulder to shoulder, they filled the back wall and continued marching toward the door.

The shelves weren't stuffed with books. They were crammed with clocks.

There were carriage clocks, pocket clocks, mantel clocks, standing clocks, station clocks, wall clocks lying on their backs, and table clocks of every shape, size, and design.

Nora's heart did a little somersault as she recalled the first riddle from *The Little Lost Library.*

The book was still tucked in its hidey-hole in her tiny house, but she remembered a line about hands without fingers.

"And something about a painted face," she murmured to herself. "And moonlight mariners."

As she panned the light from one corner of the room to the other and back again, she noticed a human-sized space in the far corner of the room. When she thrust her lantern toward the space, the light bounced off a piece of glass covering the face of a grandfather clock. She wondered if any of the clocks had maritime-themed decorations.

She knew Bea or Fuentes would appear in the doorway any minute now to tell her that it was time to go, but for some reason, she was determined to get a closer look at the grandfather clock.

There was no way to move the books. It would take too

long. But if she could move a few boxes and bags, she might be able to squeeze her way through the towers of stuff.

The first bag in her way was full of batting and fabric squares. The next bag contained plastic hangers. Nora tossed both bags on top of the hoard to her left and investigated the box that had been sitting under the bags. A quick glance showed that it was stuffed with blank sheets of paper. It was too heavy for Nora to pick up, so she pulled it backward a few inches and stepped over it.

She repeated this process with the next group of impediments, getting sweatier and dirtier every time she dislodged a bag or box that seemed to have rooted itself in place.

She was within three feet of the clock when she walked through a huge cobweb. It covered her hair and face like a veil.

"Get off!" She swiped at the sticky, gossamer fibers, but they clung to her clammy skin. Sweat rolled down her cheeks and dampened her shirt. There was a persistent itch in the middle of her back. Ignoring her discomfort, she pressed forward.

Now that she was closer, she could see the white clockface peering out at her from behind the dust-coated glass. The painting perched above the face, like a bowler hat, was obscured by grime, but Nora wanted to see it, so she sucked in her stomach and pushed past another stack of books.

Once she finally stood directly in front of the clock, she reached up to rub the glass with her gloved hand. As the beam of her light caressed the seascape, excitement bolted through her.

The painting featured a schooner in a dark and roiling sea. The ghost of a moon hovered behind the tallest mast.

"Moonlight mariners," Nora whispered.

The moment felt weighted with meaning. She'd found a

clue from the book Lucille's father had written. The book Lucille had bequeathed to Nora.

She wanted me to do this—to follow the clues and solve the riddles in her book. But why?

Nora stared at the clock, willing it to reveal its secret to her. Nancy Drew had found a will inside an old clock. What were the odds that she'd be as fortunate?

She had zero chance of discovering a treasure behind the weights and pendulums, because she couldn't possibly open the case door. She'd have to move dozens of books out of the way first, and it was a miracle Bea hadn't already come to fetch her.

Raising the lantern again, she passed it slowly over the clockface.

The painting of the night ship was remarkably well pre-served, as were the painted shells. Every corner featured the same shells. A rose-colored scallop, a milky conch, and a halved oyster. The center of each oyster shell was painted a deep indigo. In the middle of this blue-purple hue was a small sphere of blackness.

As if to represent a missing pearl, Nora thought as her gaze traveled from one group of shells to the next.

When she made it to the final set—to the shells in the corner between the numbers nine and twelve—her breath caught.

The oyster shell in this group did not have a black spot. Its pearl sat in its bed of deep blue like the moon in the sky above the schooner.

Brushing the pearl with her fingertip, Nora discovered that it was not a painting. It was three-dimensional. Moving her finger over it again, she felt how it rose out of the shell like an island rising from the sea.

It's a button.

Tugging her glove off, Nora stood on tiptoe and pushed

on the smooth surface of the pearl. She didn't really expect anything to happen, but following a soft click, the schooner moved.

The whole boat collapsed, folding over so that the topmast kissed the X in the Roman numeral XII. In the middle of the tumbling waves where the ship used to be was a black cavity.

Nora's pinkie finger tingled. It was a subtle sensation—a frisson of feeling above the knuckle—that most people would ignore. However, that part of Nora's finger had been so badly burned that it had been amputated, and phantom tingles were hard to ignore.

Nora balled her hand into a fist, hoping against hope that the feeling would go away. She'd felt it the day she'd found Lucille's body. She'd felt it other times too. It was an omen. A warning. Something terrible was going to happen, and somehow she'd be involved.

She had no idea how a partially amputated finger could be a portent of violence, but the world was full of unexplained mysteries. Animals would take flight days before an earthquake. An old woman with a rheumatic hip would brace for an incoming storm that didn't appear on a single radar map. Some people could smell snow long before the clouds gathered.

"Nora!"

Nora heard the edge in Bea's voice. She was out of time. She reached into the hole in the clockface, grasped the object inside, and shoved it into her pocket. She then righted the ship, closed the glass cover, and stepped over the box directly behind her.

"Coming!" she shouted, pushing boxes and tossing bags, this way and that, to erase the path she'd made to the back wall.

"Girl, I thought you fell through the floor!" Bea exclaimed

from the doorway. "I've gotta get you out of here. The Harpy just showed up."

The two women hurried outside.

Nora was turning toward the driveway when Bea grabbed her arm and pointed at the side of the house. "You'd better go around the other way. There might be snakes in the grass, but I'd rather pet a copperhead than spend five minutes in Harper Wynter's company."

"Good luck. And thank you," Nora said before darting around the corner.

Picking her way through the tall grass, she tried not to think about snakes. Or chiggers. Or ticks. She planned to shower as soon as she got home, and all of her clothes would be going straight into the washing machine.

Instinctively, her hand went to her pocket. She felt the lump through the fabric and quickened her pace.

The Junk Hunk trucks and most of the cars lining the street were gone, and Nora's colorful truck stood out like a sore thumb. She unlocked the doors, pulled the mystery object out of her pocket, and climbed into the driver's seat.

There was no one around, so Nora uncurled her hand and looked at the small black box sitting on her palm.

She knew it was a box because she saw a pair of hinges, but this was no regular box. The shape was too unique.

It was a coffin.

Peering closer, Nora saw that there was a glass panel on the lid. She used the hem of her shirt to clean off the dust and let out a high-pitched squeak of surprise.

A tiny human skull stared back at her.

"What the hell?"

She opened the coffin lid.

Inside were the remains of a woman. Her long red hair clung to her skull. Her skeletal hands were neatly folded over a brown book. She wore a white dress and slippers, both of which had yellowed with age.

On a label glued to the inside of the coffin lid, someone had written the word *Mother* in delicate script.

Nora was unnerved. Who would make a dollhouse-sized coffin? Who'd create such a realistic skeleton that it raised the hair on the back of Nora's neck? Who'd open the mouth and turn the head slightly to one side as if the doll had died in agony?

It was one of the creepiest things Nora had ever seen.

Her gaze landed on the book. It appeared to be leather bound and had no title on the cover.

Nora didn't dare touch it without thoroughly washing her hands first, so she placed the coffin on the passenger seat and drove away from Wynter House.

At every stop sign or red light, she glanced over at the coffin. The lid was closed, and she hoped it stayed that way. She didn't want the tiny eyes of that tiny skull watching her.

As soon as she got home, she showered and put on her pajamas. She didn't care that it wasn't even dark yet. She'd had a long and eventful day, and it was time for a glass of wine and a quick dinner.

But first, she had to examine the coffin more thoroughly.

After covering her kitchen table with a towel, Nora opened the coffin lid and carefully wiggled the book out from under the skeleton's bony fingers.

Next she put on her magnifying glasses. She always felt like a character in a sci-fi novel when she wore these glasses. With their thick lenses and built-in LED lights, she could read the tiniest print.

There were no letters on the cover of the coffin book, but a scrap of red stuck out from between the pages like a lizard's tongue.

A bookmark ribbon? Nora wondered as she turned to the page.

It wasn't a ribbon, but a bit of paper, no bigger than a dime. The paper was folded in half, and because Nora didn't think she could safely unfold it with her fingers, she grabbed a pair of tweezers and a cotton swab from the bathroom and used them, instead.

Once unfolded, the paper revealed a message. The elegant letters were handwritten in faded black ink.

You found me.

Chapter 9

Some places speak distinctly. Certain dark gardens cry aloud for a murder; certain old houses demand to be haunted . . .

—Robert Louis Stevenson

Unlike most of the workforce, Sheldon loved Mondays.

He'd come in early to examine, clean, and price the shelf enhancers Nora had bought over the weekend. She'd handle all the opening tasks, while he bustled around the shop, rearranging displays and fussing over where to put the new acquisitions. He'd flit from one shelf to another, swaying his hips to a spicy salsa playlist.

This morning, he was in an exceptionally good mood. He caught Nora in his arms when she came out of the ticket agent's booth and danced her around the Readers' Circle.

"You're full of it today," she observed with a laugh.

"I had *three* nights of unbroken sleep. Three days with no pain. No flare-ups. Nothing! Yesterday I baked bread and muffins. Then I cleaned the house and went on a long walk. Yes, you heard that right. I exercised outside—*on purpose.*"

Nora widened her eyes. "Outside? Did you get sweaty? Because I know you hate that."

"*Mi amor,* I don't sweat. I sparkle. I channel Edward

Cullen. Or Tinker Bell." He straightened his favorite bow tie—the one with the pink flamingos on a cobalt background—and smoothed his cream-colored sweater vest over the soft hill of his belly. "Guess what kind of muffins I made. If you can guess correctly, I'll make you a latte."

"If you make me a latte, I'll tell you about my visit to Wynter House last night."

Sheldon held Nora by the shoulders. "You took the job?"

"No, Bea did. She's the one who let me in."

Inside the ticket agent's booth, Sheldon scooped grounds into the portafilter. While he was tamping those, he pointed at a row of muffin tins lined up on the counter. "Try one."

Nora freed what appeared to be a chocolate chip muffin from its red wrapper and took a bite. The buttery muffin was still warm and the silky chocolate melted on her tongue.

Reading the pleasure on Nora's face, Sheldon said, "They're good, right? My *abuelita* made these all the time, but without the chocolate chips. They're called *mantecada* muffins. They must have a dome with a perfect golden crust and insides so soft you didn't need teeth to eat them."

"We should serve these on Thursdays. The storytime crowd would gobble them up."

"I'll give Hester the recipe," Sheldon said, raising his voice over the hiss of the milk frother.

Nora put the rest of the muffin aside and told Sheldon about seeing Andrews and Hollowell together.

"You need to tell her," Sheldon said as he poured the milk into a heart design.

"I know, but it's not something I can say over the phone. I'll see what she's up to today. Maybe she can stop by after work, or we can grab a pizza tonight."

Sheldon placed Nora's latte on the counter. Turning to the pegboard, he selected a canary-yellow mug with the text I AM A RAY OF F*CKING SUNSHINE and filled it to the brim with dark roast.

"Hollowell doesn't even want Jasper," he said. "She just wants to win a contest Hester never agreed to play. I've known people like her before. They're black holes. Everywhere they go, they swallow the light."

The metaphor seemed fitting. A black hole was one of the most destructive forces in the universe. When seen through a powerful telescope, it looked like a coal-black eye ringed in flame. To those with an active imagination, it resembled the Eye of Sauron from the Lord of the Rings series.

Sheldon waved a finger at Nora. "We're not going to let that human tornado ruin our day. Tell me about the haunted mansion. Any skeletons?"

"Actually, yes."

Nora wanted to draw out the telling for dramatic effect, but didn't have the time. Forty minutes from now, the Monday Moms would be waiting at the door, eager to come inside and spend the next two hours chatting over coffee and pastries. So Nora gave Sheldon a stripped-down version of her experience.

When she reached the part about the hidden compartment in the clockface, he said, "Stop pulling my leg. I know you're just repeating Carolyn Keene's secret clock scene."

"I think Lucille's clock predates Nancy Drew. And the book Lucille gave me? It led me to that clock. I'll show you what I mean."

Sheldon followed Nora to the front. She passed him *The Little Lost Library* and told him to read the first two pages.

When he was done, he whispered, "What was in the clock?"

Nora placed the coffin on the checkout counter. "She was."

"What in the world?" Sheldon carefully placed the book on the counter and picked up the little coffin. When he opened the lid, the corners of his mouth drooped. "This is some *Día de los Muertos*–type shit. Only a psychopath would give this to a child."

"I don't know why it was in the clock, but you see the book the skeleton's holding?"

Sheldon angled the coffin to catch the sunlight knifing through the front windows. "Looks fancy."

"It's old and very valuable," said Nora. "It's a Bible. A complete Dutch Bible, with a glossary and a handful of engravings."

Curiosity replaced Sheldon's initial revulsion. "How valuable?"

"Over three grand. It was printed in the Netherlands in 1750. There aren't many copies left, so it's pretty rare."

"What did Bea make of this?"

Nora's cheeks turned pink. "I haven't told her yet."

"Why not?"

"Because of the book. I think Lucille wanted me to solve the riddles in the book. I'll tell Bea about the coffin, the Bible, and anything else I find. But not yet." She laid her hand on the book. "First I need to understand why she gave this to me. If there's really a lost library at the end of this search, I'm supposed to find it. I don't know why, but that's what I think."

"What message was the old gal trying to send you with *this*?" Sheldon pointed at the coffin.

"No clue. I couldn't find any online references to antique dollhouse coffins. Lucille said her father was good with his hands. He designed Wynter House. He wrote and printed this book. Maybe he made the coffin, too. I don't think I'll understand what it means until I solve all the riddles and find all the clues."

Sheldon shook his head. "They can't all be intact. The rooms you saw were a disaster. Mold. Dirt. Rodent droppings." He shuddered. "The Junk Hunks already cleared the kitchen and dining room, so some of your clues are probably in the bottom of a dumpster by now."

"That's why I'm going to close an hour early today. I need to get back inside that house."

"We never close early in the summer. It's festival season. It's . . . Are you sure you want to do this? Get sucked into that house?"

Nora scowled. "I know it's festival season, but this weekend is a beer festival. In another town. We won't see people passing through until Thursday. Besides, what's the point of being your own boss if you can't close an hour early every now and then?"

Sheldon picked up Nora's latte and pressed it into her hands. "Drink up, boss babe."

The morning passed quickly. Nora was busy from the moment the Monday Moms entered the shop until she told Sheldon to take a lunch break at noon. A group of guests from The Lodge, who were shuttled downtown by trolley and given free tote bags to fill with purchases from local businesses, had scooped up nearly half of the vintage items Nora had bought yesterday at the flea market.

"The shelves are looking bare, and it's only Monday," Sheldon moaned.

Nora knew she needed to invest more time searching eBay, Etsy, and neighborhood websites for vintage knick-knacks, but her regular to-do list was already a mile long.

"I need to hire someone," she murmured as the sleigh bell chimed and a fresh bunch of customers with teal tote bags streamed into the store.

She'd done the calculations. She could bring on a part-time employee. Someone who could work fifteen to twenty hours a week. A friendly and reliable book lover. Someone who could operate the espresso machine, recommend books, and deal with all kinds of people.

"I'm going to stop talking about it and make it happen," Nora declared.

She was in the middle of typing up a classified ad when a woman placed a stack of thrillers on the checkout counter and said, "These are for my daughter's birthday. She asked me to get her six thrillers by female writers. I've got four. Who should I add?"

She'd selected books by Deepti Kapoor, Stacy Willingham, Rachel Howzell Hall, and Jane Harper, so Nora suggested she add the latest titles by Lisa Jewell and Liane Moriarty.

If every customer bought six hardcovers and a candle, I could afford a full-time employee.

When Nora returned her attention to the classified ad, she found that she no longer knew what to write.

She and Sheldon worked so well together. They were close friends and confidants. On top of that, Sheldon loved Miracle Books. He gave his heart and soul to the store. He cared about each and every customer. He made coffee for them. He baked for them. He ran the Blind Date Book Club and hosted a weekly storytime. He filled the bookstore with music and energy. His booming laugh was infectious. His ability to listen and to make people feel welcome was unparalleled.

Could she possibly trust someone new the way she trusted Sheldon?

You're hiring a part-time employee, not a therapist. Just write the damn ad, her inner voice chided.

When Sheldon came to the front to tell her that he was back from lunch, she told him about the ad. "It'll go online tomorrow and appear in print in this Sunday's paper."

"You should put a sign in the window too," he said. "We

want a reader, so why not hire someone who comes in here all the time?"

"Good point. I'll buy a sign after I eat my sandwich."

The hardware store was on the same block as Miracle Books, so Nora had time to eat outside and do her errand. She crossed the street, sat on a park bench, and unpacked her lunch tote.

Her bench faced the playground, and she watched kids climb the jungle gym and race in and out of a wooden castle. Two little girls were on the swings, pumping their legs and laughing, their long white-blond hair streaming out behind them like two comet tails.

A handful of mourning doves waddled over to Nora's bench, cooing in anticipation of a snack. She pulled the crust off a slice of bread and tore it into small pieces. As she tossed the pieces to the birds, a shadow fell across her face. She glanced up to see Hester grinning down at her.

"It's so weird to see you outside during shop hours," she said, dropping onto the bench.

Nora smiled. "It's weird to feel the sun on my face."

Hester touched the brim of her baseball cap. "It takes me five minutes to get a new freckle, I swear, but I was on my way to the hardware store when I spotted you giving your lunch to the birds. Was it that bad?"

"No, I just want to stay on the birds' good side. You've read the Daphne du Maurier story. You know they all talk to each other." She lowered her voice to a whisper. "Let me finish my food, and I'll walk to the store with you. I need to buy a Help Wanted sign."

Hester pushed on Nora's arm. "No way! You finally realized that you need a little more time to yourself?"

"I need more time to find shelf enhancers. I don't know if shabby chic is trendy right now, but I can't keep up with the demand for vintage keepsakes."

"If you didn't work every Saturday morning, you could hit up the flea market in Maggie Valley or the antiques malls in Asheville. The stuff is out there. You just have to go get it."

Nora was about to tell Hester what she saw at the diner last night, but Hester leaned back on the bench and started complaining about how Andrews had canceled their movie date on Sunday afternoon. He also canceled their dinner plans because he got called into work.

"I knew he wasn't excited about seeing *The Princess Bride,* but come on! The throwback movies are half price, and who wouldn't want to escape reality while inhaling a bucket of popcorn and a huge pack of Twizzlers?"

"I hate Twizzlers. They taste like plastic straws flavored with cough medicine."

Hester giggled. "Jasper hates them too. He always gets Sour Patch Kids, but he doesn't like the yellow ones, so I get to eat those and my plastic cough syrup straws."

Nora handed Hester the rest of her crust and watched her feed the doves. When she'd tossed the last piece to the birds, Nora said, "Sorry that your Sunday was a washout. What about Saturday night? Did you do anything fun?"

Hester snorted. "If you mean reading in the bathtub for an hour, then yeah, Saturday was fun. Jasper was hanging out with people from work, so I didn't see him. That was fine because I was in my pajamas by eight. I had two wedding cakes, three baby shower cakes, and four custom birthday cakes due on Saturday. Every part of my body was sore. All I wanted was a bath, a book, and bed. After a day like that, I'm not much fun."

Though Hester kept her voice light, a shadow of unhappiness surfaced in her eyes.

Taking her hand, Nora said, "McCabe and I were at the Pink Lady Saturday night, and we bumped into Jasper. He was there with Hollowell. They were at the counter, having a beer. Hollowell was being flirty. A little handsy. Like this." Nora touched Hester's shoulder and leaned her body close to her friend's. "It might not mean anything, but I thought you should know."

Hester scissored her legs in frustration. The motion startled the doves, and they burst into the air, grunting in agitation.

"She's been after him from the moment they met. But if he's encouraging her . . . well, that says something, doesn't it?" Pulling her hand free, she began twisting a strand of honey-colored hair around her index finger. "He said he was going to his parents' house on Sunday to help his dad take down a dead tree. And his mom wanted him to cart stuff to the dump. I couldn't be mad at him for canceling our movie date—not when he was being such a good son. I thought, 'My man is so sweet.'"

She began to cry.

Nora put her arms around her friend and whispered, "Hey. You don't know what's going on, and the only way you'll find out is by talking to him. You two have been through too much to give up without a fight."

Hester's head moved from side to side, her cheek rubbing against Nora's shoulder. "That's just it. Ever since I broke off the engagement, everything between us has been a struggle. We've been to therapy. We've talked about our feelings. We've done the work, but that's just it. It's been work. The fun, spontaneous, sexy, silly easiness of us isn't there anymore."

In the playground, a child squealed with elation as his mother spun him on the roundabout. Clutching the rail, he tilted his head up to the sky and whooped with delight. The wind snatched his baseball hat and tossed it into the dirt, but neither he nor his mom seemed to notice. She spun him faster, her laughter mingling with his.

Hester stared in their direction, but didn't react. At this

moment, she was blind to joy. Jasper Andrews, the man she'd loved for years, was drifting away like an untethered boat. And it sounded like she was going to let the current carry him away.

"I'm sorry," Nora said.

"Me too." Hester dragged a palm across her tear-slick cheeks and ran her fingers through her curls. She sniffed, gave Nora's hand a squeeze, and stood up. "I'm gonna go. I need to go on a hike, or clean out my closet, or organize my recipes. I need to think."

Nora stood up, enveloped Hester in her arms, and said, "I love you."

She watched Hester walk away, her hair shining like a halo in the sunshine, and wished she could mend the new crack in her friend's heart.

When Hester reached the end of the block, she turned the corner and disappeared from view. For a minute, Nora stared at the empty space where her friend had been, then glanced at her watch.

She no longer had time to buy a sign at the hardware store, which was fine with her. Suddenly the idea of hiring part-time help felt like a mistake. Did she really want to invite someone new into the fold? New people were so much work. Nora would have to tiptoe around the person until they felt comfortable with each other. And she didn't want to tiptoe around anyone in her own store.

This has nothing to do with a future employee, her inner voice chided. *You're in a funk because of Hester and Andrews.*

On her way back to the bookstore, Nora called McCabe.

She knew he was busy. She'd already sent him a text, which had gone unread, but still hoped he'd answer her call. There was something about the very real possibility that Hester and Andrews were about to split up that made Nora want to hear McCabe's voice. His deep, steady, reassuring voice.

When she heard him say, "Hey, sweetheart," she felt like she could breathe a little easier. There was so much she wanted to tell him, but she was crossing the street and would be inside Miracle Books in under a minute, so she decided to focus entirely on him.

"Hey, love. How's your day going?"

Nora heard voices in the background, followed by the solid *thunk* of a door closing. "I'm drowning in paperwork. Not mine, but Lucille Wynter's. Four of us are here at the morgue, going through pounds of receipts, bills, lists—you name it. Some of it's pretty nasty, which is why we're using a surface we can hose off when we're done."

"Found anything helpful?"

"Not yet. There's so much to go through. It's going to take days—maybe the whole week." McCabe sighed. "I don't know if I'm running an investigation or working as an unofficial member of the Junk Hunks team. I need to get back to it, but I want to see you tonight. What do you say?"

That was all Nora wanted to hear. And yet, Wynter House called to her. "I'll stop by work to see you when I get done."

"Sounds good. We can have takeout. What are you in the mood for?"

"Anything. I just want to hang out with you."

"That made my day. See you later, Book Lady."

He rang off, and Nora entered the shop to find a line forming at the checkout counter.

When Sheldon offered to run to the hardware store before he left for the day, she let him. He taped the HELP WANTED sign to the bottom corner of the front window and stood back to survey his handiwork.

"Are you ready for this, boss?"

Nora flashed him a hopeful smile and said, "To quote Maurice Sendak, 'Let the wild rumpus start!'"

It felt strange to be ushering customers out of the shop at ten past five. Nora had always made a point of letting people linger in the stacks until six or even six thirty.

Usually, after closing and locking the front door, she'd wipe down the counters in the kitchen, vacuum the carpet and the alphabet rug in the Children's Corner, and clean the restroom. Tonight, however, she didn't do any of these things. She turned off the lights, hopped in her truck, and headed for Wynter House.

The purple Junk Hunk trucks were lined up along the curb, along with a white Honda Civic with a Tennessee plate. Nora saw a small rental car decal affixed to the rear window and steeled herself for another unpleasant interaction with Harper.

But it was Beck she ran into first, and he was evidently delighted to see her.

"I'm glad you're here," he said. "I can't thank you enough for putting us in touch with Bea. She and Cricket are incredible. They have so much energy and obviously love what they do."

"It's true. If you offered them tickets to Disney World, they'd pass because they wouldn't want to leave this job. This is their idea of fun."

The light in Beck's eyes dimmed a little. "That's how Harper feels about her job. You too, I imagine. I'm proud of what I do—I'm a chiropractor—but I don't bounce out of bed every day, eager to get to the office. Guess I'm a bit jealous, but never mind all that. Come in."

He held out an arm, inviting Nora to precede him into the house. She grabbed a mask and a pair of gloves and waited for him to join her in the kitchen.

"The team's done in here, the dining room, and the clock room. Would you like to see it?"

"Sure."

Beck led her into the dining room and paused to take in her reaction to the empty space.

Obediently, she glanced around. "Wow. That fireplace is beautiful. So are those sconces. And the wallpaper—are those Greek gods?"

She knew what they were, of course, but hoped to draw Beck into telling her what it had been like living in this house.

"Yeah." Beck chuckled. "I always thought it was too busy. It's hard to focus on your food with a bunch of muscle heads in togas flying across the walls. I just wish the table had survived. I thought we'd get some real money for it, but it was too damaged by the books."

For a moment, Beck looked like he was the one who'd been crushed beneath the piles of books. His shoulders drooped and his arms hung limply at his sides.

What happened to this family? Nora wondered for the umpteenth time.

"It can't be easy to see the place you grew up in full of clutter," she said. "But it's probably just as hard to see it cleared out."

He moved his hand up and down, simulating a wave. "It's an emotional roller coaster. And not all of it's bad. I was really happy to see the clocks. I wound a few of them just to see if they still worked, and they do. Bea's uncle is coming to pack them up tomorrow."

All the boxes and bags had been removed from the office, leaving only the shelves stuffed with clocks. Nora's eyes went right to the grandfather clock with the ship on its face.

Beck followed her gaze. "My grandfather's longcase clock. The ship actually rocks on the waves. When I was a kid, I thought it was magic."

It still is, Nora thought. Aloud, she said, "Are you going to keep any of the clocks?"

"Can't afford to. We have to pay off Mom's debts and the cost of the cleanup. And we won't see a dime until this stuff is sold."

Hearing movement from the dining room, Beck turned to see two Junk Hunk employees pass by. Hurrying to the doorway, he said, "Are you working upstairs now?"

"Yes, sir. Since the stairs are cleared, the deputy said we could start on the bedroom at the end of the hall."

"That's my dad's room," Beck explained to Nora. "He left when I was eleven. Harper was nine and Clem? He was just a toddler. We never heard from my father again. It totally wrecked my mom. She barely functioned after that. Harper and I had to grow up real fast. We had to take care of Mom and Clem."

And there it was. The trauma that had left Lucille broken and bereft. She'd been abandoned—left to raise three children on her own.

She touched Beck lightly on the arm. "I'm sorry. Did you and your dad ever reconnect?"

His face clouded with anger. "I have no idea where he is. He never reached out to us. To be honest, we all hope he's dead. He turned our world into a shit show. Excuse my French."

"Beck! Are you down there?"

Beck's head swiveled toward the stairs. "That's Harper. Let's go up."

Following him into the hall, Nora was startled by the sight of the uncluttered staircase. She could picture a debutante descending its wide steps, her white dress glowing against the dark wood, her dainty hand sliding down the polished banister.

There was no girl at the top of the stairs, but rather a small woman in denim shorts and an Outer Banks T-shirt.

"Hey, lady!" Bea called down to Nora.

Nora waited for Beck to climb the stairs and disappear down the hall before joining Bea on the landing. "What happened to the crime scene tape?" she murmured.

"Your man took it down hours ago—said we could go on with the cleanout, as long as one of his people approved of everything we moved first. It's a real circus here, between us and the deputies and the family members. We can't toss personal papers or pictures, and we can't go in the front parlor or the library because they haven't finished processing and taking pictures in there, but that's fine by us. We've got plenty to do up here."

"Beck said you're working in his father's room."

Bea nodded. "It's the worst room on this floor. It looks like Lucille was trying to smother any evidence of his existence—not that I blame her. Harper told me how he left them in the middle of the night. Emptied the bank account, filled a suitcase, and was gone for good. What kind of man leaves his family high and dry like that?"

Cricket poked her head out of the room at the end of the hall. "Bea! Bring Nora in here. I want her to take a look at these books."

A line of Junk Hunk workers streamed past, their arms laden with boxes. Cricket deposited a stuffed garbage bag in the hall and stepped aside to let Nora into the room.

The other doors in the dim hallway were closed. The air smelled like old clothes and wet dog, but was slightly less noxious than the odor suffusing the main floor.

"Harper and Beck are in there, so let's give them a minute," Cricket whispered. "Harper told me how their mama locked the bedroom and bathroom after their daddy left. The kids never found the key and haven't stepped foot in here since they were knee high. They must be feeling all kinds of feelings right now."

Eventually Beck and Harper emerged from behind a

mound of boxes. Beck had his arm around his sister. Her head was bent, so he gently pulled her through the clutter and steered her toward the stairs, murmuring softly to her the whole while.

Once they were out of sight, Bea and Nora picked their way to the bathroom.

Though a layer of dust coated every surface, it was a surprisingly tidy space. It looked like any other bathroom, except for the claw-foot tub, which was filled with books.

"May I?" asked Nora.

Pointing at the tub, Bea said, "Dive in."

Nora selected a black book. Cradling the spine, she opened to the title page. The book she held was a King James Bible from 1964.

The book Bea picked up was also a Bible. As was the next book Nora examined.

She and Bea removed Bible after Bible, stacking them on a clean towel. The editions were printed between the 1940s to the 1970s. None were of particular value. None were inscribed. In short, the tub was filled with dozens and dozens of old, unsellable Bibles.

"I don't get . . ." Nora trailed off, her attention caught by a wink of metal. Removing another Bible from the very bottom of the tub, she saw that the glint came from a ring. A gold ring.

A wedding band, Nora thought.

And then, she noticed how the ring was wrapped around a yellow twiglike shape.

But it wasn't a twig.

It was a finger bone.

Chapter 10

People have to live and die somewhere, after all,
and a house can hardly stand for eighty years
without seeing some of its inhabitants die within
its walls.

—Shirley Jackson

Bea reached out to remove more books from the claw-foot
tub, but Nora stayed her hand.

"We can't touch anything else. If there are more bones
under these Bibles . . ."

The two women stared at the pathetic remains of the ring
finger in silence. It was deeply unsettling to think they were
gazing down at a grave.

If there was a body in this cast-iron coffin, it had not been
cushioned by a pillow or wrapped in satin cloth. Its shroud
was made of books. Hundreds of heavy, smothering books.

"I'll get the deputy," Bea said.

There were no bathtub riddles in *The Little Lost Library,*
but Nora knew she'd unwittingly exposed one of Wynter
House's dark secrets.

Getting to her feet, she retreated to the threshold and
thought about what Beck had said—how this room had been
off-limits to Lucille's children. How Lucille always kept it
locked.

Ever since her husband, Frederick, had left.

The door was made of thick wood. The original hardware, a glass knob affixed to a brass doorplate, was intact. Below the knob was a keyhole.

Nora could imagine Lucille fitting a skeleton key into the hole, locking the door, and tucking the key into a hidden compartment in her dresser or some other place where her children would never find it.

Because Lucille must have locked this door. She knew what was in the bathroom and decided to seal it away—to hide it from sight. Is this the reason Frederick left? Had he fled because he was responsible for the body in the claw-foot tub?

"What the hell are you doing in here?" a woman barked.

Nora swung around to face Paula Hollowell. "I was helping Bea." She pointed at the bathroom. "She asked me to look at those books. We stopped as soon as we saw the bones."

"You have to be in the middle of everything, don't you?" Hollowell sneered. "Always in the spotlight. Go downstairs and wait. You'll have to give a statement."

She pushed past Nora, bumping her roughly on the shoulder on her way into the bathroom.

Heat flowered in Nora's chest, and her hands tightened into fists. She wanted to shove Hollowell off her feet and send her careening into the tub. She wanted to see her pinwheel her arms like a cartoon character before she crashed onto the remaining Bibles with a cry.

Nora's fantasy was abruptly shattered by a commotion in the hallway.

Suddenly Beck and Harper were squeezing through the mounds of debris like two oversized ants wriggling through a tunnel of sand. Their movements were urgent, their faces etched with apprehension.

"Sorry," Nora murmured, pressing herself against an un-yielding piece of furniture covered by a mound of linens.

Harper's glance skittered over her like she was just an-other item to be removed by the Junk Hunks, but Beck paused to whisper, "You okay?"

He had the decency to listen to her reply before following his sister into the bathroom.

Bea was waiting for Nora in the hall. She removed her gloves and dropped them into the trashcan next to the door. After motioning for Nora to do the same, she said, "Cricket and her team are calling it a day, but I'm supposed to stay. Deputy Congeniality said we have to give statements before we can go. Said her backup is ten minutes away. I have some things to pack up in the tents, so that's where I'll be."

Ten minutes until more officers arrived.

With the Junk Hunks gone, Bea working outside, and Beck, Harper, and Hollowell preoccupied in Mr. Vander-camp's bathroom, Nora had ten minutes to search for the next clue.

She hurried down the hallway and stopped at the top of the stairs. Taking *The Little Lost Library* from the small messenger bag she used as a crossbody purse, Nora opened to the clock riddle. Skimming to the end, she read the next riddle:

My cap has scales, but I am not a snake,
When I shed the gardener must fetch his rake.
No squirrel can steal me for his sport,
As my purpose is to provide support
For those who climb both up and down,
In white satin slippers or boots of brown.

Nora hadn't paid much attention to the details of the staircase. She knew that its rails and posts were made of wood and that its single newel post featured decorative carving and a domed top.

The day she'd found Lucille's body, Nora had noticed the newel post at the bottom of the stairs, but only because she couldn't help wondering if Lucille had struck her head on the solid piece of wood before landing on the floor.

In the riddle, the words *up and down* could also be a ladder or another set of stairs. In a house with three stories, there was a staircase to the basement and, most likely, another staircase leading to the servants' quarters or an attic. Nora had watched *Downton Abbey* and *The Gilded Age* enough times to know that the stairs and passages used by servants were typically poorly lit and unadorned.

Based on the line about the gardener, Nora assumed she was looking for leaves. Putting her hand on the banister, she descended the stairs, her gaze locked on the newel post at the bottom.

At the end of the handrail, she ran her hand up the newel post, her fingers tracing what appeared to be a row of oak leaves in the wood. The domed cap was made of a cluster of leaves, and sitting on the top of the dome, like a finial on a peaked roof, was a small acorn.

> *My cap has scales, but I am not a snake.*

Using the flashlight on her phone, Nora examined the acorn. It definitely had scales. They were faint and coated in layers of beeswax and dirt, but they were there.

She felt a thrill of excitement, which was immediately followed by a prick of guilt. Here she was, searching for clues while everyone else in the house was preoccupied with the body in the bathtub.

Shoving the guilt aside, she ran the flashlight beam over the acorn. It was small and appeared to be a solid piece of wood. Was the clue inside?

It's too small, Nora thought dismissively. *It must be under the dome.*

Nora pressed on the oak leaf carvings, hoping to engage a mechanism concealed inside the newel post, but nothing happened.

She saw no hinges, and when she tried to twist the dome counterclockwise, as if loosening a screw, the domed cap didn't budge. Twisting it in the opposite direction had no effect either.

Aware that her time was running out, Nora ran her hands down the length of the post, probing every nook and cranny of the decorative floret-and-leaf carvings.

"Where are you?" she whispered, moving her flashlight over the wood.

Finding nothing, she took a moment to re-read the riddle.

It's all about the acorn, she decided.

She cupped the acorn in the middle of her hands and, instead of turning the domed cap, tried to pull it away from its base.

She felt movement.

It was just a subtle shift, but it felt right, so she gave the cap another tug and a tiny crack appeared between the cap and the post.

You're going to break it, her inner voice scolded.

Nora paused.

Lucille would never forgive her for damaging her beloved house. If she so much as nicked the wood of this newel post, it would feel like a betrayal.

She needed to be quick, but careful.

I need a tool—something to widen the crack in the post without harming the wood.

Opening her wallet, she searched for the plastic loyalty card from her grocery store and slid it into the crack. Then she wriggled the card back and forth until the opening began to widen.

She repeated this motion on all four sides until she finally felt a noticeable loosening.

Again she cupped her hands around the cap and pulled. With a sigh of air that sounded like a breath of wind moving through the pine boughs, the cap came off.

At the same moment, Nora heard voices from the second-floor hallway. She also heard another voice coming from the kitchen. Hollowell's backup had arrived.

Nora peered into the top of the newel post and saw a small cavity. An object wrapped in white cloth was tucked into this hollow, like an egg in a nest. She plucked it out, gently lowered it into her bag, and pushed the post cap back in place.

She'd just removed her hands from the post when Deputy Andrews strode through the dining-room doorway.

"Hey, Nora." He jerked a thumb at the stairs. "Can you tell me where to find Hollowell?"

"When you get to the top, turn left and go all the way to the end of the hall."

Avoiding Nora's gaze, Andrews said, "The boss asked you to swing by the station on your way home."

"Bea too?"

"Yep. She already left," Andrews said as he jogged up the stairs.

Nora was taken aback by this terse exchange. Andrews had always been exceedingly friendly to her.

He knows I told Hester about him and Hollowell.

Nora hurried out to her truck. Struck by a powerful sense of déjà vu, she rooted around in her console for hand-sanitizing wipes. Once she'd removed any trace of dirt, she dried her hands with a paper napkin and unzipped her purse.

The cloth-wrapped object weighed next to nothing, but Nora unrolled it very slowly, as if loose gems might be hidden in its folds.

However, there was only one item inside the cloth. Another miniature.

Nora expelled a breath of relief at the sight of the innocuous object. It was a barrel. A plain wooden barrel with metal bands and a tiny metal spout.

Using her phone flashlight again, she took a closer look at the lid. It was hinged, so she pried it open with her fingernail.

Inside the barrel was a book.

Nora wanted to examine the book, then and there, but refused to give in to temptation. Not only did she lack the proper lighting and magnifying tools, but she had to wash her hands thoroughly first.

She rewrapped the barrel in its original cloth and tucked it back into her bag. She drew her seat belt across her body, and had just clicked it into the buckle, when she saw a flash of movement outside the passenger window.

Suddenly a face filled the glass.

A man she'd never seen before glowered in at her. His dark eyes were narrowed, and as Nora stared, he peeled his lips back from his teeth in an animalistic sneer. As Nora grabbed for her phone, the man slammed his fist against the glass.

"I'm calling 911!" she shouted, fumbling with her phone.

But just as suddenly as he'd appeared, the man was gone.

Nora swiveled in her seat, searching for him in her rearview and side mirrors.

She saw him for a split second—a burly figure in jeans, a black T-shirt, and a knit hat—before he leaped off the sidewalk and vanished behind one of the giant magnolia trees near the cemetery's entrance.

Nora jerked her truck into gear and pulled away from the curb, her heart rattling like a snare drum.

"What the hell?" she murmured, casting backward glances

in her mirror. All she saw was the unruly bulk of the hedge in front of Wynter House.

Behind her, the streetlights fizzled on. The first shadows of the night seeped through the grass and slithered across the asphalt. It was time for dinner and homework and flickering TV screens. A time for softer voices. For warm baths and pajamas.

As Nora drove toward McCabe, she thought about the bones in the bathtub and the rumors that had always swirled around Wynter House. Perhaps there was some truth behind those rumors. Perhaps the old mansion really *was* haunted.

Not with ghosts moving from room to room, casting a spectral glow, but in subtler ways. Groans from the floorboards or whispers in the drainpipes. Creaks on the stairs. Scratching behind the walls. Rustling in the eaves. The sound of secrets rotting the house from the inside.

Nora rested her hand on her messenger bag.

She had her own secrets. And even though she knew the damage keeping secrets could cause, she wasn't ready to share them just yet. Later, after she'd solved the riddles and completed the scavenger hunt, she'd come clean to McCabe, her friends, and Lucille's children. But for now, the tiny objects hidden in the ruins of Lucille Wynter's home belonged to her.

Not only was McCabe waiting for Nora in his office at the sheriff's department, but he'd ordered dinner. He'd also made space on his round table for two place settings.

"If this is a new strategy to put witnesses at ease, it's brilliant," she teased, kissing him hello.

"It's only for the sassy ones," he said, holding her for several heartbeats before letting her go. He then pulled out her chair and waited until she was seated before removing the lid from an aluminum bowl. The scent of lemons and white wine billowed into the air.

Nora's stomach gave an appreciative rumble. "Chicken piccata?"

"With extra capers. And a side salad big enough to feed a small village."

Nora leaned over to kiss his cheek. "You're the most thoughtful man I've ever met." She started to unroll her napkin and then stopped. "I need to wash my hands. Should I get us glasses of water from the kitchen while I'm up?"

McCabe nodded and began to plate the food.

When Nora returned with the water, the chicken was still too hot to eat, so she recounted her movements at Wynter House, being as detailed as possible.

When she got to the part about the Bibles, McCabe cocked his head and said, "Wait. *All* the books in the tub were Bibles?"

"All the ones I saw. We stopped removing them after I saw the finger bone."

McCabe contemplated this while cutting his chicken. "It feels like a judgment—being covered in Bibles. Like the person in the tub had committed a major sin."

"I thought the same thing." Nora speared a caper with her fork. "According to Beck, their father left when he was a kid. I think he said he was eleven. Anyway, they never heard from him again. Lucille locked up his room and hid the key. But the ring I saw in the tub? It looked like a wedding band to me."

"So maybe he didn't leave," McCabe said. "Maybe he's still there."

The chicken Nora swallowed stuck in her throat. She took a long drink of water and sat back in her chair. "First there was Lucille. Now these old bones. It's like something inside that house has woken up. Something dark. And evil."

"A ghost didn't choke Lucille. A living, breathing human did that, and I need to find that person."

Nora glanced at the whiteboard in the far corner of the room and wondered if there were reports and photos from Lucille's autopsy taped to the other side.

She pushed her plate away, unable to eat another bite.

McCabe laid his hand on Nora's arm. "I know you want to find out what happened to her, sweetheart, and we will. In the meantime, I wish you'd keep your distance from that house."

"It's not like I'm alone in there. You have people there, and there's Bea, the Junk Hunks and—" She stopped, suddenly remembering the man with dark, hostile eyes and bared teeth. She didn't think she needed to tell McCabe about the riddles in *The Little Lost Library* yet, because they had nothing to do with his investigation, but she wasn't going to withhold any other information.

She told him about the stranger who'd slammed his fist against her passenger window.

"What about his age?" McCabe asked when she was done.

"I'm not sure. Late twenties? Early thirties?"

McCabe fetched a notebook from his desk. "Any tattoos or piercings? Moles or scars? What about his teeth?"

"There was a space between his front teeth. That's all I remember. His eyes were dark brown. He had brown or black hair, which was long enough to stick out from under his knit hat. There was some kind of logo on the hat. It was red and black, but I only saw it for a second."

Dropping his notebook, McCabe walked behind his desk and pulled up a file on his computer. Seconds later, his printer whirred. He grabbed the single sheet of paper and placed it in front of Nora.

"Did it look like this?"

Nora examined the image of a wolf head. Half of its face

was red. The other half was black. Its mouth was open in a toothy snarl, and it glowered out from inside the confines of a circle. To Nora, it looked like the wicked wolf from a fairy tale.

"I'm pretty sure that's what I saw, but I'm not one hundred percent. What does it mean?"

"It's the symbol used by the Red Wolves, a drug ring operating throughout the Appalachians. Their territory covers Virginia, North Carolina, Tennessee, and Northern Georgia. They get more brazen all the time. We keep arresting petty dealers covered in wolf tattoos just like this. We've seen T-shirts and hoodies too. I guess they're branching out into outerwear now."

"We don't even have red wolves in North Carolina anymore, do we?"

McCabe pulled a face. "I thought they were on the brink of extinction, which makes them an odd choice for a mascot."

Nora remembered how the man had darted behind the magnolia trees in the cemetery. There could only be one reason for why he'd be hanging around Wynter House.

"If the man with the hat was a dealer, he was probably looking for Clem. Maybe seeing two sheriff's department cruisers made him think twice about knocking on his door."

"Thankfully, Clem's still in detox," McCabe said. "He can check himself out as early as tomorrow, and there's no telling what he'll do after that. I hope his siblings keep an eye on him."

McCabe's phone buzzed. He glanced at the incoming text and frowned. "It's Andrews. He's having a tough time with Beck and Harper. They're pitching a fit over having another restricted area in the house. I'd better go over there and smooth things over."

"It sounds like I'm not going to see you later, so I'd better kiss you good night now."

Opening his arms, McCabe said, "Best offer I've had all day."

Before heading home, Nora stopped by McCabe's house to feed his cats. The two tabbies, Magnum and Higgins, took turns making infinity symbols around her ankles while she opened cans of Fancy Feast.

Higgins ate in the laundry room, but Magnum was such a messy eater that all his meals were served on the dishwasher lid. After giving the cats fresh water and cleaning their litter box, Nora turned on the automatic laser toy. The cats would chase the little red dot for a solid twenty minutes, and Mc-Cabe would play with them when he got home, no matter how late that might be. He adored his cats and had worn the CAT DAD T-shirt Nora got him for Christmas so often that its bright blue hue had faded to a dull gray.

When Magnum finished his dinner, he ignored the laser. Jumping on the sofa, he gave Nora an expectant stare. When she didn't immediately approach him, he let out a plaintive meow.

"No snuggling tonight, Mags," she said.

She felt like a heel walking away from the lonely animal, but she wanted to go home, put her pajamas on, and examine the tiny book inside her bag.

It was almost nine by the time she'd settled in at her kitchen table. She'd arranged her magnifying glass, headlamp, and the miniature barrel or beer cask on a clean hand towel. Her laptop was within easy reach, and she'd left her glass of Cava on the counter behind her to avoid an accidental spill.

"Let's see what Lucille's dolls read about while enjoying a tipple."

When she turned the barrel over and opened its lid, the miniature book dropped onto the towel.

Examining the book through her magnifying glass, she saw a title stamped into the burnt-sienna leather cover.

"Bryce's Thumb English Dictionary," she said to her empty room.

Nora gently opened the cover. On the title page, she read: *Comprising: Besides the ordinary and newest words in the language, short explanations of a large number of scientific, philosophical, literary, and technical terms.*

The book, which was no bigger than a matchbook, was published by David Bryce and Son, Glasgow.

Nora looked at a few entries before searching for the book online. She found several old miniature dictionaries, but only one auction listing was a perfect match. The auction had taken place several years ago, and the book had sold for a little over three hundred dollars.

Not nearly as valuable as the miniature Bible.

Nora picked up the book again and fanned the pages. She saw a flash of red and stopped, but not quickly enough. She had to backtrack several pages to find the scrap of red ribbon tucked between two pages of words starting with H. The ribbon wasn't attached to the book, and Nora had no idea if its placement was important.

She read the list of words, hoping something would jump out at her: *hunger, hunt, hurdle, hurl, hurrah, hurricane, hurry, hurt, hurtle, hurtleberry, husband, hush, husk, husky.*

Was there a mark next to *husband*? And another next to *hurt*? She leaned closer to the magnifier, but that didn't help. She sat back in her chair, closed her eyes, and tried to think. If there was a connection between the coffin and the barrel or between the tiny Bible and dictionary, she wasn't seeing it.

For the next hour, she drank Cava and researched the history of miniature books. She looked at image after image until she was too tired to digest any more information.

After stowing the dollhouse barrel in the hidden nook where she'd placed the tiny coffin, Nora climbed into bed.

She was too tired to read, so she switched off the light and turned on her side, waiting for sleep to come.

Her mind jumped from thought to thought. It flashed from the finger bone in the tub to the man peering into her window, to Hollowell's face. And then, Nora thought of Hester. And of how she'd neglected to call and check in on her friend.

At any other time, this realization would've jolted her awake, but other, shinier images rose to the surface of her subconscious. She fell asleep, dreaming of a pile of Bibles with gold titles and glittery page edges. And somewhere under those books, like the pea beneath the princess's mattress, was a crushed bone and a wedding ring.

Chapter 11

*Book collecting is an obsession, an occupation, a
disease, an addiction, a fascination, an absurdity, a
fate. It is not a hobby. Those who do it must do it.*
                              —Jeanette Winterson

The next morning, Nora texted Sheldon to tell him she'd be
picking up the pastries from the bakery.

She knocked on the delivery door, bright and early, holding a grocery store bouquet of sunflowers.

When Gus opened the door, his gruff face broke into a
smile.

"Those for me?" he asked, pointing at the flowers. "I like
flowers as much as the next fellow, but I'm a bit long in the
tooth for you, don't you think?"

Stepping inside, Nora was immediately enveloped by the
scent of freshly baked bread. She inhaled the comforting aroma
of butter, cinnamon, and the yeasty tang of warm dough. It
conjured images of family dinners. Of apple-cheeked grand-
mothers in checkered aprons. Of shared memories.

"Estella told me about Ms. Wynter. That must've been hard
on you," Gus said. "Grab a stool and I'll make you some tea.
I was just putting the kettle on when you knocked."

Nora pulled a stool up to the massive butcher block in the

center of the kitchen and watched Gus wipe the flour off its scarred surface. Gus's calloused hands were as nicked as the wood he was cleaning, and his face was equally marked with lines and furrows.

Gazing at his tattoo sleeve, a collage of images from *Alice in Wonderland,* Nora said, "Where's Hester?"

Gus dropped tea bags into a pair of plain white mugs and filled them with hot water. While the tea steeped, he cut Nora a thick slice of chocolate babka. It was so fresh that steam still rose from its golden crust.

"Running an errand. She won't be a minute. Want me to put those flowers in water?"

Nora nodded. "They won't make up for me being a shitty friend, but they're a start."

"I'll fix her a cup of tea and you two can hash things out." Gus freed the sunflowers from their plastic wrap and arranged them in a glass pitcher. "I need to go home and get cleaned up. I'm taking Estella to her doctor's appointment today because Jack has to meet with the health inspector. We're going to grab lunch after her appointment and do a little food shopping. I'm making Korean short ribs tonight."

"That sounds like a good day."

Gus carried the pitcher of flowers to the front, where Hester would see them. Before he could return to the kitchen, a chime sounded, and a customer entered the bakery. Nora caught a glimpse of the mayor and heard her greet Gus in a voice infused with warmth.

Nora sipped her tea and listened as the mayor tried to decide whether to treat her staff to cinnamon buns or muffins.

"I have another suggestion," Gus said. "Try a sample of my chocolate babka. I doubled the chocolate this time, so it just melts in your mouth."

The mayor popped a piece in her mouth and moaned.

The noise was loud enough to travel past the ovens, the

cooling racks, and the prep counters, to where Hester stood just inside the delivery door. She dumped a brown paper bag on the floor just outside the walk-in fridge and shot Nora a look that said, "What's going on?"

Nora pointed to the front and mouthed, "The mayor."

Hester grabbed one of her many aprons from a rack next to the sink and slipped it over her head. After washing her hands, she took the stool across from Nora and whispered, "She's sweet on him."

"Who could blame her? He looks like a burly Patrick Stewart and bakes like Martha Stewart. The man's a catch."

"You and I know that, but most people still see him as an ex-offender. My customers have no problem with him baking their bread, but most don't want him to serve their kids or swipe their credit cards."

Nora waved this off. "Give them time. They'll come around. If the mayor can recognize what a special person he is, then others will too. Maybe he'll ask her out and they'll end up falling madly in love."

Seeing Hester's face fall, Nora instantly regretted her words. "Let me get you some tea."

She sprang to her feet and prepared Hester's tea. After placing the hot mug on the butcher block, she wrapped her arms around her friend and whispered, "I'm a jerk for not asking you before now, but how are you?"

Hester leaned back against Nora's chest and sighed. "I don't know. One minute, I'm resigned and gloomy. The next minute, I feel totally fine. A little optimistic even. Like I'm ready to be free—to be done with the guessing and the wondering—to finally let this go. I love Jasper, and I know he loves me, but something got lost between us and we can't seem to get it back."

"Do you think he wants to move on?"

Hester dropped a sugar cube into her tea and watched it

dissolve, granule by granule. "Yeah, I do. I can see why Hollowell appeals to him. She's offering something fun and easy, with no strings attached. Camping trips and hikes with the dogs and beers at the ballpark."

"That woman has nothing to offer but heartache. You're the real deal, Hester. You're one in a million. You have the biggest, purest heart of anyone I've ever met—so whatever it's telling you, listen to it."

Hester reached for Nora's hand. "Thanks. I needed to hear that today. I'm glad you came to see me, but you don't owe me an apology. You have plenty of drama going on without having to worry about mine." She gestured at Nora's empty plate. "Was Gus using you as a guinea pig?"

"Yes, and I enjoyed every bite of his experiment. No wonder Sheldon always wants to pick up the pastries."

The mayor's tinkling laugh floated back to them, and the two women exchanged knowing smiles. As they sipped their tea, Nora told Hester about the bones in the bathtub.

When she was done, Hester was indignant. "Jasper didn't say a word about this. Then again, we *were* trying to figure out if we should break up, so it probably wasn't the right time to talk about Wynter House."

"Are you breaking up?"

Hester shrugged. "I don't know. We're going to revisit the topic this weekend. We're going to take the Blue Ridge Parkway to one of the lookout spots with a picnic area. I'm hoping we'll both find a little clarity up there. There's something about that view that helps put things in perspective, you know?"

Nora knew exactly what she meant. "That's how I feel when I hike. It's nothing but woods for over a mile, but then I come to that big clearing with all the boulders huddled together like trolls that've been turned to stone. I like to sit on one of those big rocks and look down at the valley. All the stuff I'm worrying about seems less important from that vantage point."

"Well, you're going to need that hike if you keep going back to Wynter House. You've found two bodies there already. Maybe the universe is telling you to stay away."

Nora couldn't even entertain the possibility. She had to solve the next riddle. Another clue was waiting for her. And perhaps another tiny book. She had to go back. Tonight, if possible. There were so many other rooms to explore. The front parlor. The library. The other bedrooms. The attic. The basement.

The bakery door chime snapped Nora out of her reverie. She met Hester's expectant gaze and quickly changed the subject.

"I hear Gus is taking Estella to the doctor today. He's going to be the world's best grandpa, isn't he?"

Hester glanced up at the wall clock. "He needs to get going."

"So do I," said Nora, getting to her feet. "Call me if you want to talk. Any hour of the day. Okay?"

"Okay."

Nora collected the bakery boxes stacked next to the delivery door and left. She walked the two blocks to Miracle Books, using the alley that ran behind the buildings. When she reached the public parking lot reserved for customers of the bookshop and hardware store, she spotted McCabe's SUV.

He got out of his truck, kissed her hello, and relieved her of the bakery boxes. "Can I buy you a cup of coffee?"

"Yes, please, but I might have to put you to work while it's brewing. I didn't finish the closing tasks last night."

In truth, she hadn't done anything beyond turning off the lights and locking the doors. There were crumbs on the carpet, paper towels on the restroom floor, stray books deposited on chairs and tables, and unwashed dishes in the sink. The counters in the ticket agent's booth were sticky with spilled coffee, and the trashcan was overflowing. The sour scent of food waste polluted the air.

"I'll take the trash out," McCabe offered.

Nora worked quickly to erase the evidence of her neglect. If Sheldon saw the state of his domain, she'd never hear the end of it.

She had the first urn of coffee brewing by the time McCabe returned, wheeling the vacuum.

"You don't have to do that," Nora protested.

"What if vacuuming is my love language? You need to let me express myself." McCabe winked and turned on the machine.

Nora watched him for a moment, her heart flooding with tenderness. Then she looked away, ashamed. McCabe was in uniform, cleaning her floor, and she was brewing coffee and keeping secrets.

He's the sheriff first and my partner second, she told herself. *He won't understand why I withheld evidence.*

Because that's what *The Little Lost Library* was. *Evidence.* It was a potential clue in a murder investigation.

Someone had choked Lucille and pushed her down the stairs. Someone had deliberately hurt her. And her killer was still in the house while Nora had held her lifeless hand.

Nora picked a random mug from the pegboard, filled it with coffee, and placed it on the shelf of the pass-through window.

McCabe switched off the vacuum and read the text on the mug out loud, "'Once in a while something amazing comes along and here I am.'" He grinned. "Accurate."

"Did you have breakfast?"

"I grabbed a protein bar on my way out the door. The cats didn't want me to leave—I had to detach them from my pants. I can't blame them if they shred the curtains while I'm gone, because they've been alone too much lately. I feel like a negligent parent."

Nora carried her Weird Barbie coffee mug to the Readers' Circle. "You could hire a pet sitter. I bet there are plenty of people who'd love to earn a few bucks hanging out with your cats. A retiree or a high school kid?"

"That's not a bad idea. I'll look into it when I get a second." He took a sip of coffee. "I know we talked last night, but you were probably still taking everything in, so I wanted to make sure you were okay."

"I'm fine," Nora assured him. "All I saw was that little finger bone. Were there more bones under the rest of those Bibles?"

"Yes. Or, more accurately, remnants of bones. It looks like the rest were dissolved in lye a long time ago. The Bibles crushed whatever remained, but a few pieces survived. Small bones—from fingers and toes."

Nora stared at McCabe over the rim of her coffee cup. "Is it Lucille's husband? Or is it impossible to know from a finger bone?"

"Forensics might be able to determine the gender and approximate age from the pieces we found, but they're not going to fast-track this case. I have no idea when we'll hear back from them, so we'll have to find out where Frederick Vandercamp went after he left Wynter House. *If* he left Wynter House."

"Vandercamp," Nora repeated. "I never heard Lucille use that name. She told me to call her Ms. Wynter."

"She dropped her married name after her husband disappeared," McCabe said. "Legally changed the kids' last names too. If Frederick mistreated or abandoned his family, I can see why Lucille would want to erase all traces of the guy, but she never had him declared dead. I guess it's because she had nothing to gain. The house was in her name, and each kid had a small trust fund set up by Lucille's father. Beck and Harper used theirs to pay for college. Clem made it through two years at NC State before moving into the garage. From the looks of his apartment, he spent a pretty penny on gaming computers and other forms of entertainment. The money his grandfather left is gone. I don't know what he's been living on."

Nora recalled her first sight of Clem. She remembered how his sleepy-eyed stare had sharpened into anger. "He knows every inch of Wynter House. He could've been inside when I was with Lucille and slipped out before anyone noticed. If he's broke and owes the Red Wolves money . . ."

"We're looking into his movements and those of his brother and sister too. According to their statements, Beck was with a patient at his Cincinnati-based practice at the time of his mother's death. Harper spent the day at the office and went to a yoga class in the evening. We're making calls to confirm their alibis, but so far, they look solid."

"Maybe none of her kids were involved," said Nora. "If there was something worth stealing in Wynter House, Clem could've taken it whenever he wanted to."

McCabe shrugged. "At this point, it's hard to say if Lucille owned anything worth killing for. I know some of her books are valuable, but from what Bea says, we're not talking about significant amounts of money."

This was it. This was the moment Nora should tell McCabe about the treasure hunt.

If the next tiny book I find is worth as much as the tiny Bible, I'll come clean, she silently vowed. Aloud, she said, "There are still lots of rooms and piles upon piles of stuff to sort through."

McCabe grunted in agreement and drank another slug of coffee. Nora had never seen anyone drink hot coffee the way McCabe did. He seemed utterly immune to its heat.

Lowering the mug to his lap, he said, "It might be a good idea for you to avoid Wynter House for a few days."

"Because of the man at my truck window? Or because I found Lucille and the bones in the tub?"

"All of the above," McCabe said. "If anything else is found with a link to these deaths—it would be better if you weren't on-site when it happens."

Nora bristled. "Bea was there when I found those bones. Are you asking her to avoid the house?"

"She needs to be there. Cricket and the Junk Hunks need to be there. They have a job to do."

"As do I," Nora argued. "I'm advising Bea about the books, remember? And I'm not spending all day there. Just an hour or two after work."

"I knew I didn't stand a chance of keeping you out, when there are so many books inside, but it was worth a try." He smiled. "Just let someone else find the next body, okay?"

"Are you expecting another one?"

McCabe's smile vanished. "That house—I'm not ashamed to admit that it gives me bad vibes. Lucille's kids couldn't wait to get away from it. Lucille refused to leave it. We already have two open investigations, and there's still plenty of house left to examine. I don't know if we'll find more bones, but I think there are plenty of secrets tucked away in its walls."

"I do too," Nora agreed, her mind conjuring an image of a library of miniature books.

Later, when the bookshop was bustling with customers, Estella and June stopped by to deliver a surprise lunch.

"We brought victuals," June declared in an exaggerated drawl.

Estella held up a brown bag. "Club sandwiches and fruit salad from Jack. He was so happy to hear that the baby is fine that I had to give him a job to calm him down. I thought he'd relax a little, now that we're in the second trimester, but he's more keyed up than ever. I mean, shouldn't I be more nervous than him?"

"I don't think there are any rules when it comes to pregnancy," Nora said.

June gave Estella a gentle nudge. "Introduce Nora to our little Butter Bean."

Nora gave June a puzzled look. "Butter bean?"

Estella placed a black-and-white photograph on the counter. "June's nicknamed the baby 'Butter Bean.' Jack thinks it's cute, so we're stuck with it. This is what he or she looks like right now."

Nora couldn't make sense of the fuzzy image until Estella traced the outline of the baby's head and the oval of its stomach.

"When my dad heard the heartbeat, he started to cry," she said. "What am I going to do with these men?"

"What men?" asked Sheldon.

June waved him over. "The ones we like to spoil. See? We brought lunch."

"You're a saint." Sheldon stepped back and made a big show of taking Estella in. "And you. You're a redheaded fertility goddess. You're glowing like a full moon. But where are you hiding the baby bump?"

"It's here." Estella put a hand to her belly. "I can hide it under this dress for now, but eventually I'll need clothes with a lot more stretch."

Sheldon offered to watch the store, while Nora ate with her friends in the stockroom. Eager to update Estella and June about the recent events at Wynter House, she happily accepted.

In the stockroom, Nora arranged three folding chairs around a short stack of unopened boxes. Estella distributed the sandwiches, while June passed out napkins and bottles of iced tea. Jack had also sent along pickles, potato chips, and fruit cups.

"If he packs lunch for Butter Bean, that kid is going to be the envy of the school," June said.

As they ate, the three friends speculated over the future of Hester's relationship. Though there was little hope that Hester and Andrews would reconcile, no one wanted to see Andrews with Hollowell. They were all fond of Andrews and shared a mutual aversion to the K9 handler.

"Remember earlier this summer? How she twisted the truth, hoping to get you in hot water with McCabe?" June said to Nora. "She wasn't able to ruin your life, so she set her sights on Hester, instead. She'd better stay away from the Gingerbread House, or Hester might make her a custom scone she'll never forget."

Estella smirked. "I could suggest a few flavors. Kitty litter, old socks, used flypaper, a fresh urine sample . . ."

The women guffawed.

"Nora could probably find some choice ingredients in Lucille's house," June said. "Sounds like the contents of the refrigerator were pretty nasty."

"The bathtubs are even worse. One of them was full of bones. Human bones."

Estella's eyes widened in horror. "What?"

Nora told her friends about the body in the bathtub. She also told them how McCabe had asked her to stay away from Wynter House for a few days.

June dropped a handful of potato chips on Nora's napkin. "Are you going to listen to the man? Because you *do* have a knack for being in the wrong place at the wrong time."

"I'm not, because I made a commitment. In fact, I'm going back tonight. I can't decide if I'm going to close the shop early or not, but I'm definitely going back."

Estella pointed at Nora with her pickle spear. "What

aren't you telling us? Did you find more creepy clues, like that tiny coffin?"

Nora didn't want to tell McCabe about her findings, for fear he'd take the items and force her to stop hunting for more, but she was more than ready to talk to her friends about them. "Yes. I found a little barrel. A beer or wine barrel, with a lid that opens. There was a tiny dictionary inside, and a red ribbon was used to bookmark two pages of words starting with the letter H. I'd show it to you, but it's at home."

"Just how many clues are there?" asked June.

"Eight, I think. I can't solve the riddles unless I'm actually in the house, and I'm not sure I'll find all of them."

June set her jaw in determination. "What's the next riddle? Let's try to figure it out right now."

Nora took out her phone. "I took photos of each riddle, and this one's next. See what you make of it."

Estella scooted her chair closer to June's, and the two women read the lines marching across the screen:

> One of these tiles of white and blue
> Will lead you to a hidden clue.
> Is it the farmer toiling in his field?
> The soldier with his spear and shield?
> Is it the fisherman making his hopeful
> cast?
> Or the ship with the flag flying atop its
> mast?
> Is it the goose, so slow and fat?
> Being chased by the man with the
> feathered hat?
> Look closely at every detail,
> If your eyes are sharp, you will not fail.

"Aha," said June. "You need to find a room with blue-and-white tiles. Like a bathroom? What are you looking up over there?"

Nora made a swiping motion. "There's more to the riddle. Keep reading."

"I see. There's a cat and something that's head and shoulders above the rest. What's white and blue and tall? A UNC basketball player?" June laughed.

Estella, who'd been too busy scrolling through images on her phone to catch the joke, made a squeaking noise. "Look! I searched for blue-and-white tiles with a farmer, and this popped up."

Leaning over the makeshift table, Nora examined the image of a Delft tile showing a farmer in a field. The only other objects were a tree and a cow.

"Look up Delft tile with goose," urged June.

Estella complied and was rewarded with a page full of images.

"See? I have to get into the house and look for Delft tiles," said Nora.

"We'll come with you! What time are you going tonight?"

Nora vehemently shook her head. "You're pregnant, which means you're not stepping foot in that house. I'm sorry, but the place is a hotbed of mold and rot."

June bumped shoulders with Estella. "You can still help. You found the tiles on your phone. Maybe you can find images to match the other riddles." She threw a hopeful glance at Nora. "What about me? Can I go? And Hester? A treasure hunt would be a great distraction for her."

"I'd have to clear it with Beck, but what reason can I give him for bringing you two along? If I tell him about *The Little Lost Library*, he'll search for the clues himself, and then I'll never know what message Lucille was trying to send me."

They contemplated this hurdle in silence for several minutes.

Then Estella snapped her fingers. "I think I've got it. Lucille's kids want to put the house on the market, right? Maybe the owners of the Lodge caught wind of this and think Wynter House might be a good space for, I don't know, yoga or meditation workshops. That might get June in the door. As the Guest Experience Manager, it makes sense that she'd be scoping out the house on behalf of her employers."

"And Hester's a member of the Miracle Springs Historical Society," June added, her eyes shimmering with excitement. "She can say that the society is looking for a historic home to use as a visitor's center or museum."

After mulling over their ideas, Nora said, "I know Beck and Harper want to clean out the house before putting it on the market, but I also know they're both impatient to get back to their lives. It's worth a shot. Are you free tonight, June?"

Standing up, June began cleaning up their lunch items. "I have Bible study, but I can miss it this time. Even though Jesus is the only *real* treasure in this life, this believer still wants to help you search for the one hidden in Lucille's house."

The thought of June and Hester joining in the hunt made Nora feel positively buoyant. With her friends by her side, she could find clues more quickly. And when all the clues were discovered, the Secret, Book, and Scone Society could work together to decipher their meaning.

"This needs to be kept between us for now," she told June and Estella as they walked through the stacks. "I'll tell McCabe about it later—after we've found the lost library."

Laying a hand on Nora's arm, Estella whispered, "Are you sure this is a secret worth keeping?"

Acting as if she hadn't heard the question, Nora thanked her friends for lunch and slipped behind the checkout counter to help the next customer in line. When she glanced up from the register to wave goodbye to June and Estella, they were already walking out the door.

Chapter 12

We came to the house, and it is an old house, full of great chimneys where wood is burnt on ancient dogs upon the hearth, and grim portraits (some of them with grim legends, too) lower distrustfully from the oaken panels of the walls.
— Charles Dickens

During a brief lull before the after-school rush, Nora called Beck. When he didn't answer, she left a voicemail message, hoping he'd get back to her before she closed for the night.

She didn't expect to see him in person, but he showed up at Miracle Books around five, with his sister in tow.

"I wish I could order a cup of coffee, but I'd be up all night," he lamented after saying hello to Nora.

"You'll be up half the night, anyway," Harper grumbled.

The siblings looked tired. No amount of concealer could hide the bags under Harper's eyes, and Beck's whole face was etched with weariness.

"How about a glass of wine?" Nora suggested. "I have a bottle of Chardonnay in the fridge."

"Do you normally drink on the job?" jeered Harper.

Refusing to be goaded, Nora said, "It's from last week's Blind Date Book Club. They read Kristin Harmel's *The Winemaker's Wife*, and each member brought a bottle to—"

"I'd love a glass," Beck interrupted. "My sister would too. We've been sorting stuff all day, and the idea of sitting in a calm, organized place sounds like heaven."

Nora led them to the Readers' Circle. After whisking away the YA books strewn across the coffee table, she uncorked the Chardonnay and rummaged around in the book club supply cupboard for a snack. The only thing she could find was a can of mixed nuts, so she dumped them in a bowl and placed them on the coffee table. She served wine to the Wynter siblings, but filled her own glass with sparkling water.

Harper raised her glass in a toast. "To Mommie Dearest's books. May they be worth the hell she's putting us through. It's what she did best. Putting her kids through hell."

She drank without waiting for an acknowledgment from her brother, but Beck didn't seem to mind. He thanked Nora for the wine, took a small sip, and sank deeper into his chair.

Nora wanted to analyze Harper's toast. What did she mean by the Mommie Dearest reference? How had Lucille put her kids through hell before now?

Beck met Nora's puzzled gaze and swiftly changed the subject. "I got your message, and we'd love to have the ladies from the hotel and the historical society look at the house, but not yet. It has to be emptied and thoroughly cleaned first."

"Or we could just spill some gas on the floor and light a cigarette," Harper said, draining the rest of her wine in two swallows.

Nora kept her attention fixed on Beck. "The organizations these women represent have budgets to cover a full renovation, so the current condition of the house isn't an issue. They're eager to see the layout—the size of the rooms and the way things flow. If the floor plan meets their needs, they can prepare an offer. Maybe you can sell the house without a broker."

"That would be wonderful, but we don't feel comfortable showing the house while our father's bathroom is cordoned off," Beck said. "We're dealing with . . . other security issues as well. We had a break-in last night."

Nora glanced from Beck to Harper. "Was anything taken?"

Harper barked out a laugh. "How would we even know?"

"Right?" Beck smiled at his sister before turning back to Nora. "We've been focusing our efforts on Mom's papers. Our main goal is to help the authorities figure out what happened to her. She wasn't the mom we needed or deserved as kids, but she was still our mom. We want to know why someone would do . . . what they did."

"And the sooner we can tackle the papers in the front parlor and the library, the sooner we can be done with this shit show," added Harper. "Pass me the nuts."

Beck pushed the bowl of nuts closer to his sister and continued. "Harper and I are staying at a B and B, so we didn't notice that one of the basement windows had been smashed. Clem spotted it. You'd have to be pretty small to squeeze in through one of those windows, so it could've been a kid doing the stupid stuff that kids do. A dare or something. We know people call the place the Haunted Mansion."

"The cops found a rock and broken glass in the basement. There were marks in the dust on the floor too. But whoever made them smeared their footprints as they went. Doesn't sound like kids to me," said Harper.

"Are there valuables in the basement?" asked Nora. "Something a person could see if they looked through the window?"

Beck shook his head. "Nothing. A small printing press, full of cobwebs. Old tools and other junk."

"Did the intruder go upstairs?"

Harper slammed the bowl of nuts on the table. "We didn't come here for an interrogation, okay? This isn't the plot of a mystery novel, and we're not here to give you juicy gossip to spread around the town." She plucked Beck's sleeve. "Let's go. I need something more substantial than a glass of horse piss and a handful of stale nuts."

Beck laid a hand on his sister's arm. "Be nice, Harp. I'm almost done. Just give me a sec." He gave Nora an apologetic look. "Bea and Cricket still need your help when it comes to the books. The books that aren't ruined, that is. I understand you have a business to run, but I'm worried that you don't have enough time to advise them because you can't get over to the house until late. Can you come any earlier? Harper and I both have lives to get back to. Jobs to get back to. We need to finish this as soon as possible."

"She can't leave someone else in charge if there isn't anyone else," Harper stage-whispered.

Nora was seized by the urge to dump the rest of Beck's wine over Harper's head. Instead, she grabbed a handful of nuts from the bowl and squeezed them in her fist. "I can come early in the morning. That way, I can put in a few hours before opening the shop. When do the Junk Hunks get there?"

"At eight, but if you want to show up at seven, I'll let you in." Beck smiled, looking pleased.

Harper stood and dusted off her white cotton pants. "Don't expect coffee and donuts. If you want breakfast, eat it before you show up."

She walked away without another word, but Beck hung back.

"I'm sorry about my sister. Being back in Wynter House has opened old wounds, and she's lashing out. It's not an excuse. It's more of a warning to give her a wide berth. She's going to be wound tight as a clock until this job is done."

"It can't be easy on you either," Nora said softly. "Not only are you dealing with the loss of your mom, but you must have so many questions about your father's disappearance too."

Beck's mouth contorted with pain. "I recognized the ring the second I saw it. It's my father's, which means the bones in that bathtub are probably his. I think . . . I think my mom killed him. I don't know how, but she bought all those Bibles after he supposedly ran away. I bet she burned his clothes and took the money out of the bank herself. Of course, it's all gone now. She spent it on all the stuff we're wading through now. She just kept piling it on and piling it on, but in the end, she couldn't hide the truth. Our father didn't abandon us. He never *left*."

The last word came out as a choked whisper. Beck turned away, but not before Nora saw the anguish in his eyes.

"I'm sorry," she said. "For everything you went through as a kid and for everything you're going through now."

Visibly pulling himself together, Beck murmured, "Thank you. You've been very kind, and I appreciate it." He dabbed at the corner of one eye. "It'll all be over soon. Then Harper and I can leave this place and never look back."

"And Clem?"

Beck shrugged. "I really don't know. He's in a good place right now. He's clearheaded and full of plans. But it won't last. It never does. If he gets his hands on any money, he'll piss it away on drugs. Harper and I have tried to help him before, but none of the treatments ever stick. He wants to blur life at the edges—to keep his memories foggy. He wants to sleepwalk through his days. It's sad, but it's what he wants."

"Beck!" Harper's shout rang through the store.

"We'll be back at the house after dinner. See you there," Beck said before following his sister out the door.

Nora was tempted to close the store right then, but there was no way she could run off without tidying up. It wouldn't be fair to Sheldon to leave him with all the opening tasks and a messy store to boot.

She cleaned up the ticket agent's booth in record time and grabbed the stack of YA books that needed to be reshelved. As she began slotting the books into their respective spots, it quickly became clear that there were more holes than books.

The thief had struck again.

"Damn it!" Nora growled as she realized there were now two copies of *Red, White & Royal Blue* instead of three. She'd just received the special editions that morning and knew she hadn't sold any yet.

Sitting on the floor, she tried to picture the faces of every teenager she'd seen that afternoon. The majority were regulars she knew by name.

Had any of them worn backpacks or carried tote bags? Probably. The high schoolers often studied together or did their homework at the store.

"That's it!" she raged, albeit quietly because there were customers in the sci-fi section and another perusing the mystery shelves. "That's the last book you'll steal from my shop!"

Nora hung up the CLOSED sign and locked the door to prevent new customers from entering. She then turned off the music and told her remaining customers that she was closing early. They left without buying anything, but Nora didn't care. She needed to get to Blue Ridge Provisions before they closed.

She made it with five minutes to spare, and when the

salesperson asked if she needed help, she pointed at a display of trail cameras. "I need one of those."

"Sure thing. Is there a particular animal you're hoping to track?"

"Yes. A human."

Though Sheldon was perfectly willing to set up the trail cam, he was less amenable to opening the bookstore on his own.

"It's fine for one day, maybe two, but what about Thursdays? I can't run storytime, make coffee, and handle checkout. And what if I wake up with a flare that just won't quit? Are you just going to keep the store closed until you're done digging through piles of trash?"

The book thief had put Nora in an especially foul mood. She didn't feel like listening to Sheldon's arguments, so her reply was unusually brusque. "If you have a flare, we'll handle it. Maybe someone will apply for the part-time position, and we'll both get a break. I've gotta go."

She hung up and rushed home to make herself a sandwich, which she wolfed down in the truck. She chased the sandwich with a Coke, hoping the caffeine would give her a jolt of energy. All she got for her efforts was an upset stomach.

She parked behind a sheriff's department cruiser and walked to the end of the driveway to find Bea and Harper conferring in one of the tents.

Bea looked up with obvious relief. "Just the woman I was hoping to see. Can you tell us if this is worth anything? There's no date, and I can't find this edition online."

Nora accepted an old book with red cloth and gilt lettering called *The Defence of Guenevere and Other Poems.*

"It's by William Morris," she said, examining the title page. Not only was the book filled with lovely black-and-white illustrations, but the pages had minimal foxing.

After a quick online search, Nora was pleased to inform Harper that a similar copy had recently sold for seven hundred dollars.

"Thank God Clem didn't get his hands on this one," Harper groused, snatching the book away. "That's how he's paid for his drug habit all these years, you know. He sold Mom's books. Not the dog-eared paperbacks or Costco hardcovers she bought from you, but the ones her parents collected."

"Where did he sell them?"

Harper shrugged. "Online marketplaces like eBay. I doubt he got a fraction of what they were worth. He would've been in a hurry to get paid. Poor screwed-up Clem. At least Beck and I had memories of a time before my mom lost her marbles. Clem doesn't even have that. He was too young."

Bea cleared her throat. "I'll take Nora to the front parlor. If we can get those books sorted real quick, I might make it home for dinner."

Harper waved them off like a queen dismissing her servants.

Following Bea into the house, Nora said, "I wish you didn't have to wait for me."

"Honey, the Budweiser Clydesdales couldn't drag me away from this place. With every room we clear, I can see how beautiful this place used to be. I can feel it breathing in relief. Sounds crazy, I know, but there you have it."

It didn't sound at all crazy to Nora. The house seemed to be drinking in the fresh air and soaking up the light streaming through the windows. In every room, Nora noticed little architectural details she hadn't noticed before. Ceiling medallions and wall sconces. Delicate inlaid borders and medallions in the wood floors. Ornate mantelpieces.

Without the books and other items, the main hallway

looked twice as wide. Someone had thrown open the double front doors, and the September sunlight pooled in the entranceway.

Bea led Nora into the front parlor, which was empty, save for a row of moving boxes pressed against one wall and a set of threadbare dark blue curtains framing the tall windows.

"I think Lucille slept here," Bea said, pointing to the spot near the center of the room. "We found blankets and pillows on an old sofa. Looked like a nest. We trashed the sofa. Same goes for the chairs and a needlepoint rug that would've been worth a pretty penny if it hadn't been chewed to bits by mice. They got the fireplace screen as well, but there's a nice antique mirror and a marble-top table for the family to sell. Some quality oil paintings too, mostly portraits, covered in sheets. I guess Lucille didn't like looking at her dead relatives."

While Bea talked, Nora's gaze moved over the room. It took a Herculean effort to tear her eyes away from the fireplace tiles and focus on the boxes of books.

Opening the flaps of the first box, Bea said, "We've got a bunch of sets here. This one's Shakespeare, but every box has a different author. Problem is, some of the volumes were too damaged to save. Are they worth anything as a partial set?"

Nora took out her phone. "Let's see what I can find on the edition."

Bea handed her a yellow legal pad and a pen. "I need to finish up outside. Can you write down estimates for the books we should keep and make a pile of books to be trashed? Cricket wants to finish this room so she can concentrate on the bedrooms."

"Is the bathroom still off-limits?"

"Yep. And that ray-of-sunshine Hollowell spent all day going through the papers from the hall and front parlor. I don't think she found much, because she left about an hour ago carrying a thin file folder and a scowl as deep as the Grand Canyon."

Nora dropped to her knees in front of the first box. "Did you hear anything about the bones?"

"Just that the tests they run to see how old they are will take a while. Weeks, maybe." Bea cocked her head. "Hasn't your man told you this?"

"I've barely seen or talked to him since Lucille died." Nora waved an arm around. "This house seems to be taking over all of our lives."

Bea snorted. "Ain't that the truth. I'll be outside if you need me, but not for long. Beck and Clem are in the library. If you wanna talk to them, you've gotta knock because they keep the door locked. I haven't been inside yet, so you know I'm dying to get in there."

As soon as the sound of Bea's footsteps receded, Nora closed the parlor door and crossed the room to the fireplace. She squatted in front of the hearth and examined the blue-and-white tiles surrounding the firebox. The designs on the Delft tiles matched the designs described in *The Little Lost Library*.

There was the farmer, the fisherman, the soldier, the ship, the goose, and the man with the feathered hat. She also saw a cat, which seemed to be lunging like it wanted to grab the goose from another tile. Each tile was unique and none of the designs repeated.

Nora didn't need to consult the riddle. She'd read it so many times that she knew it word for word. Her goal was to find the tile that stood out from the others. One that was "head and shoulders above the rest."

She scanned the tiles, one at a time, searching for an anomaly.

The minutes raced by, and the images of fields, water, and villages began to blur together. As the sunlight waned, the shadows stretched across the floorboards and distorted the shapes in the tiles. Suddenly the lunging cat seemed sinister. The soldier with the pointed spear glowered. The farmer in the pasture looked inhospitable.

Hearing the echo of voices in the hallway, Nora darted back to the book boxes and set to work researching the Shakespeare set. She estimated the value of the incomplete set, moved on to a series on the history of England, and then evaluated ten beautifully bound volumes of philosophy books.

A door slammed somewhere, and the voices she'd heard fell quiet.

After waiting a minute, Nora returned to the fireplace.

" 'Head and shoulders above the rest,' " she whispered.

She looked for the tallest person, tree, or building in every tile. And then, her gaze landed on the ship with the two masts. On top of the tallest mast was a flag. The Dutch flag. And it was in color.

It's the only tile with colors other than blue and white.

She zoomed in on the tile, using her phone's camera, and saw a pair of minuscule hinges attached to its left side.

"Bingo."

For a moment, she simply stared at the tile. When had it last been opened? Was she willing to ruin a piece of antique Delft in hopes of finding another clue?

The answer was yes, she absolutely was.

She curled her fingers under the right corner of the tile and pulled. A frisson of dust fell onto her jeans as she felt the tile give way by a few centimeters. After another firm pull, it opened with a creak, revealing a cavity in the stone.

Having seen all of the Indiana Jones movies, Nora knew it

was unwise to thrust her bare hand into an unknown space, but she was pressed for time, so she stretched out her fingers, hoping they wouldn't brush against the unyielding carapace of a beetle or the needle-thin legs of a spider.

What she felt instead was another cloth-wrapped bundle. She scooped it into her hand, pushed the tile back in place, and scurried over to her purse. With her heart thumping against her rib cage, she tucked the object in her bag.

Exhaling slowly, she continued to appraise the books.

She was on the last box when she heard footsteps in the hall. It wasn't Bea, who stepped lightly on small, sneakered feet. This was the tread of a heavier person wearing boots.

Don't be Hollowell, Nora prayed.

McCabe poked his head into the room and smiled. "There you are. Bea was about to file a missing person's report on you." He jerked his head at the boxes. "Almost done?"

"I'm on the last box." Nora scribbled a number on the legal pad.

She could feel McCabe's eyes on her as she scrolled an auction site featuring an incomplete set of *Birds of North America.*

"Are they valuable?" McCabe asked.

"Every set in these boxes is worth between four and six hundred dollars. Their antique leather bindings make them desirable."

McCabe wandered over to the windows and looked at the darkening sky. "The birds around here have all gone to bed."

Taking the hint, Nora finished her estimate and grabbed her purse. "All done."

"Have you eaten yet? I thought I'd pick up beef and broccoli from Dumpling King on the way home."

"I had a sandwich, but I could use some greens."

McCabe waved Nora into the hall. "I'll get a side of Szechuan green beans. When we first met, I remember you telling me that you liked lots of spice in your food, but not so much in your books."

Nora grabbed McCabe's elbow. "I remember that. We were on one of our lunch dates at Pearl's. Did you come here to find me?"

"No. I wanted to update the family on our progress. I knew they wouldn't want to stop what they were doing and drive to the station, so I came to them. When I saw your truck out front, I wasn't surprised."

There was no censure in McCabe's tone. Nora tried to see beyond his inscrutable expression, but couldn't. "I'm going to grab some clean clothes from my place. Should I shower there or at your place?"

Seeing the invitation in her eyes, McCabe said, "Mine."

As she drove home, Nora kept glancing at her purse, which sat squarely in the middle of the passenger seat.

At the next red light, she reached over and plunged her hand inside her bag. Her fingers fumbled around, brushing against her wallet, a tube of lip gloss, and a pen. Just as she encountered the edge of the cloth-wrapped object, the light turned green.

For the rest of the drive, she distracted herself by trying to guess what McCabe had discussed with Beck, Harper, and Clem.

Had the siblings found a clue among Lucille's papers? A threatening letter? A legal document or a diary entry?

Nora would ask McCabe after they'd eaten. She'd wait until they were moving around the kitchen, rinsing dirty dishes or scooping ice cream into bowls, and casually work the subject into the conversation. If he couldn't share the information with her, he'd let her know, and her curiosity would remain unsatisfied.

Except that it was more than curiosity.

Nora felt like she was being haunted by Lucille. She couldn't stop thinking about her. She couldn't stop looking for clues from *The Little Lost Library.* And she couldn't stay away from Lucille's house.

Nora didn't believe in ghosts, but she believed that a person could leave a deep imprint on a place. Lucille was a part of Wynter House, and her presence had not been diminished by death. Quite the opposite. The emptier the house became, the more Lucille's restless spirit seemed to fill it: *Find me,* it seemed to say. *See me. Know me. Understand me. Free me.*

After parking in the lot behind Miracle Books, Nora turned on the dome light, removed the mystery object from her bag, and unwrapped the dingy cloth.

This time, the piece of dollhouse furniture was a cradle. Carved as a single piece of wood, the cradle had a hood and a flat base. Its two curved feet were designed for rocking, but the blue blanket inside the cradle swaddled a book, not a baby.

Nora could tell from the illustrated cover that it was an alphabet book. She wasn't going to handle it beyond that initial glance until her hands were thoroughly cleaned, so she carefully bundled the book and cradle in a paper napkin and put them back in her purse.

As she walked up the path to her tiny house, she noticed that her mailbox was open. A stack of catalogs and letters was in danger of falling out. Nora collected the mail, unlocked her front door, and hurried inside. She dropped the mail and house keys on the coffee table before continuing into her kitchen.

When her hands were clean, she examined the tiny book.

It was called *Kate Greenaway's Alphabet.* Printed in London, the slim book featured color illustrations of each letter. There was also a boy or girl dressed in Victorian clothes on each page.

A quick online search valued the book at $250.

"A Bible, a dictionary, and an alphabet book. A coffin, a beer barrel, and a cradle. A mother, a husband or father, and a child." Nora gazed at the tiny blue blanket and added, "A son."

If the dollhouse belonged to Lucille when she was a child, then Nora couldn't see a connection between the objects. Lucille didn't have a brother. She had a sister. She'd married Frederick Vandercamp and given birth to two sons and a daughter. Had the cradle belonged to Beck or Clem? Was Lucille trying to tell her that one of her sons was a murderer?

"Is there a life-sized version of this cradle?" Nora wondered aloud.

She removed the other items from the hidden nook in her bookshelf and lined them up on her counter. She took a photo of each object before squirreling them away again, threw a change of clothes in a duffel, and bent to retrieve her keys from the coffee table.

That's when the corner of a letter with a yellow and white gingham pattern caught her eye. She pulled it out from under an office supply catalog and frowned.

It wasn't a letter. It was a thin piece of cardboard—a rectangle torn off a cookie box. The cookies were Lorna Doones.

Nora turned the lid over and read the message written there. The letters were written in thick black marker. They silently shouted: *STAY AWAY FROM WYNTER HOUSE! IF YOU DON'T, YOU'LL BE SORRY!*

Shoving the missive in her purse, Nora ran to her truck.

Her heart thundered as she unlocked the doors and fired up the engine. She kept glancing in her rearview mirror, then out each side mirror, expecting to see a figure standing just outside the ring of the streetlamps.

Was the person who'd threatened her out there right now? Watching her from the shadows?

Nora wasn't going to stick around to find out. She put the truck in drive and peeled out of the parking lot, her tires burning black scars into the asphalt.

Chapter 13

"If your house were burning down and you could take away one thing, what would it be?"
"I'd take the fire."
  —Jean Cocteau, interviewed by André Fraigneau

Nora burst into McCabe's house and shouted his name. He didn't answer.

One of the cats sauntered into the hall and rubbed against Nora's leg. She scooped him into her arms and nuzzled his soft face. When he started to purr, she let out a breath, releasing some of her fear into his silky coat.

The cat squirmed in her arms, so she lowered him gently to the floor and followed him into the kitchen. He made a beeline for his food dish, but Nora walked through to the living room.

McCabe was asleep in his recliner, one hand curled loosely around a water glass. The TV remote sat on his thigh, and the remains of his dinner were spread out on the coffee table. He'd fallen asleep watching The Weather Channel, and as Nora picked up the remote and aimed it at the screen, she caught a glimpse of tomorrow's forecast. The remnants of a tropical storm would arrive in the early hours of the morning and stay put for the next two days. Residents should expect wind and rain, along with localized flooding.

Rainy days were busy days at the bookstore. Sheldon always brewed extra coffee, and the pastries would be gone before noon. Nora would put on a playlist of dreamy instrumental music, burn a candle at the checkout counter, and speak softly when interacting with customers.

Tonight the forecast didn't make her think about the store. It made her think of Wynter House.

Will the Junk Hunks work in the rain? What if the power goes out? Will Bea still meet me at seven?

For a moment, she was mesmerized by the graphic playing over and over again on the screen. The radar showed the incoming storm moving up through Georgia. The bright green mass with a red-and-orange center looked like an ectoplasmic cloud.

Nora turned off the TV.

She was calmer now, so she decided not to wake McCabe just yet. Making as little noise as possible, she cleaned up the boxes of takeout from his dinner and gave the cats their nighttime kibble.

Her Szechuan beans were on the counter next to an empty bowl, a fork, and a napkin. Nora stuck the beans in the fridge and put the rest of the items back in their respective drawers and cupboards. After washing McCabe's travel mug, she turned off all the lights except for the one over the sink. Then she took a quick shower, relieved that the bathroom mirror got too foggy for her to see how wan she looked.

By the time she padded back to the quiet kitchen, she felt leaden with fatigue. All she wanted to do was crawl into bed and sleep until morning

But that wouldn't happen if she told McCabe about the note. There'd be questions and phone calls. McCabe would send a patrol car to Nora's house. He'd be up for hours when what he needed most—what they both needed—was sleep. Blessed, healing sleep.

What if I hadn't gotten the mail? The note would still be there, so I can pretend to find it tomorrow.

Tomorrow, after they'd both had a chance to rest.

Tomorrow, after she found another clue.

She tiptoed into the living room and gave McCabe's shoulder a gentle shake. "Hey, sleepy head."

McCabe blinked. His gaze was foggy, as if still in the middle of a dream. Closing his eyes again, he murmured, "What time is it?"

"Time for bed."

She waited for him to sit up before she took the water glass out of his hand and refilled it for him. After placing the glass on McCabe's nightstand, she took her turn in the bathroom and then slipped into bed. Within seconds, one of the cats settled near her feet. The second cat stood on McCabe's chest, silently demanding affection. He stroked the tabby's soft fur and told him he was a good boy before depositing him on the nightstand.

After bathing himself for a few minutes, the cat jumped from the nightstand to the cardboard box under the window. He let out a chirp, which his brother interpreted as an invitation because he walked over McCabe like he was a human mountain range before leaping into the box. The cats tussled for a solid minute before racing out of the room.

"They always get the rips when I'm just about to drift off," McCabe whispered.

Nora planted a feather-light kiss on his lips. "If you turn over, I'll scratch your back."

McCabe's arm slid around Nora's waist. "I'd rather spoon."

Noises came from another part of the house, but Nora wasn't alarmed. She was used to the cats zipping around at all hours of the night.

McCabe tightened his hold.

"Worried about you," he mumbled. "In that house."

"Shh. It's okay. Everything's okay," she whispered, brushing the back of his hand with her fingertips.

The words felt familiar on her tongue. And then it came to her. She'd murmured the same assurances to Lucille, even though the old woman was already dead.

Outside McCabe's window, a light wind slipped through the branches of the giant oak. The rustle of dry leaves sounded like hundreds of book pages being turned at once.

The wind intensified, tearing the leaves loose and separating acorns from their stalks. They struck the brick patio like stones. Far away, there was a rumble of thunder.

The storm was coming.

When Nora opened her eyes again, the bedroom was still dark. She heard McCabe in the kitchen, talking to someone. His tone was clipped. Urgent.

As he burst into the room, flooding it with light from the hall, she was already sitting up.

"What's wrong?" she croaked.

Thrusting his legs into his pants, McCabe said, "I just got a call from the fire chief. They're at your house."

"*What?*" Her shrill cry pierced the early-morning calm.

McCabe kept talking as he fastened his belt. "They got the call ten minutes ago. Someone saw smoke. I told the chief you weren't inside." Yanking a clean shirt over his head, he added, "Thank God."

Nora didn't bother getting dressed. She grabbed one of McCabe's sweatshirts and her sneakers and ran for the door.

"Get in my truck! I'll use the siren!" McCabe called.

Rain pelted down as McCabe drove down the quiet street. He didn't put his lights or siren on until he hit the business district, and with so few cars on the road, they were almost unnecessary. Still, the eight minutes it took him to drive from his house to the parking lot behind the bookstore seemed to take forever.

The fire engine blocked Nora's view of her house, but she could smell the smoke.

"No," she moaned, flinging herself out of the car.

McCabe yelled for her to stop, but she ignored him.

She had to look. She had to know what was happening to her house.

She sprinted around the back of the fire engine, right into the arms of a firefighter.

"Whoa." His hands clamped down on her shoulders. "Ma'am. You need to get back behind the truck."

"That's my house!" Nora protested.

She tried to wriggle away from the firefighter, but his hands gripped her with viselike strength. "It's not safe. You have to stay back."

Nora knew he was just doing his job, but she couldn't stop the anger rising within her. She lunged toward her house and let out a bellow of frustration when she couldn't break free from the firefighter's hold.

Suddenly McCabe was at her side. He calmly told her to stay where she was and promised that the firefighters had everything under control.

"You're not helping by getting in their way," he said, pulling her to the side.

Nora wasn't listening. All of her senses were focused on the sight of flames chewing through her roof and swimming around the window frame in her bedroom. Smoke ballooned through a gaping hole in the glass, merging into the darkness.

She felt like she was watching the scene from a great distance. Firefighters bellowed directives and dragged heavy hoses toward her house. Her sense of detachment continued as jets of water from the high-pressure hoses smacked into the flames. For a moment, the fire seemed to burn brighter. It stretched its gold-and-orange fingers toward the sky before the water slowly beat it back.

As the firefighters shouted to one another, a few phrases penetrated Nora's shock.

". . . the rain's helping . . ."

". . . started in the bedroom . . ."

". . . through the window. Homemade."

Nora smelled charred wood and the acrid scent of burning plastic. Even after the fire was doused, she felt its heat pulsating out of the blackened walls and perforated roof of her tiny house.

Her sweet little red caboose.

She wanted to wrap her home in a wet blanket. She wanted to put salve on its wounds and rock it like a child in her arms. But all she could do was stand there while a curtain of rain dropped over the valley.

McCabe tried to get her to put on one of the firefighter's jackets. When she didn't reach for it, he draped it over her shoulders like a cape and held an umbrella over her head.

Nora didn't know how much time had passed before the smoke morphed from a dark, roiling cloud to a thin, feathery plume. As she watched a firefighter enter her house through the front door, McCabe pressed a cup of coffee into her hands. Though the heat felt good, she was shivering too violently to hold it without spilling its contents.

McCabe poured out some of the coffee on the ground. "The chief wants to show me something inside the house. You can't go in yet, and I don't want to leave you outside. You're going to sit in the chief's truck and stay warm, okay? Do that for me, and I'll come right back out and tell you what I saw."

Nora got in the truck. After turning on the heat, McCabe put the coffee in a cup holder and followed the chief up the stairs to Nora's deck.

The front half of the house was undamaged, and it was surreal to see the verdant green of the potted plants on the deck or the silver pipes of her wind chimes waving in the breeze. The back of her caboose was still a bright, cheerful red. It was a happy red. The red of Christmases and cardinals. Dorothy's magical shoes and Honeycrisp apples. Ladybugs and Valentine's Day hearts.

The back half of her house was covered in black smudges. There were holes in the roof. The bedroom window was shattered. She pictured the dresser under that window and the row of her favorite books lined up on its surface. She knew they were ruined. *Jane Eyre, The Color Purple, Persuasion,* and her special edition of *The Hobbit*—all turned to ash.

" 'In a hole in the ground there lived a hobbit,' " she whispered, her eyes flooding with tears.

She mourned the loss of her cozy, snug bedroom, with its fluffy comforter and soft pillows. She thought of how the buttery morning light would slant in through the window, gilding her furniture and books. The pastel hues of her braided rug and the blanket June had knit added an extra dose of warmth to her room.

All of these things were gone. Now they were the smoldering, charred artifacts of the room where she'd slept, dressed, made love, read, and dreamed for so many years.

When people heard about the fire, they'd console her by saying, "It's just stuff," or "The important thing is that you weren't hurt."

And they'd be right. Nora wasn't home, fast asleep, when her house had caught fire.

The fire was no accident, though. Someone had tried to destroy her tiny home. She couldn't understand why someone would do such a thing.

McCabe kept his head down as he ran back to her through the rain. He hopped into the driver's seat and wiped water off his brow. "Your bedroom, bathroom, and laundry closet took the brunt of the damage. They're checking your kitchen now, but all I saw were smoke stains. No structural issues. I'm not going to sugarcoat this, Nora. This was arson. Someone threw a Molotov cocktail through your bedroom window. It landed on your bed."

"Oh, God."

McCabe grabbed her hand and held it to his heart. "If you were home last night—" He shook his head, unable to finish the thought.

Nora's brain finished it for him.

If I'd been home, I'd probably be dead right now.

"Do you have any idea who'd do this? Has anyone threatened you? If they have, you need to tell me." McCabe put a finger under Nora's chin and raised her head, forcing her to meet his imploring gaze. "You have to tell me whatever it is you've been keeping from me."

Nora expelled the air trapped in her lungs and nodded. The moment had come before she'd wanted it to, but now that it was here, she was relieved.

While firefighters moved in and out of her house, Nora told McCabe everything. From the riddles in *The Little Lost Library* to the miniature books and dollhouse furniture. Finally she told him about the note she'd found in her mailbox—the threatening message penned on the back of a box of Lorna Doone cookies.

"Is that everything?" he asked when she fell silent.

"Yes."

Still holding her hand, McCabe looked toward her house. "The clues you found—are they inside?"

"Yes. In one of the hidey-holes in my living room."

"For your sake, Nora, I hope they're intact. I'm investigating a murder. These toys could be evidence. Same goes for the book Lucille gave you." When his glance moved back to her face, Nora saw hurt in his eyes. "Why didn't you tell me?"

"I had to follow Lucille's breadcrumb trail. If you knew, you wouldn't have let me."

McCabe shook his head. "You know better than anyone that those trails only lead to trouble. Wynter House is like the scary forests in all the old fairy tales. People get lost inside. You've been getting lost in there, Nora. Closing the shop early, eating dinner in your truck, getting Lucille's kids to give you access in the morning. What did you expect to find by solving all the riddles?"

"The lost library."

"Meaning what? Expensive books? Rare books? Tiny books? Is that really worth an obstruction of justice charge or the loss of your house?"

Nora freed her hand from McCabe's and sagged deeper into the seat. Closing her eyes, she said, "Lucille gave me that book for a reason. I think she wanted me to know who she really was. The good, the bad, and the ugly. She wanted to be seen after being invisible for decades. She never said so, but that's how I interpreted her gift."

"And from the moment you read her letter, the clock has been ticking."

Opening her eyes, Nora turned to McCabe and nodded.

The fire chief opened the driver's door and poked his head into the car. "Okay, folks. We're clearing out. Ms. Pennington, your house is not fit to live in right now. First thing you need to do is call your insurance company and file a claim. They'll want to talk to the fire investigator. That's me. We've already called the utility companies. They'll suspend services until further notice. Your bedroom and bathroom are off-limits. Do not enter. The areas may not be structurally sound, and as I'm sure you've heard, the bedroom is a crime scene. I'm sorry, ma'am."

"Thank you for rescuing what you could," Nora said humbly.

The chief shifted his gaze to McCabe. "Sheriff. A word?"

"Please take my seat," said Nora. "Grant, I'll be in the car."

Because she ran out of McCabe's house without her purse or phone, Nora didn't have her keys, which meant she couldn't go inside the store and sit among the books. She couldn't call Sheldon or take her mind off her ruined house by brewing a latte or filling the rolling cart with new releases.

She climbed into McCabe's truck and watched the emergency vehicles drive away. When they were gone, the only sound was the slap of rain against the windshield. Nora was glad for the storm. It echoed her tumultuous thoughts and the rage she felt against the arsonist.

Staring between the drops clinging to the window, she imagined someone creeping up to her house and hurling a bottle with a flaming rag stuffed in its neck through her window.

Who would do such a thing?

Who wanted to keep her from going back to Wynter House?

Someone who knows I am looking for the lost library.

The most likely suspects were Lucille's children.

Lucille hadn't left *The Little Lost Library* to any of them. Surely, if Beck, Harper, or Clem owned a copy of the book, they would've collected the clues by now. Beck and Harper had been working in the house for almost twelve hours a day, and Clem had had access to it for years.

True, Clem had been out of the picture recently, but his only income came from selling his mother's books. It stood to reason that he'd want to squirrel away the most valuable books instead of selling them at auction and splitting the profits with his siblings. Beck and Harper were staying at the Inn of Mist and Roses, which meant Clem could enter Wynter House at night and remove whatever he wanted.

Clem was an addict, and his addiction was a demanding

master. It would take everything from him: his money, his loyalty, and his judgment. He would betray his family to appease it. He would be jailed because of it. And he would lose his future to it.

Nora felt sorry for Clem. He wasn't like June's son, Tyson, who had a mother willing to do anything to get him the best treatment and would support him during his recovery. Because of June's unwavering faith and devotion, Tyson's life was full of possibility. He had a job he loved and was dating a wonderful woman named Jasmine. He was saving up to buy his first house, and June expected him to propose to Jasmine very soon.

According to Beck, Clem had been an addict for his entire adult life. And even though he was approaching fifty, it wasn't too late for him. He could start over—live an entirely different life. Nora knew this better than most. She also knew that he couldn't do it alone.

Would his siblings invest in a residential treatment facility for him? Nora doubted it. Beck and Harper had made it clear that they wanted to empty Wynter House and get back to their lives as soon as possible. Their childhood home was a weight about their necks. Clem was part of a past they were both eager to leave behind.

Nora didn't fight the sadness washing over her. She let her tears flow again, unsure if she was crying over Clem, Lucille, her house, or all three. She felt hopeless and defeated. She'd failed to help Lucille in life or in death. She'd ignored her business and her friends. She'd kept things from McCabe and burned the candle from both ends trying to solve the riddles in a children's book. She'd done all of this and had nothing to show for her efforts.

Worse than nothing, I've lost my house. My precious tiny house.

By the time McCabe returned to the truck, Nora had composed herself.

"Let's get you back to my place," he said, rubbing her shoulder. "You need a hot shower and breakfast. After that, we'll deal with the insurance company. We'll fix this together, okay?" He smoothed her hair and then wiped away the tear marks on her cheek with such tenderness that she almost started crying again.

"I'm sorry," she whispered.

McCabe held his warm palm against her cheek. "We'll make it right. As soon as we can, we'll get the clues from your house. You can show me where you found them, and I'll see if they have any relevance to the investigation."

"Wait. You want me to go back to Wynter House?"

"With me, and me alone. We'll go tonight, after dinner. You'll bring the book Lucille gave you, and we'll find as many clues as we can. If we can't make sense of the clues we find, I'll have no choice but to bring Lucille's children into the mix. I doubt they'll be happy to learn you've been tearing their mother's house apart because you believe she was trying to tell you something."

Nora stiffened. "She was. I *know* she was. I just don't have the full picture yet. Maybe tonight . . ."

Relenting, McCabe softened his tone. "Maybe tonight."

Nora squeezed McCabe's hand in gratitude, then glanced back at her house. Seeing the charred roof and the black stains on the red paint refueled her anger.

The anger felt good. It felt better than sorrow. Better than grief. It had heat, like the fire that had chewed through her bedroom. She embraced her fury. Held it close. She needed it right now. As long as she was angry, there'd be no room for grief.

"The lowlife that tried to burn my house down didn't even give me a chance to respond to their threat," she growled. "What's the point of threatening me if they were going to punish me on the same day? Why bother? Just skip the note on the cookie box and go straight to the point where you're throwing a flaming bottle through my window."

McCabe contemplated this in silence for a moment. Then he frowned. "Have you gotten your mail every day? Or have you missed a day?"

She stared at him blankly. "I can't remember. I think it's been at least two days, which means—oh, God, Grant. If I'd gotten the note, we could have done something. My house—I might have saved it."

"Don't do that to yourself," McCabe commanded. "You are *not* responsible for the fire. You're the victim of a crime, and I'm going to find out who committed it. You have my word. But until I do, I want you to be safe."

Nora couldn't help but smile. "I don't think my living arrangements could be much safer. My roommate is an expert marksman, and even if he weren't home, any intruder would trip over his cats."

McCabe let out a laugh, and when Nora heard the familiar sound, the world regained a little balance.

Reaching across the center console, he opened his arms and said, "Come here, love."

Nora sank into his embrace.

It would be a long time before things felt normal again, but she and McCabe were okay. They would work together to find a killer, an arsonist, and the lost library. And when all was said and done, the ghosts trapped inside Wynter House would finally be set free.

Chapter 14

Love grows best in little houses, with fewer walls to separate.

—Doug Stone

Two hours later, Sheldon found Nora sitting behind the checkout counter, staring into space. She was supposed to have gone to Wynter House before work, but the only house she could think about was her own.

Sheldon laid his hand over Nora's. "I smelled the smoke on my way here. I couldn't believe my eyes when I saw your house! What happened?"

Nora didn't look at him. She sat hunched on her stool, gazing listlessly out the window. "It was arson. Someone was trying to scare me. I thought I was lucky. I didn't get hurt, and I'd get my house fixed, and things would go back to normal. But I don't have enough savings to cover the repairs. I'll have to take out a loan. We won't be able to hire anyone for the shop."

Sheldon wrapped an arm around her shoulders. "What about your insurance?"

"It doesn't cover acts of arson."

"*Pobrecita.* That isn't fair!" He pressed her head into the soft wool of his sweater vest. "Everything will be okay. I know it will. You'll find a way to fix your house—make it better than ever—because you get things done. This is not the moment for tackling such a big thing, though. This is a moment for a very strong cup of coffee and a very sweet donut. Luckily, I can give you both of those things."

Nora murmured, "Not hungry."

"You only think that because you're still in shock. I bet you don't even remember putting on the clothes you're wearing or unlocking the store, do you?"

"No."

Sheldon smoothed Nora's hair. "*Exactamente.* But I love your mismatched socks. It could be a new trend. You should show them to all the customers today."

Nora stuck her legs out. She was wearing one blue sock with white stripes and one purple sock with white flowers.

"Shit," she muttered, which made Sheldon laugh. He pulled Nora against him so she could feel how the laughter made his belly jiggle. Impossibly, it made her smile.

"There you are," Sheldon said, his voice warm with affection. "You will figure this out, and you'll have plenty of help. From me, from your friends, from everyone who loves you. In the meantime, you're going to eat something, drink something, and watch me set up the spy camera. Identifying the book thief will solve one mystery, at least, and that will feel good."

Nora allowed Sheldon to lead her to the Readers' Circle. He brewed her such a strong cup of coffee that she had to add cream and four sugar cubes just to make it palatable. Then he stood over her, his arms folded, until she ate one of Hester's famous apple cider donuts.

By the time she greeted her first customers, she felt almost human. And when a woman came in seeking books for a social media reading challenge, Nora became so caught up in the subject that she actually started enjoying herself.

"I need a spooky classic to read in the fall, but I've read *Dracula* and *Frankenstein,* Poe and Wilkie Collins—most of the famous ones. I'm trying to figure out what I missed," the woman said.

Nora showed her several books, including *Rebecca, The Picture of Dorian Gray,* and *The Haunting of Hill House,* but the woman had read them all. She'd also read *The Phantom of the Opera* and every subsequent book Nora suggested.

"How about *Northanger Abbey*? It has a Gothic vibe."

"I re-read Austen's canon every year. I love the Brontës too. Except for *Wuthering Heights.* I've never enjoyed that one. Can you find me something more obscure?"

Happily rising to the challenge, Nora found a short book in the used section that the woman hadn't read yet called *The Best Ghost Stories of Algernon Blackwood.*

"This book belonged to another customer, who reads nothing but horror. He told me about one of these stories. It's about two sailors traveling on the Danube. They stop for the night to rest on an island full of willow trees. They think they're alone, but strange things start happening that make them question their sanity."

"I like it, but I wish it were longer. I feel like I'd be cheating if I read something so short. Unless I read two."

Nora scrolled through a mental Rolodex of spooky story collections. "How about 'The Yellow Wallpaper' by Charlotte Perkins Gilman?"

"I've heard of it, but I don't think I've read it. What's it about?"

"Well, it's more of a psychological thriller than horror. It's about a woman with postpartum depression back in the times when anything wrong with a woman was given a diagnosis of hysteria. After the woman is locked in a room with peeling yellow wallpaper, she starts seeing shapes in the wallpaper and tries to figure out where they're coming from."

The woman nodded enthusiastically. "A creepy classic written by a female writer. I'll take it."

They moved on to the next category in the challenge, which was a book with apples or a pumpkin on the cover.

"I have several cozy mysteries that'll fit the bill," Nora said. "I was actually going to make a fall-themed cozy display this afternoon, so you're helping me."

For fall romances, Nora recommended a number of titles, of which the woman selected Ashley Poston's *The Dead Romantics*, Jessica Booth's *A Match Made in Autumn*, and Sarah Addison Allen's *First Frost.*

After finding books for ten of the twelve categories on the list, the woman ended up purchasing a whopping twenty-two books, both new and used, as well as a candle and a handful of bookmarks. While narrowing down her choices, she'd had a cappuccino and a chocolate book pocket.

"If all of my customers were like her, I could afford to fix my house," Nora told Sheldon later that day.

"Not everyone has her book budget, but we could encourage more spending if we printed out that challenge. We could even offer a prize for customers who complete it. Nothing huge. We could have three winners. Our prizes could be a candle, a coffee and bookmark, and a gift card."

Nora liked the idea. "I can make copies after I close."

"Or I can ask June. You know she has color-copy machines at work."

"I don't want her to get in trouble."

Sheldon pulled a face. "Trouble? The woman practically runs the place. If she doesn't feel comfortable, she'll just say no. After what happened to your house, your friends will want to help you. And you should let them. I'll call her, okay?"

He retreated to the ticket agent's office to make the call, and while Nora couldn't hear what he was saying, the conversation went on for a long time. Sheldon was up to something, but Nora didn't have the energy to give much thought to what that something could be.

At four thirty, Sheldon was gone, and the shop was buzzing with high school students, tourists in search of wine-themed books preceding a local vineyard tour, a bridal party staying at the Inn of Mist and Roses, and festivalgoers who'd stopped in Miracle Springs on their way to a bluegrass-and-barbecue event in Asheville. There were customers in every part of the store.

Nora was bagging three Richard Osman mysteries for a bridesmaid when June suddenly appeared at the checkout counter and told Nora to shoo.

"You trained me on this machine a few months ago, so I know exactly how to take these fine people's money. There's a line of folks waiting for drinks. Hester is handling the coffee and tea orders, but she's rusty on the espresso machine."

"Hester's here too?"

June hip-checked Nora out from behind the counter. "Honey, someone tried to roast you like a Thanksgiving turkey, so, of course, we came as soon as we could. Estella will be here as soon as she finishes with her last client of the day. The three of us are going to sell the hell out of everything you've got for the next hour and a half. Then we're going to sit down and figure out what you need to get your life back to normal. Now beat it. This gentleman has places to be and doesn't need to be kept waiting while we yammer on."

As Nora walked away, she overheard June say, "Good evening, sir. This is our fall reading challenge. If you check off all the categories, you might win a prize. I'll give you two copies, in case you'd like to hang one up at work, the gym, or anyplace with a public message board."

Back in the ticket agent's booth, Hester was passing out checklists with every cup of coffee or tea.

"You should start carrying wine," she said as Nora entered the room. "You could have a cocktail hour from five to six and offer something besides sweet treats. You're totally out of food, and it's not even five. I'm going to talk to Gus about coming up with some afternoon snacks. He's been wanting to experiment with more savory recipes, anyway. The man works in a bakery and has absolutely no sweet tooth."

Hester placed an iced tea on the ledge of the pass-through window. After it was collected by a pretty high schooler, with Dutch braids and a READ BANNED BOOKS sweatshirt, Hester took the next customer's order.

For the next ten minutes, the women moved around the small space like dancers, pouring coffee, tamping grounds, grabbing clean mugs from the pegboard, and dumping dirty mugs in the sink.

When there were no more customers in line, Hester finally pulled Nora into a hug and whispered, "I'm sorry about your house, but I am *so* relieved that you're okay." She wiped away the tears beading her lashes. "I never imagined that someone would come after you because of Lucille. Is it because of the book she gave you?"

"It could be," Nora said. "I didn't think anyone knew I was searching for clues, but I guess I was seen. By whom? I don't know. One of Lucille's kids? A Junk Hunks worker?"

"Or Bea?"

Nora shook her head. "She would've asked me straight out. Same goes for Cricket. Maybe one of the Junk Hunks has ties to the Red Wolves. Maybe Clem isn't the only person mixed up with them."

They fell silent as a man approached the window and asked for cookbooks with food-and-wine pairings. After showing him the three she had in stock, Nora headed to the

YA section to search for strays and to make her presence known to any potential shoplifters.

Rounding the corner of a set of display shelves featuring new nonfiction releases, Nora came upon a familiar group of girls sitting on the ground. They all had backpacks and appeared to be engaged in several activities at once. Nora took in the textbooks, binders, and calculators and realized that these girls were doing homework, while also scrolling through images on their phones and flipping through a stack of novels.

"What's new on Bookstagram, ladies?" Nora asked.

"An author has lost her freaking mind," said a girl named Brit. "She went after a reader for posting a negative review—which was totally legit, by the way—and harassed this woman on all her socials. People are calling out the author for bullying readers, and she's trying to play the victim. She's, like, one post away from being canceled."

The girl across from Brit, whose name was Taylor, showed Nora her phone. "That's already happening. See? Here's a pic of someone returning her books to Barnes and Noble."

Nora leaned down to get a closer look at a young woman with glasses standing in front of a register, looking peeved. She recognized the books in the young woman's hand. The author wasn't on par with the James Pattersons and Colleen Hoovers of the world, but she was one of the better-known authors of her genre.

"Considering she's written five books, I'm surprised she let a negative review get under her skin," said Nora.

On one hand, she felt sorry for the author because this single mistake could lead to the end of her career. On the other hand, she'd crossed a line by attacking a reviewer on a public platform.

Doesn't everyone deserve a second chance? Especially if they own up to their mistakes.

As if guessing the direction of Nora's thoughts, Taylor

said, "If she apologized, people would've already moved on. I mean, we all say dumb stuff on social media. Maybe she had too many margaritas when she went after that reviewer."

"Nah, she's done this before," Brit interjected. "Other readers are posting messages she wrote in response to their reviews. Some of them weren't even negative! They were mostly neutral, like, three stars, but she still went after them. She has a history of being nasty to reviewers."

The girls were completely invested in the drama. They exchanged animated whispers and searched for other examples of bad behavior by the author. The whole thing brought Nora down. She tried to change the subject by asking the girls which of the books on the floor were currently popular with Bookstagrammers. They responded, but their answers were brief and unenthusiastic. Knowing they were eager to get back to their phones, Nora left them to it.

However, she'd made a mental note of the books poking out from under the girls' backpacks. If any of those books disappeared before closing, Nora would have no choice but to view the girls with suspicion.

I hope it's not them. I like those young ladies.

The rest of the workday passed quickly. Estella showed up a few minutes before closing with a take-out bag in each hand. She and Hester cleaned the kitchen, while June insisted on running the vacuum. All Nora had to do was shelve strays and run an inventory report on YA sales for the day. She was pleased to discover that the high school girls were not book thieves.

In fact, Brit and Taylor were good for business. They'd each purchased a book and posted a photo of the cover on Instagram. Both girls had tagged Miracle Books in their posts, and several of their friends had left comments saying that they were excited to hang out at the bookstore on Saturday.

"Are you smiling?" June asked as she bent over to plug in the vacuum.

"I overheard an older woman complaining to her husband about the younger generations. She doesn't think any of them read for pleasure, which is simply not true. They *do* read." She held out her phone for June to see the social media post. "They also post photos and reviews. They attend author events, festivals, and conferences. They actually influence market trends. This current generation might just be the biggest book advocates ever."

June nodded. "They've definitely made sure we have more diverse reads. I hardly ever saw a Black woman on the cover of the books I read when I was in high school. Granted, I wasn't reading Toni Morrison or Zora Neale Hurston back then. I was checking out as many romance paperbacks from the library as I could get. I remember when I saw a Harlequin with a Black couple on the cover. Lord, I thought it was so beautiful. I still remember the title. *Adam and Eva.*"

"You'll have to find a picture of that and show us while we eat," Estella said as she emerged from the fiction section and made a beeline for Nora. "Come on, darlin'. You must be wrecked. When I think about how your day started, it's a miracle you're still on your feet. And helping customers for the past eight hours like nothing happened. Jack made dinner for all of us, so we're going to stuff our faces and talk. Two things we do extremely well."

Hester and Estella laid out a feast of comfort foods in the Readers' Circle. There was cottage pie topped with a crust of golden mashed potatoes, Jack's famous biscuits, autumn squash risotto, a green salad with apples and walnuts, three bottles of hard cider, and a bottle of sparkling apple juice for Estella.

June dimmed the lights and lit the tea light candles scattered around the coffee table. When all the candles were lit, she grabbed her bottle of hard cider and raised it in a toast. "To quote the wise and wonderful Oprah, 'Turn your wounds into wisdom.' "

"And may your wisdom help send the bastard who set fire to your house to jail," added Hester.

The women knocked the necks of their bottles together.

As June loaded food onto Nora's plate, she said, "We've been through so much together, ladies, and we'll get through this too. Let's start with the practical stuff. You have a home with McCabe, thank goodness, but you still need everyday types of stuff. Which is why I picked up a few things for you."

After putting the loaded plate in front of Nora, June went to the Children's Corner and returned with a pair of bulging shopping bags. "You can look through these later, but your immediate clothing needs are covered. Bras, underwear, socks, jeans, and a few tops. I even found a pair of Chuck Taylors in your size."

Before Nora had the chance to thank June, Estella cried, "My turn!" and grabbed the bag she'd stashed in the ticket agent's booth.

"I was in charge of toiletries, so prepare yourself. Most of these are from the salon. There's a boar's hair brush, shampoo, conditioner, body lotion, face wash, sunscreen, moisturizer, serums, exfoliating wash, masks, and makeup. I know you tend to stick with lipstick and mascara, but I added a few more things, like blush, shadow, eye pencils, concealer, and a manicure kit with some neutral polish. Just in case you need an extra dose of self-care."

Nora gaped at Estella. "You can't give me all of those products. It's too much."

"I got every item at cost, remember? Besides, I can't wait to see how you look with a dark brown smoky eye look or vamp-punk lips."

Peering into the bag, Hester said, "What's vamp-punk?"

"A statement lip in deep red or a reddish brown."

Hester turned to Nora. "My contribution isn't mine alone, but I'll explain more over dessert."

Hester disappeared into the ticket agent's office, emerging a few minutes later with a casserole dish. She placed the dish on a folded tea towel and headed back into the kitchen. "I just have to grab the ice cream."

"Is this what I think it is?" Nora asked hopefully.

"Yep. Apple-and-mixed-berry crumble." Hester removed the foil from the casserole dish and plunged a spoon through the oat-and-brown-sugar topping. "Still warm enough to melt the ice cream. June, would you do the honors?"

June added perfect scoops of vanilla ice cream to each serving of apple-and-berry crumble.

Nora smiled at Hester. "I keep a special compartment in my stomach reserved for your desserts. Thanks for making my absolute favorite."

Hester, who'd served herself a smaller portion than anyone else, was the first to put down her spoon and dab her lips with her napkin. "That *is* good. Wanna know what else is good?" she asked Nora.

"The three of you. I feel a million times better than I did this morning."

"A lot can happen in a day." Hester exchanged cryptic glances with Estella and June before continuing. "Jasper called to tell me about your house late this morning. Apparently, the sheriff gathered his officers together and said that he wouldn't rest until he apprehended the arsonist. He seemed perfectly calm on the outside, but he was obviously furious."

Nora nodded. "The thought that I might've been home, in bed, when that bottle crashed through the window scared him. It scared me, too, but I got tired of feeling like a victim pretty quickly. I'm not scared anymore. I'm angry. I want to know who did that to my home."

"You have to be a monster to torch a red caboose," Estella grumbled.

Hester said, "Sheldon shared the bad news about your insurance. They really won't cover the damage?"

Nora visibly deflated. "Nope. The store is covered, but not my house."

June let out a frustrated sigh. "The CEO of your insurance company should share a cell with the arsonist because that's just criminal."

"Luckily, you're part of a pretty special community," Hester went on. "A community that loves your caboose cottage. And you. Which is why people have already contributed to the crowdfunding site I set up earlier today."

June showed Nora one of the fall reading challenge handouts. "You haven't seen this yet, because we knew you wouldn't like it. Not the reading challenge. We knew you'd like that. I'm talking about what's on the back of the sheet."

Nora flipped the sheet over and paled. "You gave this to my customers today?"

"You bet your ass we did," said June.

Estella pointed her sparkling apple juice at Nora. "*You* help people every day. You listen, you comfort, you offer advice and bibliotherapy. You don't know how many lives you've changed with your magical book matchmaking, but judging by the contributions to your fundraiser, the answer is lots."

"It's going to take a few days to spread the word about this campaign, but it's already started off with a bang. Do you want to know how much people have donated in one afternoon?"

Despite Hester's enthusiasm, Nora shook her head. "I know you all mean well, but this feels wrong. Fundraisers are for sick kids or pets in need of a lifesaving surgery. They're for families who've lost everything in a natural disaster. I have a job. I have a place to stay. I have McCabe and all of you. I've lost my house, but only temporarily."

"While we're counting your blessings, let's count a few other things." June held out her right hand, fingers splayed. "How many vacations have you taken in the past five years? Zero. How many times has someone else closed the store for you? Zero. How many times have you called in sick? Zero."

"If you drain your savings, you and Grant will never visit his sister in Texas. And didn't you say you wanted to drop by that bookstore in Houston?"

"Murder by the Book," said Nora. "Yes, I want to go there. I want to go to Booksellers' Row in London too. But they're bucket list trips."

Hester gave her a stern look. "A vacation shouldn't be on your bucket list. Vacations are something people do to stay sane."

June raised her hands to the heavens and cried, "Amen."

Seeing Nora's stricken expression, Estella leaned across the table and patted her knee. "We're not going to take advantage of people's generosity. Once you have the money you need to rebuild and furnish your new and improved space, we'll cancel the fundraiser. One of my clients is the only female contractor in town, and I already called her to see if she'd give you an estimate. I'll share her contact info with you before I leave."

Nora passed her hands over her face. It was one thing for her friends to help out in the store for a few hours or bring her dinner, but it was quite another to take donations from her customers and neighbors.

"We know we've hit you with a lot," Hester said softly. "But we wanted your day to end on a better note than it started."

Nora stood up to hug her friends. She held each of them for several seconds, hoping her touch could convey a fraction of the gratitude she felt.

"I hate to break this up, but I'm meeting McCabe in thirty minutes." She quickly explained that she and McCabe would be hunting together for the rest of the clues from *The Little Lost Library*.

Estella began stacking their dessert plates. "In that case, we'd better clean up."

"I hope you find the library," Hester said as she collected their empty glasses. "It wouldn't make up for Lucille's death or the damage to your house, but I feel like the books need to be rescued."

Glancing around at the book spines neatly tucked into their warm wooden shelves, Nora whispered, "Me too."

Chapter 15

No person who can read is ever successful at clean-
ing out an attic.

— Ann Landers

When Nora arrived at Wynter House, McCabe's SUV was already parked in the driveway, so she pulled her truck behind his. She locked her car and walked around the dumpsters toward the row of tents.

It was too dark to see clearly, but the tables appeared to be empty. Nora wondered if Bea and Cricket were moving the valuables to a storage facility or securing them in Lucille's garage.

She glanced to her right. The detached garage was a low, squat, windowless building surrounded by weeds and lanky grass. In the darkness, it looked like a cat waiting to pounce.

When a branch snapped near the entrance of Clem's apartment, Nora stiffened.

Is he watching me again?

She saw the firefly glow of a cigarette and knew he was there. She couldn't see his face, only the outline of his body. He stood in a pool of shadow, unmoving.

What if it's not Clem?

The thought shivered through her, and she almost scurried away in fear. But then she remembered the smoke rushing out of her tiny house. She remembered the flames. And anger overwhelmed her fear.

She glared at the pinprick of light in the distance, willing the smoker to see that she was unafraid, before turning toward Wynter House. Though she maintained an even gait, she fervently hoped McCabe had left the door unlocked. She wouldn't look so tough if she had to call him on the phone and beg to be let in.

The door was unlocked, and Nora slid the dead bolt in place as soon as she was inside. A single bulb burned in the kitchen, and the only source of light in the dining room came from a battery-powered lantern sitting on a wooden stool. The lantern failed to illuminate the full length of the walls, and the shapes of the Greco-Roman figures floating across the wallpaper became distorted the closer they were to the ceiling. They became Rorschach inkblots, bleeding into one another until the gods and heroes were indistinguishable from the monsters.

"Grant? Where are you?"

Nora's voice boomed back at her like cannon fire. As it ricocheted off every corner, she cringed.

A floorboard groaned overhead, as if the house were complaining about the disturbance. Nora stood still, listening for the sound of footsteps, but the noises she heard were not generated by McCabe or any other human.

Spidery branches scratched against the window glass. Air sighed up through the floor vents and down from the chimney into the cavernous fireplace, and there was a clicking behind the walls like someone drumming their long fingernails against a hard surface.

The lantern light seemed to glow brighter for a moment before suddenly flickering. The strobe effect gave the impression that the figures on the wallpaper were moving. When it seemed like the serpent heads of every Hydra in the room were wriggling, Nora fumbled for her phone and called McCabe.

He answered right away. "Sorry. I was in a bedroom upstairs and didn't hear you. Be right down."

"Is anyone else in the house?" she asked, unwilling to sever their connection until they were in the same room.

"No. I just sent Deputy Fuentes home and Beck and Harper are gone for the night. Clem's in his apartment. I spoke to him about ten minutes ago."

Nora heard McCabe's tread on the stairs. "Was he outside? Smoking?"

"He was eating pizza in front of the TV."

McCabe hung up as he entered the dining room. After embracing Nora, he said, "I've read the riddles a dozen times today, so I think I know where to find the next clue."

"You do? I figured the lines 'the tree that is forever green' and 'the fibers are glued and then bleached clean' refer to making paper out of pine wood, but I haven't seen a 'glass made of rainbows' in this house."

"That's because you've only seen a few rooms. Anyway, this one is probably more of a closet than a room."

Nora felt a surge of excitement. "Like the one under the stairs?"

"That one was full of broken furniture. Nothing interesting at all." He tapped his phone, which was tucked into his breast pocket. "Thanks to Gladys from the permit office, I now have a copy of the blueprints for this house. There's a space near the front door called the butler's closet. Today we'd probably use it as a coat closet. If we were watching *Downton Abbey*, I'd expect a footman to be waiting inside until he heard the crunch of car tires on the gravel. He'd have to spring out and be ready to open the car doors for visitors. The Wynters weren't on par with the peerage, but they were one of the wealthiest families in the area."

McCabe handed Nora a Maglite flashlight and led her down the hall to the front door.

None of the wall sconces in the hall were turned on, but six portable work lights mimicked the daylight. Nora could see every mark, scuff, and scratch on the walls and floor.

McCabe pointed at the front door and said, "There's a round stained-glass window next to this door. No one can see it from the outside because the branches from the magnolias have basically formed a curtain over that side of the house. I asked Andrews to come out here with a chain saw earlier today, and there was the window, pretty as you please."

"How do you hide a clue inside stained glass?"

"One thing at a time. We need to open the closet first."

With the lights shining directly on the walls, the outline of the hidden door was obvious. As were the hinges. And while there was no knob or handle, Nora spotted a keyhole just above the chair rail.

"They used a painting to hide the keyhole," Nora said, tracing the rectangular ghost marks. "Clever. But how do we get in without a key?"

McCabe gestured at a toolbox sitting on the floor. He bent down, pulled out a small case, and showed Nora its contents. "Behold the Allen wrench—a layman's way of dealing with skeleton locks. As long as the spring inside the lock mechanism still works, I should be able to mimic a skeleton key."

He went on to explain that the first Allen wrench he inserted would apply pressure to the lever. Once the lever was engaged, he'd insert a second wrench and twist it clockwise to move the dead bolt.

It took several tries, but eventually McCabe succeeded in unlocking the door. Without the dead bolt holding it in place, the door swung open a few inches. The effect was eerie, and Nora hung back while McCabe probed around inside with the beam of his flashlight.

Unlike the rest of the house, the closet held no signs of Lucille's hoard. Two moth-eaten umbrellas leaned against the far corner, and a pair of tattered leather boots, robed in dust and cobwebs, sat on the floor.

When McCabe first pointed his light at the round window, the yellow, green, and blue design looked like a map of the world. But as Nora's eyes adjusted, she realized that the blue glass had been used to make the sky and a river winding through the center of the window. On either side of the river were yellow mountains and five pine trees with green foliage and dark yellow trunks.

"I'll grab the stepladder," McCabe said.

Nora took his place inside the closet and slowly swept the beam of her flashlight across the window.

Like everything else in Wynter House, it was covered in a layer of grime. Nora wished she could clean the window and reveal the true colors of the glass. McCabe passed her one of the work lights, and when she held it up to the glass, the glare made her wince.

Pulling the stepladder into the closet, she climbed up until her face was level with the window.

"Anything?" McCabe asked.

Nora studied the hills, pine trees, and river. She ran a hand around the black metal frame. The thick lead was notched at regular intervals, like the hours on a clock, but none of the sections moved when she pushed on them.

"Nothing yet. Maybe it would help if we cleaned it. Cricket left rags in the kitchen. Want to take my place while I grab some?"

"You know I do," McCabe said.

It didn't take Nora long to fetch a few rags. She ran one under the kitchen tap, hoping to soak it in hot water, but the water stayed cold. Balling the rag in her fist, she squeezed out the excess water and carried the rags back to McCabe.

Though he did his best to clean the glass, his efforts revealed no secret words or symbols.

"*The Little Lost Library* was written for children. I'm a grown-ass man, but I can't figure this out," he grumbled.

Nora was about to suggest they move on to the next riddle, and come back to this one later, when she was struck by a memory.

"Grant, do you remember that terrible fire at Notre Dame?"

"I do. The footage of the roof burning was terrible to see." He climbed down from the stepladder and moved close to her. "Are you thinking about your house?"

She shook her head. "I was thinking more about the restoration than the destruction, actually. I have this crazy memory of watching a video about a round stained-glass window with a secret compartment in the frame. I can't remember if it was from Notre Dame or another famous landmark."

McCabe's eyes lit up. "How did it work?"

"You have to turn the metal frame—kind of like a ship's wheel."

"Clockwise or counterclockwise?" McCabe asked as he ascended the stepladder.

Nora didn't know, so McCabe tried clockwise first. When the frame didn't budge, he tried turning it in the opposite direction.

"It's moving," he whispered.

Nora heard a brief shriek of metal followed by a soft gasp from McCabe.

"There's a hollow space up here. Right at eleven o'clock. See the tip of the tallest tree? It's right above that. I feel something . . . Got it!"

He passed a cloth-wrapped bundle down to Nora, took a

few photos of the cavity in the window, and hopped off the stepladder. Nora edged closer to the light and unwound the soiled cloth concealing a miniature steamer trunk.

Nora pivoted the leather trunk, admiring the tiny metal studs, handles, and latch. Gently she raised the lid. Inside were two porcelain dolls and a book.

"We should look at these later, using a clean pair of gloves," McCabe said. He reclaimed the bundle from Nora and put it in his toolbox.

"To the mirror on the wall?" asked Nora.

"Yes." McCabe headed for the stairs. "Other than the bathrooms, there's only one room with a mirror on the wall. It's the biggest bedroom. According to Harper, it used to be Lucille's. There's a mirror over the fireplace that slides up and down. Harper showed it to me."

Nora grabbed McCabe's arm. "Why?"

"It came up during her interview. I asked if there were places in the house where her mother might have hidden letters or important documents. Harper said that her mother was always squirreling things away. She'd toss things in the laundry chute, in the closet under the stairs, and behind the mirror in her bedroom. Lucille didn't think her kids knew about the mirror, but they did."

Nora was both relieved and disappointed to have been handed the answer to the next riddle.

Cricket and the Junk Hunks had finished clearing out the bedrooms, so all that remained in Lucille's room was a marble-top dresser, a matching nightstand, and a four-poster bed. The bed had been taken apart, the mattress and linens discarded. The floor was bare, as were the walls. Nora opened a closet door and saw another door at the back of the closet.

"It leads to the bedroom next door," said McCabe. "I guess that's how couples did things back in the day. If my snoring gets worse and I have to sleep in another room, will you come through the closet for conjugal visits?"

"Maybe." She smiled at him. "And if I'm not in the mood, I'll send in the cats for a snuggle."

McCabe took her gloved hand in his and led her to the mirror over the fireplace. It was a horizontal piece measuring about four feet long and a foot high. McCabe grasped the sides of the wood frame and raised the mirror.

The space behind it was empty.

Nora aimed her flashlight into the cavity. "Someone cleaned this. You can see where they missed spots—in the back and in the corners. Do you think Harper removed whatever was in here?"

"It's possible."

McCabe pushed on the wood lining the back of the nook, but it was solid and unyielding.

"The riddle says, 'Behind the mirror on the wall, once it's raised, don't let it fall.'" Nora pointed at the bottom edge of the mirror. "Is there a way to make it stay open?"

"No. There's no catch or anything. I think that's why the next line is a warning to watch your fingers."

Nora sighed in defeat. "I guess someone took this clue. We have two left to go, right?"

"We do, but let's save the garden riddle for last. Are you okay going out of order?" McCabe asked. "If we follow the book, we should go from the mirror in the bedroom to the attic. After that, we're supposed to go to the garden and finally the library."

"We're already on the second floor, so let's get the riddle in the rafters. Have you been to the attic before?"

McCabe pulled a face. "I stood in the doorway and peeked in, but it was so packed that I couldn't make out the forest for the trees. According to Cricket, it's a gold mine of antiques. I saw the list of the things they removed today. It's mostly furniture, but there was also a huge birdcage, a gramophone, boxes of china, photo albums, and souvenirs from family trips. You'll see."

McCabe led the way up a narrow staircase and through an equally narrow door to the attic. Just inside the door, he hit the wall switch. A row of bare light bulbs dangling from the ceiling winked on. Nora heard a sizzle and a pop as the bulb closest to the door burned out.

"That's not creepy at all," McCabe said as he put a reassuring hand on Nora's back.

The attic had high rafters and lots of floor space. As Nora stepped deeper into the room, she felt like she was walking inside an Egyptian tomb. The room was festooned in dirt and cobwebs. Insect carcasses were mounded in every corner and under every window. Webs were strung between the light bulbs like party garlands, the ends disappearing into the dark.

Cricket's team had cleared everything up to the second light bulb. Beyond that point, a collection of shapes emerged from the gloom. Boxes, suitcases, chairs, chests—the relics of many lives huddled together, clothed in decades of dust and shadow.

McCabe pointed at the light bulbs. "Some fast-working spiders in here."

"I'd rather not think about them."

There was a broom leaning against the wall next to the door. McCabe picked it up and used the bristle end to gesture to the left. "You can see outside from that window." He pointed the broom in front of him. "And that window."

Nora was already turning her head to the right. "Is there a third window?"

"It's on the blueprints."

"Which means there's a hidden room, and the entrance must be on that side."

McCabe picked up his battery-powered lantern. "Exactly. But let me sweep the rafters before we get any closer. I don't want things with lots of legs dropping onto our heads."

Nora was tempted to peer into the boxes and chests, but they still had to search for the garden clue, so she followed behind McCabe, holding her lantern aloft as he swiped at web after web.

"I love that Lucille's father made this book for her—or for both of his daughters—but it's *really* eccentric. I mean, did he add all these secret compartments to the house so he could invent scavenger hunts, or did he hide other things in these places? Like stolen coins or rare stamps or jewels?"

McCabe lowered the broom and looked at her. "I've thought about that too. Especially in light of the scandal at the paper mill. If he embezzled a bunch of money, he could've hidden it behind the mirror in the bedroom. But I don't think that was the case. That scandal happened after Lucille was married. The house was built long before then. And most of the hiding places are pretty small."

Nora thought about all the hiding spots she'd seen up to this point. "The frame of a stained-glass window or a tile in the fireplace is one thing, but to wall up an actual room—that goes beyond eccentric. I liked Hugo Wynter better when I thought of him as a very indulgent father versus a criminal hiding things in the walls."

"He was clever, I'll give him that," said McCabe. "I don't even see a door. All I see is wood. Wood slats with wood rafters in between. No hinges. No handle. No keyhole. No seams. If there's a door in this wall, it's invisible."

We're so close to another clue, Nora thought.

Forgetting about the gloom and the dust and the legion of insect skeletons, she knocked on the wall adjacent to the rear corner. The wood sounded solid under her knuckles, and when she pushed against it with the flat of her hand, it didn't give at all.

Ducking under a thick rafter that angled toward the floor like a sailboat boom on a loose line, she repeated these motions on the next section of wall.

After watching her for several seconds, McCabe mirrored her movements. They were both banging and pushing and probing when Nora's knocking suddenly produced a different sound.

McCabe cocked his head to listen.

"You're onto something," he encouraged. "Give it a push."

Nora didn't need to be told twice.

She pressed both hands to the wall and gave it a shove. The wood creaked. As she continued to apply pressure, she felt a subtle shift of air.

Coming closer, McCabe said, "Try higher or lower. Maybe it tilts like a spinner target."

Nora shot McCabe a questioning look.

Rotating his hands around each other, he said, "You know that old pinball machine we used to have in the station? When the ball passed through the spinning targets, you'd get extra points. They were like a door rotating around a central piston."

"So don't push in the middle," Nora murmured, lowering into a catcher's stance.

This time, when she pushed, the whole panel moved an inch. She pushed harder and gained four or five inches.

"That's it. I'm getting down and dirty."

Sitting on the floor, she thrust her feet forward. The wood splintered as her heels went right through the slats.

"Oops."

A piece of wood hung like a loose tooth next to the hole Nora had made. McCabe hesitated for a second before wrenching it free.

He got on his hands and knees and held the lantern in front of the cavity. Scooting back a few feet, he said, "Some of these boards are warped. That's why the tilting mechanism didn't work. If I can get this rotten board off, we should be able to swing the whole piece inward."

Getting on his hands and knees, McCabe mule-kicked the board in question. It thudded to the floor, raising a cloud of dust.

After exchanging excited glances, Nora and McCabe pushed their lanterns into the tiny room and crawled in after them.

"Watch your head," McCabe cautioned.

The slant of the roof kept them from standing upright, so they hunched over like gargoyles and gazed at the only object in the cramped space.

"It looks just like the miniature version," Nora whispered, taking in the details of the steamer chest.

"Seems like a good place to store a bunch of stolen cash."

Nora pointed at the padlock. "What about that?"

He shook his head. "I have a warrant to search every inch of this house, but I can't destroy property without a damn good reason. The hole in the wall is already out of line. I'll have to admit to that damage and show this trunk to Lucille's kids. They need to be here when it's opened."

Nora suppressed a sigh. Though she was disappointed, she knew there were rules McCabe had to follow. "I don't think these bitty books and pieces of dollhouse furniture were ever going to lead us to Lucille's killer, and solving that riddle matters way more than a lost library. *If* the lost library exists at all."

McCabe moved his lantern closer to the trunk. "It could be in here."

"I hope not. Look at all the holes in the bottom." Nora squatted down to examine an area that had clearly been chewed by an animal, which is when she noticed the rust coating the metal bands and handle. Aiming her lantern at the back of the trunk, she saw that the hinges were also orange with rust.

Nora tried to wiggle one of the hinges, but the moment she made contact, the hinge came away from the chest and clattered to the floor.

"What are you doing?" McCabe asked sharply.

"The hinges are wrecked. Can I lift up the lid from the back? Just to see what's inside?"

McCabe held out a hand. "Wait. A car's coming."

He ducked out of the cramped space and hurried over to the front window. Nora stayed where she was and tried to raise the trunk lid. However, it wouldn't budge because the other hinge still clung to the trunk's body.

Suddenly a howl sliced through the quiet of the night.

A wolf howl.

"Stay here!" McCabe shouted as he raced for the stairs.

Fear rippled up Nora's spine. Abandoning the trunk, she scuttled out of the hidden room and rushed to the front window.

The glass was veiled by dirt. Nora rubbed at it with her sleeve with little effect.

All she could see were the dark outlines of the magnolias and, beyond the trees, a glimpse of the tall hedge lining the road. She located the driveway to her left before swinging her gaze back to the street.

She heard the low rumble of an engine. It sounded like a truck or a motorcycle. Or one of those cars with a dual exhaust.

Another wolf howl split the night air.

Nora craned her neck, searching for McCabe somewhere below her.

She thought she saw a man-sized shadow in the driveway, but as she tried to hone in on the shape, her vision was suddenly filled with a searing explosion of light.

The window glass cracked, and she jerked away from it. But even as she reared back, she saw that the magnolias crowding the front yard were drenched in flame.

"Grant!" she screamed.

She hurled herself down two flights of stairs, pulling out her phone as she ran. She hit the emergency button on her screen while wrenching the boot room door open.

"There's a fire at Wynter House!" she shouted into the phone. Cutting off the responder before he could speak, Nora rattled off the address. "Sheriff McCabe is here!" she yelled. "He needs help!"

Nora tore across the backyard to the driveway, screaming Grant's name.

A figure appeared in the alley between their trucks.

"I'm here! Nora, I'm here!"

McCabe rushed to Nora and cupped her face in his hands. "Are you okay?"

She threw her arms around his neck and kissed him. She tasted dirt and sweat and didn't care. Grant was there in front of her, whole and uninjured.

"I saw the fire, and I thought . . ."

"I know."

Nora clung to him. "I love you."

"I love you too."

They held each other while the trees burned.

Chapter 16

It has not been in the pursuit of pleasure that I have periled life and reputation and reason. It has been the desperate attempt to escape from torturing memories, from a sense of insupportable loneliness and a dread of some strange impending doom
—Edgar Allan Poe

The fire station was close by, so it wasn't long before the wail of sirens echoed through the night.

McCabe pointed at the garage. "I need to check on Clem."

Nora followed him to the back of the structure and listened to him bang on the door. As he called Clem's name, Nora turned to watch the smoke from the burning trees rise above the roof of Wynter House and drift toward the cemetery. The same wind pushing the smoke to the east whispered against the scarred skin of Nora's neck. Her entire right side felt hot. The scars swimming across her skin from wrist to shoulder itched so badly that Nora wanted to tear off her shirt and rake her fingernails up and down her arm.

It was as if her body remembered being burned. It remembered how Nora had deliberately reached into the flames to pull a mother and toddler to safety. She'd been responsible for that fire. She'd been drunk. She'd forced another car off the road and had almost killed two innocent people.

Tonight's fire was different. It was no accident. It wasn't the result of rage fueled by alcohol. It was a targeted attack. Just like the fire at Nora's house was a targeted attack.

This realization hit Nora on a cellular level. Heat rose through her layers of tissue and flamed her skin. Every scar itched while the healthy skin tingled with a pins-and-needles intensity. She felt like she'd swallowed the fire. Sweat dampened her clothes and pearled her forehead. Her throat was chalk dry.

"Clem! I'm coming in!"

McCabe's voice broke through the smoke clouds in Nora's head. When he pushed Clem's door open, adrenaline swept through her body, obliterating all traces of numbness.

She was right behind McCabe as he entered the apartment. The only light came from a floor lamp in the corner of the living room, but Nora had no trouble seeing a torn and sagging leather sofa, a coffee table, and a TV sitting on a makeshift stand of plywood and plastic crates.

More crates rose up along the length of the wall. Each one was filled with books.

McCabe moved toward the kitchen, which was divided from the living room by a half wall. He flicked on a ceiling light, took a quick glance around, and headed for the bedroom.

Nora had been distracted by the books, so she was still in the living room when she heard McCabe swear.

From his tone, she knew that Clem was either dead or injured. She entered the room to find McCabe leaning over Clem's body, his fingers pressed to Clem's neck.

"Is he . . . ?"

"Yeah. He's gone."

Clem was on his back, his face turned toward the wall. His arms and legs were loosely splayed. His feet were bare. The lava lamp on the nightstand bathed him in blue-green light, and Nora could imagine him floating in a clear, calm pool of water.

As if he had the same thought, McCabe murmured, "He just went under and never surfaced again."

Nora saw the band of rubber tied around Clem's left arm, just above the elbow, and the syringe on the floor next to the bed. There was a piece of paper on the nightstand, resting on top of a short stack of books.

Noticing the direction of her stare, McCabe held up a finger. "Stay where you are and don't touch anything." Leaning over the piece of paper, he said, "The note says, 'I killed my mom. The wolves were coming for me, so I asked her for money. Or for something to sell. But she said the treasure wasn't for me. She'd let me die to keep her secrets safe. She made me so mad that I lost control. If there's a hell, it'll feel just like home.'"

Nora looked down at Clem's silhouette. The blue light smoothed the lines of his face and she could see shades of the boy he used to be. A boy whose mom suffered from a mental illness. He'd lived with her addiction until he'd developed one of his own. After his siblings moved away, it had been just the two of them. Lucille had hidden inside Wynter House, while Clem was cloistered in the garage. They were simultaneously a few hundred feet and a world apart, each trying to escape the demons that refused to cease their relentless haunting.

"I wish he hadn't been alone," Nora whispered.

From the moment she'd first seen him in the backyard, Clem had unnerved her. She hadn't liked the idea of him watching her. His proximity to Lucille and his involvement with the Red Wolves convinced Nora that he'd had a hand in

Lucille's death. Now that she knew this was true, she felt no relief. Just sorrow.

The sirens were close. Firefighters and other first responders would be there in less than a minute. They'd douse the trees and stray sparks with water. They'd save Wynter House.

Does it even matter? Nora wondered bleakly.

Lucille was gone. Clem was gone. Beck and Harper would sell, then up and leave. There would be no Wynters left in Miracle Springs. And what of Wynter House? Would it be torn down? Replaced by another three-story apartment complex or strip mall?

Maybe it would've been better to let it burn. The spirits in its walls would finally be set free.

While she'd been lost in her dark ruminations, McCabe had been snapping photos with his phone.

"Let's go," he said, taking Nora's hand on his way out of the room.

"Did he set the fires?"

McCabe kept walking. "No. He's been dead for hours."

"What he said about Lucille—about them both going to hell—do you think he's talking about the body in the bathtub? Like, he knew that his mom killed his dad?"

They exited the apartment and were immediately engulfed by a cacophony of sirens and flashing lights.

"Maybe he knew, or he was condemning her for being a bad mom," McCabe shouted over the din. "Maybe it was both. He knew what she'd done and hated her for it. I'm sure he hated how he had to rely on her, just as she had to rely on him, to survive."

Though Nora had never been able to picture Lucille as a murderer, her resolve was beginning to weaken. Lucille was an addict. If her addiction had corrupted her relationship with her children, it had probably tainted her marriage as well.

What if her husband threatened to get rid of her stuff? Maybe Lucille lashed out. Had she killed him in a fit of rage and then suffered the same fate at the hands of her son?

In the street, firefighters shouted to one another. Doors slammed as other first responders exited their vehicles. Red lights whirled through the darkness, boomeranging off the asphalt and the dense line of trees on the other side of the road.

Nora stood off to the side as McCabe conferred with the fire chief. She couldn't hear what they were saying, but when McCabe pointed at the attic window and used his hands to mime an explosion, her gaze traveled from the burning trees to the peaked roof of Wynter House.

If the house caught fire, no one would ever see what was inside the locked chest, and the answer to that riddle might die with Lucille.

The fire chief moved off to supervise his team, and McCabe beckoned for Deputy Andrews and a team of paramedics to follow him into Clem's apartment.

There was nothing Nora could do to help, so she sat on the curb in front of the cemetery and watched the firefighters turn the flaming trees into smoldering black sticks. Her eyes smarted from the smoke, so she put her head down, pressing her face to her knees.

Curled up like an egg, she suddenly realized how tired she was. Her bones were so leaden that she could probably fall asleep in the middle of all the chaos.

"There you are."

Hearing McCabe's voice, she raised her head.

He handed her a bottle of water and told her to drink. When she was done, he helped her to her feet and swept her hair out of her face.

"Andrews will run you home. We've got a long night

ahead of us and I'm not going to have you falling asleep on the grass."

"He doesn't need to do that. I can drive myself."

McCabe pointed at the cluster of vehicles blocking the driveway. "You won't get out for hours, and you've been through two fires in two nights. You need a shower and a good night's sleep. And cat snuggles."

"You need rest as much as I do, but I know you won't get it."

He gestured around at the other first responders. "This is what we signed up for. Adrenaline will see us through, and when that wears off, there's coffee." His hand slid down her arm and closed around her wrist. "Andrews will drop you off on his way to pick up the ME. The doc's car is in the shop and she's right around the corner from my place. *Our* place."

Nora felt the warmth of his smile as he opened the door to Andrews's cruiser.

"Sheriff!" One of the firefighters waved at McCabe. "You need to see this."

Nora glanced through the open door and saw columns of smoke rising from the blackened trees. The firefighters had extinguished the flames and were now using chain saws to cut the charred branches stretching toward Wynter House.

Other than smudges left behind by the smoke, which darkened the peeling paint in places, the house appeared undamaged.

One of the firefighters held a rake, and something was caught in its metal teeth. He walked to the edge of the driveway and stopped to show his discovery to his chief.

McCabe shut the car door and slapped a palm against the roof, signaling for Andrews to leave. Andrews put the car in gear, but hesitated for several seconds before crawling forward. As they moved past the circle of men studying the object in the rake, both Andrews and Nora craned their necks to see what it was.

With the strobing lights, Nora caught a glimpse of black fabric.

"Looks like a balled-up sock," she muttered.

As the lights hit the rake again, she saw a glint of red and white. She felt like she'd seen the color combination before, but before she could sift through her memory, Andrews hit the gas.

Nora sagged against the back of the seat and closed her eyes.

Andrews drove in silence until he paused at a stop sign on a quiet residential street. "I'm sorry about your house, Nora. I know it isn't much consolation, but we're going to nail the guys who threw that bottle bomb."

Suddenly the red-and-white threads stitched themselves together in Nora's memory. "The Red Wolves," she said in an icy voice. "Their logo was on that thing in the rake. A hat or something."

"Yeah."

"Why would they set fire to Wynter House? Clem couldn't pay them whatever he owed if he was dead."

Andrews darted a glance at her in the rearview mirror. "It was a threat. Their way of telling him he was out of time. That's why they went for the trees and not the garage."

"They're not going to get a dime from him now." Nora gazed out the window. "But they're still out there, wanting someone to pay up. Does that mean Beck and Harper are in danger?"

"Don't worry, we're going to get whoever threw that Molotov cocktail because we have them on camera. We set up cameras all around the property, which is why we knew about the fire before the sheriff called it in."

The unspoken question hung between them. When the silence stretched on long enough to become uncomfortable, Nora said, "I've been searching Wynter House for clues based on a book Lucille gave me."

"Something about a lost library, right? Was it in that bag I gave you the day she died?"

"It was. The clues are hidden around the house." She shook her head. "Actually, more like *in* the house. So far each clue has been a piece of dollhouse furniture and a miniature book. We were about to find the clue in the attic, when the fire started."

Andrews turned onto McCabe's street and reduced his speed. "Why didn't you tell Lucille's kids about the book?"

"Because she left it to *me*. There's a reason she sent me on that wild-goose chase, and I wanted to get to the end and see what that reason was before I told anyone else about it."

"Except the sheriff, that is."

Nora made a chuffing noise. "Only *after* those Red Wolves bastards tried to burn my house down. Tonight was the last time he was going to let me look for clues. He was hoping they'd explain the bones in the bathtub. Or why Lucille was killed. But I guess we know what happened to her now."

Andrews pulled into McCabe's driveway and kept the engine running while he opened the back door for Nora.

"Will Grant tell Beck and Harper about their brother tonight?"

"He'll go to the Inn of Mist and Roses as soon as I get back with the ME," he said as he walked Nora to the front door. "They've lost half their family in the same week, and I know this sounds weird, but maybe, after some time goes by, they can finally let go of the past. All the memories. All the grief and guilt."

Nora wondered if Andrews was talking about the Wynter siblings or himself.

A moth bumped against the porch light, its wings beating furiously as it searched for a way to get closer to the small sun inside the glass.

She didn't think Beck and Harper would ever be free of their memories. They were as much a part of them as their blood type or eye color. They were like tattoos inked on the inside of the skin and could never be completely removed.

"I just hope all of this will bring them closer together." Nora gave Andrews a weary smile. "Thanks for the ride."

Andrews hesitated as if he had more to say, but seemed to change his mind. He touched the brim of his hat, wished Nora a good night, and jogged back to his idling car.

Nora had barely closed the front door behind her when McCabe's cats came running. They meowed and purred, weaving around her ankles and dragging their tails across her shins.

After giving them some kibble, she took a quick shower and fell into bed. The cats hopped up too. Magnum, who had an uncanny way of sensing when people needed comfort, pressed his face to Nora's cheek. She stroked the fur on the back of his neck while he nuzzled her, his purrs rumbling into her ear. Finally he curled up next to her and began to lick his front paws. Every now and then, his rough tongue would move over her hand as if saying, "There, there."

Nora had never had a pet, and when she and McCabe first got together, she wasn't sure if his cats would accept her. They'd always been happy for her to feed them and would sit on her lap from time to time, but they rarely cuddled with her the way Magnum did now.

Usually, when McCabe worked late, the cats spread themselves across his side of the bed. Tonight, however, they gravitated toward Nora, lying so close that she felt the weight of their warm bodies. They purred until her breathing slowed and she drifted into sleep. Even then, they didn't leave her. They orbited around her slumbering form, their eyes probing the darkness for threats. Bookended by her feline sentinels, Nora slept without stirring until McCabe woke her with a kiss.

Though he'd only grabbed four hours of sleep, McCabe dropped Nora off at the Gingerbread House before heading back to the station.

Gus ushered her into the bakery and insisted on making her a cup of tea. "I've been experimenting again, so if you'd try my peanut-butter, chocolate-chip bread, I'd be real grateful."

Nora had finished her tea and was on her second slice of bread when Hester entered the kitchen. Despite the flour and scraps of dough, she dropped her purse and keys on the butcher block and put her arms around Nora.

"Gus told me about the fire at Wynter House," she said. "The chief was here a little while ago getting treats for his team. Are you okay?"

"I'm better now. I'm pretty sure this bread has healing powers."

Hester moved her purse and selected one of a dozen aprons hanging from a row of hooks near the sink. She tied the strings of a vintage-style apron decorated with pumpkins and fall leaves and smoothed the pleated skirt. "I'm so ready for fall. I know it's still apple everything season, so I made two dozen apple spice muffins for the shop, but I'm itching to skip ahead to pumpkin season."

Gus laid a hand on Hester's arm. "Don't wish your time away, darlin'. It goes fast enough, all on its own."

"Can I wish for a cup of tea, instead?"

"I think I can manage that before I go." He filled a mug for Hester and put it on the butcher block. "I'll man the counter for a spell so you two can chat."

Hester thanked him and turned an expectant gaze on Nora. "So, what happened last night?"

Nora told her everything. While she talked, Hester listened attentively, taking the occasional sip of tea. When Nora was done, Hester stared at her in astonishment.

"Are you safe? First your house and now this?"

"The sheriff's department set up cameras around Wynter House, so they've got the make and model of the bottle bomber's car on camera. The license plate was covered, but there can only be so many cars like that in town."

Hester frowned. "If these guys are drug traffickers trying to scare Clem, then why go after you?"

"Maybe they knew he sold books to fund his habit and figured I might be able to influence him. I really don't know."

"And Grant is sure it's a suicide?"

Nora tried to recall if McCabe had ever said as much, but couldn't. "He hardly got any sleep last night, so I didn't ask about the ME's findings or anything like that. There was a note next to Clem's bed. I assume he wrote it."

"How sad." Hester gazed down at her tea. "People always said Wynter House was haunted. Maybe that wasn't the right word. Maybe it's *cursed.*"

Nora thought about the bones in the bathtub. "People filled that house with secrets, and I don't think all of them have been uncovered yet."

"I feel sorry for Beck and Harper. I know Harper's been awful to you, but she must be in a world of pain today." Hester carried their empty mugs to the sink and hung her purse on the hook neck to the supply shelves. "Do you think you'll see either of them again?"

"Only if they want to confront me for keeping *The Little Lost Library* to myself."

Hester put on a clean apron covered with cheerful yellow

lemons. "And after all this, you didn't get to finish the scavenger hunt. It's not fair. I know I'm a terrible person for saying this, but I want to know what was inside the trunk in the attic. And what about the library? You never even got a peek!"

Gus poked his head into the kitchen and said, "Sorry to interrupt, but Mrs. Lowry wants to order a gravity-defying birthday cake for her son, and I have no clue what that is."

"Tell her I'll be right there."

Hester loaded Nora's arms with bakery boxes and walked her to the door. "I know you don't mind books with ambiguous endings, but it's not always entertaining in real life. I hope you see Beck and Harper before they leave. Even if they blast you for snooping around their house, I hope they tell you the secret of the lost library. If not, that house might haunt you too."

It already does, Nora thought.

Aloud she said, "I don't think I'll see the Wynters or their house again. And that's okay with me. Now go find out what Mrs. Lowry wants. If a gravity-defying cake requires a magic touch, then she's come to the right place."

Nora was wrong about the Wynter siblings. She would see both of them again, starting with Beck.

The shop had been teeming with customers all day long. Not only were early-weekend visitors flooding the town, but locals kept pouring in, eager to hear the story of Nora's house fire and to offer her sympathy and support. By three, she was completely out of candles and had only a handful of shelf enhancers left in the entire store.

After bagging a stack of expensive cookbooks for the general manager of the grocery store, Nora hurried back to the ticket agent's booth to see if Sheldon was still alive.

"I can't feel my hands or feet, but I'm here," he said when

she asked how he was doing. "We ran out of food before noon and we're almost out of milk again."

"Again?"

"Yeah. I bribed one of the Monday Moms to do a milk run for me. I told her she could have free drinks all next week, but she said she wanted to help you out and refused to let me pay her for the milk. Even though she stocked the fridge, we're on our last cartons of whole and skim." He gestured at the coffee urns. "They're getting low too. Can you refill them and then go out and buy us a cow?"

Knowing she couldn't leave Sheldon alone, Nora said, "We just need to make it until the high school kids show up. I can think of several who'd be happy to get us milk in exchange for a free paperback."

Sheldon gasped. "*¡Dios mío!* It was so crazy when I got here this morning that I didn't have the chance to tell you about the book thief. I know who it is!"

"Who?"

"A boy. A small, skinny kid with Harry Potter glasses. He looks so much like HP that I wouldn't be surprised if he lived in a closet under the stairs."

Nora paused in the act of scooping grounds into the filter basket. "Did you catch him on camera?"

"Yep. He helped himself to a Leigh Bardugo paperback. Guess the kid has a thing for feisty fantasy heroines."

"I'll deal with him later. Right now, I need to help you with this line and then shut down service for the day. You need to go home and I need to concentrate on selling books."

Sheldon jerked his head toward the Readers' Circle. "I don't think he's here for coffee or books."

Nora followed his gaze. Beck Wynter sat in the mustard-colored chair, an unopened book in his lap. His skin was gray with fatigue and his silver-streaked red hair was un-combed.

"He looks like a tired hedgehog," Sheldon muttered. "Give that man a coffee."

Taking Sheldon's advice, Nora filled a take-out cup and carried it to Beck. "This is a lame peace offering," she began.

Beck stood up and accepted the cup. "You're slammed and, from what I can see, shorthanded, but Harper and I need your help."

A woman rounded the fiction shelves and waved at Nora. "Sorry, but can you ring me up?"

"Do you mind coming behind the checkout counter with me?" Nora asked Beck. "We can talk as soon as I whittle down the line."

Not only was Beck willing to accompany her, but he volunteered to bag books. With his help, Nora served six customers in under ten minutes.

"You're good with people," she told him as the sleigh bells jangled for what seemed like the thousandth time that day.

"I have to be. My patients trust me to crack their necks." He mustered a small smile that instantly faded. "Part of me understands why my mom gave you *The Little Lost Library.* You were the one person she could talk to about books. The other part of me resents her choice. Her dad wrote that book and gave each of his daughters a copy. Mom should've left it for one of us. It's about *our* house. She kept secrets from all three of us. That book was a chance for us to discover things we've always wondered about."

Nora lowered her gaze in contrition. "I'm sorry. I got swept up in the mystery. I thought I'd understand Lucille better if I found the lost library. *If* there is one. Is there?"

"Yes. I remember Mom showing me a bunch of tiny books. I was really young, but I remember. Sheriff McCabe showed us the clues you found. There was another piece of dollhouse furniture in the attic trunk. It was a bed and a tiny book called *The Two Sisters*." He raked his hands through his hair. "Harper and I have no idea what these things mean."

Two sisters. Lucille and Lynette. Two copies of *The Little Lost Library*. A collection of miniature books. A dollhouse. Whispers of stolen money, of some kind of treasure, hidden inside Wynter House.

"What about the mirror in your mom's room? When the sheriff and I searched for the clue, it was missing. Did you find it?"

Beck shook his head. "I think Clem found it a long time ago, but I don't know what it was or what he did with it. Sorry."

"How can I help?"

"The answer to the whole mystery must be in the library. It was Mom's favorite room. We weren't allowed to enter unless she let us in. She kept the door locked at all times and wore the key like a necklace."

Nora had never seen the key, but Lucille tended to wear high-necked blouses and thick cardigans, even during the summer.

"Forgive me for asking, but was she wearing the key when she died?"

His face tightened with grief. "Whoever killed her took the key. They opened the library, but I don't think they found what they were looking for. There were so many books. And paper. Boxes and boxes of paper from the mill. The Junk Hunks have cleared all of that away, which took forever because the sheriff's department had to document and examine every item first, but we still can't find the last clue."

One of Nora's regulars entered the shop and smiled at her. She smiled back, but didn't ask the woman if she needed help. Now was not the time to interrupt Beck.

"Harper doesn't want to look anymore," he continued.

"Losing Clem—it was too much. She totally shut down. But *I'm* fired up." He balled his fists and struck the countertop. "I'm *furious*! I had no control over my life when I lived in that house. I *still* have no control. I want to understand *why* this happened. *All* of it. Can you come back to the house tonight? Mom wanted you to find these clues. Will you finish what you started?"

The air above Nora's pinkie finger tingled. The phantom sensation was a warning. A bad omen. She knew this to be true, but it didn't matter. She had to go. She couldn't walk away without knowing the whole story.

And so, she placed her hand on Beck's hand and said, "Yes. I'll come back to Wynter House."

Chapter 17

To add a library to a house is to give that house a soul.

—Cicero

"**Y**ou can't go back there alone."

Nora placed a bowl of chicken and corn chowder in front of McCabe. He thanked her and reached for the loaf of sourdough bread, which sat on a scarred cutting board. McCabe worked a serrated knife through the loaf's crust, speckling the table with crumbs. He put the heel on Nora's plate and helped himself to two thick slices. Then he laid the knife down and met her quizzical gaze.

She said, "I won't be alone. I'll be with Beck."

"Clem's death may look like a suicide, but I have my doubts. So does the ME. Before moving to Miracle Springs, she was in Baltimore, where she saw dozens of overdose cases. After getting her take on certain details, we can't rule his death a suicide."

Wisps of steam rose from Nora's chowder bowl, so she spread butter on her bread and took a generous bite. She told Beck she'd be at Wynter House at seven thirty, which meant she needed to eat her dinner quickly and go.

If not for the kindness of Val and Kirk Walsh, the couple

who owned Tea Flowers, Nora would be slurping soup from a can, while McCabe made do with a sub sandwich from the grocery store. Instead, they were feasting on fresh greens with herbs, homemade chowder, and a loaf of Gus's crusty bread.

Nora had already finished her salad and was surprised that McCabe, whose last meal had been a fast-food breakfast biscuit at nine that morning, had yet to touch his food.

"What about the note?" she asked. It had sounded genuine to her, but she didn't know Clem. Maybe Harper or Beck had doubts that it had been written by their brother.

"The note was typed on his computer and printed on his printer, using what appeared to be the last piece of standard printer paper. That's the first oddity in my eyes. I don't think Clem bought a package of printer paper in his life. All the paper in his apartment came from his grandfather's mill. He trimmed it to make it fit in the printer tray, and he used the scraps as bookmarks." McCabe swallowed a spoonful of chowder. "Every book in his place has a paper bookmark listing the copyright information and estimated value."

"What else?"

"The biggest red flag is that Clem had a tourniquet around his arm." McCabe tore off a piece of bread and popped it in his mouth. Picking up his soupspoon again, he said, "Do you know how an injection works?"

Nora considered the question. She had a vague sense of how it was done, but her knowledge was based mostly on novels or BBC crime shows. "People use the tourniquet because it helps them find a vein, right?"

"Exactly. The blood flow going to the heart is blocked, so the veins get backed up. That makes them dilate, which makes them easier to see and feel." McCabe pushed up the sleeve of his uniform shirt and pointed at the prominent vein on the inside of his elbow. "Let's say I inject liquid meth into this bad boy here. The needle goes in, and I'll know it's a good stick if I get a little blood when I pull back on the stopper."

Nora had no problem reading about grisly topics while she was eating, but listening to McCabe talk about syringes and needles, while miming the actions on his arm, had a visceral effect on her. Abandoning her spoon in her bowl, she wiped her mouth with her napkin and signaled for McCabe to keep talking.

"Once the needle is in, I hold it there with one hand and take the tourniquet off with the other. If the tourniquet stays in place, the drugs aren't going to flood my bloodstream. I'll push the plunger, but the liquid won't go into my veins like I want it to. It'll go into the surrounding tissue instead. That won't feel good. Not at all. It's the opposite of feeling good."

"Clem's syringe—was it empty?"

"Yes. The plunger had been pushed, and the meth had backflowed into the surrounding tissue. That's a red flag. It's not like this was Clem's first injection. The needle was his delivery method of choice."

McCabe unrolled his shirtsleeve. "Another thing that seemed off was the tourniquet itself. It's the kind you see at a doctor's office. You can buy them online from any number of pharmacies, but most addicts don't buy their gear online, when they can get something similar for free. We don't need to go into detail about that while we're eating."

Nora pushed her bowl away. "Go ahead. I'm done."

"People use belts, strips of clothing, or tie two condoms together. Clem preferred the latter. He got the condoms from the free clinic. We found quite a stockpile in his bedroom." McCabe shrugged. "I'm sure he was sexually active, but I doubt he was *that* active. The password and lock screen on his computer were disabled, so we had a look at his files.

There's no record of Clem buying a box of rubber tourniquets online and no one sells them locally."

"I see why you can't rule it a suicide," Nora said.

Higgins sauntered out of the kitchen, making a beeline for McCabe's chair. The cat sat on his haunches and gazed up at his cat dad through slitted eyes until McCabe scratched the tabby's head. Nora could see the tension ebb from McCabe's shoulders. He smiled at his cat and reached for his beer. His fingers picked at the corner of the label as he said, "I think Clem was murdered."

"By the Red Wolves?"

"They're the logical suspects, but I'd expect them to do a better job faking a suicide by overdose. Clem had enough meth in his body to fell a horse. The ME thinks he was given a fatal dose before the tourniquet was tied on. His blood alcohol levels were sky-high too, and we found two empty bottles of grain alcohol in the kitchen. There's nothing suspicious about empty bottles. There's a mountain of the same brand in the grass behind the garage. Clem's been buying the stuff for years. Everyone at the ABC store knows him by name. The problem with the bottles in the kitchen is that they were wiped clean."

Magnum padded into the room and directed a meow at Nora. She'd fed the cats as soon as she got home from work, but they'd taken two licks of wet food before turning up their noses and walking away from their dinner dishes. Magnum had been complaining on and off for the past hour, to no avail.

"If you don't lick that plate clean, there'll be no treats tonight," McCabe told the dissatisfied feline.

Nora darted a glance at her watch. If she was going to leave, she had to go soon.

She carried her bowl of unfinished chowder to the sink

and returned to the table to collect McCabe's bowl. She laid her hand on his shoulder, instead. "Are you worried about me going back to Wynter House because Beck or Harper might be dangerous, or because the killer might have unfinished business with them?"

"All of the above."

Nora felt knots between McCabe's shoulder blades. Pressing her thumbs into his muscles, she tried to ease some of the tension. "If Clem didn't take his own life, why was he killed? Is it because he knew who murdered Lucille?"

"Possibly. He was silenced out of anger or fear, but until we find the person responsible, we won't know which one."

The thought of Harper or Beck pushing a needle into Clem's arm made Nora shudder. "The other day, you said your team was checking alibis for Harper and Beck. Are they in the clear? Or is there a chance one of them strangled their own mother? I know Beck isn't the kind of health care professional using syringes or prescribing medication, but he understands human anatomy. And Harper strikes me as the type of person who'd kill someone for cutting her in line at Starbucks."

"Harper was in a yoga class that evening. Not only is there a record of her signing in, but the instructor definitely remembers seeing her. Beck's office manager confirmed his claim that he had two appointments that afternoon. Both siblings were in other states, hours away from here, when Lucille was killed."

This made Nora feel much better about being in Wynter House with them.

"Which deputy is watching the house tonight?"

McCabe said, "Hollowell and her K9 partner. But if you're going there, I'm going too."

Nora bent over and kissed his cheek. "You're running on

what, four hours of sleep? And you'll be up at six tomorrow, ready to face another twelve-hour day. Stay here. Watch TV with a cat on your lap. If there's any trouble, Hollowell will call you. Or I'll call you."

"You must really want to see this through if you're willing to hang out with Hollowell."

Nora kissed him again. "We're so close to the end."

McCabe pushed back from the table and carried the remains of the bread and the crock of whipped butter into the kitchen. After covering the bread with plastic wrap, he pressed his fingers into his bloodshot eyes.

"Okay, here's what's going to happen," he said. "I'm going to take a power nap in my recliner. I'm setting my phone alarm for ten. If you aren't home when I wake up, I'm coming to Wynter House to get you. At any time before ten, if you get the slightest vibe that something isn't right, you need to call me. Where's your pepper spray?"

"In my purse."

"Put it in your pocket."

Nora said she would and kissed McCabe once more before heading out into the night. She knew she should be wary, if not downright scared. But all she could think about was that she was finally going to see the library. Lucille had owned thousands of books, but Nora was certain that the books in the library were special. If they hadn't completely deteriorated, a collection belonging to Lucille's parents could be worth a small fortune.

Not only that, but Nora had a strong feeling that the little lost library was somewhere inside that room. She had visions of a secret room behind one of the bookcases or a trapdoor hidden under a moldy rug. These were pure Nancy Drew–style fantasies, but as Nora drove through town, she indulged in the fantasy that Wynter House had been waiting to reveal its biggest secret to her, and her alone.

Lucille had given *The Little Lost Library* to her because of their shared love of books. Lucille's decision to make Nora the custodian of what could prove to be her most treasured possession was intentional. This is what Nora believed in her heart of hearts.

She hoped Beck and Harper would find a box full of money. She hoped Wynter House could be restored. But what she cared about most were the tiny books and the story behind the dollhouse miniatures.

As she drove past the cemetery, her thoughts of a story-book library were pushed aside by the memory of Clem lying in bed, bathed in the blue light.

If the Red Wolves hadn't murdered Clem because he couldn't pay his debt, then the most likely suspect was a relative. A brother or a sister. A long-lost aunt. Or a missing father.

No one knew if the bones in the bathtub belonged to Lucille's husband or to someone else.

No one knew what had become of Lynette Wynter. Mc-Cabe had tried to locate her—to inform her of her sister's death, but Lynette had vanished without a trace, not long after Beck was born. Other than a birth certificate, social security number, and school documents, there were no official records of a Lynette Wynters of Miracle Springs, North Carolina. Unofficially, she was mentioned in the local paper as being the maid-of-honor in Lucille's wedding to Frederick, but after that, she seemed to have vanished into thin air.

Years later, Frederick also disappeared.

If Lynette or Frederick were still alive, they'd be in their eighties by now.

Nora had a hard time imagining an octogenarian staging Clem's suicide, but she supposed it was possible.

However, Beck and Harper were the more likely suspects. They were here, in Miracle Springs. They both had a reason to kill Clem and plenty of opportunity to fake his suicide. With Clem out of the picture, the profits made from the sale of Lucille's possessions would now be divided between two siblings instead of three.

Was Clem's share worth killing over?

Nora hoped to have that answer by the end of the night.

Nora parked next to Hollowell's SUV and, after patting her pockets to make sure she had her phone and pepper spray, knocked on the kitchen door.

From somewhere inside the house, a dog barked. Hollowell's K9 partner, an all-black German shepherd named Rambo, was on duty.

Hollowell appeared in the kitchen with Rambo at her heel. Standing squarely in the doorway, she gave Nora a lengthy once-over. "The sheriff said you'd be coming. Why are you always in the middle of *so* many investigations? Is this how you get your kicks?"

"Is poaching other women's boyfriends how you get yours?" Nora retorted.

As soon as the words were out of her mouth, she regretted them. She knew better than to respond to Hollowell's taunts.

A joker's smile spread across Hollowell's face. "Guess I have something she doesn't."

"Yeah, you're the gray sprinkles on a rainbow cupcake. Now, can you move so I can ignore you for the rest of the night?"

Hollowell stepped aside, leaving just enough room for Nora to squeeze past her. "Relax, Rambo," she murmured, putting a hand on the dog's head. "This one's no threat."

Rambo wagged his tail and gazed at Hollowell, affection shining from his nutmeg-colored eyes.

Nora waited until she was in the dining room before calling out for Beck.

"I'm in the library!" he yelled back.

Moving swiftly, Nora crossed the hall. The room she'd been waiting to see since she'd heard of its existence was a bibliophile's paradise.

There were bookcases on every wall. Each shelf was made of thick, polished wood. The sections were divided by fluted columns that rose toward a carved cornice. Carved leaves decorated the molding on the bottom of every case.

The shelves were deep and held roughly twelve to sixteen books each. A few were empty, but most were still stuffed with books.

Nora saw row after row of fine leather bindings and gilt titles. The rich wood and dark spines told a story of wealth and privilege. It was like stepping into the library of a British estate. It was the picture on a puzzle box. The setting of a movie. It was incredibly beautiful.

"You should've seen it back in the day," Beck said, his voice full of pride. "When there were velvet curtains and brocade chairs. There was a globe on a stand in that corner and a library ladder in the other corner. There was a desk in front of the window, with lots of drawers, and a huge, hand-knotted Turkish rug, with birds and flower designs."

Nora drifted over to where Beck stood. "You and Harper must've worked really hard to get this room looking like this."

"We went through pounds of paper, but none of it was helpful. Mom kept every newspaper. Every piece of junk mail. We filled a box with bills—paid and unpaid—but we only found a handful of letters from people she actually knew. A few birthday and Christmas cards. That's it."

"Nothing from her sister?"

Beck gave her a sharp look. "What makes you ask about Lynette?"

"Because people don't just disappear without a reason.

You told me earlier that she'd left, but where did she go? And did you ever hear from her again?"

"No. I only know her from photos and from what my mother told me about her. Apparently, she and Lynette were really close. So close that Lynette stuck around after the news of the mill scandal broke even though she wanted to leave. But after I was born, Lynette had had enough of the neighbors whispering behind her back. She left and Mom didn't say where she went. My mom probably cut her off—told her not to come back or contact her again. That's what she did to her former friends."

Like Ida Fleming, Nora thought, remembering the old woman from the estate sale.

Keeping her eyes on the shelves, she said, "It must've been hard, after your dad left, to know you had an aunt somewhere in the world. It sounds like you, Harper, and Clem could've used another adult in your life."

"Instead, my sister and brother had to rely on me. I was an eleven-year-old trying to raise a nine-year-old and a toddler. Look how that turned out."

The agony in his voice pierced Nora's heart. "You were just a kid with no support system. You did your best. And then you got an education and built a life. You should be proud of that."

Beck slumped against a bookcase. "What life? My dying practice? My crappy apartment? A string of broken relationships? What did I know about building a life? My mom was crazy. My dad abandoned us—or so we thought. Now it looks like Mom killed him. She poured lye over his body and covered him with a bunch of Bibles."

Very quietly Nora said, "Was he abusive?"

"I never saw him lay a hand on her, but there was lots of yelling. Lots of tears. My dad was an alcoholic, and he could be a mean drunk. No, not mean. He was cruel. He used to look at me like I was a pile of dogshit on the lawn—something that disgusted him. He'd call me the Changeling. He called Harper a useless girl. And he'd tell my mother that it was her fault Lynette went away. He also threatened to burn her books if she did anything to make him mad."

This story does have a villain. It's Frederick Vandercamp, Nora thought.

"I'm glad he didn't act on that threat, because I see a room of really fine books. Look at all the classics. Shakespeare, Dickens, Austen—they'll all sell well. But let's find the rest of them. You and Harper need to cover your expenses, but you also deserve to live a little. Go on a vacation or open up a business in a new place."

Beck turned away to compose himself. After wiping an errant tear off his cheek, he said, "Sorry, it's been a long day. I'm grateful to you for coming here to help. Let's hope you can make more sense of my grandpa's stupid riddles than I could."

Nora pulled up the final riddle on her phone and tried to focus on the words. It was hard to think in the presence of so many old, rare books. She wanted to page through each and every one. She wanted to examine their age, assess their condition, and admire their illustrations.

The books weren't the only distractions. She also heard footsteps in the hall, along with the *click, click* of a dog's nails on the bare floorboards.

"She's doing her rounds," said Beck.

Nora didn't want to engage with Hollowell, so she turned her back to the door and asked Beck if he'd already searched the books for possible clues.

"Harper and I opened every book and fanned the pages, even though the sheriff's people already did that. Nothing fell out. None of them were fake or hollowed out. They're just books."

Just books. Nora glanced around. *This room is a treasure trove of stories. Of history, science, philosophy, and religious studies. These books could tell me so much about Lucille's parents. A library is such a personal place. If only I had more time . . .*

"We also took the books off the shelves, shelf by shelf, to check for hollow spaces behind the bookcases," Beck continued. "We looked for any book with a number on the spine or in the title. Because of the clue."

Nora read the clue out loud: " 'To solve the last riddle, count one and then two. Consider your commandments and nudge the yew.' "

Beck threw his hands in the air. "See? It makes no sense. Was everyone on my mom's side of the family off their rocker?"

"When your mom and her sister were kids, they would've recognized the first line. If I'm right, it's from a nursery rhyme that starts with 'One, two, buckle my shoe.' "

"I've heard it before too, but what does it mean? Are we looking for shoes? Buckles?"

"You were right to focus on numbers. Ten Commandments. Nora pointed at her feet. "Ten toes."

"Okay," Beck whispered, edging closer.

Dropping to her knees, Nora put her hand on the line of carved leaves running the length of the baseboard. "These look like oak leaves to me. We're looking for a yew."

"We had to google it, and even after we did, we couldn't figure out why it mattered. I mean, you don't get paper from yew trees, and they don't grow around here, so the bookcases aren't made from their wood."

"According to the clue, we need to bump the yew with our toes. I think we need to find a yew carving on one of these baseboards."

Beck held up a flashlight. "What's it look like?"

"It's an evergreen. Two rows of needlelike leaves. Like a Christmas tree." Nora showed him an image on her phone.

"You're a genius," he cried, beaming. The gloom clinging to him earlier was suddenly gone. "You check this wall. I'll check the other side. We should both start from the window and work our way to the door."

Nora got on all fours and crawled over the floor, examining the leaves as she moved. It was slow going, because the baseboard was caked with dust. In some places, it was so thick that it distorted the shape of the leaf. Whoever had swept the library floor had pushed the dirt toward the baseboards and left it there.

Luckily, Nora had brought a pair of gloves with her. She wriggled her hands into them and swiped at the dust piles until she could identify the leaves. She'd reached the last bookcase on the wall, and was fighting off a sense of despondency, when she swept away a clump of dust to reveal the yew carving.

The thin, needle-covered twig was no bigger than her pinkie. Entwined with an oak leaf, it was cleverly camouflaged. Bending closer, Nora saw lines in the wood on either end of the twig.

"It's here!" she cried.

Beck was at her side in seconds.

"No wonder I never noticed this before. My mom's reading chair was in this corner. And like I said, she never let anyone in this room unless she was here too." His fingertips traced the yew branch. "This must be some kind of button."

Nora pointed at his feet. "Nudge the yew with your shoe."

With a childlike grin, Beck pushed the baseboard with the toe of his sneaker. It moved a few centimeters and then stopped.

"Could be warped after all this time," Beck said, applying more force.

The panel refused to budge.

Nora sat back on her heels and re-read the riddle once more.

"Ten Commandments. Ten toes." She glanced up at Beck. "You're using five, not ten. Is there another panel?"

Without waiting for him to join her, she wiped the worst of the dust away from the remaining baseboard. The last oak leaf on the wall was also entangled with a yew leaf.

"Here it is!" She looked from Beck to the baseboard. "One person couldn't do this alone. I guess your grandfather wanted your mom and her sister to work together."

Beck helped Nora to her feet. "Good thing you're here, or I'd have to ask the deputy for help. Ready?" At Nora's nod, he said, "One, two, three, push!"

The wood in front of her shoe slowly gave way as noises echoed behind the bookcase. After a series of whirrs and clicks, the columns flanking the shelves popped forward.

Beck stuck his flashlight into the cavity behind the columns. "There's a lever back here. Is there one on your side too?"

Thrusting her phone into the aperture, Nora saw a glint of metal. The lever was almost an arm's length away, but she was able to wrap her hand around it. Even through her glove, it felt cold.

"Got it?" Beck asked breathlessly.

"Got it."

Based on how the lever was mounted, it was clear that Nora was supposed to push down on the handle. After another countdown, she tightened her grip and pushed.

The lever didn't move, but she heard a lock or other mechanism disengage on Beck's side of the bookcase.

"My side's stuck," she told him.

Taking her place, he reached into the hole. She watched the cords in his neck stand out as he struggled to move the lever. Grunting through clenched teeth, he applied all the force he could muster.

"Dammit!" He withdrew his arm, gave it a shake, and stuck it back in the opening. "Whatever gears are behind this wall are probably rusted to hell. I'm so close. *So* close!"

As he strained, his face reddened, and veins stood out on his forehead. His whole upper body shook, but the lever didn't move. He let out a bellow of frustration, which brought Hollowell running.

"What's going on?" she demanded.

Rambo was in high alert mode, ears pricked and nostrils quivering.

"Can't. Open. This." Beck panted.

Hollowell freed her Maglite from her utility belt and investigated the opening. She then passed her flashlight to Beck and told him to give her some room. She waited for him to take two steps back before she reached into the hole.

Hollowell was younger and stronger than Beck, and when she bore down on the lever, it gave way with a nails-on-chalkboard shriek. Rambo barked in protest until Hollowell silenced him with a command.

As Beck, Nora, and Hollowell held their collective breaths, the bookcase seemed to let out a sigh. Then Nora felt a stirring of air against the back of her hand.

"Now what?" Beck examined the bookcase with feverish intensity. "Should we try pulling it away from the wall?"

Nora didn't think that was the answer because the floor under their feet had no track marks, but she grabbed the lever and pulled as hard as she could. Hollowell pulled from her side, and Beck gripped the center shelf and leaned backward, using his body weight to increase his power.

Nothing happened.

Nora said, "We used ten toes to push. Maybe we're supposed to push with ten fingers too."

Beck and Nora planted their palms against the bookcase and shoved. The wood groaned. Metal scraped against metal behind the wall. And the bookcase moved.

At first, it sank into the wall by several scant inches. Then those inches widened to a foot.

A frame of darkness now outlined the case, and Nora could see grooves in a stone floor.

"The bookcase is on wheels," she whispered.

Long ago, two little girls had been able to move the entire bookcase. Back then, the mechanisms were new and undoubtedly well oiled. Left to the ravages of time, they didn't function as they should, and though three adults gave it their all, the bookcase was stuck.

Beck put his hands on his knees and glared at the floor as his chest ballooned in and out. "So. Damn. Close."

Rambo stuck his head into the black void behind the wall.

"What do you see, Rambo?" asked Hollowell.

The dog barked. The sound bounced around the space directly behind Nora's hands. Her Nancy Drew fantasies resurfaced, and she pictured an entire room filled with cases of tiny books.

"Another few inches and we'll be able to see what's there. Can we try again?" Beck pleaded.

Once more, they pushed with all their might.

The bookcase moaned. The wheels screeched. The opening widened inch by excruciating inch.

"I can squeeze through!" Beck shouted before disappearing into the darkness.

Before Hollowell could say a word, Nora slipped around the corner of the bookcase. Holding her phone out to light her way, she shuffled toward the outline of Beck's body.

As her eyes adjusted to the gloom, she could make out another shape.

A house.

A Southern Gothic house, with a pointed roof, multiple chimneys, and a wide front porch.

Wynter House.

"It's a dollhouse," said Beck. "Our miserable house in miniature."

Ignoring him, Nora unfastened the hooks attaching the sides of the house to the front panel. The house opened its arms as if offering an embrace. Nora saw the dining room, the central hallway, and the front parlor. On the second floor were two bedrooms and a bathroom. When Nora released the hooks on the back of the dollhouse, more rooms were revealed. There was the kitchen, the clock room, more bedrooms, and baths. And the library. The beautiful, beautiful library.

Tears swam in Nora's eyes.

I found it, Lucille.

I found the little lost library.

Chapter 18

Words accumulate indoors, trapped by walls and ceilings.

—Diane Setterfield

The dollhouse library was an exact replica of the library in Wynter House, only the miniature version of the old mansion was much better preserved.

Nora couldn't take her eyes off the little library. She stared at the desk under the window, the standing globe, and the upholstered chairs and settee. Turning to Beck, she pointed at one of the bookcases. "May I?"

"Go ahead."

Nora removed her dirty gloves and pulled a random book from the shelf. The diminutive volume wasn't much bigger than a penny. Beck kept his flashlight trained on her hands while she squinted at the gilt letters on the cobalt-blue cloth cover.

"'Bijou Illustrations of the Holy Land,'" she read the title aloud.

Beck eyed the book hungrily. "Is it valuable?"

Opening the book, Nora showed him the engravings of various holy sites. "I don't know, but it's in great condition."

"Can you look it up while I see if there's anything else hidden in this space?"

Reluctantly Nora shelved the tiny book and picked up her phone. To her surprise, she found a similar copy of the miniature book right away.

"Beck. A similar copy sold two years ago for five hundred dollars. Since yours is in better condition, you'd probably get closer to six hundred."

Having found nothing else of interest in the small space behind the dollhouse, Beck returned to Nora's side.

"I thought we'd find the money here, but maybe Harper was right. There is no money. Maybe my grandpa spent it. Or Mom. Clem never found it, and he had years to look." Beck hung his head. "We're going to end up with nothing."

"That's not true," Nora gently argued. "If every book in this little library is worth five hundred dollars, then you're looking at quite a windfall."

Behind them, in the real library, Rambo began to bark.

"A car just pulled in," Hollowell announced. "I'm going to see who it is."

It's McCabe was Nora's panicked thought. But when she glanced at her watch, she saw that it wasn't even nine. McCabe should still be dozing in his recliner, and Nora was too fixated on the dollhouse library to care who else might be visiting at such a late hour.

"Is this where all the money went?" Beck glared at the dollhouse.

He obviously didn't view it in the same light as Nora. To her, the dollhouse was a marvel of artistry and engineering. It was so much more than a model house. It was a time capsule and a repository of secrets. It was a museum-caliber work of art. From the stained-glass window next to the front door, to the carved porch railing, to the hundreds of roof shingles, the miniature Wynter House was unlike any doll-house Nora had ever seen. The handmade furniture, paint-ings, textiles, and decorative accessories were remarkably detailed.

What a labor of love this is.

She peered into the other rooms, taking in the furniture, rugs, wallpaper, and tiny objects. For the first time, she saw the Wynter House Lucille had known. The house of her childhood—the house where she lived with her parents and her sister—was a place of elegance and beauty.

Then Lucille's parents died, and she married Frederick. After that, everything changed.

As Nora stared at the dollhouse bathtub, she knew that the body destroyed by lye must be Frederick's. Those bones were the reason Lucille never left Wynter House. This secret kept her prisoner. Guilt and fear were her jailers.

Beck picked up the miniature printing press from the doll-house basement and cranked the handle. When the rollers turned, Nora pictured fresh ink making tiny words on a tiny piece of paper.

Hugo Wynter had loved paper. He'd loved the combina-tion of paper and words. He and his wife had made books together, and together they'd written and illustrated a book for their daughters. Nora had no idea if Hugo had embez-zled money from the paper mill or not. She could only judge him by what Lucille had told her and by the objects he'd left behind, and based on this evidence, he seemed like a man who cherished his family and did everything he could to build a comfortable life for them.

Studying Beck's glum expression, she said, "I know this isn't what you were looking for, but this dollhouse is a prize. I wish I had time to examine every book in this little library so I could show you what a find this is. Beck, there are tons of miniature book collectors out there. You might be able to sell this entire collection at auction without breaking it up."

Hope rekindled in Beck's eyes. "I've spent my whole life just scraping by. I'm fifty-six, and I haven't done anything or gone anywhere. I have a job and an apartment, but no *life*. No romance. No excitement. Nothing. I can't go back to that existence. I just can't."

Nora put a hand on his arm. "Things will get better. You've been through so much in the past few days. After the house cleanup is done and your mom's things are sold, you can have a fresh start. Same goes for Harper."

"Oh, God! I have to call Harper." Beck reached out and clutched Nora's hand. "I want to give my sister some good news, so could you stay a little longer? Please? Maybe you could take the books into the kitchen? See what they're worth?"

Nora couldn't think of anything she'd rather do. "Sure."

"Thank you. I didn't expect to come back to this town and make a friend, but I have."

For a moment, Nora thought he might try to kiss her, so she gave his hand a brief squeeze and stepped away. "I'll get a clean pair of gloves and look for a box to hold these bookshelves."

Slipping out through the narrow opening into the library, she felt a strange mixture of satisfaction and grief.

On one hand, she'd completed the scavenger hunt. Even though she didn't find the clue behind the bathroom mirror, or the clue hidden in the garden, she'd found the little lost library, and it was just as magical as she'd dreamed it would be.

And yet her discovery also spelled its doom. The little library would be removed from the dollhouse, dismantled, and sold, book by precious book, to collectors all over the world.

"Someone will cherish these books the way they were meant to be cherished," she murmured resolutely to herself. "No book should sit on a shelf in the dark. Those words will finally see the light of day. It's a good thing."

Is this why Lucille had given *The Little Lost Library* to her? Because she wanted Nora to find a home for her books? The ones her parents had collected, along with the miniature books in her dollhouse? If so, why send her on a wild-goose chase? Why not just tell her where they were and be done with it?

In the kitchen, she lined an empty rubber bin with paper towels. Then she stepped out to the boot room to get a new pair of gloves.

For a moment, she saw Lucille in her chair, holding a Lorna Doone in one hand and a porcelain teacup in the other. The image was so vivid that Nora's heart knotted with grief.

Of course, you're still here. You're still tied to this house and to its secrets.

From somewhere in the yard, Rambo let out a single bark. Nora turned toward the sound, and when she looked back to where Lucille's chair had once been, nothing was there.

She returned to the library to find Beck taking photos of the dollhouse. The bright flash of his camera repeatedly illuminated the darkness behind the bookcase.

"I have a bin," Nora called.

Beck pushed his way through the opening and held out his phone. "I thought I should make a photographic inventory before you leave with the books. I trust you completely, but it just seemed like the smart thing to do." He glanced over her shoulder. "Is Harper here?"

"She hadn't come inside yet."

Beck rolled his eyes. "I'm dying to show this to her, and she's probably out in the driveway, fawning over Rambo.

She has two German shepherds back in Dallas. She keeps calling the kennel to see how they're doing."

Tucking the box under her arm, Nora said, "Should I wait until she sees the dollhouse before moving any of the books?"

"You know how she feels about books. I'm sure she'd rather see the house without them." He waved at the little library. "I'll find out what's keeping her."

Nora squeezed behind the bookcase, the rubber bin trailing after her. Balancing the bin on the edge of the table holding the dollhouse, she took a long moment to drink in the details of each room again. Then she snapped a few images with her phone and sent them to McCabe, along with the text **Guess what? We found the library! All is well. Be home by ten**.

She hoped he wouldn't hear the incoming text alert chime. She hoped he'd go right on sleeping until she tiptoed into the house and covered him with a blanket. She hoped he wouldn't wake up while she stayed up well past midnight, researching a priceless collection of miniature books.

Pocketing her phone, she took hold of the first set of bookcases and gave them a hesitant pull. Though she was eager to examine the books, she wasn't willing to damage the dollhouse or its furniture.

When the bookcases didn't yield, Nora assumed they'd either been nailed or glued to the wall.

"What now?" she mumbled.

She already knew the answer. She had to wait for Beck and Harper. They had to decide if they wanted her to remove the books, one by one, or remove the bookcases by force.

In the meantime, she took more photographs of the dollhouse. She shot a short video as well, knowing her friends would want to see every detail.

As she zoomed the camera in to capture the Delft tiles surrounding the fireplace in the front parlor, she couldn't help but wonder if Hugo had created secret nooks in this version of Wynter House too. However, when she wiggled the tile with the ship, it didn't budge. The trunk in the attic was empty, the clock in the office didn't have a pearl button, and the newel post of the stairs was solid. She didn't bother trying to twist the frame around the stained-glass window, as she didn't want to damage the delicate glass.

She was about to pull out another book, just to read the title, when she was struck by a thought. She gripped the edges of the bookcase that was the tiny twin of the bookcase directly behind her and pulled. It separated from the wall with ease.

Nora glanced from the piece of furniture cradled in her hand to the shallow nook carved into the interior wall. An envelope no bigger than a domino tile filled the space.

The ghost tingle in Nora's pinkie started up again, but nothing could stop her from reaching for that envelope.

It wasn't sealed, so she eased the letter from the envelope, unfolded it, and tried to read the cursive writing. But in the dim light, the minuscule words looked like ants marching across the page.

Luckily, her phone camera was able to focus on the tiny words. Nora took photos of both front and back before reading the letter's contents:

> *My name is Lynette Shirley Wynter. I leave this letter in the care of my sister, Lucille, to give to my son, John Steinbeck, when the time is right.*
>
> *John, my darling boy, I loved you from the moment I knew of your existence. At the time*

of your conception, I was an unmarried school-teacher. I could not claim you as my own. But you were my whole world.

Your father is Frederick Vandercamp. I am your mother. One night, when my sister was in the first stage of pregnancy and suffering terribly from morning sickness, Frederick got very drunk and took me by force.

When I, too, became pregnant, I hid it for as long as possible—for how could I explain my circumstance? One night, in the middle of a January blizzard, Lucille went into labor. As the roads were impassable, Frederick and I had to deliver her child. He was born with the cord wrapped around his neck, blue and lifeless. My sister was inconsolable with grief. Frederick buried his son in the garden, under the statue of the angel, and threatened to kill my sister and me, should we ever speak of what happened. Even then, he meant to replace the child he'd lost with the one
I was carrying. This is exactly what he did.

You were also born at Wynter House, sweet John. Frederick hired a doctor who knew nothing of our family and told him that I was his wife. After your birth, Frederick hired a wet nurse to take care of you and refused to let me near. I tried everything I could to get close to you until Frederick grew tired of me and locked me in my room.

Lucille couldn't help me. The loss of her son had broken her spirit. When the wet nurse brought meals to my room, she told me how

Lucille wouldn't leave her bed. She wasn't speaking and was barely eating.

One day, Frederick decided my presence was inhibiting my sister's recovery. He told me to leave and never return, saying he'd kill me if I did. He gave me money from a large sum of cash hidden in my father's old desk. Here was the money stolen from the mill! The thief was not my father, but Frederick!

I agreed to leave, but I'd never abandon you, John. I stayed away for one night and have now snuck back into the house. I write this letter from my hiding place in the dollhouse cupboard. Frederick is in the parlor, drinking himself into a stupor. As soon as he blacks out, I will make sure he never wakes again.

Though I fear for my life, I must rescue you and my sister. As long as we three are together, there is hope. If I fail, know that I am—
Always,
Your Loving Mother

Nora had no idea how long she stood next to the dollhouse, staring at the letter. Her chest swelled with emotion until there was no room for air in her lungs. The small space seemed to be closing in on her, and she reached out to touch the wall as if she could push it back. The cool stone felt good against her clammy skin.

Leaning against the wall, she took a breath.

The revelations in the letter were a tangle in her brain, but after a few moments of concentrating only on inhaling and exhaling, thoughts began to separate.

Beck's mother was Lynette Wynter. Lynette was raped by

her sister's husband. Lucille's baby was stillborn. Frederick Vandercamp was a monster. Hugo Wynter never stole money from the mill. Lynette tried to save her sister and her son from Frederick and had clearly failed. What price had she paid?

Nora lowered her head and let out a sob. At last, the source of Lucille's trauma was evident to her.

Frederick Vandercamp.

Nora had no doubt that he'd killed Lynette. And afterward? Had he threatened to do the same to Lucille if she didn't fall in line?

No wonder she cut off contact with the outside world. She had three children to protect. "Oh, Lucille. I am so sorry."

Even after disposing of Frederick, Lucille couldn't leave Wynter House. Crippled by trauma, she'd buried herself in books. She'd built walls of boxes and bags, avoiding human interactions unless strictly necessary. It was understandable why she'd legally changed her children's surnames, wanting to scrub the Vandercamp name from her memory.

"So much pain," Nora whispered.

Wynter House had witnessed so many deaths. Lucille and her baby. Lynette. Clem. And the man in the bathtub, a monster called Frederick Vandercamp.

Nora slowly refolded the note, slid it back into the envelope, and tucked it back inside the wall of the dollhouse library.

Then she called McCabe.

He answered on the third ring. "Are you on your way home?"

Home.

Home was a place of safety. It was a place to dream. A place to make memories. A place where one could build a life. It was the place where people dared to be themselves. Where they gave love and were loved in return.

"Grant. I need you." Nora knew she sounded bereft, but didn't care. "I need you to come here."

McCabe was already moving. "Are you in danger?"

"No, it's nothing like that. It's just . . . I found what Lucille wanted me to find, and it's . . . too much. Can you just come?"

"I'm on my way."

Nora put her phone in her back pocket, tucked the rubber bin under her arm, and sidestepped back into the library.

She emerged to find Harper standing in the middle of the room. She had a flashlight in one hand and a gun in her other. The gun was aimed directly at Nora's chest.

"*You.*" Harper spat the word. "You are *always* here. *Always* sticking your nose where it doesn't belong. You pretend to be *so* sympathetic. *So* understanding and helpful. But I was right about you all along. You're nothing but a thief."

Nora's eyes went wide with fear. "*No!* Beck asked me to come. He knows I'm here."

"I don't care what Beck asked you to do. He's so busy playing nice that he doesn't see what's right in front of his face." Harper took a step toward Nora. Anger rippled off her body. Her eyes were cold sparks of hatred. "*You* have been coming here for *years,* selling books to a hoarder so you could gain access to this house. You've been looking for the money all along, but you lost patience, didn't you? You killed Mom. You killed her and then made sure your friends got the cleanup job. I know you and Bea go way back. Are you going to split the money two ways? Or is it three ways? Is Cricket in on it, too?"

With every question, Harper's voice rose, and she jabbed the gun in the air like a boxer throwing punches.

Nora searched for something to say to tamp down Harper's fury, but terror made her mute. Her eyes followed the black maw at the end of the gun, and all she could think about was the bullet waiting in the chamber. It was such a small thing to have so much power. If Harper applied pressure with a single finger, Nora's life would be over.

Say something! screamed a voice inside her head. And suddenly the words were there.

"I would never hurt your mom! And I never wanted to steal from her or from you! Beck asked me to help him find the lost library, and we did. The tiny books—they're worth a lot of money. You can—"

"LIAR!" Harper shrieked.

Beck appeared in the doorway. He stared into the room, his eyes bulging, and it felt like an eternity before he shouted his sister's name.

"HARPER! What the hell are you doing? Put that damn thing away!"

Harper jerked her head in refusal. "She's after our money. She—"

"I know why your mother started hoarding!" Nora cut in. "Lynette left a letter in the dollhouse. It was in the wall behind the bookcase." She shot a desperate glance at Beck. "She wrote it for you."

Beck crossed the room until he was standing in front of Nora. "I mean it, Harper. Put that damn thing away before you get arrested. Why do you even have a gun?"

"I'm a Texan. We like to defend ourselves and our property." She lowered the gun to her side, but kept her finger on the trigger. "Too much shit has gone down in this house to walk around unarmed."

With Beck shielding her, Nora felt a measure of safety. Peering around Beck's shoulder, she said, "Horrible things have been happening here since before you were born. It's all in the letter."

Beck advanced toward Harper. "I want to know what it says, but I can't get it while you're on the other side of the bookcase with a loaded gun. Will you please put it away so I can show you what's behind that wall?"

Harper hesitated a long moment before saying, "Fine, but I'm leaving the safety off. If she tries anything, she's going down." Harper slid the gun inside her crossbody bag and glared at Nora. "Go get the letter. I'm not going back there until I know you're telling the truth."

Nora returned the glare. "If Hollowell sees you—wait, where *is* Hollowell?"

"She's chasing a nonexistent intruder in the cemetery. The cops in this town are absolute morons. How many Wynters have to die before they make an arrest?"

Beck turned to Nora. "I won't let anything happen to you. I promise. Please get the letter."

Nora stared at him for a long moment before relenting.

The moment she was out of sight, she sent a text to McCabe. Only when she saw that it had been read did she retrieve Lynette's letter from the dollhouse.

She returned to the library to find Beck and Harper exactly as she'd left them. Holding the letter out to Beck, she said, "You should read this before you share it with anyone."

Harper's hand moved toward her bag. "Listen, you little—"

"Stop!" Beck thundered. "Can you just stop for two minutes?"

Without waiting for Harper's reply, Beck opened the envelope, unfolded the letter, and began to read. Nora watched the range of emotions flash over his face. By the time he reached the end, his skin was covered in red blotches, and his lips were trembling.

"Beck," Harper whispered. "What does it say?"

Tears streamed down Beck's cheeks as he arched his neck and let out a howl of despair. His eyes were wild as he crumpled the letter and threw it to the floor.

In three steps, he moved to his sister's side and grabbed

her by the elbow. "You were right. The letter is a trick."
Pointing at Nora, he croaked, "*She* murdered our mom. *She*
killed Clem. They're gone because of *her*. The money's gone
because of *her.* Our lives are ruined because of *her*!"

Whipping the revolver out of her bag, Harper hissed at
Nora, "Good thing you like this house so much. Because
you're gonna die here."

Chapter 19

Now I know what a ghost is. Unfinished business,
that's what.

—Salman Rushdie

Nora was shaking all over. Her hands shook. Her teeth
chattered. When she spoke, her trembling voice made her
sound like a liar. "*No!* I did *not* kill your mom! I would
never hurt her!"

Though Harper's eyes were hard as flint, she hesitated.

Seeing this, Beck gestured feverishly at his sister. "Harper! Do it now, before Hollowell and her dog come back!
We'll tell the cops we caught her trying to steal the books,
and when we confronted her, she attacked you. It'll be self-
defense, plain and simple. But if you wait, she'll get away
with killing Mom and Clem. Do you think her sheriff
boyfriend will ever convict her? If we want justice, this is the
only way!"

Nora dragged her gaze from the gun barrel to Beck's face.
"It was *you*. You killed Lucille. But why? Did you know she
wasn't your birth mother?"

Stunned, Harper looked at her brother. "What the hell is
she talking about?"

"She'll say anything to save her skin! She's been after
Mom's money for *years*."

"There isn't any money!" cried Nora. How she wished she'd kept her promise to McCabe and moved the pepper spray from her purse to her pocket, but in her eagerness to find the lost library, she'd left it where it was. She was defenseless and had only herself to blame.

Harper narrowed her eyes like a cat sizing up a wounded bird. "What?"

"The treasure you've been looking for is in this room! There must be two hundred grand's worth of books here." Nora knew that if she didn't say the right thing right now, she might never have the chance to speak again. "Read the letter, Harper. Before you commit a crime that will send you to prison for the rest of your life, read the letter."

Panicking, Beck lunged for the letter, but Harper was quicker. She scooped it off the floor and thrust it at Nora. "Read it to me."

Beck howled, "*No!* Just shoot her, Harp!"

Ignoring her brother, Harper jerked her gun in a "hurry up" gesture. Nora uncrumpled the paper and began to read.

The letter felt like a shield. With every sentence, Nora's voice became steadier. She thought Beck might run, but the words seemed to pin him like an insect on a spreading board.

By the time she reached the end, he'd sunk to his knees.

As silence swept over the room, he seemed to shrink. He dropped from his knees to his rear, pulling his legs in close and wrapping his arms around them. His chin fell to his chest, and his shoulders curled inward until he looked more egg than man.

Harper lowered her gun. She stared at her brother, her face a mask of confusion and shock, but didn't make a sound.

This was the scene Sheriff McCabe encountered when he entered the library. His weapon was drawn, and he announced himself with all the authority of his office.

"Drop your weapon!" he boomed.

Seeing McCabe in the doorway, with Hollowell right beside him, her hand holding Rambo by the collar to keep him from rocketing into the room, Harper let her gun clatter to the floor.

"Hands where I can see them! You too!" McCabe shouted at Beck.

Neither sibling offered any resistance. In no time at all, Harper and Beck were in restraints, and Nora was in McCabe's arms.

"You're late," she murmured into his shoulder.

"I know," he whispered, tightening the lasso of his arms. "Hollowell flagged me down outside the cemetery. Thank God, you're okay."

Hollowell walked Beck out of the room and then returned for Harper. McCabe bagged Lynette's letter and Harper's gun. More deputies arrived, and the Wynter siblings were carted off to the station. McCabe and Nora were the last to leave Wynter House.

"It's going to be another long night," he told her as they drove to the station. "The last one for a while, I hope."

Nora gave her statement to Fuentes while McCabe and Hollowell interviewed Beck.

After answering all of Fuentes's questions, Nora sat in the conference room and sipped hot chocolate from one of McCabe's mugs. Though she was free to leave, she wasn't ready yet. She just wanted to sit and think for a moment.

And what she thought about was Frederick Vandercamp. He was only one man, but his actions had created a legacy of deceit and dysfunction. He'd been responsible for the ruination of an entire family and, in the end, had become one of many ghosts haunting the rooms of Wynter House.

Fuentes poked his head in the room and asked if she wanted to press charges against Harper Wynter.

"No," Nora said.

Fuentes arched his brows in surprise. "You sure?"

Nora didn't like Harper. She hadn't liked her from the moment they'd met. The woman had been unforgivably rude. She'd accused her of doing terrible things. She'd pointed a loaded gun at her and come very close to using it. And yet, Nora pitied her.

"She's been through enough."

"Okay. We'll cut her loose."

Fuentes left and Nora sat there until the hot chocolate was gone. After all that had happened that night, she expected to feel a huge measure of relief or sorrow.

Instead, she felt hollow. Tired and hollow.

"Things are always better in the morning," a voice inside her head whispered. The words were familiar. And there was comfort in their familiarity. As Nora walked out of the station under a river of stars and a bright hunter's moon, she remembered the source of the book quote and had to smile just a little. The words were from *To Kill a Mockingbird*. By Harper Lee.

Nora woke the following morning to find a fully clothed McCabe in bed beside her.

Wanting to safeguard his sleep, she gathered her clothes and toiletries and showered in the guest bedroom. Then she fed the cats, made a pot of coffee, and carried her cup outside. Sitting on the front steps, she breathed in the mountain air. The light was gentle. It slanted through the trees, painting shadows on the pine needles and brown leaves. In McCabe's front yard, the dogwoods and Japanese maples were putting on coats of gold and scarlet. Squirrels raced across the grass, and a cloud of sparrows danced overhead, bound for places where it never snowed.

The coffee worked its magic, and by the time her cup was empty, Nora was ready to face the day.

Though she felt surprisingly rested as she drove to Miracle Books, she kept searching her feelings for signs that she wasn't okay. It was like prodding a canker sore with her tongue. She couldn't stop poking at the tender place, which was the thought of Lucille living with a monster of a man and raising her sister's son as her own.

Beck hadn't known that Lynette was his birth mother. Nor had he understood why his adoptive mother had been so unstable. Like any child, he'd wanted love and affection. He'd wanted to be cared for and cherished, but Lucille had been too traumatized to give him or his half siblings what they needed.

As a result, he and his siblings had drifted through their childhoods like leaves in a fast-moving river, only to become bitter, disillusioned, and angry adults.

Nora felt sorry for Beck, but she couldn't forgive him for resorting to violence when Lucille couldn't give him what he wanted most. She couldn't forgive him for wrapping his hands around Lucille's neck or injecting a lethal dose of drugs into Clem's veins.

Unlocking the delivery door, Nora entered Miracle Books. She walked to the Children's Corner, sat down on the alphabet rug, and stared at the fall-themed waterfall display Sheldon had created before Lucille's death. The bright colors of the covers, the sweet titles, and the wholesome stories called to her.

Drawn to a picture book called *The Very Last Leaf,* Nora read the story of Lance Cottonwood, a leaf at the top of his class. Unfortunately for Lance, his final exam required that he fall, and he was afraid of falling.

Nora was instantly invested in Lance's plight. His anxiety

was presented in a way that children could recognize, and when he decided to face his fears and fall, Nora felt strangely moved. By the last page, she was smiling.

This was the medicinal quality of books. With all she'd been through as of late, a simple story about a leaf had whisked her away to a world of color, humor, and hope. It had reminded her that it was okay to be afraid. It also reminded her that she could call upon her reserves of courage and grit. She could feel sad and angry and mournful over the tragic fate of one family, but she didn't have to succumb to those feelings completely.

Here, in her bookstore, she was strong.

Here, surrounded by the stories she loved and all those she'd yet to fall in love with, there was hope.

And so she turned on the lights, brewed coffee, and selected a music playlist titled "Gilmore Girls Autumn."

She opened boxes from eight different publishers and loaded wheeled carts with new releases and popular titles that continued to sell out, month after month.

It was impossible to fill all the holes on the shelves. People had been buying so robustly that her inventory was at an all-time low. The front display table was practically bare, and as she stood over it, making notes on titles she needed to reorder right away, Sheldon arrived.

"*Mi amor?*" he called. "Where are you?"

"Checkout counter," she called back.

Sheldon rounded the corner of the fiction section, followed by Hester and June.

"Estella would've come, but she doesn't know what went down last night," Hester said. "I only know because Jasper called me."

June slipped an arm around Nora's waist. "How you doing, girl?"

Nora leaned into her friend. "I'm okay."

"Wanna talk about it?" asked Sheldon.

Nora thought of all the work she needed to do. She glanced at the disheveled display tables and the cart full of books and almost said no, but then she pictured herself sitting in the Readers' Circle with her friends—her found family—and said yes, instead.

Sheldon distributed mugs of coffee and loaded small plates with Hester's Autumn Spice scones. In between sips of strong, rich coffee and bites of scone that tasted like cinnamon-glazed spice cake, Nora told them everything.

Her friends responded with shock, horror, and sympathy. They asked questions and offered comfort. They exchanged theories as to what would become of Beck, Wynter House, and the contents of the little lost library.

"I'm sure everything will be sold," said Nora. "Harper will probably use the money to revive her interior design business and Beck will spend his half on attorneys."

"At least there won't be a trial. He made a full confession last night. He's tucked away in a nice, cozy jail cell until the plea bargain gets ironed out. After that, he'll be sentenced and transferred to a nice, cozy prison cell." Seeing Nora's look of surprise, Hester said, "Didn't McCabe tell you?"

"He was dead to the world when I left the house this morning. But if Jasper told you, does that mean you two are okay?"

Hester nodded. "Yeah, we're okay. We're not together anymore, but we're okay. We really are. Separating feels like the right thing for both of us right now. We care about each other, and that'll never change, which is why he called me. He wanted me to know that you were safe and could use a dose of sugar and a friendly face or two this morning."

Sheldon said, "Good man."

"That he is," agreed Hester.

Nora studied her friend. She didn't look like she'd spent the night grieving the loss of her relationship. She looked like a woman at peace with herself and the world, and this allowed Nora to shift the conversation back to Beck. "What exactly did he confess to?"

Hester counted off his transgressions on her fingers. "Murdering his mama. His brother. Paying the Red Wolves to torch your house and the trees in front of Wynter House."

Nora was floored by the latter two revelations. "Was he trying to kill me?"

"He swears that he wasn't. The Molotov cocktail was meant for your truck. He wanted you and everyone else to assume the Wolves murdered Lucille and, later, Clem."

"But my truck wasn't here because I was at McCabe's, so—"

June threw her hands in the air. "They set fire to your house, instead! Not the brightest bulbs in the bunch, are they?"

"I hope Beck names names," said Sheldon. "Then all those boys can hang out together in jail. Start a crochet club or a book group."

Ignoring his snide tone, Hester said, "That's not a bad idea. Readers have more empathy than nonreaders. Anyway, I know there are at least two Red Wolves in custody."

Nora glanced at June, who was strumming the raised stitching on the JUST ONE MORE CHAPTER throw pillow on her lap.

Following Nora's gaze, Sheldon said, "What are you thinking about, Mama?"

"I try not to hate," said June. "I try to find the good in people. But these Wolves, and the thousands of other scumbags like them, prey on weak people. They take advantage of their pain and lead them down dark and lonely roads. I think of how Tyson almost lost his life to drugs and I want these lowlifes to pay for what they've done."

In a hushed voice, Sheldon asked, "You want God's wrath-style justice? Like the scene from *Raiders of the Lost Ark* when they open the Ark and people's faces melt?"

"I'd prefer a come-to-Jesus moment. If they came out of prison and helped the folks they once tried to hurt, that'd be enough for me."

Nora pictured Beck as she'd last seen him. On his knees, his head bowed like a penitent. He'd been crushed by guilt. Shrunken and hollow.

"Was it all about money?" she asked Hester.

"I guess. Beck thought his mom was hiding cash stolen from the mill, including coins that would be pretty valuable today. Buffalo nickels, mercury dimes, silver dollars, and some special penny from 1930."

"Sounds like wishful thinking. If I wanted to hide stolen money, it'd be in cash. Or maybe a gold bar," said Sheldon.

Hester shrugged. "Beck's granddaddy had a small coin collection. Beck remembers looking at it when he was a boy, but Clem told him that he already sold all the coins. Sounds like he sold anything he could get his hands on. Didn't give a penny to his mama either."

"He was angry at her—they all were," Nora said softly. "They wanted so much more than she was capable of giving. That family needed help, and they didn't get it. They needed friendship, counseling, prayer—all of the above. This community failed them."

"You're right," said June. "But you did more than most. You visited Lucille. You collected food and clothes and brought them to her. You gave her your time and your attention."

Nora's cheeks burned with shame. "I didn't do nearly enough."

Sheldon emerged from the ticket agent's booth carrying a fresh latte for Nora and a second cappuccino for Hester. He placed the mugs on the coffee table a little too roughly, causing foamed milk to crest over the rim like a storm wave and dribble down the side of the mugs. Standing tall, he put his hands on his hips and glowered at Nora.

"Stop beating yourself up, woman!" he barked. "You can't change the past, and even if you could, you couldn't fix all that was broken in Lucille's life. How about asking yourself this: Is there anything you can do now? Any action you can take to help her or her children?"

Nora seized on his question. She'd rather take some kind of action than sit around, feeling mopey and regretful.

"There's the books," she began.

"What about them?" pressed Sheldon.

In her mind's eye, Nora saw the library at Wynter House. There were hundreds and hundreds of rare and valuable books in that room and in the secret room behind the bookcase.

"They're beyond the scope of Bea's cousin," she said. "They need to be appraised, cataloged, and sold by a premier auction house."

Hester passed her hands over her face. "I'm getting serious déjà vu right now. It feels like we've had the same conversation, but back then, you were telling us about the collection Tucker's grandma left him."

Nora smiled as she always did at the mention of Tucker's name. The ten-year-old boy who'd lost his mother several months ago was a regular visitor to Miracle Books. He lived with his aunt and uncle, the owners of Tea Flowers, and had inherited his grandmother's book collection. That collection was being sold in Sotheby's upcoming book and manuscript auction. The proceeds, which were destined for Tucker's educational fund, were estimated to be in the high six figures.

Harper was a grown woman, but she and Tucker had both lost loved ones to violence. Harper's losses didn't stop there. She also had to say goodbye to her brothers. One would be buried, while the other was destined for prison. She didn't have a loving aunt and uncle to take care of her. If she had close friends, they were far away. Harper was all alone.

How could this broken woman manage the Herculean tasks awaiting her? How could she bury her mother and brother, oversee the removal and sale of items from her childhood home, and make hundreds of decisions while turned inside out by grief?

She can't. She needs help.

Glancing at her friends, Nora thought about a line from the book she was currently reading. In the latest installment of Alexander McCall Smith's series about a Botswanan amateur sleuth named Precious Ramotswe, a client told Precious a sad tale, to which Precious responded, "I'm sorry, my sister."

The sincerity and compassion in this simple phrase warmed Nora's heart. As a bookseller and amateur bibliotherapist, she'd heard her fair share of difficult stories, and there were so many times when she wished she could offer comfort with a phrase similar to Precious Ramotswe's.

She couldn't imagine putting a hand on Harper's arm and saying, "I'm sorry, my sister." However, she could speak with the same sincerity and compassion. She could offer help and support her. She could be what June, Hester, and Estella were to her. A sister.

For the rest of the morning, she was energized by this idea.

During her lunch break, she looked up the few miniature books she remembered seeing in the dollhouse library. They were all quite valuable, which reaffirmed Nora's belief that the entire collection should be handled by one of the major auction houses.

Steeling herself, she called Bea.

"I was just about to call you," said Bea. "Someone from the sheriff's department was on the horn with Cricket bright and early. They told her no one could go in the house today, but asked her to come over and take down all her tents. Do you know why? They wouldn't tell her a damn thing."

Nora went very still.

"You there?" Bea asked after the silence went on a beat too long.

"Yeah, I'm here. There's a body buried in the garden. It's a very sad story."

Bea let out a sigh. "Okay, let's hear it."

Nora told Bea about Lynette's letter. After answering as many of Bea's questions as she could, she described the rest of last night's events. When she was done, she added, "Which leads me to the reason I called. We need to talk about what's best for Harper."

Bea, who was a salt-of-the-earth woman with a generous heart, immediately agreed that the best books should go to Sotheby's.

"Reach out to the folks in New York today. I'll handle things with my people," she said. "And Nora? I'm real sorry I called the woman a harpy. My granny used to say that folks who held on to anger like a mule chewing a mouthful of bumblebees were folks who needed grace most. I forget that sometimes."

A grin tugged the corners of Nora's mouth upward. "You need to print T-shirts with your granny's sayings. You'd make a fortune."

Bea snorted. "I'll add it to my list. If I don't see you before Sunday, come straight to my booth. My brother just got his hands on a whole collection you're gonna want to see."

"My shelves are bare, so that's music to my ears. What's the collection?"

"Bookends. Over a hundred pairs. Ceramic, brass, cast iron, wood. Animals, globes, buildings, ships—you name it."

Knowing what Sheldon would say at this moment, Nora asked Bea to give her a price on the whole collection. "You don't need to tell me now. Let's save the haggling for Sunday."

She'd just ended the call when a teenage boy approached the checkout counter.

Nora recognized his lean frame, raven-black hair, and round spectacles. She'd seen him lounging near the YA section before, but she didn't think he'd ever bought a book from her. Noting his flushed cheeks and the way he picked at a torn cuticle on his left hand, she suddenly knew what he was about to tell her.

"Um, hello," he began nervously. "My name's Charlie Kim. I'm, um, Mr. Vega told me to talk to you. He said you might—that I might be able to work here."

Nora gestured at the HELP WANTED sign in the window. "Have you filled out an application?"

Charlie lowered his voice to a nearly inaudible whisper. "I was hoping I could work to, um, pay you back. For the books."

He seemed unwilling to elaborate, but Nora wasn't going to make things easy for him. She wanted to see him squirm a little.

Folding her arms across her chest, she gave him a fierce stare. "What books?"

He glanced around before murmuring, "The ones I stole."

"Ah." Nora nodded. "I see."

A deep flush spread across Charlie's face, but he held Nora's unflinching gaze. "I knew it was wrong," he said. "But I did it, anyway."

"Why those books in particular?"

Charlie's cheeks turned crimson. "There's this girl." He lowered his gaze and spoke so quickly that Nora had trouble understanding him. "She comes here a lot, so I wanted to read the books she was reading. I thought if I could talk to her about them, or, I don't know, *be* more like the guys in those books, she might notice me."

Nora suppressed a smile. "Okay, so you were studying these books to impress a girl. Sounds reasonable to me. But why steal them?"

"I can't afford them, and I couldn't ask my mom for money because she doesn't have extra. It's just her and me and my baby sister." He continued shredding his cuticle. "I've been wanting to get a job since I turned sixteen, but I have to watch my sister after school. And I was never going to keep the books. I was going to bring them back—I swear! It was wrong, and I was stupid, and I'm really sorry."

Softening her expression, Nora asked, "Did the books help you get the girl?"

"No."

The word was infused with misery.

Nora scrutinized the shame-faced young man in front of her. Being a teenager wasn't easy, and being a teenager in love was pure hell. "Look, Charlie, I'd be happy to have the books back, and I'd be happy to consider you for employment. However, it doesn't sound like you're available to work after school."

"I can work Fridays after school and every Saturday. My mom works a half day on Friday, and I don't have class last period, so I could be here at three. If my sister makes the soccer team, I can work other days after school too."

Nora tried to picture Charlie making espressos. Sheldon could teach him how to use the machine, but could he chat with a variety of customers? Or was he too shy?

"Give me a minute to talk to Sheldon."

"Yeah, of course." He waved toward the back of the store. "I brought the books with me. They're by the back door."

Nora nodded. "Great. I'll find an empty cart for you to put them on."

Sheldon was busy with a customer when Nora led Charlie to the delivery door, but he gave her a wink as she passed by. Judging by the twinkle in his eye, he liked Charlie and wanted Nora to give him a chance.

She left Charlie to his task and returned to the ticket agent's booth.

"Do you think he can do what you do?" she asked Sheldon.

"Of course not! No one can reach my level of magnificence, but the boy can aspire to it." His smile turned wistful. "I see so much of my angsty teenage self in him, Nora. A job like this would've been so good for me, and I know it'll be good for Charlie. It's going to be awkward and scary and weird. He's going to make mistakes. Lots of them, but I'm willing to be his Yoda."

Nora shook her head in mock disgust. "You're soft on him because he lost his ever-loving mind over a crush."

"Is there a better reason?" Sheldon challenged. "The kid has a passionate heart. He's sweet, sensitive, and shy. Everyone's going to love him."

"Okay, Yoda. Have him fill out his paperwork."

She left the ticket agent's booth and walked back down the hallway toward the delivery door. Though Charlie was nowhere in sight, Nora spied an empty red Radio Flyer wagon parked next to the book cart.

Moving as quietly as she could, Nora crept up to the stockroom door and peered in.

There was Charlie, standing over an open box of new releases. As she watched, he ran a hand over the vibrant, glossy covers. She saw the smile playing on his lips and the glint of curiosity in his eyes. She saw the respect in his touch. And when he carefully flipped one of the books over to read every word of the back cover blurb, his smile grew, and he nodded as if he and the author shared a secret.

In that instant, Nora knew that he belonged at Miracle Books.

Stepping into the room, she offered him her hand. "Charlie Kim. Welcome to the family."

Chapter 20

Life becomes easier when you learn to accept an apology you never got.

—Robert Brault

It was almost closing time, and Nora was putting away strays when Bea and Cricket entered the bookstore. She didn't see them come in, but heard the sleigh bells jingle and headed to the front to greet her last-minute customers.

"Hello, ladies. What's this?" she asked, noticing the boxes on her checkout counter.

"The miniature library," said Bea.

Cricket patted the counter. "It's all here. Harper was hoping you'd give us a rough estimate of the value. She's willing to pay you for your time."

Nora moved toward the boxes, her fingers itching to open the flaps. "This is a surprise."

"The woman's had the wind knocked out of her," said Bea. "She was like an angry dog before. Barking all the time and snapping at people's heels. Now she's quiet. There's no fight left in her."

"We're hoping that you can give her some good news," added Cricket. "Maybe that'll rouse her a bit."

Nora didn't think she'd see the books from the little library again, and now the entire collection was here in her shop. Not only could she examine each and every book, but she could do so with Harper's blessing. The idea of spending her evening with the little library filled her with delight. Then she immediately felt guilty for experiencing joy in the face of Harper's heartache.

Bea saw the emotional shift in Nora's eyes. "I know what you're thinking. You feel like a vulture, feeding off the dead. But that's not what you're doing. Folks die. They leave things behind for their relatives to deal with. We help the living by packing, sorting, and selling their loved one's things. It's important work. And we love what we do. There's no reason to feel guilty about loving what you do."

"The only way we can help Harper is to deal with the stuff in Wynter House," Cricket said. "The sooner we can finish this job, the sooner she can go back to her life in Dallas. We're hoping to get back in the house tomorrow, but Harper's going to stay at the inn until we're done."

"I'll visit her there, after I've got an estimate for the collection." Nora looked at Cricket. "Did Bea tell you that these books need to be sold by Sotheby's or Christie's?"

"She did. She told Harper the same thing. What about the dollhouse?"

Nora sighed. "I wish it could stay in Miracle Springs. I wish the town would buy Wynter House, turn it into a museum or an art gallery, and put the dollhouse on display. It's a nice fantasy, but I doubt it'll happen. The auction company that sells the miniature books might sell the dollhouse too."

"Could you imagine playing with that as a kid?" asked Bea. "Or having a daddy who could make such a beautiful thing? I wonder how long it's been since that house has seen the light of day?"

The same question had crossed Nora's mind as well. "I

think it's been a long time. I think Lucille hid the clues decades ago—probably after she killed her husband. If something happened to her, the horrible history of the house could be made known as long as someone tried to solve the riddles in *The Little Lost Library.*"

Cricket frowned. "Why not just write a letter?"

"Lucille once told me that ever since she was a little girl, her favorite books included a hero's quest, where the hero had to follow a set of clues or solve difficult problems to discover a long-hidden truth, save the girl, or find a treasure. I think she wanted to create her own hero's quest inside Wynter House because she knew she was never going to leave. She was never going to experience a storybook adventure, so she used the one her father wrote for her and Lynette when they were girls as a way of telling the right person what she'd been through and what she'd done to her husband."

Bea smiled warmly at Nora. "And that person turned out to be you. So, what were the clues?"

"The first one I found was the coffin marked 'mother.' That represented Lynette. There was a beer cask, which probably represented Frederick. A cradle with a blue blanket, which could've stood for John, the child Lucille lost, or both children. The book about sisters was a tribute to Lynette. I didn't find the clue hidden in the garden statue, but McCabe sent me a photo of it. It was a tiny dollhouse."

Cricket whispered, "Could you imagine making all those little pieces of furniture? Hugo Wynter sure loved his daughters. I wonder what kind of things he put in those hiding places for them when they were little. Silly notes? Candy? Jewelry? I guess we'll never know."

"Was there a tiny book with the tiny dollhouse?" asked Bea.

Very quietly Nora said, "Yes. A book of prayer."

The three women reflected on this in silence until a man

holding the hand of a young boy opened the front door. The sleigh bells jingled, and the boy said, "It sounds like Christmas!"

Nora exchanged grins with Cricket and Bea.

The women chatted for a few more minutes before Bea said they needed to get going. "Before I skedaddle, I want you to know that you did right by Lucille in the end. She knew you wouldn't let her down, and you didn't. Despite everything that's happened, that's got to be worth something. Enjoy looking at those little books."

When the store was empty, Nora locked the door and loaded the boxes into the back seat of her truck. Leaves crackled under her feet, and a gust of wind chased more leaves across the parking lot. She glanced at the mountains rising above the town. They were still green, but patches of yellow and orange were spreading across the wooded slopes like spilled paint.

Night was slowly descending, and the streetlamps winked on, casting her tiny house in shadow.

Nora wished she could go inside, pour herself a glass of wine, and kick off her shoes. She wished she could have a bowl of chicken and rice soup and a hunk of Hester's pumpernickel-rye bread for dinner before settling down to examine the miniature books. But she wouldn't be sitting at her own kitchen table anytime soon. Instead, she'd go to McCabe's. She'd feed the cats and order a pizza. When McCabe came home, they'd talk about their day. But until he walked through the front door, all of her concentration would be focused on the contents of the little library.

She needed the magnifying light, tweezers, and other tools from her house, so she unlocked the door and stepped inside.

It no longer smelled like home.

It smelled of smoke, burned wood, and chemicals.

Pausing just inside the door, Nora put her hand on the wall and remembered how she'd bought her caboose and hired a builder to transform it into the cheerful, minimalistic home of her dreams.

The caboose could be transformed again. All it needed was time, love, and money. Like Nora, it had been scarred by fire. Damaged, but not ruined. Like her, it would be forever changed, and change could be good.

As Nora loaded the things she needed into a bag, she thought about the online fundraiser her friends had launched and groaned. She was humbled by all the donations, but she was also reluctant to accept money from her friends, neighbors, and customers.

"You would've done the same thing if it had been my house," June said when Nora had shared her feelings about accepting charity.

Hester had her own take on the subject. "I know you're more comfortable giving than receiving, but people from this community want to support you. They're contributing because they care about you and want to see your house restored. But they're also doing it because Caboose Cottage is a Miracle Springs landmark. Everybody loves it. Everybody refers to it as the house where the book lady lives. Downtown wouldn't be downtown without it. Why not let them preserve a building that makes them happy?"

As Nora locked her door, she wondered if the residents of Miracle Springs might be persuaded to save Wynter House. If not them, perhaps the National Trust.

It couldn't hurt to send them an email.

Nora locked her house and ordered a pizza and a large Greek salad. By the time the delivery person knocked on McCabe's front door, she'd already researched a dozen titles.

When McCabe got home, he marched straight to the refrigerator for a beer. He popped the cap, took a long pull, and loaded two slices of pizza onto a plate.

"Am I allowed in?" he asked, tentatively stepping into the living room.

Smiling, Nora pointed at his chair. "As long as you don't spill your beer, you can stay."

"After the day I've had, this beer isn't gonna last long." He sat down with a sigh. "But I have nothing to complain about. I came home to pizza and you. I love pulling into the driveway and seeing lights through the windows. It's the best thing—having you here at the end of the day."

Nora stretched out her hand and he grasped it.

"How did it go with Beck?"

McCabe picked up a slice of pizza and eyed it longingly. "I'm pretty talked out right now. Why don't you tell me about those bitty books instead?"

"Where to start?" Nora looked down at the books spread out over a sheet of white paper. "I've never seen anything like this collection. It's incredible."

"How so?"

Nora began pointing at books. "This Bible has a sterling-silver cover. This prayer book has a mother-of-pearl cover. This alphabet book has accordion-style pages. This dictionary set comes with a magnifying glass. And look at this cookbook! It's bound in leather, but the cover is a silver plaque stamped with a steaming cauldron. Here's a souvenir book full of tiny photos, and *this* is a fairy tale in the Lilliputian Library series. This one can teach you how to play whist, and this one can teach you how to be a ventriloquist."

"Oh, good. That could be a new interrogation technique," quipped McCabe. "I could carry a ventriloquist dummy into the room. The suspect would be so freaked out, they'd confess right away."

Nora laughed. "That would be terrifying. Anyway, I

won't bore you with the details of every book. All I can say is this collection is going to sell for a boatload of money. Miniature books are highly sought after, and the people who collect them will pay top dollar for the contents of these two boxes."

"How much are we talking about?"

Swiveling her laptop to face him, Nora clicked on a page from an auction house in England. "The contents of this miniature library, which were printed by a Scottish publisher in the late 1800s, were sold as one lot. Want to guess how much it went for?"

"Fifty grand?"

"Multiply that by two."

McCabe whistled. "Are you telling me you've got a hundred grand's worth of itsy-bitsy books on my dining table right now?"

"At least."

McCabe made a show of slowly rising to his feet. Exaggerating his movements, he picked up his plate and bottle and retreated to the kitchen. "I'm going to finish my pizza in here. Then I'm going to take a shower and watch TV. Will that bother you?"

"Not a bit. I only have so much time with these books and want to learn as much as I can about their worth in hopes of bringing Harper some good news tomorrow. I'm going to drop by the Inn of Mist and Roses in the morning."

"I spoke with Patty earlier," McCabe said, referring to one of the inn's proprietors. "Harper hasn't left her room at all today. They brought her breakfast and lunch on a tray, but she didn't touch either meal."

Joining McCabe in the kitchen, Nora poured herself half a glass of wine and opened a fresh beer for McCabe. The two of them leaned against the counter and sipped their beverages in silence.

Eventually McCabe said, "This has to be one of the saddest investigations I've ever seen." Moving closer to Nora, he told her about exhuming the bodies in the garden.

"It's hard to imagine a garden under all those weeds, but we found evidence of a path and several broken statues. Lucille's boy was buried under an angel statue. The dollhouse clue was hidden inside a sphere held by the angel. The remains of a woman were there too. Not two feet away."

"Lynette," Nora whispered.

McCabe nodded. "It'll take time to extract her DNA and compare it to Lucille's. Same goes for the baby. Once that's done, they can be laid to rest together."

Nora put an arm around McCabe's waist. She could feel the weight of the day's events clinging to him. The community may have failed Lucille and her family once, but he wasn't going to let it happen again.

Resting her head on McCabe's shoulder, Nora said, "I wonder what Beck's life would've looked like if Lynette had lived. I'm disgusted with him for what he did to Lucille, but I feel sorry for him too."

"I think he's always been unhappy. He's actually relieved by the thought of a long prison sentence."

Nora raised her head to look at McCabe. "Are you serious?"

"I am. He says he's tired of trying to make his way through a world that never wanted him. He called himself a zombie." McCabe took a sip of beer before continuing. "He thought money was the answer. If he could travel, buy a nice house and car—all that stuff—he thought it would fill the hole inside him. It never dawned on him that he needed to connect to other people to do that. I guess he never learned how to let someone in."

"So, did he just snap one day and decide to confront his mom?"

McCabe seesawed his hand. "His client base was shrinking. It wouldn't be long before he couldn't pay the rent for his apartment or his office space. He'd already sold his car to keep the creditors at bay, but time was running out. Since he had several days with no scheduled appointments, he rented a car and drove down from Cincinnati. He went straight to Wynter House and begged Lucille to give him the money stolen from the mill. When she told him it was long gone, he left. He spent the night at Clem's place and tried again the next day."

"And in between those visits, Lucille wrote me the note and put *The Little Lost Library* in the bag of books she meant for me to take. She was scared of Beck. She must've sensed that his turning up in Miracle Springs wouldn't end well."

McCabe made a noise of agreement and then tossed his empty bottle in the recycling bin.

Nora held up a hand. "Wait. Didn't Beck have an alibi for the day of Lucille's murder?"

"He did. It was solid, but not so solid that I didn't call the authorities in Cincy for help proving it. Unfortunately, we got held up trying to reach two of Beck's clients."

"I'm not following."

"Beck used an answering service to book his appointments because it's much cheaper than hiring someone," McCabe said. "Even though the service handled his bookings, he still had access to the online calendar. It was easy for him to log on and add a few appointments on the day of Lucille's murder. When we called to check his alibi, we didn't realize we were speaking with an answering service. The young woman who answered identified herself as the office manager. According to her, Beck was with a patient when Lucille died. She refused to give us the patient's name because Wynter Chiropractic is a medical practice, and Beck's clients were protected by patient privacy laws."

Nora recalled her first impression of Beck. He'd seemed so humble and kind. Compared to Harper, the man was practically Gandhi. The truth was Nora didn't want him to be the bad guy, but when she thought about her tiny house, she knew that she'd been a fool to accept him at face value.

"He's smart, I'll give him that," she muttered. "He knew it would take you time to see through his alibi, and while you were waiting for judges to sign documents, and the cops in Cincinnati to get back to you, he drew your attention elsewhere by hiring some local lowlifes to throw a Molotov cocktail at my house."

"Exactly," McCabe said. "But it was a mistake. The Red Wolves wanted him to settle Clem's debt, but Beck was tapped out. He needed more time to search for money or other valuables in Wynter House—something he could give to the Wolves. As you can imagine, they didn't want books. However, he did find some jewelry behind the mirror in Lucille's room, which he used to buy enough meth to kill a horse. He left a dose in Clem's apartment and waited for his brother to shoot up. Beck used the rest to finish him off."

Nora remembered how Beck had slumped to his knees in the library. How his remorse had pressed down on him, stiffening his body like a hunk of stone or a piece of petrified wood.

Picturing him this way, Nora could believe that he was ready to accept whatever punishment he was given. He was ready to lose his freedom—to be told what to do and how to do it every hour or every day for the rest of his life.

Once he's in the system, he'll be truly lost. His only tie to the outside world is Harper, and she may never return to North Carolina. There's nothing but bad memories for her here.

"Hey." McCabe smoothed Nora's hair. "Where'd you go?"

She didn't want to dwell on the tragic fate of the Wynter family anymore today. She wanted to look at miniature books until she was too tired to stay awake. After that, she wanted to climb into bed with McCabe and hold him until they both fell asleep.

"I'm right here." She kissed him and then nudged him toward the door. "Go shower. It'll feel good to wash off the day. I'll leave the pizza out in case you want more later, and there's ice cream for dessert."

His eyes gleamed. "Mint chocolate chip?"

"Yep."

He let out a soft sigh of contentment. "It's the little things, you know? The little things that make life better."

Nora knew that too. It was a hot shower, a bowl of ice cream, and a ball game on TV. It was a cat sleeping on the corner of the bed, the golden glow of a lamp, and a warm house. It was knowing that tomorrow was a fresh start. It was an unopened book, waiting to be read.

For now, though, the little library was calling, so Nora washed her hands and got back to work.

The next morning, Nora showed up at the Inn of Mist and Roses and asked the owners if Harper was still in her room.

"She came down for breakfast this morning," said Patty.

"Thank goodness," added her partner, Louisa, who went by Lou. "When I got up today, I just knew I had to make her my famous pumpkin pancakes. She didn't eat much, but it was something. She's out in the garden now, nursing a cup of coffee. I'm sure it's gone cold. Would you bring her a fresh pot?"

Lou loaded a tray with a small carafe of coffee, a pitcher of milk, and a pair of clean mugs. She carried the tray outside and handed it off to Nora.

"Go down the center path and make a left at the sundial. Harper's sitting in a chair just past the bed of Autumn Sunset roses. They're the color of apricots, with a touch of marigold."

Nora headed down the gravel garden path, marveling over the stunning display of flowers. She didn't expect so many roses to be in bloom, but she was surrounded by vibrant shades of pink, red, yellow, and orange.

Passing a lush group of bushes with bright, ruffled, apricot-colored flowers, Nora spotted the curve of Harper's back. She was sitting on a stone garden bench, her hands cradling a coffee cup. For once, she was casually dressed in jeans and a white T-shirt. A dove-gray shawl was draped over her shoulders.

At Nora's approach, she looked up, but didn't speak. Her face was as blank as a painter's canvas. Her gaze was listless.

"Lou thought you could use a fresh coffee."

Nora put the tray down on a little side table and filled one of the two mugs. "Milk?"

Harper dipped her chin in the ghost of a nod.

Nora took Harper's used mug and placed it on the tray. When Harper gripped the new mug, it began to shake. Fearing Harper would be burned by the hot coffee, she quickly covered Harper's hand with her own, steadying the mug.

"It's okay. You've got it." She coaxed Harper into taking a sip of coffee.

"Lace it with arsenic and I'll drink it all," Harper muttered.

Nora patted her pockets. "I'm all out, but I do have some news."

Harper didn't seem to hear. She stared past Nora, her flat eyes fixed on the mist-covered mountains rising over the valley.

"Before I get to that, I wanted to ask you a question," Nora continued as if she had Harper's full attention. "I'm going to rebuild my house and thought I might make some improvements. I could use more storage, for example. And I want new paint colors. I'd like the whole space to feel calmer."

"Are you trying to hire me?" Harper asked.

Hearing the note of astonishment in her voice, Nora pressed on. "I don't know a thing about interior design, but I've seen your website. You do beautiful work. And since you'll be in a position to pump funds into your business pretty soon, you're going to be too busy to help me, which is why I'm asking you now. So, what do you say?"

Harper barked out a laugh. "You can't afford me."

Nora smiled to herself. She wanted to elicit a reaction— any reaction—and she'd succeeded. "Probably not. But maybe you could suggest a color palette before you go back to Dallas. If not, I'll probably just paint the whole interior white."

"It has to be the right white," Harper said. "You don't want one with too many pink or green undertones. You want a chameleon white—a shade that looks just as beautiful at night as it does in bright sunlight." She finally looked at Nora. "What's your news?"

"I spent hours last night researching the collection of books from the dollhouse."

Harper's stare sharpened. "And?"

"The collection is worth well over a hundred grand. I've already put in a call to Sotheby's in New York, and they're interested in selling it for you. I can box up all the books and ship them out today if you want."

"Okay."

Seeing that Harper had finished her coffee, Nora offered her a refill.

Harper shook her head in refusal. "I need to go inside and call the funeral parlor. The sooner I say goodbye to Mom and Clem, the sooner I can leave this place."

"Are you planning on a service?"

"They're being cremated, and I suppose I'll bury their ashes at Wynter House. It seems fitting. After all, they never went anywhere else."

Nora thought about this for a long moment before saying, "What if you could change that for them?"

"What do you mean?"

"I read an article about your grandfather's paper mill. It was a few miles south of Miracle Springs. On the river. You could scatter the ashes there. I can drive you if you want," she added.

Harper got to her feet and pulled her shawl tighter around her shoulders. "Why would you? We're not friends. Never will be. So, why are you here, trying to solve my problems? Don't you have a store to run?"

Harper's prickly demeanor pleased Nora. It meant she still had some fight in her. Her spirit was wounded, but not entirely crushed.

"I'm on my way to work right now. I just wanted to give you something first."

"Is it a book? Because I think I've made it pretty clear that I hate books."

Nora grinned. "You have, but I have a feeling this one will change your mind."

She pulled a gift-wrapped book from her tote bag and placed it on the bench. She then picked up the coffee tray and walked away.

The book she'd given Harper was Kassia St. Clair's *The Secret Lives of Color.* It was divided into chapters based on color and explored the history and social significance of each shade. In the chapter on chrome yellow, Nora had left a scrap of paper that said: *Van Gogh used this color to make his sunflowers. Where could I use it in my house?*

Nora had no idea if Harper would ever answer her question, but it didn't matter. Before she even opened its cover, Harper would see a rainbow of colors on its page edges. Unable to stifle her curiosity, she'd flip to a random page and learn the history of Imperial Yellow or Mountbatten Pink. She'd read about how these shades came to represent different emotions, ideals, and meanings. Even if she only read the Yellow chapter, it would be enough. Inspiration was there, in those pages, waiting for Harper Wynter.

This book, with its polka dots of color on a cloud-white cover, might just stitch some of the tears in Harper's heart together.

It was just a beginning, really, because hers would be a long road to recovery. But the book would be a start. Word by word. Page by page. It would distract and inspire her. It would fill her mind with ideas and permeate her dreams with images. It would fill the cracks in her soul with the light of hope.

This was the magic of books.

As Nora walked past an explosion of yellow roses, their perfume became entangled with the autumn breeze. She inhaled deeply, feeling electrified by the scents and the crispness of the air. Her thoughts turned to the bookshop, and she hastened back to her truck.

There was so much to do. And she couldn't wait to get started.

Chapter 21

One of the best cures for a reluctant reader, after all, is a tale they cannot stop themselves from reading.

— Neil Gaiman

Nora took a step back and once again admired the display of pumpkins in the red wagon directly below the main display window.

The wagon had been Charlie's idea. After seeing an illustration of a pumpkin-filled wagon in a children's book he'd been shelving, he'd offered to wheel his wagon to the farmers' market, load it up with gourds of every size, shape, and color, and park it in front of the store. As soon as this task was done, he went back to the market for hay bales and potted mums, spending the good part of his Saturday morning transforming the bookstore's facade.

When Nora saw the results of his efforts, she'd showered him with praise and bought him a huge sub sandwich for lunch.

Hiring Charlie Kim had been one of the best decisions of her life. Though still somewhat shy with the customers, he was a hard worker and keenly eager to please Nora. He was more relaxed with Sheldon, who joked around with Charlie

until he smiled or let out one of his rare, high-pitched guf-
faws.

Nora had never spent much time with a teenage boy.
Judging them from afar, she'd always assumed they were a
whirlwind of hormones, hunger, and untidiness. Charlie did
have a voracious appetite and devoted the majority of his
headspace to his crush, but he wasn't messy. Quite the opposite, in fact.

Charlie couldn't stand the sight of books lying around on
side tables or reading chairs. And he was always scanning the
shelves for books that had been placed in the wrong section
or out of alphabetical order. Not only did he like order, but
he liked tidiness as well. He dusted, vacuumed, and cleaned
the kitchen and restroom without being asked. He organized the stockroom.

After two weeks on the job, he'd worked up the nerve to
ask Nora for permission to make a few changes to the shop's
social media accounts. Soon he was posting every day.

"You need to keep a record of the time you spend on
those posts so I can add the hours to your paycheck," Nora
told him one Friday afternoon.

Charlie, who'd been unwrapping a chocolate bar the size
of Nora's shoe, paused to say, "You don't need to pay me. I
like taking photos and making videos. And guess what? *She*
likes all of my posts."

Though Charlie had never identified his crush, Nora
knew that her name was Tilly. Tilly had moved to Miracle
Springs in July and spent many a languid summer afternoon
at Miracle Books. She liked iced tea, the color pink, Hello
Kitty, young adult books featuring fierce female protago-
nists, and Greek retellings with a feminist spin. Tilly was
smart, confident, and had no problems making friends. Nora
heard her introduce herself to other kids her age, and it wasn't

long before she started showing up at Miracle Books with two or three other girls.

By October, she'd made it a habit to stop by the bookstore every Friday after school. She was always friendly to Charlie, but he barely spoke in her presence. He blushed and stammered and seemed unable to look her directly in the eye.

He was in the ticket agent's office, helping Sheldon winnow down the line of people waiting for coffee, hot chocolate, and pastries, when Tilly's pretty face appeared in the pass-through window.

"Hey, Charlie," she said, tucking a lock of espresso-brown hair behind her ear, "were you at the farmers' market with the red wagon last Saturday?"

Charlie blushed. "Um. Yeah. I was getting, um—"

"Pumpkins," she said helpfully. "I saw them outside. I took a pic of the wagon and sent it to my mom. She wants to do the same thing on our front porch. You have a really good eye for color."

"Um. Thanks." Charlie stared at a point just past Tilly's shoulder. "Can I get you anything?"

Tilly glanced at the menu board. "I'm not sure. What goes with a story about a Greek queen who's been unfairly vilified for centuries?"

Charlie reached for a rag and wiped a speck of sugar off the counter. "Are you talking about Clytemnestra?"

Tilly stared at him in astonishment. "Yes! How'd you know?"

"I read Costanza Casati's retelling. It was awesome."

"I can't believe it!" Tilly squealed. "Are you *into* retellings?"

Charlie nodded. "Greek myth, yes. Fairy tales? Not so much." Pointing at the menu, he said, "I recommend Agatha

Chris-Tea with honey. You know, because the Greeks loved their honey."

"Okay. I'll get that." Tilly leaned on the counter and smiled at Charlie. "Hey, when do you have a break? We could drink tea and talk books. I'm dying to know what other retellings you've read."

"Um . . ." Charlie began.

Sheldon shoved Charlie to the side. "Give him five minutes. Since all the chairs in the Readers' Circle are taken, he'll bring your tea to the YA section."

"Perfect," said Tilly, plunking a ten on the counter. "Keep the change."

As soon as she was out of sight, Charlie darted to the front of the store and slipped behind the checkout counter.

"Could I talk to you?" he whispered.

Hearing the panic in his voice, Nora said, "Sure. Is everything okay?"

"No," Charlie hissed. "*She's* here, and I can't remember a single Greek retelling. My mind has gone totally blank."

Nora was about to tell him to wait until she was done bagging Mrs. D'Agostino's order when the elderly lady raised a hand and cried, "Don't ring me up yet! I don't want to leave without one of those fall candles."

Charlie offered to get the candle, but Mrs. D'Agostino couldn't remember which scent she liked best. "I'll just waddle back to the mystery section and smell them all again."

As soon as she was out of earshot, Nora put a hand on Charlie's arm. "Relax. You've got this. You've been preparing for this moment for months. You've read *Atalanta*. What else?"

"*Circe,* of course. And *Ithaca.*" Charlie gazed upward as if the answers were written on the ceiling. "Also, *Ariadne,* and my favorite, *Stone Blind.*"

Nora picked up a pen and used it to draw a squiggly line

on Charlie's palm. "If you forget the titles when you start talking to her, just look at this. It'll make you think of a snake. Medusa will pop in your head and you'll be off to the races. And, Charlie, remember what the goddesses and queens in those books wanted most."

"They wanted to be treated as equals."

"Exactly. She doesn't want to be put on a pedestal. She wants to talk to you, reader to reader, human to human. Got it?"

"Okay. Um, I gotta go make her tea. Thanks."

When Charlie's break ended up being over an hour long, Nora and Sheldon exchanged high fives in the ticket agent's booth.

That night, Nora recounted the story to her friends during a lull in their discussion of Daniel Mason's *North Woods*.

"I'm glad that girl finally paid him some attention. He's such a sweet boy," said June.

Hester placed a wineglass filled with pumpkin mousse in front of Nora. "So, what happened? Did he ask her out?"

Nora couldn't wait to drive her spoon through the cloud of cinnamon-dusted whipped cream perched on top of the glass, but she restrained herself in order to satisfy Hester's curiosity. "They just talked about books, but Charlie was dancing on air for the rest of the day."

"I'm proud of you for hiring him," said Estella. "At first, I thought you were crazy—hiring the kid who stole from you—but you're all about second chances. And look how well it's working out."

As the women dug into their dessert, they went around the circle, sharing their favorite quotes from *North Woods*.

When it was her turn, Hester said, "Am I the only one who thought about Wynter House while reading this book? I mean, there was so much history in Mason's yellow house in the woods, and a lot of that history was sad. The ghosts of the two sisters who never left the house reminded me of Lucille and Lynette."

"Me too," said Nora. "I loved how their bond survived beyond the grave. I found it strangely comforting."

Estella stirred milk into her decaf coffee. "I saw the ad for Wynter House in the paper. I guess the National Trust isn't going to rescue it?"

Nora shook her head. "Too many houses need saving, and there aren't enough funds to go around. I don't know what'll happen to the house."

"I like the thought of it becoming a visitors' center or a museum. I don't think people should live there anymore," June stated.

Hester gave her a quizzical look. "What about a hotel or a vacation rental?"

"Nobody's going to sleep soundly in that house," June insisted. "Don't get me wrong. It should be preserved because it's part of our history, but it needs a new identity. Otherwise, it'll always be our town's haunted mansion."

"I wish a famous writer would buy it," said Nora. "Someone with tons of money and talent. Like Stephen King or Neil Gaiman."

Hester gazed at Nora over the rim of her mug. "Stranger things have happened. Charlie could do a social media post on Wynter House, the post could go viral, and the next thing we know, the house becomes a writers' retreat or a miniature-book museum."

Nora brightened. "Speaking of miniature books, there's a good chance Lucille's dollhouse and collection of miniature books will come back to North Carolina."

"How do you know?" asked Estella. "The auction isn't until November."

"Because I got an email from Harper. She was told that a

North Carolina state senator flew to New York to preview the dollhouse and the book collection. The senator told the folks at Sotheby's that her grandfather had made her a similar dollhouse, but it had been destroyed when a tree fell on her house. She's a tobacco heiress, so if she wants the Wynter House dollhouse and all the books, she can afford to buy it."

"I hope she does," said Estella. "I never had a dollhouse, but I loved my Barbie Dreamhouse. It was a used one that belonged to a girl down the street. She gave it to me when she stopped playing with her Barbies, and I loved giving my Barbie the beautiful, happy home I didn't have. I know it sounds silly, but those dolls helped me survive some bad times."

June smiled at her. "Doesn't sound silly at all."

The four friends talked about their favorite childhood toys until the conversation circled back to Harper.

"I didn't think you'd ever hear from her again," said June. "She wasn't exactly your biggest fan."

Nora snorted. "Still isn't, but she did email me a few paint swatches she thought would look nice in my bedroom. They're all soothing shades of blue, green, or yellow. I'm leaning toward a blue called Lullaby."

"Oh! Maybe I should use that color in the nursery," said Estella.

The conversation changed course once again as the women weighed in on which shades should and shouldn't be used in a bedroom.

"You could paint every inch of my room in Lullaby, and I *still* wouldn't sleep," complained June. "These night sweats are killing me. How am I supposed to age gracefully when I'm dripping with sweat at two in the morning and wake up to find a new hair on my chin?"

Estella darted a nervous glance at June. "You've been

dealing with insomnia ever since we met. I've always slept like the dead, so I don't know how I'm going to function when I'm sleep deprived."

"Not well," said June. "But we'll be here for you. I can't wait to watch that baby while you take a nap or do whatever you want to do."

"Same here!" echoed Hester.

Estella looked at Nora. "I know you're not a baby person, so you can babysit when he or she is old enough to read."

"Deal. I'll make sure your kid has the best library in town."

Eyes shining, Hester told them how she'd already done a sketch of Estella's baby shower cake.

"I've been knitting things for this child since August," laughed June.

"Three doting aunties. This kid is going to be so lucky." Estella laid a hand on the soft mound of her belly and smiled at Hester. "How is your baby doing?"

"Good. She's decided to go back to school for her teaching certificate. I'm going to spend Thanksgiving week with her, and she'll tell me about her plans when I'm there. Can you believe she's still writing me letters instead of calling or emailing me? I thought she might get tired of the Mennonite lifestyle as time went on, but she loves it. She's thriving, too, and that's all I care about."

For a moment, Hester looked so vulnerable that Nora wanted to enfold her friend in her arms.

Catching Nora's eye, Hester said, "I'm okay. I really am. I know you're worried about me, but I'm fine. It was awkward at first—seeing Jasper around town—but when he comes to the bakery now, we can talk and laugh like we used to. I'll always love him, and I want him to be happy."

"With Hollowell?" Estella asked in horror.

Hester gave a little shudder. "God, no. But he won't stay

with her for long. I honestly think he likes her dog better than he likes her."

Everyone laughed.

"You know I've been kind of sad for months," Hester told Nora. "But not anymore. I'm not lonely either. I'm enjoying my own company, which is something I learned from you."

Nora's heart swelled with affection for her friend. "And I learned something from you—that I needed to hire some help and have a life outside the bookstore. Because of you, I'm taking this Sunday off. Grant and I are heading up to the Shenandoah Valley for a day of leaf peeping, hiking, and flea market shopping."

"I know *all* about your day trip," June muttered. "Sheldon won't shut up about it. He thinks you're going to come back with a truck full of treasures for him to polish, price, and display. He must've been an antiques dealer in another life."

"Or a crow," said Nora. "It would explain his penchant for disco balls and glittery things."

Estella gestured at Nora with her mug. "You and Grant should spend Saturday night at some romantic B and B. The Wynter case was really rough on both of you. You could use some sexual healing."

The room erupted in giggles, squeals, and groans.

Hester started scrolling on her phone. Within minutes, she'd picked out several Airbnbs for Nora.

"You should totally spend the night at this place. It has a fire pit, an outdoor movie screen, and a hot tub. Look at the view! You could sit in the hot tub, drinking bubbly, and watch the sun go down behind the mountains."

Taking the phone from her, Nora thought about how tired McCabe had been lately. The Wynter case had stretched on long after Beck's arrest. It had taken weeks to identify

Lynette's body, as well as the remains of the child buried beside her. The bones in the bathtub were also tested, and DNA analysis confirmed that the fragments belonged to Frederick Vandercamp.

With no family to claim him, his remains were sent to Raleigh for cremation. Lucille's sister and child were also cremated, but Harper had their ashes placed in a family vault alongside Lucille and Clem.

Long after the Wynters were laid to rest, McCabe was still dealing with the paperwork. A change of scenery would do him good, and as long as Nora could get someone to take care of his cats, she could surprise him with a night away.

"Let's do it," she told Hester. "I want to book that place."

While Hester typed in Nora's information and credit card, June suggested Nora hire her son to feed McCabe's cats. "Tyson's got half-a-dozen side hustles going on right now, and pet sitting is one of them. You know he's been saving up for a house down payment, and he's getting real close. I am so proud of that boy."

Nora couldn't help but think of Beck and what his life would've been like if he'd been raised by someone like June. She felt the dual pangs of sympathy and anger she always felt when she thought about Beck, and for a moment, it was September again, and she was in the library of Wynter House, staring down the barrel of a gun.

"Hey, boo," June whispered, recognizing the pained expression on Nora's face. "Those bad days are behind you. Time to look ahead. And Beck? Well, the things he's done will haunt him for the rest of his life. But that doesn't mean his life is ruined. He can still grow and change. He can still lead a purposeful life."

Nora leaned into her friend's shoulder. "Maybe he's already started. Harper told me how much he loves working in the prison library. He sent her a long list of books to buy using his share of the money from the estate—when everything is settled."

"Improving the library won't erase his guilt, but it might ease it a bit. Especially if he sees the other inmates benefiting from the materials he buys," said Hester. "Libraries are all about community. Maybe he can help create one."

Estella bobbed her head in agreement. "My daddy became a reader while he was incarcerated, and look at him now, he reads more than I do."

Hester told the group how Gus listened to audiobooks at the bakery. Every morning, well before dawn, he was in the bakery's kitchen, mixing, kneading, and sliding pans into the ovens. Because the movements were second nature to him, he could listen to novels while he worked. At this point, he was listening to one or two books a week. At night, he read the books in print he'd purchased from Miracle Books.

"What about Harper?" asked June. "Do you think she'll ever become a reader?"

Nora's lips curved upward as she thought of the book she'd gifted to Harper. Based on what she'd written in her email, Harper had read several chapters.

"I never thought that woman's name would make you smile," said Hester.

"I'm smiling because of her email. At the very end of it, she made a request."

Estella tapped her chin. "Let me guess. She wants you to donate a kidney."

"Or fly to Dallas to walk her dogs."

"Or get a red wine stain out of her white shag carpet."

Laughing, Nora held up her hands. "It's a good thing. Actually, it's a great thing. It's my reason for being. *My* purpose in life. The thing I do best and never get tired of doing. Harper Wynter asked me for a book recommendation."

The other women stared at her in surprise. And then, June picked up her coffee cup and said, "To the new reader."

"To the new reader," the other women echoed.

The four friends gazed at the stacks, their eyes shining with tenderness as they moved over the books. The whole shop was aglow with light and color. The air smelled of coffee and autumn leaves. Music tiptoed through the speakers. The women in the Readers' Circle were full and warm, relaxed and happy.

This is my favorite time of the week, every week, thought Nora.

She knew her friends were thinking the same thing. For an hour or two every week, they had this time together. A time of food, sisterhood, and books. A time worth more than any treasure.

Waving her hand toward the shelves, Nora said, "So. What should we read next?"

The Little Lost Library:
A Secret, Book, and Scone Society Mystery Reader's Guide

1. Wynter House is known as the town's haunted house. Is there one in your area? How does a house gain such a reputation?

2. Name some signs that Lucille Wynter wasn't living her best life—things Nora later realized she should have noticed and acted upon.

3. Hoarding impacts so many people. Do you have any experience with hoarding?

4. Nora feels compelled to search for the riddles in *The Little Lost Library*. What is driving her to ignore her bookshop and her friends? How could she have handled the situation differently?

5. Did you have any theories about the clues hidden around Wynter House?

6. What is the appeal of miniatures? Do you collect any miniatures? Have you seen any remarkable examples in a museum or shop? Were you surprised to learn that miniature books can be extremely valuable?

7. How did trauma shape certain characters in this novel?

8. What are your thoughts on Paula Hollowell? What motivates her? Do you think she and Jasper Andrews are suitable?

9. Speaking of couples, what are your thoughts on Nora and Grant?

10. Every chapter in *The Little Lost Library* leads off with a quote. Which is your favorite?

Bibliotherapy & Book Lists from
The Little Lost Library

Books About Toxic Women
Jessica George, *Maame*
Heather Hodsden, *Women Who Hate Other Women*
Nella Larsen, *Passing*
Nikki May, *Wahala*
Toni Morrison, *Sula*

Nora Recommends: Female Thriller Writers
Rachel Howzell Hall
Jane Harper
Lisa Jewell
Deepti Kapoor
Liane Moriarty
Stacy Willingham

Spooky Classics
Jane Austen, *Northanger Abbey*
Algernon Blackwood, *The Best Ghost Stories of Algernon Blackwood*
Charlotte Perkins Gilman, "The Yellow Wallpaper"
Shirley Jackson, *The Haunting of Hill House*
Gaston Leroux, *The Phantom of the Opera*
Daphne du Maurier, *Rebecca*
Oscar Wilde, *The Picture of Dorian Gray*

Romances with Autumn Vibes

Sarah Addison Allen, *First Frost*
Jessica Booth, *A Match Made in Autumn*
Linsey Hall, *The Modern Girl's Guide to Magic*
Ashley Poston, *The Dead Romantics*
Farrah Rochon, *The Dating Playbook*

Other Books Mentioned

Kristin Harmel, *The Winemaker's Wife*
Barbara Kingsolver, *Demon Copperhead*
Sandra Kitt, *Adam and Eva*
T.J. Klune, The Extraordinaries series
Daniel Mason, *North Woods*
Ann Napolitano, *Hello Beautiful*
Kassia St. Clair, *The Secret Lives of Colors*
Stef Wade, *The Very Last Leaf*
Rebecca Yarros, *Fourth Wing* and *Iron Flame*